His hand latched on to her wrist again. "Rocks," his voice called close into her ear.

Birle had no time to think. The boat was thrown into the middle of white-crested waves. Her hand grabbed for his wrist as they tumbled into the water. Her shoulder hit something hard, his wrist slipped out from her numb fingers, her head was taken by the waves. She turned over, her head pulled down, down into darkness underwater. Her legs rolled heavy above her. She had no choice but to go where the water took her, turning in the icy water like a leaf in stormy air. She tried to struggle against it, struggle up into the air. Blackness struck her on the back of the head and she tumbled into it, like falling into water. . . .

Named by the A.L.A. as a Best Book for Young Adults

By Cynthia Voigt
Published by Fawcett Juniper Books:

ON FORTUNE'S WHEEL

Cynthia Voigt

FAWCETT JUNIPER • NEW YORK

A Fawcett Juniper Book
Published by Ballantine Books
Copyright © 1990 by Cynthia Voigt

Library of Congress Catalog Card Number: 89-39010

ISBN 0-449-70391-6

This edition published by arrangement with Atheneum Publishers, an imprint of Macmillan Publishing Company

Manufactured in the United States of America

First Ballantine Books Edition: April 1991

10 9 8

FOR NICK & JUDY & EMILY—
two proven romantics, and one probable

Contents

🏚	The Inn
🏰	Corbel's city
👑	The Kingdom
💎	The Port
🦅	Sutherland's castle
- - -	Route of journey
✚	Meeting with Damall
◉	Forest camp

Part One

---∞---

The Innkeeper's Daughter

One

What she saw first was a moving shadow. In the trees that bordered the meadow, among their dark trunks, something moved.

She heard nothing to alarm—not over the rush of water and the sweep of wind—but she saw a dark, crouched shape, moving.

The shadow, no more than a darker darkness in the night, crept out from the mass of trees, crept low across the long grass toward the docking place.

No man of the village would move so. A man of the village, come out to check a hastily secured boat, would carry a light. He would come along the path that ran from the village through the Innyard, the path she stood on. No fisherman would be setting off, not at this hour, not on a moonless night when all the stars shining together couldn't penetrate the dark, windy air. Birle stood motionless, watching.

She herself ought not to be out in the night. Da and Nan would not be pleased to know how she had left her small sisters asleep in the bed they shared, pulled on her skirt and overshirt, and latched the door stealthily behind her to tiptoe past the room where her brothers slept, past the room where Da and Nan slept, down the broad staircase, and across the empty public room. In the kitchen, where the banked fire glowed in its ashes, she had put on her boots and taken her cloak from its hook. The dogs, if they heard anything, knew

3

her steps and took no alarm. Da and Nan, if they knew, would be mightily displeased, and they would lay angry words across her shoulders. Aye, they were counting the days left to the spring fair, when they would have her married and gone from their care. Aye, and Birle was counting them, too.

The shadow was human, she had no doubt of that. Only a man or woman would move so, hunched over, gliding along the edge of the river like a beast on the hunt among the long grasses. Watching, Birle let the wind urge her down the path to the docking place. Whatever else, the shadow was up to nothing lawful.

Soaking spring rains had turned the path to mud. Her boots made squishing sounds, so she stepped off the path into the grass. As soundlessly as the shadow before her, but more swiftly, she approached the river.

She should return to the sleeping Inn, she knew that, and rouse her brothers. At the least, she should turn and call out an alarm, to set the dogs barking. But the mystery of the intruder, like the mystery of the night, which had called her from sleep, kept her from doing what she ought.

It wasn't that she hadn't heard the tales. There was no child who hadn't been warned. Some of the warnings spoke of robbers, dangerous especially to a woman, murderous to all; others told of servants so hard used, or so proud-spirited, that they fled their masters, fled even knowing that if the law caught up with them—man or woman—they might be hanged, or have branded on their right palm the mark of the renegade servant. This shadow, she thought, wasn't a robber. Robbers moved in bands, like wolves. Anyway, robbers were few, here in the remote southern lands of the Kingdom, where the cleared land was rich to farm and the goats and pigs fed to fatness; where even in the sharpest days of winter fish might be taken from beneath the ice of the river; where the forests were filled with game, and the Earl's huntsmen kept the pathways safe. This was no robber, she was sure of that.

If it was an escaping servant, Birle wouldn't be the one to return a man or woman to the servant's life. For all that she was the Innkeeper's daughter, her own life tasted more like

4

service than freedom—and that was sour in the mouth. But it wasn't long now, she reminded herself, not many days and she would be wed and away.

Because she moved erect and quickly, she stepped onto the planks of the dock just as the shadow-shape bent over an iron cleat at the far end. The thick boards creaked in the river's currents. The boats tied there bounced and slapped upon the dark, wind-troubled water. The river was running high and fast, in its spring flood.

The wooden planks echoed her footsteps, making them even louder. The shadow heard her now, and now had arms she could see—gathering in the rope that pulled a boat's narrow bow to the dock. Secrecy lost, Birle ran to prevent the theft of the boat. The thief did not concern her. She had no desire to catch the thief.

It was too late. Just as she reached it, the shadow—turning an alarmed, pale face—jumped out into the boat and scrambled onto the rowing seat. It dropped its pack onto the floorboards, then bent down to pick up the oar handles. Its arms pushed out, rowing backward. The oars banged against the sides of the boats tied alongside. Not a fisherman, Birle knew, neither a boatman; someone who knew boats would let the current carry him free before trying to put his oars into the water. She stretched her hands out, kneeling on the rough wood, to catch the bow with her hands.

The oars found water, and dug into it. That stroke, aided by the swift current under the boat, was more than Birle could resist. She raised her head to call out, already knowing what they would say to her for not raising the alarm sooner. She filled her chest with air for a sound loud enough to rouse the dogs, who would then rouse the sleeping Inn—and felt her body pulled off-balance, pulled out over the black water, pulled up from the planks and dropped into the river.

Water rose up around her. Birle kept her head, and kept her strong grip on the bow of the boat. She could swim. She had no reason to be afraid. The rowing shadow made grunting noises and she knew why—with her weight at the bow of the boat, it would be hard work at the oars. Her boots filled with cold water, her cloak and skirt were logged down with it, her own weight pulled heavy at her arms. She could imagine how heavy a burden she was to the rower, and the thought pleased her. Slowly, hand over hand, she worked her way around to the side.

An oar fell down upon her shoulder, just missing her head. She grabbed the blade with one hand, and held it. "Thief!" she cried. "Thief!"

The thief pulled at the oar, but she held firm. The cloaked shape turned to face her. She couldn't see the riverbank, but she knew the boat was moving swiftly; the water pulled at her skirt and cloak and boots. She couldn't see the face but she guessed, from the way the figure sat and turned, that this was a man. His voice confirmed it.

"Let go," he grunted. "Let go! I've no wish to harm you but I will. I warn you. Go off, let go, go away now. You can swim, can't you?"

Water flooded into Birle's mouth and prevented her from answering. Her boots were filled with water, and if she had not had one hand on the side of the boat, it would have been hard work to stay afloat. She spat her mouth empty and realized the truth: "Aye, I can, but not dressed as I am." Because she had no choice, she let go of the oar to have both hands free, and started to haul herself up over the side and into the boat.

The boat rocked under her weight. The thief moved away from her—but for balance, she thought, not for fear. Birle rolled herself over into the boat, thumping down onto the floorboards. Once she was safely in, she moved to crouch in the bow, her legs under her in case she needed to spring. He was a dark shape at the stern, himself crouched.

"I wish you hadn't done that," he said, moving toward her. His voice sounded genuinely regretful. "You better take your boots off, because I'm going to have to throw you back into the river. But know this: I am no thief."

"Oh aye," Birle answered. She didn't need to say more. A man taking a boat that wasn't his was a thief. She tensed her legs and gripped the two sides of the boat. "Try to throw

6

me into the water and you'll find you've tipped the boat as well, and yourself too.''

He froze in place, considering. She was ready for whatever move he might make. ''And you,'' she asked, ''can you swim? I doubt it. It's not many who have the skill. I doubt you swim any better than you row. Thief.''

''Believe what you like, I've told you true,'' his voice answered, out of the windy darkness. ''Since you're kind enough to be concerned,'' he said, not meaning the words at all, ''I'll promise you I can swim, and strongly.''

Birle was sorry to hear that, but it wouldn't do to let him guess it. ''Aye,'' she said, ''and which bank will you choose? Or will it be the current choosing for you, and you helpless. You've your own boots to take off, that too, before they pull you under.''

He moved, but only to sit down to the oars again. Facing her, he had to row with the broad, flat stern of the boat facing clumsily forward. ''I'll take you to shore.'' The bow swung around.

''You'll not get rid of me without a fight,'' Birle promised him. He ignored her, and struggled with the oars. ''And what if you lose the boat, with the bears come out from their winter sleep, coming down south where the grubs and berries are more plentiful, and the wolves behind them still carrying their long winter hunger. There's naught but forest here, one bank or the other, unless you know your way. A man alone in a forest is a sorry creature.''

He lifted the oars out of the rushing water and Birle felt the bow swing, as the current caught it. She smiled to herself: That battle had been won. She stretched her legs out, settling herself more comfortably—if you could call this wet cold comfortable. He sat hunched over, thinking, the oars in his hands. Let him think. Let him see where it would get him. He was a stranger to the river and she was not.

He lifted his head and once again put the oars into the water, once again turning the stern of the boat. She pulled her legs back under her, ready.

''There will be holdings along the river,'' he said.

7

"No, none. Not in this part of the Kingdom, not in the forest. You've left the last village behind you."

He didn't know whether to believe her. He left the oars in the water but ceased his attempts to row. The boat swung around again. He ought to believe her.

The thick-growing trees made a dark wall on either side of the broad river. The boat moved swiftly, racing the waves that pushed it along. Birle wrung what water she could from her cloak, and waited. She could wish for a fire.

"All right then," he asked, finally, "what would you do?"

She knew before she spoke it how her answer would anger him. "I'd take the boat to shore."

"So. There are no bears, no wolves."

"That I didn't say. Do you want to hear what I'd do, or do you want to go along in your own unknowing way?"

"I always go my own way," he announced. "But I'll hear yours," he said, for all the world as if he were the Steward listening to a man's plea for lower taxes.

"I would tie up for the night," she told him. "There will be a tree or a low branch at the shore. I'd tie up there, to await daylight—you can use the rope you loosed, when you were stealing the boat."

"I have told you what I am not."

He spoke too well for a robber, she thought, or a common servant. He was, at a guess, a city man, one of the Lord's household servants. She couldn't think why he would flee from the ease of such a life, but she assured him, "It's only the boat I want." She would let him go on his way southward and herself return the boat to its owner. She was shivering over her entire body, with cold. Tied up to the bank, she would at least have protection from the wind. "I'll row," she said.

"Thank you, no. I'm fine with it."

He wasn't fine. The little boat twisted and rocked with his clumsy rowing. "The work would warm me," she said.

Without a word he moved himself onto the board that made a seat at the stern of the boat. Shivering, keeping low so as not to upset the balance, Birle settled herself onto the rowing

8

seat, facing him. The oars waited for her hands. She brought the bow around, and pulled strongly for shore. These fishing boats were built to ride high and light on quiet waters, so it would have been foolishness to try to take it back upriver, against the waves and current. She made straight for the low bank. Close enough, she could see a young, straight tree they might safely tie up to.

Up near the bank, the wind spent itself among the trees, and the heat of her body made the wetness of her clothes at least not cold. She left the oars and leaned out from the bow to loop the rope around the tree and then, quickly, before he might get up to mischief, turned back.

He sat watching her, silent.

She settled down into the bow. This was a double safety. He couldn't untie the boat without waking her, and should he decide to attack she could be out of the boat and in the shelter of the forest before he might do her harm. Bears there were, and wolves, that was true, but not many in this well-hunted forest. On the other side of the river, where no men had settled, such dangers were more common. Birle shivered again, along the whole length of her body.

"You might lend me your cloak," she asked. He lay on his back along the seat at the stern, with his pack to make a pillow under his head.

"And why might I do that?"

"Aye, my clothes are wet, and cold."

"Since that results from jumping into the river of your own free choice, it makes no persuasion," he told her.

"Aye," she pointed out, "I was chasing after a thief."

He didn't answer. Birle fumed: When light came she would be able to identify this boat, which belonged to one of the village fishermen, or might even be one of the Inn's boats. She tried to think of what to say to this runaway, to show her scorn of him, but no words came to her. Besides, she could hear in his silence that he had fallen asleep. It was easy for him to go to sleep, she thought, wrapped as he was in a dry, warm cloak.

Two

BIRLE didn't know how he could sleep. The boat was barely wide enough for two abreast on the rowing seat at its center, so he must have been uncomfortably cramped on the stern seat. Waves moved under the boat, rocking it like a cradle, and maybe that lulled him. She was not lulled.

Stars shone overhead. Looked at from where she sat unsleeping, the sky seemed walled in by forest. It looked as if there was a river of sky matching the water river below. The white stars floated on that sky river. Birle leaned back into the bow of the boat and rested her head on an outstretched arm. She closed her eyes.

What had she been thinking of, to follow him? He slept, the wind blew, the river slapped against its bank—she could be out of the boat and gone before he could stop her. If she kept to the riverbank she could make her way back to the Inn, even in the dark. She had no concern for what her family would say, but she did wonder—briefly—about Muir. Muir might make this night's work an excuse to turn his back to her.

If she followed the river, she couldn't get lost. She could be back at the Inn by first light. She could be back building up the fires, drawing buckets of water from the well, and only her own fatigue to say she had ever been away.

But when she recalled the morning chores, Birle had no desire to return. Let someone else do them, for once, and scold her later. Aye, and they did that anyway. Her brothers and Da, and Nan especially, drove her through the days, scolding. Why should she want to hurry back to that?

Besides, if she left now, the boat would be lost. The boat, and the oars built through the sides of it, and the net that might lie folded under the seat the runaway slept on, and maybe also the owner's short-handled fishing spear, with its five sharp prongs—If she gave up now, a man's livelihood would be lost.

Birle had nothing to fear. She knew the forest, even if she couldn't know just where she was presently, and she knew the river. She could run and she could swim. The man was no danger to her. She had her knife, safe at her boot, and she had as well two brothers, so she knew how, and where, to hurt a man so that he would be able to think of nothing but his own pain. Besides, living at the Inn as she had, seeing all manner of people, she knew how to judge a man. The blood that signaled her warning—at the way eyes watched, or the way a voice spoke, or the words a voice chose—had not given her any alarm.

Not just men, women too. There were some women who, when they had risen from the table, Nan counted the metal spoons; or women who, when they departed in the morning, you had to study them carefully to see that they hadn't over-night become round under their cloaks, grown fat with the Inn's bedclothes. Some men, and some women too, her father would not allow to sleep within the barred Inn doors. Man or woman, Birle trusted her blood to warn her. This man, her blood said, was no danger. She had no reason to fear him. Thus, she should not allow him to make off with this boat.

She might have been in the wrong to be outside in the night, or, rather, they might say she was wrong to go outside alone; but she was right to stay with the boat. In the morning she would deal with this runaway.

Birle doubted the man knew what his destination might be. Little as she knew of the lands to the south, she knew more than most people because of the caravans that traveled into the Kingdom, for the spring and fall fairs, bringing word

11

of the world beyond the Kingdom. She knew from those merchants and entertainers that a few days' journey downstream, the river emptied into the sea—and the sea, they said, stretched out empty farther than any boat had ever traveled. Even before the sea, there was a port. Its size was no larger than three villages put together, they said, but in danger it exceeded its size. No Lord claimed rule over the port. No law governed it. This was a place of thieves, cutpurses, murderers; it was the home to pirates, and to soldiers who had deserted their officers or had been sent away, too wild even for soldiery. No merchant traveled alone near the port. No entertainer entered it willingly. Near the port, night and the forest were safer than day and the river. Birle told herself to remember to warn this runaway that he should go wide around the port, unless he wanted to find himself run away from servitude into slavery.

Thinking that, she slipped into sleep.

She opened her eyes to darkness. Was it moments or hours she'd slept? Overhead, the river of night was crowded with stars.

No man had mapped the sky, although some few had mapped the land. Birle had seen these maps, from her grandparents' cupboard. It was safe to think of them, although not to put those thoughts into words. Some things were never to be spoken of.

Maybe the Lords had maps of the sky, she thought. She might ask this runaway servant that, before she sent him on his way. She had no idea where his way would lead him, except south. To hear the merchants talk, and the tales of the entertainers, the lands to the south were more strange than people of the Kingdom could imagine. Such tales were quickly cut off, because the people of the Inn and of the village were frightened by strangeness. Just as they feared the night, Birle thought. Birle had been taught that fear, and believed it, when she was a child. But now—

Sometimes, on a winter morning, when she opened the kitchen door to go out and draw water, the stars hung so close outside the door that she thought she would be able to step out among them, and she felt her blood racing at the possibility. What was known, and safe, seemed then to her like a cell in one of the Lords' dungeons. All the fear she lived among seemed then like a yoke across her shoulders, a heavy burden that kept her from moving swiftly, freely. Aye, men carried fears like great stones strapped on their backs, she thought. Why else had Da and Nan protested so when she said yes to Muir?

Birle shifted against the boat-ribs behind her, to find more comfort. Whatever others might say, she had nothing to fear from the night. People just felt safe with known things, things fixed and regular as the sun's passage across the sky. Night too had its one light, the moon; but the moon didn't move in the sun's orderly pattern. The moon even changed its shape, growing and shrinking—sickle to circle to sickle, to darkness. Darkness, Birle thought, looking up through dark air to the tiny lights of the stars, needed no map, because men avoided darkness. The work of darkness differed from the work of day. People slept away the dark, the long nights of winter, the short nights of summer. She wished she could sleep this night away, she thought, her eyelids closing down heavily.

When she awoke again and raised her head from her chest, Birle's neck was painfully stiff. Opening her eyes, she wondered if the sun had set forever, yesterevening, and would never rise again. Still, the stars shone white in a black sky. Birle pulled herself up to sit straight against the bow. She gathered her cloak around her. It was as if the sun and the moon had been blown out, like candles, but by what giant's breath? Granda had asked her once, "There might be people living up there, in the stars, think you?"

Granda had a way of saying and doing odd things, so Birle wasn't surprised at the question. "Aye, no," she promised him. "The stars are only lights in the sky. A man can't live in a light, any more than in a candle." They had gone outside into the cold, to bring in wood for the fire. Three winters

13

ago that had been, Birle calculated. A fall baby, Birle was then in her eleventh winter. Granda was an old man standing beside her, his breath floating white in the air before him, watching the moon sail among the stars.

"Aye, and you're probably right, although I like to think it," he had answered, his voice as warm as summer. He had still been strong enough, that winter, to go out with her to fetch wood from the pile he built up in summer and fall. He had still been alive. "Although," his voice went on as he piled logs into her arms, "when I saw your mother, with her hair like starlight netted, I sometimes wondered."

It was that same night that they had told her about the treasure.

Sitting on the warm hearthstone, the door bolted fast against the night and the little high windows shuttered safe, Birle had looked up to where her grandparents sat at the table, both of their faces turned to her. "What treasure?" she had asked. "The Inn doesn't have any treasure. I never heard about any treasure."

"The secret held safest is the one no one even thinks to wonder of," Gran said.

"Where is it? What is it? Did you bring it with you when you left the Inn?"

"Aye, we did," Gran answered, looking over to Granda, who said at the same time, "We left it with your father, for it is the Inn's treasure." Then Gran smiled—a girl's smile on her old-woman's face, the smile of a girl in springtime, a girl in springtime dancing at the fair. Gran's smile never grew old. Birle didn't know what to make of what they were saying, but that didn't trouble her. She sat contented, her back toasted by the fire, growing sleepy, and glad to be away from the unending labor of the Inn.

"It isn't any treasure you'd guess," Gran said, rising from the stool she sat on to go to the cupboard under the bed. Bending down, she lifted out bedclothes, and then a long sheet of paper, which she carried over to the table as carefully as she would a baby.

Birle didn't know what to think. It wasn't that she didn't

know what paper was, or what it was used for. But it was the Lords who owned and used it. The Steward kept his records, not in his head, as Da did, but in long books, a stack of paper sewn together and then placed between thin pieces of wood. The Lords wrote proclamations on paper, then rolled them up and tied them with strips of cloth, and the Lord who was riding as messenger would unroll the paper and read off what it was the Lords wanted their people to know. Birle couldn't think what her grandparents were doing with this sheet of paper, how they had come to possess it. But it wasn't anything to call a treasure, she thought, getting up to look closely at it; only the Lords would have a use or value for it, and she wouldn't dare to offer it to a Lord. He might ask where she had gotten it.

The paper was drawn over with dark lines, which divided it into odd-shaped sections, and with irregular markings, which looked like the traces of birds' feet in mud. The stiff paper was spotted brown, like the backs of her grandparents' hands. That was the first map Birle had ever seen.

Her grandparents explained it to her, pointing out the different parts of the Kingdom—the mountain-walled north, where they had been born, and the forest-walled south, where they now lived; the long rivers, which divided the Kingdom between those lands the King held for his own and those he gave over to the use of his two Earls; the places where the cities had been built; the King's city, the Earls' cities, and the cities of the great Lords who served the Earls. As she learned how to see the map, Birle looked for her own place on it.

"The Inn stands here." Granda put his finger on a bend of the longest river. His finger was swollen at the joints, hooked like a bird's talons. "And this house lies—about here, think you, lass?"

"Aye, you know better than I," Gran answered him. "You could always read a map better than I. When this map was made, there was only empty forest in the south," Gran told Birle.

"Not empty," Granda corrected her. "The forest is never empty."

Gran was more interested in talking about the map than in quarreling. Her finger followed the river off to the north, to show Birle where the great mountains guarded the Kingdom. "We've stood at the feet of the mountains, your Granda and I," she said. "We lived"—her finger moved—"here." The finger stopped at a point on the King's Way midway between two cities.

"Your mother's mother also came from those parts," Granda said.

"When you journeyed north, to bring back the vines," Birle told him, to show that she remembered the story. "When Da was only a little boy."

"Aye," Gran said, in her memory-laden voice, "so that when your mother's mother died of giving birth to Lyss, and my own child died before three days were out . . ."

"Lyss filled the empty place," Granda said.

Until Lyss herself died, Birle thought, wondering if the map was a treasure because it held the key to so many memories, as if the memories themselves were somehow put into the map. Her eyes found a place on the river, above the Inn, where her mother would perhaps have capsized, on a late-winter morning when the water ran icy cold, and come home to die in fever before a fire that couldn't warm her. Birle was too young to remember her own mother; she had other peoples' memories, but none of her own. The map would be no treasure to her. For mother, Birle had Nan, who came a servant from the hiring fair before Lyss died, and then after his years of grieving were completed, came a woman to her master's bed, to have all the authority of a wife over the Inn.

You didn't need any map to hold memories, Birle thought. She didn't know why this memory-map should be a treasure.

Unless those bird scratchings above the cities and across the forest, along the bending line of river and straighter line of Way, showed secret stores of gold and jewels, buried underground in chests, or hidden deep within caves. Then the map might be a treasure. But that was as unlikely as one of

16

the old stories, where tiny deathless folk lived in trees that knew no season, or animals talked, or Jackaroo rode.

The old people talked on, their fingers moving over the map. Birle was restless. What was she to do with this treasure? If there were stores of gold marked on it, someone would have gone out to claim them already. A man like Granda, unafraid of travel. The way life would be, then, if he had, for the family that held such riches—but none of the people lived so. Only the Lords lived in that fashion.

She interrupted her grandparents. "Is this the treasure? Where can I hide it?" They must know there was no place for secrecy at the Inn.

"You won't be taking the map with you," Gran said, sharp and displeased. Her finger came down on the scratchings, one after the other, hopping like a bird over the map. "These are the treasure."

Hope rose in Birle's chest. If she had been right in her thinking, if there was even one treasure to be dug up . . . she smiled in excitement.

"She's but a greedy child. She's young to have the keeping of it," Gran said.

"I can keep secrets," Birle promised. "I'm not too young."

"It's not her youth I'm thinking of, lass," Granda said, "it's our age."

Birle made herself sit patient, or at least look patient, while Gran argued it out within herself.

Finally Gran spoke to her. "It's letters. These are letters."

Birle didn't understand.

"Words," Granda said. "These letters"—he pointed to the scratchings Birle had asked about—"name Lord Mallory. To say that this is Lord Mallory's city."

Birle backed away from the table.

"This line marks the King's Way, and these letters name it," Gran said. Her finger followed the Way to where a wide-winged falcon had been drawn. "Sutherland," Gran said. "Earl Sutherland's city."

"You mean reading." Birle looked from one old face to

the other, hoping they would deny it. She knew now why it had been kept secret. Only the Lords could know how to read.

"Aye," Granda said. "And writing."

This wasn't any treasure, Birle thought. This was knowledge, a secret like the old story of the weasel that struck out at the child come to rescue it from the trap. "Never tell me," she asked them. "I'm too young, Gran's right."

"Gran and I, we have decided," Granda said. "You are the one of our grandchildren to have the treasure. Aye, then, you must, Birle."

Birle shook her head, but even then she knew that if she must, she would have to. People had no more choice than animals about what burdens they carried. That night, however, she refused to go back to the table. She sat—sullen and afraid—before the fire. That first night they spoke no more of it. Gran put the map away, Granda took out his pipe, and the song he played moved around the little room, like sunlight left behind when summer was chased away by the cold seasons.

Over that long winter, and the next two, Birle had learned to read and to write. She started out unwilling, but helpless; then when she first wrote down the letters to make her own name, she wanted to hurry and know all there was to know. In the same cupboard as the maps, there were two long books kept by Stewards of older times, records of supplies and expenses, plantings and harvestings, taxes paid in coins, in goods, in labor. There were also two books, bound not in wood but leather, which told stories. Gran read those stories aloud to them. By the end of the third winter, Birle could take her turn reading the evening story. She was not as fast and clear as Gran, but her tongue stumbled over words less than Granda's. In these stories, animals talked and thought as people did, trying to deceive and make profit from one another. The second book they had not gotten to, although Gran told her that in it there was a story of a woman magicked into a spider, because she was so proud of her weaving, and a young herdsman deep in unwaking sleep because the

18

moon fell in love with his beauty. Birle was looking forward to reading those strange tales.

But in the spring, Granda died, as gently as he'd lived. Gran walked the long way to bring them the news, but would not come back to live there. One summer noon Da found her lying beside the stream, her hand trailing in it as if she had been reaching for the watercress that choked the water. Da reported the empty holding to the Earl through a huntsman. By the time he could send Reid and Birle to empty the supplies from the little stone house, the fall fair had come and gone, and the first frosts were on the ground. When Birle looked for the maps and books, she saw nothing there but bedclothes. Gran might have buried them, a thief might have taken them, or perhaps Da had them now. Birle didn't know. She had never dared to tell Da that she, too, held the Inn's treasure. She watched him, but he never gave away the secret. She too kept it locked inside her head, and would have forgotten it if she could.

But she couldn't. Even now, the only human creature awake in the night, she saw letters shaped by the stars—an *L*, an *E*, a *W*, and even an *A* right above her eyes. *I*'s, *T*'s, they were common. It was the bellied letters that were hard to find, like *C* and *O*. She might, she thought, making it into a game, make her own name, spell it out up among the stars, if she could find a *B* and an *R*. She stared into the sky, searching out letters, so that she might not think of the sorrow of those two deaths. As she stood at the second burning, with the ripe summer sun setting into thickly leveled trees, she had felt alone with a sharpness she had never known before.

And that, she thought, uncomfortable in the little boat, with the runaway sleeping sound at the far end of it, with the waves gentle in a dying wind, that was why she had welcomed Muir. Muir danced with her, and said she was the prettiest little thing to be seen at the fair, and asked her if she would be his wife, with an expression in his eyes that made her feel a power she hadn't known she had, and she had said yes to him. Da tried to talk her out of the wedding, saying she was too young, saying Muir was too old. Birle stood silent. Nan said that she was old enough, but not in the ways that made a man glad of his wife. "She thinks life in a city house will be easy," Nan said. "Aye, and what holding would you have for a son, or dowry for a daughter?" As much as you, Birle thought, but did not speak the words. Her mother had not been much older when she wed, she thought, and did not speak those words either. She had only to stand firm and they would have to give way to her.

So they had, in the end, and without any joy. Birle had felt no joy either, at the victory, just relief that the quarrel was ended and she could come closer to a house in Sutherland's city, and the solitary life of a wife whose husband kept the distant forests for the Earl. Her life at the Inn did not suit her. She wore it like somebody else's cast-off boots, which pinched and chafed.

In a few days, little more than a fortnight, it would be the spring fair, and Muir would await her there, to wed. Alone in the night, under the eyes of the stars, Birle felt for the first time as frightened as Nan said all sensible girls should feel before they wed. Well, she could ask him to wash as regularly as she did, and she could teach him gentler manners. Besides, he would be away—as huntsman guarding the forest, then as captain over a troop of soldiers, who must live with his men in the soldier's barracks. As for children, she need not concern herself much with that. It was the men who slept at night in their own beds, their wives at their sides, whose wives had children. If Muir did not like his intended bride to be out in the forest, with a runaway servant, for the length of a night—if he did not know how much it mattered to save a man's livelihood—well, then, he was free to not like it. He could come to the marriage place and say her nay when the priest came to them, and tell why. A man could do that, under the law.

Birle imagined that scene. She saw the faces of those who heard him. She saw her own shoulders held stiff and proud, as Muir spoke falsely of her. The imagining warmed her heart; she thought that, among the listeners, there must be many who admired this girl.

But, she thought, laying her head back down along her arm, Muir wouldn't speak those imagined words. She had imagined it as her brothers would have spoken it. Muir spoke more simply. The pictures started at the beginning again, like turning back to the first words of a story. The girl, with her hair long and loose, in her finest skirt and shirt—all unknowing of what lay before her—walked with her family to the wedding place under the walls of the city. There, her cruel bridegroom waited.

Birle slept again.

Waking suddenly, she didn't have to wonder if she had been asleep. It was birdsongs that had warned her, and she opened her eyes cautiously. Light was spreading out gray along the sky overhead.

Birle kept motionless. The runaway slept on. His booted legs hung out over the side of the boat, and she saw how muddy those boots were. He slept with an arm flung over his face, as if to hide himself.

In her deep sleep, Birle had understood two things, which waking had concealed. She understood first that she must get back to the Inn. It was not courage but foolhardiness that had counseled her to act as she had. Without turning her head she could see how close to shore the boat lay. Two steps through shallow water and she would be away—back to the Inn and her family there, back to her wedding day, and Muir.

This was, she now understood, a wedding she no longer wished to be bride for. Muir was not the man she would wed, but he was the man she must wed. The promise she had given couldn't be altered. A man had the right, but a girl did not.

All the years to come seemed to Birle a dark cloak, heavy as iron. How she would carry this mistake, she did not know. Maybe, she thought, he would get her with child, and she would die, as many women did, of carrying it or having it.

Then at least she would not have long to bear the weight of her ill-chosen life.

For now, before abandoning the boat, Birle wanted to know whose it was, so she could carry word back to its owner. The fishing spear, if he had left it under the seat, would identify him.

She crept toward the stern, low over the rowing seat, cautious not to wake the runaway. Without trying to put her hand on the spear, she twisted her head to see its handle. It was the Inn's mark burned into the wood, a falcon's wing outspread. It was Da's boat.

Birle didn't know if that made things worse or better, and she wished she could find a way to return the boat. But to linger under a lightening sky, which must surely awaken him if the noisy birds didn't, was foolish. She drew back with as much care as she had approached the man—for this runaway was armed. A short sword lay unsheathed across his chest.

Despite her care, the boat rocked sharply. As Birle crouched watching and afraid, his eyes opened. He sat up, the sword ready in his hand. When he saw her, he smiled.

Why he should smile so, Birle did not know. All she knew was that his smile lit up the morning as the rising sun does. For a moment, looking at his face, it was as if her ribs were empty, hollow, as if the world had stopped forever while she looked into his eyes as blue as the bellflowers that grew wild across the meadows. For a moment, just until her beating heart had returned to her chest, Birle thought she understood everything about herself that she had never understood before.

Three

BIRLE crouched in the bow. The little river waves wept against the stony bank.

"Don't be frightened," he said at last. "There's no need for you to fear me. I'm just surprised—dumbfounded, more like. I thought—" His smile faded. "You're a child. Last night, in the dark, you sounded—I thought—" He scolded her, "You made me think you were older."

What Birle was thinking she couldn't say. "I'm no child. I was fourteen years this fall, and I'm to wed at the spring fair," she told him. Aye, and with her heart breaking within her at such a wedding, it wouldn't be many days until she died, wed to Muir. Never before had she felt so bitterly helpless.

For this runaway had no beard. A light stubble dusted his cheeks and chin, a lighter brown than the dark hair of his head and his dark eyebrows—and his eyelashes were gold-tipped, she saw. But he had no beard, for all that he was a man grown.

"What were you doing?" he asked her, more curious than cross. "What did you think you were doing? Wandering around in the night when you should have been in your own bed, dreaming whatever it is girls dream of in the days before they wed. Why did you follow me?"

"The boat," she said. "You were stealing the boat."

The mouth tightened and she knew she had displeased him. Back along the river, the way they had come in darkness

23

and haste, the sun lifted its slumbering head to send rosy light flowing down along the water.

"And now what am I to do with you?" he asked.

Birle didn't know what he might do. For he was no runaway servant.

What he was doing, creeping through the world like a thief—where he was going to, in secrecy—what he might be fleeing from—those questions also she didn't know the answer to. But she did know that only the Lords went beardless.

This young man, with his bellflower eyes and a smile to light every corner of the world, was a Lord. He had her heart, and he was a Lord.

"Well," he said, sheathing his sword, "I doubt I have any choice in the matter." He wore no crested ring, nor any other sign about him to name the house he was son to. "I'll take you back to your people."

Birle closed her teeth against the words she wished to say. She knew she must go home.

"You've had nothing to break the night's fast with, my Lord," she said.

He looked surprised when she spoke his title, and then not surprised but resigned. "I thought to hoard what cheese I have left, and the bread can't get any staler. I've not enough for two."

He had misunderstood her. "I thought I would catch fish," Birle said.

"How?"

"The fishing spear is under your seat. I know how to use it and if you look over there—" She pointed to the distant bank, where sunlight hadn't yet penetrated the overhanging bushes, and some large boulders broke through the gilded surface of the water. "A good place for fish."

"I'm not hungry enough to eat raw fish," he said. "Not yet, anyway, although I'm beginning to understand that I might come to that."

"I'll build a fire. It's simple to cook fish."

"And the smoke from that fire will summon all the huntsmen and herdsmen of the area," he said.

24

"There's nothing for you to fear, my Lord," Birle told him. Why should a Lord fear huntsman or herdsman? No man of the people would dare lay unfriendly hands upon a Lord. "This is empty forest, unclaimed forest. There's no holding after the Inn."

"What Inn?"

"The Falcon's Wing. That's where you took the boat," she said, speaking swiftly on, "which is so far off now that even if there should be anyone sharp-eyed enough to see a little smoke rising, he wouldn't investigate. Aye, my Lord, this part of the forest is safe enough, from human dangers."

"Are we beyond the Earl's lands?"

"I think we must be. So we are beyond Mallory's grasp, and even, I think, beyond the King's reach."

He studied the muddy toes of his boots while he thought about that. Birle sat quiet, studying him. His hair was the color of the leaf mold that lay on the forest floor, a rich, dark color. His wrists and hands were slim, for a man—but not for a Lord, she thought. In their bodies, as in the skin of their faces, the ease of life for the Lords was evident. At last, he raised his face to her, smiling. She waited, wordless. "In that case, I would like some fish, if you can catch them."

Birle stood up. First, she would go into the trees for privacy. She could gather wood for a fire on her way back.

"Where are you going?" He too stood, ready. The boat rocked but they stood facing each other, Birle surprised and the Lord wary. Why should he fear her? "I asked you a question," he warned her.

"I would relieve myself, my Lord."

"Oh." His eyes looked down in embarrassment. Birle was sorry to have embarrassed him. Lords, she thought, must not speak of such things as the people did. "Then I will do likewise," he said, his cheeks pink.

As she made her way back through the trees and saw him waiting, Birle almost laughed aloud at the glad surprise, to see him there, tall and slim and straight. "We'll need wood, for the fire," she suggested.

"While you make off with the boat? I'm not so easily gulled."

"Aye, you can trust me, my Lord," she promised him, meeting his eyes.

He considered her. "Aye then, I will," he said, mimicking her speech. "You have a name," he asked.

"Birle," she told him.

"Well then, Birle," he said, "if you can catch us some fish, I can make us a fire. Pass the sack out to me; I've a tinderbox in it."

The bag he traveled with was of thick woven cloth, gathered together at the top with a leather strap. It was not heavy, nor was it large to contain whatever of his life a Lord would take with him, running away. Birle lifted it over to him before she untied the boat, and sat down to take the oars into her hands.

When she returned with six silver fish on the seat before her, each one gutted and washed clean in the river, and her knife wiped dry and back in its sheath in her boot, he rose from the ground to greet her and tie the boat's rope around the sapling. Birle, her fingers clumsy under his attention, fixed two of the fish on the spear prongs. She crouched beside the fire, which blazed crisply. He sat down beside his sack, to wait.

The morning warmed around them. The Lord ate the first two fish and then cooked the final pair while Birle ate hers. He took the last two for himself when she told him, almost truthfully, that she wasn't hungry. "I've learned about hunger, even in these few days. If it is not now, I've learned, it lies in wait," he told her. He sat cross-legged on the ground, picking off pieces of flesh until the supple bones lay clean. Birle threw their scraps into the river and then washed her hands in the running water. He followed her example. Birle thought, watching him dry his fingers on his cloak, that if she must leave his presence and lose sight of him forever— she could not bear that, even though she knew she must.

"My Lord," she said, meaning to warn him about the

port, but at the same time he said her name—"Birle"—and she could say nothing, hearing his voice speak her name.

"There's a stone, a jewel, much prized, called beryl. Are you named for that? If your eyes were green, I'd think you were. It's a pretty idea, to name girls after precious stones."

Birle stomped on the coals, and scattered them with her boots until the fire was destroyed. "I can leave you the spear, to fish with, when I take the boat back." Before he could argue she explained: "The spear is my father's, a small thing for a gift. There is no need for you to retrace your way back to the dock." Almost, she wished he had already gone off into the forest, because knowing he would soon go was like a stone crushing down on her.

"That's not the way I've planned things, Birle."

"You should be warned." She ignored what he said. "Near the mouth of the river, where they say the river empties into a sea, there's a port that's—dangerous, unsafe. It's a place for lawless men, and they take strangers for slavery or the sport of killing, as I've heard. It's no place for a man traveling alone, and a Lord especially I'd guess. You can go around it. Are you listening? As you follow the river, you come to a little peninsula, reaching out into the river, and there's an island just beyond its touch. This is where the land rises higher, and the banks grow steep and stony. I can't tell you how far downriver it is, because I've only heard of this place from the merchants. It's the point where they turn into the forest, as they journey south after the fairs, there, at that peninsula. It keeps them a safe distance from the port. There must be a path, and it must be visible, because they travel with laden beasts. You must not miss it. They say it's a high, barren island, very small, with a single pine at its center. You should be able to recognize it. And pass safely by the port," she concluded.

To know that he was safe, that would be something to comfort her. She would never know what became of him, just as she would never know what had driven him away from his father's house and his own lands, but she would be eased if she could think him safe.

27

"I'd heard rumors," the Lord said, "but I don't entirely believe them."

"Believe them," she urged him.

"I mean to take the boat."

If it were hers to give, she'd give it to him gladly. "My father—"

"What has your father to do with it?"

"Aye, it's his boat, my Lord."

"Well, then, that's easy. Just say I was a wild and desperate man—which is near enough the truth—and he's lucky to have his daughter returned unharmed, so he shouldn't fret over the boat."

"It's his boat." Birle didn't know why she was being so stubborn, except that as long as they were quarreling, they weren't parting.

"Is this his livelihood?"

Hope raised Birle's eyes to his, but the ready lie was more than she could say to him. She would not put an untruth between them. "No."

The Lord smiled.

"I still can't let you take the boat."

He bent to his bag, not answering. Instead of picking it up, as Birle had thought, he reached into it and pulled out first a wooden box, then a clean shirt, and then from within the folded shirt a folded piece of paper. He sat down on the ground. Birle did the same.

When he had unfolded the paper, she saw that it was a map, more hastily drawn than those in her grandparents' house, but still a map. She recognized the Kingdom, with its forking river. At the top of the map, the letter *N*, with an arrow pointing upward beneath it, indicated where north lay. The cities were marked by *X*'s, ringed round with circles: three in the north, the King's city, three in the south, with Mallory's the southernmost. This map, she saw, went on beyond the Kingdom.

"This is a kind of chart of the land," he said. Birle didn't tell him she knew that. "I'm trying to guess how far I've come."

The port was not marked on this map. Long dark lines slanted to show the forest, out of which the river emerged into open space. She had never seen a map that told of more than the Kingdom, and she wondered who had made it. Two circled *X*'s to the southwest might be two cities, at the edge of the sea, with forest stretching inland behind them. If she had been more often allowed to serve the Inn's custom, rather than being kept in the kitchen to ladle stew and wash pots, to cut cheese and bread, to take pastries out of the oven, she might know more about the land beyond the Kingdom. All she knew was that everybody, Da too, agreed that those lands were dangerous. Thinking of the danger, Birle reached out her finger—not thinking—to place it at the river's end. "Just there. That's where the port will be."

He looked up at her and she realized her mistake. "If, as I think, this line marks the river, because it curves and winds. Does it?" she asked, to distract him.

"Yes, as it happens, it does. Who told you of this port?"

"We're on the borders of the Kingdom," she explained, her words coming out fast in her hope not to have given her knowledge away. "The caravans for the fairs stop at the Inn. Ours is the first they come to, going to the cities, and the last they leave, traveling south."

"I wouldn't have expected you to know—"

He didn't finish the thought, but Birle could finish it for him: much of anything beyond your own daily work. She knew what the Lords thought of the people, from serving the Earl's Steward on his twice-yearly taxing visit to the village and Inn, from the conduct of the messengers. These were Lords of the lowest order, these stewards and messengers, so the higher Lords would be even more disdainful. At the fairs, Lords and Ladies acted as if all the world except for themselves were invisible. A man might get justice against a Lord, if he could claim it, at the Hearing Day. But those were the great Lords sitting as judges, not these everyday Lords who sometimes had little more than their birth to keep them fed. Maybe this young Lord was a lackland. Whatever he was, she didn't want him to disdain her.

29

"My father keeps the Inn, the Falcon's Wing," she told him. "So we often meet outlanders, and hear many strange things." She stood up, and brushed the twigs and dirt from the back of her cloak. "I could travel the day with you, to take you farther along, safely on the river."

"What is so important about this boat?" he asked. He remained seated, so she was looking down at him. His hair shone in the sunlight.

"The Inn is in Sutherland's gift," she answered. He should know his adversary. "The Earl has a special care over the Inn, which stands at the very end of the Kingdom, at the border of his lands."

"You have warned me, and I thank you," the Lord said. "Although I don't fear the Earl—no more than I fear any other man—he is all the more reason for me to take you safely home, before I go on. And how can we know? It might be that if the Earl knew my need, he'd give me this boat. But you must not tell your people anything about me." That thought brought him to his feet. "My safety lies in secrecy. I ask your promise."

She would make that promise, and keep it. "What would you have me say, my Lord?"

"Tell them something they will believe, but not the truth."

She could not imagine what he could have done to make flight necessary, and in such secrecy. What crimes could the Lords commit? Theft, or murder, she answered herself, a plot against the King. But he didn't have the look of a murderer. She had seen, in her time, two murderers at their hangings. Neither of them was a Lord, but she would stake her life on this man, that he was no murderer. Aye, and she wished she could stake her life on it.

"Tell them—that you went for a nighttime ride and the boat overturned, which in the wind it might well have. The current carried you downstream. You deemed it safer to sleep the night on shore rather than risk the forest at night. Wouldn't you have done that?"

"Nan would have me locked in my room if she thought I

30

was doing such things," Birle protested. He had said he was not a thief, and she would take his word on anything.

"Then you say you went to check the boat, and it was working loose, and you tried to rescue it but it got away from you."

He didn't have the look of a traitor either. Traitors were greedy, for power or wealth. There was no greed in his eyes.

"Or tell them you don't know what happened. That might be best. Tell them you awoke to find yourself in the forest, in the night. There are some who walk in their sleep and never remember how they came to be where they are when they awake. I've heard of such things."

She wished she did not have to part from him.

"I'll row you back upriver," he told her. He picked up his pack and slung it over his shoulder.

"I can row," Birle said. She could not keep her eyes from studying him, to lock all that she could see of him into her memory. "We might meet up with a fisherman," she warned him.

"Why then I'll push you into the water and he'll be so busy rescuing you I can make my escape," he answered. A quick man with a lie, and a story, and a plan; he was that, she thought, memorizing that about him too.

"My mother died of a chill she took from the river, in early spring," Birle said, remembering.

"Ah," he said. "Then I won't serve you so. We'll hope to meet no one. If hope fails, there will be some other way."

Why *did* she have to part from him?

She didn't, Birle thought, the idea entering her mind like an arrow finding its target. There was nobody here to bind her up and carry her back to the Inn, unless the Lord wished to. There was no law to rule her, here beyond the borders of the Kingdom. There was no one ever to know what became of her.

"I could travel with you. I could be your servant." The Lords needed servants.

"I don't even have enough food for one," he said. She

31

didn't dare look at him, but she took hope at the laughter in his voice.

"I also know the river, as you don't."

He didn't say anything.

"I can fish and I could teach you how. I could go with you only as far as where you enter the forest, and then I could bring the boat back. Don't you see?"

If she could just not have to part from him, she didn't care what happened after. Her family would punish her, for their shame, and the way she had shamed Muir; she would never wed, for no man would take the chance of such a girl, so she would spend her days in service at the Inn. Measured against the brightness of the present day, such gray forebodings meant little. A coward might find such threats for the future reason enough; but Birle thought it might be greater cowardice to throw away the bright treasure of the present hour.

The Lord was shaking his head. "Although I wouldn't mind learning what you could teach me, and the truth is, I also wouldn't mind the company. I'm not a man for solitude and silence."

Birle didn't expect him to desire her presence. If he didn't mind it, that was enough for her, and more than enough.

"Besides," he reminded her, "you've a husband awaiting you."

The thought of Muir sent a chill out from Birle's heart and she pulled her cloak closer around her. The thought of Muir as husband froze her tongue. There were songs about girls throwing themselves into the river because a man had spurned them, or had chosen another. She had always thought those girls fools, but now she understood what their choice was.

"Don't you wish to marry?" his voice asked. Birle's eyes were trapped at the toes of her boots and she couldn't see his face. She couldn't speak, as if her voice were trapped also, so she shook her head.

"I thought the people married from free choice," the Lord said.

If he thought she was being forced to wed, then he might take her with him, for pity. That little hope warmed her and

32

she raised her face to lie to him. But it was the truth she spoke. "So we do. I said yes to him."

"It looks to me as if you'd be better off to tell him you've changed your mind," the Lord advised her.

"That's the man's right. A girl who has given her word must keep it. What would the world come to if a promise made wasn't kept?"

At that he laughed. Birle locked the golden sound of his laughter up in her memory. "Who is this fortunate man?" he asked.

"A huntsman who serves the Earl."

His smile faded. "Didn't they warn you?"

"Aye, my family tried to persuade me against him, because he's older, because a huntsman's wife has to live in the city while he serves his Lord. Because there is no holding to inherit, if there are children."

"And did they tell you what happens to such wives, living poor and unprotected in the cities? Didn't they tell you how many such women turn to drunkenness, and the protection of men who are not their husbands? The wives of huntsmen and soldiers are a disease of the cities, turned vicious by poverty and hopelessness. Did they not tell you?"

"Is that true?"

He nodded.

"Would Muir have known this? Would he have known, when he asked me to wed, what my life would be?"

The Lord made no response to that.

"Aye, then, what can I do?" Birle didn't expect an answer.

"Not all huntsmen serve their wives so," the Lord said. "There are good men among the huntsmen, although they are few. Is your Muir such a man?"

"I don't know," Birle said, her voice a whisper. She should know that before she wed, to put her life into a man's hands. It had been enough for her to know that Muir wished to marry her, and thought her pretty. She had been more stupid than she had known, more stupid even than Nan had guessed.

"It may be that he is," the Lord said, pity in his eyes and

33

his voice. Now that he pitied her, Birle thought she didn't wish him to.

"Muir is not a bad man," she said, without confidence.

"It isn't easy for a huntsman to find a bride—and especially a young one. He must have guessed that you were ignorant."

Birle didn't know what Muir thought.

"If you tell your father what I've told you," the Lord suggested.

"I've given my word." That was the unfortunate truth; she had given her word and there was nothing now she could do to ungive it. "Maybe he'll turn his back to me, and say me nay, because I've spent this night who can say where."

"If he does that, you'll know he's one of the few good ones," the Lord said. "So I doubt he will."

Birle, remembering the expression in Muir's eyes when he asked her to wed, doubted it too. She had felt pity for the rough-mannered man, seeing how much he longed for her to say yes.

"So you had better come with me after all," the Lord said.

Birle, wrapped round in fear and anger, almost didn't understand the words. "With you?"

"Just as far as the path into the forest, but—if we travel slowly the fair will be come and gone, before you return. So the danger will be past, won't it? I can't see any other way, can you?"

Birle couldn't see anything for the sudden gladness rising in her, that she need not part from him, and that she need not marry Muir.

"And I'm not in any particular hurry, now I'm clear of the Kingdom. You aren't either. Are you?"

She would have to find her tongue, she knew, and answer him something. "Aye, my Lord," she said. "I mean, no, my Lord. I mean—I thank you."

"It's what I've been bred to do, rescue maidens in distress. From fierce dragons," he talked on, bending to pick up his bag, "or evil guardians, or wicked witches. I suppose an unwise wedding can be considered such a danger."

34

He moved with the grace of a young tree in a high wind, Birle thought, dazed with joy. Aye, and he was straight and strong as a tree, standing there.

"If we're going, let's be on our way," the Lord said.

Four

Two gentle days followed, days filled with watery sunshine. Sometimes Birle rowed, but more often she let the oars hang above the water, dipping them in only for a steering stroke to keep the boat to the center of the river, where the current ran most strongly. They traveled at the river's lazy pace. The Lord seemed content with this, and for herself, the longer they took the happier she would be. She didn't think of the journey's end, and the parting. Why should she spoil whatever hours she had by counting up the days and years to come?

They moved past banks that grew steeper as the land rose into hills. The branched trees they floated by were putting out pale green leaves. Frothy patches of wood violets appeared beneath boulders or atop grassy banks, as if the stars departing from the sky had left their scarves behind.

The two days passed slowly. The Lord could sit silent for hours at a time. Birle didn't know what he thought of as he stared into the water or into the forest. She was content to take care that they kept to the center and content to watch the way the water reflected sunlight up onto his face, in little light-filled shadows that moved over his cheeks and forehead.

At the end of each day he shaved his face clean, using the narrow dagger he wore at his belt. His right hand would grasp the hilt, to pull the sharp steel down along his cheek. With the fingers of his left hand he would follow the path the dagger had cleared. He did this not only on his cheeks, but also on his upper lip, with choppy strokes, and around the curve of his chin. Birle watched, and thought she understood why the men of the people wore beards. Let the Lords and Ladies wear their faces and hair like decorations. The people, men in beards and women with their long braids curled around their ears, had no time to spend so.

The differences between the Lords and the people—she kept seeing them, in the supple leather of his boots, in the unmarked smoothness of his hands, in her memory of the Ladies moving through the crowds at spring fairs and fall fairs in brightly colored gowns of blue, yellow, red, their long hair shining down their backs like silken rivers or dressed high as crowns on their heads.

He mastered the fishing spear easily. Perhaps this too was a difference between Lords and people—the people must be cautious lest they lose the little they had, so the people thought and spoke slowly, acted without haste. From the first, this Lord had acted and spoken differently from anyone Birle knew; she could only guess at what he was thinking. Birle thought he was a quick man, quick to learn, quick to laugh, and quick to pride. The first evening, the boat safely tied, the air still warm with sunlight and the speared fish gutted and ready for the fire, she had stood before him wondering how to ask permission to draw aside to bathe in the river. She didn't know if her request would again embarrass him.

"I would be alone here, Innkeeper's Daughter," he had said, dismissing her. She stood uncomfortably by the fire they hadn't yet put flint to. "I'm not going to take the boat and abandon you," he said.

"I could get back safely if you did," she told him, trying to think of how to frame her own request. "My Lord, I wonder—"

"I'm going to bathe, Birle," he interrupted. "Wash myself. My whole body. That's what bathing is. Without any clothes on," he added, when she didn't move.

"I know what bathing is," Birle answered. "The people of the Inn keep themselves clean, even in winter."

37

For a minute, he stared at her, as if deciding how to rebuke her. Then he decided that she meant no impertinence. "How could I know that?" he asked, a smile rising in his face. "You can go downstream and bathe. I'll stay here."

Birle went obediently along the bank, to a place where tumbled boulders formed a quiet pool of water. She had no soap, nor fresh linen to put on, but she rubbed herself well in the water and felt clean when she emerged. By the time she returned, he had lit the fire and was watching the flames take the wood.

"How did you bathe in winter, at the Inn?" he asked.

He was a quick man to curiosity. She told him how they stood in a wine barrel, brought up from the cellars, just as she had earlier that day showed him how the leather strap through which her knife slipped had been sewn onto the side of her boot. She couldn't ask him the questions she wondered about, but often he told her without asking. The Lords had metal tins, large enough to hold a seated man, which the servant carried into their bedrooms, then filled with heated water.

He tried slipping his dagger into the top of his boot, but returned it to its sheath at his belt. A knife carried so would not be deemed clean enough for use at table, he said. He said he himself didn't see much difference between boot leather and sheath leather, but he thought it had to do with the closeness to feet. "Feet," he laughed, "offend the ladies. There is much that offends the ladies."

He didn't expect her to say anything, she knew that. She wondered if it was a lady who had caused him to leave his home. The Lords, as it was said, married not for choice but for land, or dowry, or connection into a more powerful family—one closer to the King, perhaps—or to settle a quarrel between two families. The Lords married as their fathers or profit dictated. Perhaps then this Lord had been told to marry a woman not of his choice? To marry one when he would have chosen another—but it would be foolishness to throw away your inheritance for that, if you were a Lord. The Lords had much to inherit. The world was generous to the Lords.

But if a Lord were the youngest son, then he might be used to serve a father's or brother's ambitious plan, married for another's profit. Or he might be sent to serve in the King's household. They said that the King had Lords for servants. Aye, Birle thought, and he might come to the anger of hopelessness, enough to strike out against father, or brother, or even Earl. Any one of those might be reason enough for a young man to leave his own home, hoping to make his fortune elsewhere.

She looked at him, wondering if he was the kind of man whose angers might lead him to draw his sword. At the same moment, he raised his eyes from the water and looked at her. His bellflower eyes had a dark ring around their blue color, she saw, feeling lost in his eyes, as if they were a world in themselves, into which she had wandered and could not, even had she wanted to, find her way out, find her way back. "What are you thinking about, Innkeeper's Daughter?" he asked her. "What is there that a girl will think so intently about?"

"I was thinking of you, my Lord," she said.

This pleased him, and amused him, and he gave her a smile as heady as wine. She put the oars into the water and pulled firmly upon them. The boat sped forward.

"Thinking what?" he wondered.

Birle concentrated on rowing. "Thinking why you might have left your home." She didn't look at him, but over his shoulder to the trees, crowding a rocky bank, the roots of the pines bare to the air. She had no right to ask him questions.

After a time his voice told her, "I have broken no law."

She wanted to tell him that if he had broken a law, then there must be that about the law which should be broken. She would always believe him. But that raised a question and she wondered what its answer was. "If a man takes back by force, or stealth, something that has been stolen from him, is he a thief?"

"Under the law, he is," the Lord answered. "Under the law, he must bring his case to the Hearing Day."

"But it is a long time between one Hearing Day and the next," Birle argued. "Gold can be spent in that time. An animal may die."

"Or a case might be unjustly undecided," he agreed. "The Lord who judges might never see the truth. And by what right—do you ever think, Innkeeper's Daughter, why the people must pay taxes to the Lords?"

"How can they not, when the Lords own the land?"

"And by what right do they own it, when it's the people whose sweat makes it fertile, while the Lord sits in his walled castle within his walled city. You say the Inn serves the Earl—have you ever seen this Earl?"

Birle shook her head. "They say in my Granda's day that he would sometimes ride into the forest, for the hunting."

"But you never have, in your fourteen years. This is the man who takes gold coins from you, or silver, and if you don't pay it he can have you locked into a cell, even hanged, this man you've never even seen. Birle, you have no idea—I could be the Earl and you wouldn't know it."

"If you were, you wouldn't be here, my Lord,' she reminded him. "Besides, the Earl is an old man."

"So I can't be," he said. He leaned back, satisfied with her answer. "What I keep wondering about is—why none of the people ever doubts."

"Doubts what, my Lord?"

"Doubts—everything," he answered. "Doubts the right of the Lords to rule and the necessity of the people to serve them."

"In time of trouble, the people of Inn and forest can ask aid of the Earl," she pointed out.

"And he can give it," the Lord answered. "Can is not must, as anybody knows. But what if"—he leaned forward again—"there is no Earl, and no King. What if it is all just stories—like the stories of dragons in the south, great winged worms that fly over the land, breathing fire from their nostrils. You've heard such stories?"

"Aye, my Lord."

"Do you not doubt them?"

40

"I've never been where dragons might live."

"Try to think, Birle," he said. "Try to think about it. Here is a creature, a living creature, very long-lived I grant you, but still—it is hatched from an egg like a bird or snake, and it grows, like all living things. How can it carry fire within it, and not be burned?"

"There is much we don't understand," Birle pointed out to him. "I've seen," she said, remembering her grandparents' house, "a place where water just comes bubbling up out of the ground. Where does the water come from?"

"Underground," he answered quickly.

"Aye, but what is this underground? If it is filled with water why is the whole world not afloat? And how comes that water also to fill the sky?"

"Just because we don't understand something doesn't mean there is no reason for it. You can't find the reason unless you think about it. The first step in such thinking is doubt," he said. Then he looked at her, and smiled again. She had pleased him, Birle thought, glad of it.

"You think, then," he said, "that I should try to find one of these dragons, before I doubt it."

Birle had had no such thought, but she didn't tell him that.

"Even though there is nothing living that can withstand fire. Stones can, and metal can—although even metal can be made hot enough to melt, or how would we have knives and swords, or gold and silver coins. But if this beast is made of metal or stone, how can he lift his great weight off the ground?"

Birle didn't know how such a thing could be. Since there were no dragons in her world, she didn't see a need to wonder or worry about it. She had another question, and this seemed the time to ask it. "Do you go south, then, to know if there are dragons?"

At that, he laughed. "They say dragons have great hoards— of gold and jewels—which they sleep on as nests. Maybe I'm on my way to win such a treasure. Do you think that, Innkeeper's Daughter? I'm ill-armed to undertake a dragon's death, but if I have courage enough I could try it. If there are

41

dragons to be found." That was no answer to her question. He didn't want to answer her.

On the third morning a little light rain fell, in among the trees. The Lord didn't wish to go out onto the river in the rain, so they sheltered the day under the long branches of an ancient pine. Birle kept a small fire going, under the roof the branches made.

Sitting there, on opposite sides of the crackling fire, they toasted the staleness out of thick chunks of bread. The little rains drizzled down. The Lord said, "They make songs about high and noble things—the death of dragons, the love of beautiful women. But they should make songs about bread—and cheese—the way they fill an empty stomach. I wouldn't say no to a piece of cheese, would you?"

Birle shook her head. No, she wouldn't.

"Or a song about rain, as it falls. Do you ever wonder why they have never made a song about rain?"

Birle shook her head.

"What do you wonder about, then, Innkeeper's Daughter?" he asked her. "I know you are awake, behind your brown eyes."

He knew the color of her eyes. Why should he know the color of her eyes? In her confusion, she answered him, "I wonder about my mother's father. At least, I used to wonder about that. Now, I don't. But I used to wonder what man he was."

"What does that matter?" he asked. "I know my fathers, for generations past." The bitterness in his voice silenced her. He was looking into the flames, lost in his own thoughts. The rain turned the branches behind him a dark silvery green.

Later they sat, not side by side, leaning back against the prickly trunk of the tree. Rain pattered down onto branches and ground. The smoke from the fire rose slowly.

"How could you not know your mother's father? You must know every man in the village, there can be few to choose among. What does it matter to the people who father and grandfather might be?"

She was ashamed for the answer she must give, so she

gave it boldly. "My mother's mother, when she came from the north, was already with child. In those days, there wasn't even a village, only the Inn. She had no husband. There was no man to be father to her child."

"She came alone?"

"Not alone. My Granda," she turned her head to look at him, "Granda and Gran came from the north, when they were young, to keep the Inn for the Earl. When Granda wanted vines he returned to the land of his birth, for the sturdiness of the cuttings. He found my mother's mother at a Hiring Fair. He had known her when she was only a girl—unlucky in her father, a man who blamed his luck, not himself, for his misfortunes. At the Hiring Fair, she could find no master because she was sickly, and already swollen with the child, so he brought her back with him. She claimed Jackaroo for the father—as if that could be true."

"If I were a girl, and no man to step forward to claim my child, I'd name Jackaroo. Who can say you nay?"

"She was mazed," Birle said. "A loony. She died in birthing."

"And it no longer mattered who, or what, the father was. And the child?"

"My mother. My grandparents took her, and when she was old enough my father married her, and then she died too. I don't remember her, but my brothers do. Nan, too, remembers her—because she came a servant to the Inn when my mother was alive—but I have no memories."

"Nan is your father's second wife," he guessed.

"No, as you know. He can't wed again. If a man could wed again, then the second wife would want her children to be named heir, and what would become of the children of the first wife?"

"What if," he asked her, "a first wife dies childless? If there are no others, why shouldn't those children then be given the holding?"

"It's the law," Birle reminded him. "The Lords give the holdings, and it's their law the people follow. Can a Lord marry again, under the law?"

43

"Of course. My father buried three wives. A Lord must marry. Without sons—his brothers will grab up his lands for their own, or the King will. If you want to hold the lands, you need sons. The more the merrier," he said, but his voice was not merry. "And a daughter or two does no harm, either, especially if she has any beauty."

If this Lord had sisters, Birle thought, they would have beauty.

"A pretty face takes a smaller settlement when she marries," he explained. "What do you take for dowry to your huntsman, Birle?"

"Two gold pieces."

"A small price for a woman's life."

"Not small to the people, my Lord." She wouldn't have him think she was without value.

"Do you never think that it is the man should bring a dowry to the woman?" he asked.

Birle had no way to answer such foolishness. She thought he might be mocking her, so she explained, "The man brings his holding, or his labor." They spoke easily to each other. She hadn't guarded her tongue, and she hadn't needed to. So she asked him what she wondered. "Why did you run away, my Lord?"

At the words, his face closed to her. He turned his back. That was a question to which she should never have given voice. If Birle had dared, she would have asked his pardon. If she had dared, she would have apologized. Aye, but he wanted to hear nothing of her. His shoulders and silence made that clear.

Through the next two days of the journey, he spoke only to request her presence or absence, a fire, food, to be taken to shore or to set off on their way, to have his linen laundered. Birle was even more silent than he, because her response needed only to be actions. She wondered that her question had caused such a change. He wished to know no more of her. He wished her to know no more of him. The sun came out, and shone strongly, but its warmth fell down as sad as little rains.

Five

As the afternoon of the second unhappy day drew into its evening they came to their destination. The high island, with a single pine tree on its stony crest, sat so close to the right-hand riverbank that where the river ran between the two it was no more than a stream, rushing shallow over stones. A lowering sun turned the river to liquid gold.

Birle let the main current carry the boat beyond the island before she put oars into the water and turned toward land. When they lay in the lee of the island, she drew up to a low, flat rock. The Lord waited while she carried the rope over the rocks to reach one of the twisted roots. There she tied the boat fast, forcing the rope under the thick root, tying a double knot. She pulled the knot as tight as she could and turned to watch him stand, pick up his sack, and follow her path up, over the rocks.

This was the place where she must part from him, she knew that. But it need not be immediate, the parting. "My Lord," she said, when he stood tall beside her and before he could say anything to her, "let me catch some fish. Aye," she argued, seeing in his face that he would tell her to leave him straightway, "you should begin the journey with a full belly."

"True enough," he agreed, and sounded tired. He sat himself on a boulder, his pack at his feet.

He might, of course, choose to go on while she was away, thinking that the parting needed no farewells. "You might also want to bathe,'' Birle suggested. ''You don't know how long it will be before you find enough water to bathe in again.''

''True enough,'' he said, never moving his eyes from the nearby bank, with its steep incline and thick trees.

By the time they had eaten, the sun had set and the light was flowing out of the air. It was too late for him to start off, Birle thought, and was glad to think she had put off the parting for another few hours. But the Lord stood, picked up his sack by its leather drawstring, and swung it over his shoulder. His eyes, in the dim light, looked black. ''Here is where I go on alone, Innkeeper's Daughter.''

Birle rose, alarmed and afraid. ''But, my Lord,'' she protested. He already had his back to her, was already moving off toward the mainland.

Birle would have fallen down before him in the suppliant's position. That was all she could think: that she must go with him, that unless he were to strike her down and leave her unable to move, she would go with him. She could follow him secretly, she could. . . . ''My Lord,'' she called to his back. ''Take me with you.''

He turned but she couldn't see his face. ''Why?''

Birle didn't know what answer would persuade him. If she said that he needed a servant, he would refuse her in his pride. If she told him she feared being left alone, to make her way back alone, he would answer that that had been her choice. If she told him she had little wish to live in a world he had gone from, that one day in his company was worth more to her than a lifetime elsewhere, he would leave her behind for distaste, or for pity. Aye, and he might well laugh. Her mind ran helplessly, like a mouse between the cat's paws, seeking the words to convince him.

''Do you fear they'll make you marry your huntsman?'' the Lord asked.

Birle couldn't speak for the sudden tightness in her throat at his quick sympathy, for all that it was wrongly placed.

''What would I do with you?'' he asked, gently.

46

"I know the forest, what roots are good for eating, what greens."

"Hunger, they say, is an easy death. Freezing, they say, is easier."

"You must not die, my Lord."

"And you'll save me from it?" His voice was laughing now. Birle couldn't promise that, and so she said nothing.

"But what a monster this huntsman must be, if you fear him so."

Birle didn't deny it, although she could have said that Muir was no worse than other men. What she feared was not Muir himself, but Muir as husband. To live her days with him, to have him come to her as a man comes to his wife—that, she feared. It was only when she had had no longing of her own that Muir's hunger for her seemed enough reason to say yes to him. "Let me find you the path the merchants speak of. My eyes know better how to read the forest paths."

"You'll do that, and having done it you'll say, 'Let me go along it with you,' " the Lord prophesied.

Birle drew her cloak around her, against the chill of dark. "Aye, my Lord," she promised him.

"What if, at the fair, you're not there to be wed?"

Birle's spirits bubbled up, like the spring at her grandparents' house. "Muir will be shamed and mocked, and he would refuse to have me."

"Will you give me your word? When I say you must go, you'll obey?"

"Aye, my Lord." She would promise him anything.

"All right, then," he said. "Let's be on our way."

"You don't think to sleep the night here? It would be better to travel by daylight into the forest."

She felt his anger before he had time to voice it, and she didn't blame him. She was servant, not master. "I'm ready, my Lord," she said, before he needed to speak. "Let me carry the sack."

She took it, and put it over her own shoulders. He climbed down the boulders and splashed across the stream, before

47

clambering up the bank and into the forest. Birle followed. It was as she had first seen him, a dark, moving shadow.

He stepped in among the trees and she had to hurry to keep him in sight. The sack was heavy, clumsy. Twilight was deeper among the trees. It was hard to see what roots, or stones slippery with moss, waited to catch her feet. Although the Lord moved quickly, he often stumbled. It wasn't long before he stopped and let Birle catch up with him.

"You should be the one to lead," he said. "Since, as you say, you know the forest. What kind of path will this be, do you think?"

"A secret way," she answered him, "but wide enough for a small cart. The merchants have carts, and their beasts travel abreast by twos. So I think it won't be difficult to see."

"Shouldn't there be such a path for us to follow here?" he asked.

"I don't know," Birle told him. The forest crowded around them, tall looming trees whispering to themselves. What little light was left of evening leached out of the air, so quick you could almost watch it fade.

"How large are these caravans?"

"Sometimes only six folk, sometimes as many as twenty, or even more. Never fewer than six, for safety."

"Then they'll leave a track clear enough to be found. If we go on, we're bound to cross it. Lead on, Birle." He was impatient.

Birle set the sack down, to pull its drawstring loose so she could pull it over her head, as the huntsmen carried their quivers. This freed her arms. She moved more slowly than he had, but more steadily. They didn't speak. She could always hear him behind her, as her feet climbed the slope of the ground, up among trees and rocks and bushes. When she heard his steps stumble she stopped, to give him time.

He came up close and spoke in a dark whisper. "Can you smell that?"

Birle's ears and eyes had been the tools she used. She hadn't thought to smell. There was the tangy smell of pine needles and the moist odor of earth. There was the cold smell of the air, too, and with it something that she couldn't name at first. "Meat?" she whispered.

"Fowl, I think. Something roasting."

Birle sniffed the air like a dog. Faint though it was, the smell brought to her mouth the imagined taste of roasted fowl, crisp skin and juicy flesh. She'd had naught but fish for days, she thought.

"Wait," he whispered.

"It's this way," she said, sure of the direction.

"But who is it?"

Birle hadn't thought to wonder that. He was right to hesitate. "The merchant caravans, going north for the fairs?"

"Outlaws, lying in wait for those merchants?" he suggested. "But they wouldn't be building a fire, would they? And if they wanted to ambush the caravan, they'd wait until it was carrying gold, not goods. So it's likely that these are your merchants. It's not sure, but it's a good chance."

"If they were on their way back south, you could go with them."

"But they aren't. I can't be seen, Birle. Word of me must not get back to the Kingdom."

She didn't question that. She had another idea. "My Lord, they'll return by this same way. You could travel safely with them, then. It would be seasons before they could take word of you to the Kingdom." If he were to do that, then the two of them might stay in the forest, for however many weeks it took the merchants to complete their business. She would have his company for day after long day.

"If we are thinking of safety, it would be safest for you to travel north with them," he said.

"Except for the boat."

If he were to stay here, in the forest, she would be able to remain with him for the time. She waited for him to decide. He also waited, but she didn't know for what.

"I don't hear anything," he said at last, his voice pitched low.

"We shouldn't go any closer," she warned him.

"Why not?"

49

"They may have men on watch."

"Men on watch? Merchants? This isn't an army, Birle."

"They'll have dogs, it may be. Or the beasts, mules or horses, beasts hear more sharply than men."

"Nonetheless, we have to go closer. Where these men are, that's where the track is. When I've found it, I can circle around their camp."

"What about me?"

"Once we've found the track, you can return to the boat. I'd like you not to argue about this: It'll be a longer, slower trip upstream; and you can make it last as long as you need. If you delay your return home long enough, your huntsman will have found himself another bride." When she didn't say anything, he reminded her, "You gave me your word, Birle."

But she had not thought it would be so soon. She thought she had given her word in exchange for days, not hours, and she had had hope for weeks, not days.

"Tie your cloak closed, as I have," he instructed her. "For silence."

Birle obeyed. She still carried his sack on her back. Perhaps, she thought, following his shadowy figure among the trees, she would pretend to forget she carried his sack. Then, even though she would have to leave him, she would have an excuse to return. So she would see him once again, at least once again. He moved so intently that she thought there was good hope that he had forgotten his sack.

Their footsteps sounded loud, but she knew that to any human ear the sounds they made would blend into the forest noises. She peered into the shadowed dimness, to see and follow him.

They heard the voices at the same time that they saw the light of a fire, glimmering through the trees ahead. The Lord put his hand up and Birle stopped, immediately obedient. They crept forward until, by a hand on her shoulder, he directed Birle to move behind a wide tree trunk.

She moved to look around one side of the trunk, as he looked around the other. Flames from a small fire lit a clearing. Six men were seated or crouched around the fire. Two

50

held the ends of a long stick upon which the bodies of three rabbits hung, roasting. Beyond the fire, so still that Birle thought they must be hobbled, the sumpter beasts waited. Their backs were piled high with goods—wools and knives, ribbons and papers, woven cloths, spices and laces, the whole array that would be spread out on tables before the Lords, first, and then the people. Even at night, the goods stayed in their packs and the packs stayed on the beasts, piled onto the patient backs or hung down in thick woolen bags by their sides. At the end of a day's travels the men rested by the fire, but the beasts' labor had no end. They stood together with lowered heads, too tired to do more than nuzzle the bare ground for any blade of green.

Birle could see the cooking flesh, the skin growing crisp and brown, and see the sudden spurt of flames when fat dripped into the fire. She couldn't hear what the cloaked figures were saying to one another as they conversed around the fire. She stepped back behind the tree trunk.

"I think the track must come in here," the Lord said.

They were silent for a time.

"I'm tempted to join them, if only for the sake of a meal," the Lord said, speaking softly into her ear. "We won't, but I am tempted."

Birle nodded. She had felt, like the gesture of a moth, the momentary warmth of his breath on her cheek and her sadness threatened to choke her. She moved hastily away, as if to look again at the camp. The flames of the fire lit up the under-branches of the trees, and the low, curved arms of pines. The firelight moved through the surrounding darkness as restlessly as clouds through the sky.

Birle saw the dog, then. It came out from among the beasts to walk behind the men. She heard the Lord's voice pitched low to warn her, "See it?" and saw by his ears that the dog, too, had taken warning.

She didn't know whether better safety lay in drawing back so that she might be hidden, or in keeping still where she was so that she could see, and know what was happening. The dog walked out slowly from behind the men, slowly,

51

low, across the clearing, to the edge of the firelight. It was big, big as a hound. It growled, deep in its throat.

One of the men at the fire lifted his head, and turned around. He looked toward the tree, where she stood frozen. Birle thought the man must see her there, but she knew he could not, looking as he was from light into darkness.

Growling, head low, the dog came closer.

The Lord grabbed Birle's cloak and pulled her back, behind the tree. He motioned her to come with him as he backed carefully, silently, away from the dog, and the clearing, backed into the sheltering forest.

The dog stiffened, and barked. The sound cut through the night like a lightning flash. It barked again, deep and baying. The men at the fire jumped up. The rabbits fell into the flames. "Run!" the Lord said.

Birle turned and caught her foot on a root. The sack on her back unbalanced her and she fell down onto her knees. Scrambling onto her feet, she heard the Lord running loudly away and the dog's snarling pursuit. She turned to see the men at the fire, huddled together, their knives out but unsure of what to do, unwilling to risk the darkness and the forest. With her heart thundering in her ears, Birle moved slowly away from the clearing. She didn't begin to run until she was sure the merchants would not hear her, over the sound of the dog on the hunt.

So must the blind move through the world, she thought, following the sound of dog and running man. She dodged around dark shapes that rose up suddenly before her, trees, bushes, boulders, following. The ground was slippery under her feet. The burden on her back weighed her down.

The dog's voice was snarling now, and still she couldn't see. The snarling was accompanied by a rolling, thrashing sound. She heard, running blindly forward, reaching down to pull her knife from her boot, no word, no cry nor curse, no human voice. She heard only the dog, at its prey.

The roiling, dark mass she came upon was like the sight of a fish fighting the hook that brought him to the surface. It was all movement, and she couldn't see what was happening.

As she ran into that mass, she saw more clearly—the dog had leaped, and in leaping had brought the man down. They rolled like wrestlers. The dog bit, snarling, for the throat as the man tried to fend off the jaws and teeth, with his hands and arms. Birle fell down across them, reached her right hand underneath the dog's chin, placed her left hand down its muzzle and into its mouth to pull the head up and, before it could think to close its teeth on her hand, she drew her right hand back, across, and slit its throat.

Silence fell over them. The dog's head fell limp. Her hand and knife were wet with the rush of hot blood. She couldn't catch her breath, lying heavily there. She drew back to her knees and hauled the dog's body away.

The Lord scrambled to his feet. "Come on," he said. His voice was weak, filled with the air he struggled for. "The river. Can you find it? The boat? Get up!"

Birle stood up. "Aye, but—"

"Argue later," he told her. "The men—if there's another dog—"

Birle hadn't thought beyond the immediate danger. His words frightened her. She set off running, and he came crashing along close behind her. She led them to the river and then—knowing they had come in upstream from the island—down its bank, across the shallow stream. There, he stepped out ahead of her, his cloak loose now. He reached back to haul her up over boulders.

The boat was a dark shape floating out in the water, held to land by the rope. The Lord bent over to catch the rope and pull the boat to shore. "You get in," he gasped, "hold the oars. Where's the knot?" he cried.

Birle clambered into the boat, which rocked dangerously under her feet. She shed the sack and sat down, facing the island. She held the oars ready. As soon as he had his feet in the boat, she lifted the oars, dipped them into the water, and pulled, as strongly as she could. The boat shot away, into the river.

The sudden movement knocked his feet out from under him. He tumbled down onto the floor, facing her. Birle rowed backward until they were safe at midstream, then lifted her legs and swung around in the seat. She continued rowing, down the dark, southward-flowing river.

Overhead, the sickle-shaped new moon shone peacefully among stars, and after a while Birle's heart slowed, and her breathing slowed. She didn't know about his heart, but she heard his breath grow steady, until she couldn't hear it at all. "Are you hurt, my Lord?" she asked.

His answer came from behind her. "I don't think so, but— I'm covered with blood. Some might well be my own, but I don't feel any pain."

"Aye, the blood'll wash out," she assured him.

"And you?" he asked.

"I'm not hurt." She could have complained of fatigue, this night's work after the day's, but she didn't think she had anything to complain of.

"I couldn't get my knife. Couldn't get my hand to my knife. Or my sword," his voice told her. "You were handy with the dog."

"It's how pigs are slaughtered."

"I'm going to move to the seat."

The only answer she gave was to hold the oars out of the water. He climbed past her and sat down carefully, facing her. He rested his elbows on his knees and rested his head in his hands. Birle rowed steadily, along the quiet river with its dark, distant banks, closing safe around them like walls.

When the Lord raised his head it was to say, "You saved my life. The creature would have chewed my throat out. I was so frightened—afraid for my life. And with reason. I didn't know how fear tastes." He laughed then. "I've hunted with dogs, and thought I was a brave man doing it, and rode proudly back with the game carried behind me. It brought me down, that dog, like running game. I've seen deer brought down so." He seemed to be staring at her, but Birle could see only the whiteness of his face, not what his eyes saw. After a long time, the Lord said, "As if I were an animal. I've never been in battle, never killed a man. My brother is the soldier."

So it couldn't be a murder that he ran from.

"We might go to the shore now, my Lord," she said. "It's not safe to travel in darkness. I don't know how far downriver the port lies," she added. Without waiting for his order, she headed the boat to shore. She had forgotten the danger ahead.

He didn't protest. He didn't say anything, not until the bank loomed up close overhead. Then he told her. "I cut the rope."

He sounded so sorry, like one of her sisters, like little Moll caught with jam on her face saying "I was hungry," that Birle couldn't be angry. That sound of his words, with the darkness shadowing his features so that she was no longer sure of his face, led her to ask him, "How old are you, my Lord?" Immediately, she regretted the question. "Never mind the rope, we'll stay close to the bank where the current isn't strong. In the morning, when we can see, we'll see what's to be done for a rope."

"With my sword," he said, going on with his own thoughts as if she hadn't spoken at all. "I've been nineteen years in the world, Birle, and you'd think I'd have learned better sense, wouldn't you?"

"I wasn't thinking that, my Lord." He was quick to despise himself, she thought, and wondered why that should be so.

"We'll sleep in the boat," he said. Without another word, he turned to lie down on the short seat, his knees rising up like a tent.

Birle left the oars raised out of the water and moved off the rowing seat to the narrow bow. There, she arranged his sack like a pillow behind her. Somewhere ahead lay the port, but she didn't know how far. Now she knew his age. And she had saved his life, so she had given him something he would remember.

His voice floated out of the darkness, like the boat floating at the river's edge. "I have a bed with a feather mattress, and hangings to keep the cold out. So what am I doing here, with blood drying all over my cloak and my shirt." He didn't expect her to answer. Birle imagined what a mattress filled

55

with feathers might feel like. Her own was stuffed with straw, but feathers must be soft, softer than grass. "It's too bad, really," he said, laughter rising in his voice. "I would have enjoyed a rabbit. Why did we leave it behind, Birle?" he asked, laughing.

Six

During the night, a fog settled over them. Waking, Birle peered into the moist air, but could see no riverbank, on any side. The boat moved gently along, like a basket set adrift. But this was like no fog she had even seen on the river. Fogs lay down along the river like ribbons lifted on air, or the unbound hair of drowned women; river fog floated, soft and fine, until the morning brushed it away. This fog crowded gray-white around their boat. Birle knew it must be day, because it was daylight that caused fog to shine white, but how far into the day they had traveled, she had no idea.

It should have been frightening, this blindness, this ignorance, but it wasn't. She could see the Lord, where he slept, with his long legs hanging out over the flat water. She could see a little way around them. Such isolation was safety. The thickness of the fog made them invisible. At any time, she could pick up the oars and steer them to one bank or other, and it didn't matter which; but she judged that for the time they were safest in midstream. She didn't think it necessary to wake the Lord.

The moist, white world around her made no sounds except for the gentle sweep of the river, nuzzling up against the boat as a kid nuzzles up against its mother for milk. As far as Birle's senses told her, there was only the boat and its two passengers in the whole empty world.

When the Lord stretched, his heels splashed into the water. His eyes opened in surprise and he was immediately awake. He pulled his legs in, sat up, and looked around. "Is it late?" he asked. "It feels late." He rubbed at his face with his hands. "I guess you can sleep deeply even without a feather bed."

"Aye you can, my Lord," Birle agreed. If that were not so, only the Lords would get rest. "When the fog burns off, we'll see where we are."

Wrapped around by fog they drifted on. After a time, he asked for his sack, and Birle passed it to him. He took out the map and spread it out over his knees. "How near are we to this port?" he asked.

Birle had no idea. For a minute, looking at the map—at the line of river opening into the sea, at the emptiness once the sea began, and the unknown land falling away to the south—she felt a washing of fear go over her. It was a small thing, no more than a little wave washing on the river's bank. She thought of her family at the Inn, and how they might worry, and she wished she could have sent them word, somehow, that she was well. The Lord's stained cloak reminded her that those merchants might have taken word to the Inn; but there had been no chance to give them a message. It was odd, however, that the fog didn't lighten.

The Lord reached over the side of the boat to wash his face, splashing water over his eyes and cheeks and chin. His tongue licked at his lips. "Birle? Wash your face, as I have."

She wondered what marks were on her, but didn't hesitate to do as she was told. There might well be dirt, and the blood, too, which would be an ugly sight. The water was cold, and she splashed it hastily over her face. It trickled cold down her neck and into her mouth. There was a salt taste to it, she thought, dipped her hand into the gray water again and tasting it on her tongue. She turned around to ask him.

"We must be near the sea," he said.

Birle looked at the map. If it was seawater they floated on, they must have passed the port in the night, and they might be drifting out now into the landless area. "Should we turn back?" she asked. "You don't want to go out there—" Her finger hovered above the broad empty space.

"Could we have passed the port in the night and never know?"

"If I could see the sun, I could know which way is south," Birle said.

"How do you know I want to go south?"

"Aye, my Lord, that's the only direction for you, if you would come at the end to a city."

"But how do you know that the cities lie to the south?"

"Because north"—she pointed at the letter *N* with the arrow underneath it—"is that way." Then she saw her error. Her hand drew back, as if it had touched fire, and she spoke quickly. "Or so I understood from the way the map looks. Because the Inn was here, you said it, and I know the Kingdom lies to the north of the Inn, and the river—everybody says—runs to the south and west." If he knew she knew letters, and words, and how to read them, he would never trust her. "Or, is it that you don't want to go to the cities of the south?"

His bellflower eyes just stared at her, and he said nothing.

"I thought—you were looking for a dragon," she said, trying to make him smile.

He folded the map up and put it away. "No, you're right, it's to the south I'm traveling. My grandfather says, it's never wise to underestimate what the people know. But I don't think we can be at the sea, not yet."

"Why not? What do you know of it? I know only what I've heard, that it lies there at the end of the river."

"I don't know anything, but I've heard things. When entertainers come to the castles, they pay for their dinners with the tales they tell. The waves of the sea, they say, are tall, even on a calm day, tall as a table. The water rises and falls, pulled somehow by the moon, in tides—twice a day if they are to be believed. I don't believe everything they tell. Great twisting grasses grow in the water, and there are creatures that come up from the bottomless depths of it, to raid the shores or to attack boats. These long-necked creatures rise suddenly up out of the water to come crashing down on a boat. They have heads, teeth—eyes—but their heads are scaly, like snakes, without ears or hair or feathers. No man lives to tell the tale.''

Birle looked out into the fog, but could see nothing.

''Which makes you wonder how the tale gets told, doesn't it? But I think we aren't on the sea,'' the Lord said, ''because it seems to me that where the river joins into it, the sea must mix back up into the river, and that would cause the river water to taste of salt.''

Within the circle of the visible world there was the man, the boat, and the colorless water. What lay beyond Birle could not see. If she couldn't see it she couldn't concern herself with it. Thinking that, she smiled; seeing her smile, he answered it with his own, and opened his mouth to tell her something.

''Hold your oars.''

The man's voice came out of the fog. Birle couldn't say which direction it came from, before or behind them, to right or left.

''Did you hear—?'' the voice asked.

''I didn't hear nothing,'' a second voice answered. ''You, you're hearing things now.''

Birle heard the sound of oars. She peered into the fog, to see from which side danger approached, and how close it lay. She moved forward to take their oars in her hands, but ''No,'' the Lord whispered.

''There,'' the first voice spoke out of the fog.

''You're drunk.''

''I wish I were. This hag's breath of a fog is poor company for a sober man. And you're no improvement. The only thing that smells worse than your clothes is your breath, and the only thing that stinks more than your breath is the words you puff up with it.''

Birle had her knife in her hand, and looked about her, right and left, back and front. The Lord had drawn his sword. The voices were drawing closer, but she couldn't see any boat, or man. She didn't know how long she could sit still, waiting for danger to attack. She didn't know how the Lord could be so at ease, as if he were waiting for his servant to bring him a goblet of wine.

"Watch your mouth," the second voice said. Oars splashed, but the fog made sound seem to be where it was not. The sound of that other boat came from all around Birle. "Cap'n said if you was drunk I should slit your throat, and good riddance. That's his exact words."

The first voice laughed. "And you believed him? If you did, you might as well try it. But I should point out that if you succeed at the attempt—which is not highly probable— you might find the captain not entirely grateful to you. He has uses for me. For myself, I've little use for the world, and the world has no use for me, so you're free to find out for yourself if I'm sober or drunk."

Birle hoped the voices were drawing away now. She thought they were becoming fainter. But she was afraid she was deceiving herself.

"An' don't think I wouldn't," the sullen voice said.

"Although you'd be wise to hold your hand at least until we've relieved these travelers of their burdens. As the captain knows, they'd prefer to be robbed by a gentleman."

"Some gennlemun."

The voices *were* moving away. Birle's shoulders sagged with relief. She tried to catch the Lord's eye, to nod at him so that he too should know all was well, but he stared into the fog over her shoulder.

"Just row. It's what you're good for," the gentleman's voice said.

"I been rowing for two hours, I'll wager. And with the current running against me. And you too dainty to take a turn at the oars."

"It won't be so hard returning downstream. You can cheer yourself up with that thought." The voice was mocking now.

"Could be, I'll tell him you was drunk, anyway."

"He wouldn't believe you."

"Oh aye?"

"You have the mind and manners of a brute, and I can give him the word of a gentleman."

"Hoo," the second voice crowed, drifting away in the fog. "Hoo, hoo."

As the immediate danger faded, Birle remembered the stories she'd heard, the voices rising up through the floors from the public room, creeping out through the crack of a closed door. The Lord signaled her to lean toward him. She could barely find the will to obey him. They were both on their knees in the little boat; they brought their faces so close that they could speak almost without sound.

"We must go back," Birle said. "To the Kingdom."

He shook his head, the deep blue eyes staring at her, as if he would see inside of her head, to see everything that was there. What should he fear in her? Birle knew what it was she feared. Fear made her bold. "My Lord, we're near the port. What they do to the prisoners they take—aye, the women especially, but men, men too—I heard a man say that the cries from the cells—it's those cries that make the skies weep, I heard—"

He put his hand over her mouth. "Birle. Hush. Hush now. I'll keep you safe," he promised her.

She shook her head. He could not promise her that, if there were many to attack them. She had seen goats upon a nanny in her season.

"Birle," the Lord said, "I could kill you, if it were your wish, if death seemed the better fortune. But I don't understand—I thought that the people took their pleasure as it came to them."

"Why should you think that?" she asked him. "We are not animals."

"I know. I know," he said, sounding tired. "My grandfather told me that as well. It would be easier to be a Lord if the people were sheep."

The wistful quality of his smile quelled her anger as effectively as a bucket of water on a fire. Aye, and he couldn't protect her, she knew that. But his promise to do so was genuinely given. How could he know, gently raised and living so easily, how cruel men could be? It was fine in him to make the promise, and to mean it.

62

He had never seen goats going after a nanny in her season, or dogs when a bitch was in heat.

"Can we not turn back?" Her low voice had ragged edges of fear.

"I cannot, Innkeeper's Daughter."

"Or, let me take us to the opposite bank. To wait. Let the merchants return from the fairs, and whatever thieves they meet on their way, and then—then the way around the port would be safer."

"I don't know. If we make any sound—sounds carry, even the sound of muffled oars. . . . I don't know how broad the river is, if—Do they guard the port? Have the merchants said?"

"I don't know. We can't see. What time is it, think you?"

"I don't know. If we can stay hidden until dark . . . How far is it from the port to the sea?"

"I don't know." She looked at him, his face close to hers, waiting for him to decide what they should do.

"What have we gotten ourselves into, Birle?" He spoke as if it were a joke.

It was no joke. Birle would have liked to tell him that. But his smile, and his bellflower eyes close, his face so close to hers that his breath brushed her ears: The confusion of her feelings overwhelmed her. Fear and contentment, and the danger they were moving toward, and she didn't even know how close it lay, she couldn't even see where it might come from in the fog—"Please?" she said, her voice like a cry.

He clapped a hand across her mouth again, and this time held it there. She tried to push it away but he dug his fingers into her cheeks. "Hush. Listen. Hear it? There's something—get down, pull your cloak over you, stay down out of sight in the boat. In the fog—our only chance is not to be noticed, seen or heard. Hear it?"

She heard it, a creaking of wood like trees pulled by the wind, and a clanking of metal like a workhorse turning the plow on its chain. Too frightened to protest, or to think, Birle obeyed. She slid backward, to lie curled up on the floor-

63

boards. She pulled her cloak up over her until she lay in darkness, alone.

She heard the faint rustle that she thought was the Lord, arranging himself under his own cloak, and then—for minutes, or maybe an hour—she heard nothing but faraway sounds. She didn't know what those sounds were, or if it was distance, or fog, or the enveloping cloak that made them sound so far away. Her heart beat so loud in her ears she was sure it must be heard, like a drumbeat. She couldn't catch her breath and her whole body seemed to be quivering as she strained to hear.

A shriek filled the air, like lightning. Another came after it and then there was silence. The shriek echoed in her head. Who would shriek so, and what must be happening? It was as thin as a child's voice in terror. Birle strained her ears, and could hear nothing.

Something thumped against the side of the boat, rolling her sideways. She wanted to throw off the cloak and jump up, knife in hand, to face whatever danger awaited. She wanted to scream out aloud. She clamped her teeth shut. It could be another boat their boat had run into and at any moment they would be plucked up and out, like eggs taken out from under a hen.

But the boat seemed still to be moving. A log, then? Or a branch, torn from its trunk by the wind. Pilings, that held up a dock?

Fear pressed down heavy on her, her shoulders and legs, on her bent neck. In the blackness under the cloak fear was blind, a blind, groping thing struggling to get out, like a kitten taken to be drowned in a sack. Birle had never known how much fear she could feel, and she did not think she could endure it. She stared into the blackness, her hands clenched under her cheek. Fear lay down on top of her like a black cloud, trying to get into her mouth through her clenched teeth. There was nothing she could do but wait, and hope that the danger—a danger she couldn't even lift her head to meet—might not notice the little boat, drifting helpless through the fog. Birle shut her eyes, to shut out the imagined dangers. Without thought, or choice, she was asleep.

She woke to the sound of her name, spoken over her head. The darkness as her eyes opened puzzled her, and the stale air, and the way the boat was rocking. Lifting her head, remembering, throwing off the cloak to sit up, Birle saw that the Lord was sitting in the rowing seat with the oars in his hands and that the fog had closed in around them. The little visible world had grown even smaller. She held on to the side of the boat with a hand, against the rough rocking. Water sprayed into her face, and she welcomed its sharp coldness. The water tasted of salt.

"Where are we?" she asked.

"Did you faint? I thought only Ladies were given to fainting." There was no fear, no caution, in his voice.

"I was asleep. How long has it been? Are we safe?"

"Safe?" He raised his eyebrows. "We passed the port—we must have—some time back. I think now we are on the sea. If my belly is to be believed, it's late into the day. Tell me, Innkeeper's Daughter, do you prefer the known danger or the unknown?" He gave her no chance to answer the question. "Are you sorry now?"

That question he did give her time to consider. Birle could wish herself at the Inn, in familiar surroundings, with the smell of a stew in the kitchen and the sounds of custom in the public room, and Nan bursting in to scold. But that life seemed no more than a dream remembered. She was about to answer him, no, not sorry; but he answered himself.

"I am. I am sorry. I should have overpowered you that first morning, it would have been easy—or left you behind while you slept at night. I haven't served you well."

The kindness of his thought touched her even while the bitterness of his voice made her want to remind him that his way would be easy, now that the port lay behind him.

"Should we not be making toward the shore?" she asked him.

"Which way would that be?"

65

The fog drifted close, in sheets like rain, in long groping white fingers. Beyond the close, drifting fog a settled whiteness filled all the air.

"When the fog lifts we'll know which way to go," Birle said.

"The sea, as I've heard, is endless and empty. You should be sorry."

"Aye, maybe I should. And maybe I would be, if it would make any difference." Although that last she would not promise, watching his mouth's corners turn up in a reluctant smile. "When the fog lifts, when we can see the sun, then we can know. The land lies to the east of the sea."

"How do you know that?"

"It's on the map," Birle reminded him. "If we go away from the setting sun, or toward the rising sun, we must come to land, sooner or later."

"How are you so certain that's what the map says?"

Birle had not thought fear would bite him as hard as it had her. "North is marked on the map." He still stared at her. "That's what the *N* means, my Lord, with the arrow beneath it to point north."

"I thought you had recognized it."

She had fallen into his trap.

"You know *N*, that it's a letter. Do you know other letters?" He sounded curious, not angry. Birle nodded her head. "You've seen other maps too, I warrant that."

Birle nodded.

He thought about this. "And words? Can you read?"

"Aye, my Lord. And write." Maybe she shouldn't have added the last, but she was proud to surprise him.

"Who would have taught you?" he asked. "There's no danger now in answering my curiosity."

That reminded her of her own questions. "What did you do, that you must flee your own lands, your own home, your own family? There's no danger now in answering my curiosity either."

She thought he would laugh aloud, but he didn't. "What I did was be myself, be the man I am. Let me ask you a

66

question, Birle. How many just Lords can rule before the land goes to ruin?''

"Why should a Lord not be just?" she asked.

"Which is the greater good for the people, justice or safety? If the land goes to ruin, then there is no living for the people. They suffer first, and most. So that if a Lord cares feelingly for his people, he is the very one who will put them into danger. One such Lord, in several generations, might do good. But how many such Lords can the people bear?''

Birle couldn't have answered that question and he didn't seem to want her to. He might have plotted, she thought, against a Lord he thought was such a danger. Plotters, even among the Lords, were hard dealt with. If a servant turned his hand against his master the whole house trembled on the act, and what were Lords to Earl and King but servants to master.

And why, she wondered, were they talking of such things? It was as if both of them wished to be distracted from the troubles they faced and could do nothing about. If they were afloat on the sea, and blind in the fog—they didn't even know what direction they should turn in. What then did it matter that she knew reading and writing, or that he had been caught out in a plot against his overlord?

Seven

DARKNESS lowered itself down upon them, at the end of that day. Ordinarily, light and color drew up out of the air leaving darkness behind, but that evening the dark came down, flowing down into the fog, like mud into a river. The Lord did not speak.

How long it was after that that the wind came up, Birle couldn't tell. The wind blew at the fog, blowing it away. Looking up, she saw the sky stretched huge above her. She hadn't thought the sky could be so large. Thick clouds moved across it, dark shadows that showed—where they broke— glimpses of the young moon, and her attendant stars. Birle's spirits lifted. "My Lord, are you asleep?"

"No."

The boat leaped about on the sea waves, like a kid at play.

"Should I row? Think you?"

"Do you know which way the land lies?"

"I thought you might," she said.

"No, I don't," he said. She waited for him to make the choice. When he made none, said nothing, she spoke again, across the darkness.

"I think the land is over there, where the wind comes from. It feels to me as if that's where the land is." If she were rowing, then at least she could warm herself. This wind had an edge to it that cut through her cloak. Waves sprayed up, and into the boat. Aye, he was probably cold, too. "It'll be hard going against the wind. Let's each take an oar."

68

"That's better than sitting and waiting for whatever might come upon us," he said. "Well, then, Innkeeper's Daughter, we'll row. But move very carefully. This boat seems not as safe a place as once it was."

Cautiously, the Lord first, they settled themselves on the rowing seat. As they stroked with the oars to bring the boat around into the wind, waves splashed up over the side. The water was ice-cold upon Birle's fingers. She ignored it, trying to match her strokes to his.

Rowing was hard work, made harder by the spray of cold seawater over her head and neck and hands. But it did warm her. She hoped it was warming to him, as well. It must have been, because when he spoke his voice was rich with laughter. "We made it safely past your dreaded port. That's something to be proud of, if the tales you told me are true."

"Why shouldn't they be?"

"I wonder, often, about those wolves and bears you spoke of," he reminded her. "Which matter not at all, now. There'll be little danger from wolf or bear here on the sea. And what do you think of it, Innkeeper's Daughter? Do you think if we knew where our choices would lead us we would still make them as we did?"

"But we can't know," Birle said. She paid little attention to his words. She was busy with her own thoughts. Her own thoughts were uncomfortable companions. The wind, she thought, was rising, steadily rising. It might just seem that way now because they were backing into it, and thus receiving its full force—or so she hoped. But the clouds also seemed to be moving more swiftly across the sky, and to be massing together. Birle turned her head and saw—coming at them across the sky from the direction she hoped was west—an endless darkness, like a wall.

Did waves wash over the bow more frequently? More strongly? The whole back of her cloak felt wet. She bent herself to the task of rowing, both hands on the oar handle. She couldn't even see to know if they made any progress. There was no landmark against which to place the boat.

Aye, and there was no land, here on the sea.

She was afraid, again afraid. She did not dare to name her fear, for hope that it might prove groundless, for fear that naming it would give it truth. She sat with her back to her fear, as to the wind and waves. Fear blew and sprayed at her back but she dared not turn around to face it. How long they rowed thus she didn't know.

When the skies opened and rain poured down upon them, they both stopped rowing, without a word. Against wind-driven waves the oars did no work. Waves crashed into the sides of the boat. The boat bounced and fell. Water poured down over Birle's head and shoulders and legs. Water splashed over the sides of the little boat. The wind roared like water. "These boats," Birle called, "are built for quiet waters."

"If we don't bail the water out we'll sink," he called back.

They had nothing but their hands to bail with. Birle bent down and cupped her hands together, to lift water over the side of the boat. The boat rolled and bucked on the black water, under the black sky. The Lord worked beside her.

The whole world had contracted to the little boat, and the splashing of water, out of the boat and into it. She was barely aware of the sheets of water pouring down into the boat from the sky. She would have stopped the work of bailing if she could have thought of a reason to do so; although, there was no reason to continue it, none that she could think of.

When the Lord took hold of her wrist, she thought he must be thinking the same thought. But he pointed toward a patch of whiteness, moving on the water beyond his shoulder. Except that it did not lie quiet, that patch of whiteness was like a patch of snow, hidden deep among the trees from the warmth of spring.

"What is it?" Birle called. He shook his head; he didn't know.

The boat spun around, and crashed down against a wave. Birle's knee cracked against the oar that swung uselessly up and down. There was a heavier darkness waiting behind the unquiet patch of white. Something was drawing them toward

70

it. A screaming cry was making its way up from Birle's stomach, fighting its way up to her throat.

The boat rolled under them. She slid heavily against the Lord, who struggled to keep his seat in the boat. He fell off the seat and onto his knees on the floorboards. Birle slid heavily away from him.

His hand latched on to her wrist again. "Rocks," his voice called close into her ear.

Birle had no time to think. The boat was thrown into the middle of white-crested waves. Her hand grabbed for his wrist as they tumbled into the water. Her shoulder hit something hard, his wrist slipped out from her numb fingers, her head was taken by the waves. She turned over, her head pulled down, down into darkness underwater. Her legs rolled heavy above her. She had no choice but to go where the water took her, turning in the icy water like a leaf in stormy air. She tried to struggle against it, struggle up into the air. Blackness struck her on the back of the head and she tumbled into it, like falling into water.

What roused her, Birle was not sure. It might have been the sun coming up over the distant edge of the moving water. When she opened her eyes, she could see the first early curve of the sun, over the unsteady horizon. It might have been the odd sucking sound below her, or the cry above her, a wailing screech answered by another and another. Birle lifted her head to find the source of the cries, which seemed to be two large soaring birds. Or, it might have been the hardness of the rock on which she was lying facedown, and the soreness of her arms, legs, shoulders, even her head, of her back and belly. She had heard such cries before.

Remembering, she rolled over and sat up, ignoring the sudden ache of her head.

The Lord lay not far distant on the same rock—it was as large as an animal shed, the rock, and maybe even larger, since it seemed to continue on underneath the water. The fingers of one of his hands grasped the edge of her cloak. She pulled it free.

He didn't stir. She could see his back rising and falling, so she knew he lived. His cheek had been scraped. A cut on his forehead had crusted dry. His gold-tipped eyelashes lay upon his cheek, and she thought she wouldn't disturb his sleep.

Birle looked around her. The sea, and rocks; rocks tumbled down from a tall cliff behind her, or so it seemed; as endless as the sea, the sky over the top of the stony cliff face, turning pale blue before the light of the rising sun. There was no sign of the boat.

Birle sat at the edge of the flat rock, waiting. The water sucked at the toes of her boots. All around her—the ragged cliff, the ragged boulders, and even the pebbles in the shallow waters below her were ragged—was stone. The world was made of stone, and water. It was a small curved inlet where they had been thrown to shore.

She reached a hand up, to touch the throbbing pain at the back of her head. A large, tender lump had swollen up under her hair. She must have been knocked unconscious, she thought, and he must have pulled her up onto the shore. She was glad he had done that, although she thought it would have been easier to drown, unconscious and unknowing. She knew, with a dull certainty, that no living thing could live long in this stony world.

If she must die here, then she must. She wished the Lord need not, but she could do nothing about that. Aye, and for herself, his was the company she would choose. He was the one she would choose for company, in her meeting with death.

There was no need to rouse him, so she didn't. She sat still, because there was no purpose to movement, and because her body protested at every motion. The sun came up and gilded the empty surface of the restless water. In the little bay, the sun reached the stones under shallow water, so that it looked as if the floor of the sea were made up of ragged pieces of gold. Every now and then, a bird cried out overhead.

"Birle?"

She turned her head to greet him, to see him. Her braids had come loose from their coils and hung down heavy over her shoulders.

"I think you must have saved my life," she said.

"I think I must have," he answered, with a smile that lifted her spirits and eased her pains. He stood up, groaned, then moved stiffly to sit beside her. "So we know where east is. Have you found a way out of this place?"

Birle didn't answer. He could see as clearly as she how the two cliffs came down armlike around them, three times the height of the tall walls that surrounded Mallory's city, jutting out into the water.

The early sun shone over them. Little waves played against the rocks, with the same sounds that the river made playing against its banks. Birle could barely remember what had happened in the storm. She could barely believe it was the same water that now lay so docile at her feet.

"We'll have to wait for rescue then," the Lord said.

Birle turned to look at his face, scraped and cut.

"You mustn't give up hope," he said.

Hope wasn't so much to give up, Birle thought; but he must think it was. "Aye, my Lord."

"I'm hungry," he said. "Aren't you?"

"And thirsty," she realized. "But we've water in plenty."

"You mustn't drink seawater."

"Why not?"

"It's a kind of poison, or so I've heard. I've heard that men who drink seawater go mad with thirst. It only makes them thirstier, and so they drink more, and die in a fever. Clawing at their own throats." He unclasped his cloak and shook it off his shoulders. He raised his face to the sun. "Who knows if it's false, or true, that story? I heard it more than once, and think it may be true. How did you learn to read, Birle? And write?"

There was no harm in telling him now. "My grandparents taught me."

"How would they have learned it?"

"I don't know." Birle had never even thought to ask them.

"They were never like other people. They were born in the northern Kingdom. Maybe in the north, some of the people know how to read and write."

He shook his head. "But that's not so. I can't think they would have studied with the priests. Didn't the villagers ask about them? This couple, from the north, who knew reading and writing?"

"But there was no village when my grandparents came. There was only the Inn, in the Earl's gift. Besides, even if there had been a village, they kept it secret. The Inn's treasure, they called it. The village"—and for a moment, her memory brought it clearly before her eyes—"is small, and new. It isn't even really a village—there are only four families in it, fishermen's families. Although Rue, since his accident, can't fish for many hours because his arm tires and falls useless, so he sometimes makes baskets to sell at the fairs. My second brother, who will not inherit the Inn, talks sometimes of asking the Earl for a butcher's holding—because the pigs feed fat in the forest—or a blacksmith's. The village grows slowly."

"With the village so small, there wouldn't be many to choose from, for marriage."

"Aye, that's true," she said. The only boys in the village were six and ten, little boys who had yet no thought of asking a girl to wed.

"Have you sisters?" he asked her.

"Two, just little girls. Nan has had two daughters."

"The woman your father cannot marry," he remembered.

"Aye."

"And your brothers are older than you."

"Aye."

"If we talk, Birle, then we need not think. Unless you would rather not talk?"

"No, my Lord."

"What does that no mean?" he asked. "No, you would choose not to think, or no, you would choose not to talk?"

Birle thought she knew what it was he preferred not to

74

think about. "Have you brothers, my Lord?" she asked. "Have you sisters?"

He took so long to answer, she thought she had offended him again. "One brother. My mother had two sons. There are other children, but not my mother's. I don't know how it is among the people, but a Lord wants as many children as he can get. So many children die, and the strength of the family is in men who can serve the King and thereby earn its right to the estates. My father married three wives, and outlived all of them, before he died himself. He was rich in wives. The house breeds men of strong passions—in earlier times, when they turned the passion against themselves, they were known as dangerous men. The difficulty is, of course, that it's such men who make the house strong. My brother will be a man like that, and my father might have been, if he'd outlived my grandfather. But my grandfather still lives, and he is honored, more than most Lords, by his people. They don't see the harm he does them. He sometimes sees it, I think. My father saw it, and often spoke of it, although never to my grandfather, before he died."

That made too many times he had mentioned his father's death. Birle wondered why that death was so near the front of his mind.

"When did your father die, my Lord?"

"In the winter."

Near enough for grief to be fresh, Birle knew, although he didn't sound grieved. "How did he die?"

"Hunting. There was an accident, while he was hunting with his men."

"He was thrown by his horse," Birle guessed. Such accidents were not uncommon among the Lords.

"No, not that way." He told it like a story. "My father rode out, early, wrapped in furs against the cold. He had with him four Lords and a dozen huntsmen, and the snow muffled all sound of the horses' hooves. They made a line of color on the white landscape, and the twelve green cloaks of the huntsmen shone in the sunlight. It was deer they were after, meat, and they rode down a herd in the forest half a

75

day north. My father and some others followed after a young buck until it turned, exhausted, to fight what it couldn't flee. They notched arrows to bows, my father at the front. There was a singing of arrows through the air—and one went through my father's neck. At nightfall, they brought him home, dead. No man could know whose arrow killed him— the huntsmen all fletch their arrows the same way.''

Birle could think of nothing to say.

"A huntsman loves gold as much as any other man," the Lord said.

"You think the man was suborned? Who would do that?''

"At whose behest, I don't know, or if it was so. My grandfather is old, and ill, so there will soon be a new Earl. Which is, as you've probably guessed, why I had to leave.''

Birle had guessed nothing. She thought of what he had told her. If his brother became Earl, his own position would be safer. "Were you in danger? Why were you in danger? What danger was it?''

"The most perilous," he said, and laughed. "You don't know? I was sure you did, but vanity blinds us.''

"Know what?''

"Who I am. I am Orien.''

The name meant nothing to Birle.

"The next Earl Sutherland. My father's eldest son. I may even be Earl now.'' He was watching her carefully. "Or my brother will be, and I sometimes think that might be his desire. He would make a great Earl, an honor to the house.''

She didn't know what he watched for, or what he saw. In part, she was proud for him, that he should be a Lord even among the Lords, and she was not surprised to hear how great a Lord he was. And in part she was angry.

It was the anger that spoke. "Then why did you run away?'' If he had not abandoned his rightful place, she would not be here, without hope.

"How else could I make my brother Earl? Over all the lands—as I often think he should be, for the man he is.''

Aye, and if this Lord—Orien, she named him to herself— had not run away, she would never have seen him skulking through the night, and followed him. Birle didn't know what she thought. "How could you give your rightful title over to your brother?" she asked him.

"Because—look at me, I can't even bend a girl of fourteen to my will, but must listen and give way to your wishes. I meant to send you back, the first morning, and look where I've brought you. How could I rule the land, and the people? You see what would come to them, under my hand."

Birle didn't see anything. "Was it that you thought your brother would have you murdered too?" She turned her head to see his face. Orien, she thought. It was good to have a name for him.

"That, too, is my difficulty. I don't know that Gladaegal suborned the huntsmen, and I wouldn't have thought it of him; but I can't but wonder. And if he has been brought so low—I didn't like to think of his honor, lost so, his proud honor. Or do you mean because I am afraid?"

"I don't think you are afraid," Birle answered. Watching his face, she wondered if—if she had many years to serve him—she would ever tire of seeing him smile. "If you doubted your brother—that would be a crime of treason upon him, wouldn't it?"

"Could I have my own brother taken for treason?"

"Didn't you wish to be Earl?"

"Yes. Like any other man, I wanted it. But I saw, when I lived as a page in the King's household, how men will say and do what they think will please him who has power over them. The King doesn't hear the truth. The Lords live in a net of lies. And the women are worse than the men, perhaps because they have only one way to get power over a Lord— and the women servants worst of all. Even knowing, and they do know, that the best they will get is a dowry to buy them one of the Lord's creatures—to give his child a father's name. There is so much to be done, and no one does it."

"What would you do?" she asked him.

"I have such ideas," he laughed. "Why must a Lady take land with her, for dowry, when often that means she will never marry, if her father and brothers don't wish to part

77

with their land. And who can blame them? Or Stewards, did you never think that it would be better to have the Steward who collects taxes be one of the people? Chosen by the people? I'd have two Hearing Days in each year. One a year is not enough for justice, and I would have the man who speaks for the people be changed, each five years, I think. I think if a man holds power for too long, it—changes him, for the ill.''

What of the Lords, then, Birle wondered. But that was not a question to be asked of a Lord, and especially not of a man who might be an Earl.

"My brother," he said softly, as if only to himself, "is First Captain, over all the soldiers."

"You are proud of him," Birle said. But why should she not ask it, since there were only the two of them in the world, and both doomed.

"I always thought he was the best man I would ever know," Orien said, sad now.

"What about the Lords?" Birle asked.

Her question pulled him back from his own thoughts.

"Or the King?" she insisted. "Both have held power over the people for all the time in memory."

"As if the people were cattle," he said, and she thought he was pleased at her question. "You begin to understand my dilemma, Birle. What kind of a herdsman would spare his beast from the knife? Or the shears, that the creature might not feel the cold?"

"How could you run away? To leave behind you the safety of castle, servants, and food."

"My father was not safe," he pointed out. "And my own thoughts kept me uneasy."

"You ran away from thoughts? Ideas? An idea is—nothing."

"It's enough," he told her.

"Aye, it's only the Lords, whose bellies are full, for whom ideas can be reason enough. And look where this idea has brought you."

He looked. He stood up to take in everything—the steep

cliffs and the jagged rocks, and the empty sea, out of which the sun had risen.

"We must wait for rescue," he said.

Birle's mouth opened to tell him how long she thought the rescue he spoke of would take, but she closed it without saying a word. He must be used to living with hope.

The sun was up in the sky now, its light reflecting off the water. Birle lay back and let the sunlight fall over her, to finish drying her cloak and skirts. She had no hope. With her eyes closed, she could hear him clambering around on the rocks. The Earl of Sutherland—such a man wouldn't sit quiet until he had tried every way to find food. Such a man wouldn't give up easily. He would examine every inch of the barren trap they were caught in and then, even if he gave up hope of food, he wouldn't give up hope.

Hunger waited gently in Birle's stomach and she would have welcomed a mouthful of water, but she was not afraid. Orien's boots splashed now among the little rocks, as he moved away, exploring their prison. The warm sun poured down over her, and the sound of waves made a lullaby.

She would do well to be afraid, Birle thought, but she didn't have the heart for it. If they could know her situation, her family would shake their heads and say they could have foreseen it, and ask her if she was sorry now. As if she could hear their voices and they could know her answer, Birle shook her head. She was sad, but not sorry.

"Can you see any way up?" Orien asked. He had returned from his explorations. "I couldn't."

Birle tipped her head back, to study the cliff face. It was a wall of stone, uneven and rough-faced, but without pathway. The ledges formed by bulging rock did not connect with one another; the clefts, up which a strong and patient man might work his way, came to abrupt conclusions; the whole tall cliff seemed to lean outward to its topmost height, as a neck leans outward to its chin. Birle could see no pathway up the cliff face, no way around the enclosing arms of the cliff, no way across the empty sea. She could see no way for them.

79

"Because," Orien said, "if we are going to try to climb up, we ought to do so while we still have some strength."

Birle had no strength.

The bellflower eyes studied her face. He was standing, leaning against the rock. "Rest, Birle."

"What will you do?" Without food or water, their strength could only fade; he was right to think now the time for the cliff. She didn't have the heart to tell him so, but he ought to make the attempt. She couldn't, but neither could she condemn him for going on alone. She made herself ready to hear him say it.

"I'll wait, think. I'll sing you a song. Would you like me to sing you a song?"

Surprise made her smile. "Like the minstrels at the fairs."

"I lack an instrument. I didn't think to bring an instrument with me, and I might well have, now I think of it. A minstrel is welcomed, wherever he goes, and fed—if he pleases his listeners. It would have been a good idea, if I'd only thought of it. Would you like a song?"

"Aye," she said, lying back with eyes closed against the brightness of the sky, content.

"Then you shall have it." The voice had laughter in it. As soon as he began to sing, Birle recognized the song. It was one she had heard at fairs, when the minstrels performed before the Lords and Ladies, and the people stood back to listen from the proper distance.

"There were three ravens on a tree," he sang. "Down a down, hey down, hey down. There were three ravens on a tree, with a down." His voice was deep, a little rough, and pleasing. "There were three ravens on a tree. They were black as black might be, with a down, down, derry, derry down."

He sang on, to tell the story, as the ravens discussed where they might dine and hoped to dine off of a slain knight, whose body lay abandoned in a field. But the knight's hawks guarded him, and his dogs guarded him, and Birle understood that when the deer, "as great with young as she might go," appeared to take the knight away for burial, it was his lady that

80

deer was. "God send every gentleman," Orien sang, "such hawks, such hounds, and such a leman, with a down, down, derry, derry down."

This was a sad song—the knight slain, the lady dying that same day, and her babe within her. Even the downs and derry downs, which could have been so cheerful, became sorrowful.

"I could never earn my keep as a minstrel," he said, after a few minutes. "My grandfather keeps a minstrel."

Birle sat up. "You have music then, whenever you wish?"

"Unless the man can't be found."

"Can he come and go as he pleases?" Birle asked. At each question Orien answered, she asked more. He had two personal servants, to keep his clothes and answer his needs. Food was brought to him before he arose from his bed in the morning; the tailor came to his chamber to measure him for clothing, when he needed clothing made, as did the cobbler for boots. He was schooled in swordplay, and in dance. The priests had taught him from books. Birle learned who sat down at the tables in the Earl's feasting hall, and who had seats at the high table.

She learned that from boyhood Orien had been taught to read the words and figures in the Stewards' long books, so that he might understand and safeguard the wealth of the house. He preferred books of stories, like Gran's, but ability with the figures of the long books was valued more.

Orien, she learned, stood behind the Earl on Hearing Days, and sometimes spoke advice into his grandfather's ear. He might go weeks without an exchange of words with his father. On high feast days, he ate with a spoon shaped out of silver. At the King's table, he told her, even the plates were silver.

When Birle's head was so crammed with information that she could take no more in, she fell silent.

He, too, fell silent, as if he had run out of words. The sun was well up in the sky. The water had been soundlessly creeping up over the rocks, and he climbed back onto the rock, to sit beside her.

"I see no hope of food," Orien said then. "Tell me about your home."

"The Inn is beyond the village, by the river. Aye," she said, just realizing it, "it's your village." Then she realized something else. "And it was your boat, too. You are no thief."

"Aye," he mimicked her. "As I told you."

"Isn't the village written down in the Steward's long book? Or do you mistrust your Steward?"

"No, I don't. Although neither do I entirely trust him. He's a man like any other, with his own purposes to serve. I know how many families live in the village, I know what kind of living they earn from land and river. But there is so much untold by the long books. Are the hardships manageable? How do you build your houses? I know of the Inn, which was built before my grandfather's time, but how are the village houses made?"

"They build the houses of wood. A woodman will come, to cut the logs to planks. Out of these they make walls and roof. The house my granda built was made of stone, like the Inn, and there was a journeying slater who made the roof for that. The Earl paid the cost of it, Granda said. Isn't that holding in the long book? Who will have it now?"

"There's nobody who wants it, solitary as it is."

"They are fools, then," Birle said. "There's meadow, apple trees, and a spring. The forest for hunting, the river close enough to fish, a house."

"It made little for taxes. I don't know why the Earl gave the holding, except I do—because he could find no reason to say no. He was never satisfied to say no without a reason. But Birle, what about things like stools, or latches for the doors—without a blacksmith, how do you have hinges?"

Orien wondered about the growing of the grapes and the making of the wines; he asked how a smokehouse was built and how many baskets of parsnips a household would need in its cellars, for a winter. He asked her if she knew why it was that wine made men drunk but water did not; he knew no more of that than she did. He seemed disappointed that

82

she had been kept to the kitchen, and so did not know much of the Inn's custom except that it sometimes grew loud. Neither could she tell him how much of a burden the taxes were. Her father always put aside coins for the Earl, keeping them safe in a locked box. Other men were not so careful, and grumbled when the Steward had come, but somehow they found the necessary coins and then forgot about it until the weeks before the next fair, when the Steward came again. He asked about the number and manner of rooms in the Inn, and how the wine casks were built. He asked about obtaining the fishing spears, and how to keep flour free of weevils. He asked question after question, until at last he fell silent. Birle was glad to rest.

It was midafternoon before he spoke again. The sea was sliding down the side of the rocks, pulling back from the stony shore. The sun hung over their shoulders. Unlike the sun and the sea, hunger did not draw back. Birle lay on her stomach at the edge of the flat rock, looking into the water. No fish moved among the stones.

"Birle?" Orien asked. "How long do you think it will be before we are rescued?"

Eight

As the afternoon drew on, the long, cool shadows of the high cliffs chilled them, while the sky was still filled with light. The water reflected the changing colors of the sky as the sun set behind the cliffs. Then dusk swept like a wind over them, trailing darkness behind. Birle watched the sky.

The first stars came out, hesitant, shy. They were joined by more, and more, until the whole star-filled sky hung over her. Hunger burned in her belly, crowding it just as the stars crowded the sky.

"I am sorry, Birle," Orien said, breaking his long silence.

She didn't answer. All she could think of was that she could think of him, now, with his name.

"We can't get food here, or water. We can't build any shelter," he went on. "I didn't want to be who I had to be—which, without my sack and the proof of the ring hidden there, I'm not. But this needn't have been your fortune."

Birle's head was light with hunger, and it was difficult to attend to what he said. "There's a story—do you know it?—about the man who had his wishes granted." Orien didn't know the tale, so she told it to him, how the woodchopper captured one of the little men and claimed from the graybeard the three wishes that were his prize. The woodchopper told his wife the good news that evening, so joyful that he wished the turnip stew she gave him were a string of sausages. She in her anger at his stupidity wished the sausage onto the end of his nose, where it hung until the third wish

84

was spent to remove it. They shared the sausages for their meal.

Orien then told her of an ancient king who asked that everything he touched might turn to gold. The wish was granted him. So that when his beloved daughter ran to embrace him, she became a golden statue.

That story, and the rising of the moon before her, reminded Birle of the book she had never read in her grandparents' house. She asked Orien if he knew the story of the moon and the handsome shepherd. He did, and told the tale. She sang him the song of the old woman and the billy goat in the garden. Perhaps Orien was too hungry for laughter, but she heard the smile in his voice when he asked her, "What would you be doing now, Birle, if you were at the Inn?"

"Aye, we'd all be in our beds asleep."

"How could you be asleep, with the night just begun?"

"When the day's work begins in the dark of morning a man sleeps early, and easily."

"But do you rise so early?"

"There's work to do. Fires do not light themselves, a loaf of bread doesn't knead itself and run into the oven. Fields and animals must be kept."

"I thought your father was Innkeeper."

"Aye, and for that reason the work of spring is heaviest. Because the Inn's stores must be enough to feed the guests. In spring, the ground has to be turned over and the seeds sown. Spring is the season when goats and pigs have their young. Fish for the table—cheeses from the rich milk—and the bedclothes to launder, because in spring the custom at the Inn is busy, with the Steward and his men, there for the taxes, and the caravans traveling to the fairs. Life isn't meant to be easy." This was what Da and Nan, and her brothers too, had said to her, over and over.

"I am not wakened until the fire has warmed my chamber," he said. "Then the curtains are drawn back from my bed, and I am given bread warm from the oven, and wine in a goblet. At this evening hour," he went on, his smooth-flowing words making pictures in her mind, "there will be two fires in the hall, and candles on the walls and tables, for light. The Ladies would have withdrawn to their own rooms. I would be perhaps talking, perhaps having a game of chess with my grandfather or a quarrel with my brother. There might be songs from the minstrel, or—since it's the season— entertainers who, summoned from the fairs, come to the castle in the evenings and the Ladies stay to see them. Then we see a play, or puppets, or there is a man who swallows fire. I wished to be a fire-eater when I was a boy, to be able to do so wonderful a thing and to travel with the entertainers. I know better now, but—he took flame into his mouth, Birle, as if—and it may be—he were not ordinary flesh and blood. I tried it with a candle but the candle kept going out as soon as I closed my lips around it. Once I asked the fire-eater to tell me his secret, and offered him gold for it. But he wouldn't. He said I had no need of such tricks and he had need to keep them to himself, not give them away to every child who asked. I tried to get Grandfather to make him tell me—the Earl has the power—the Earl could put such a man into the dungeon until he told, or offer him so much gold he'd never need to seek his living again. But my grandfather refused me. He said the fire-eater spoke true, and he wouldn't take away from a man that which he needed to earn his bread. I would probably say the same now," Orien said.

Birle tried to imagine days where there was not always some voice telling you to hurry at your task, so the next could be started. She tried to imagine an evening of entertainment—but the nearest she could come was her grandparents' house. "My granda played music on a pipe."

"So it isn't all labor," he said.

"But it is." The work of keeping your belly filled, from one day to the next, from one season to the next—but he couldn't understand it, she thought. She was herself having just a taste of a laborless life, through the chance of having found Orien in the dark, and the mischance of being marooned.

"Last night the whole world was a storm," Orien said then. "What do you think happened to it? Do you think a

86

storm travels across the sea until it falls off the edge of the world?''

Birle had never thought about that.

''Or does it blow itself out, like a log in the fire that burns itself out, using itself up and destroying itself even while it rages?''

''I don't know,'' Birle said. ''I never wondered about a storm except when it was upon me.''

''I think I will practice that wisdom,'' Orien said, ''and sleep.''

Birle lay upon her back, her cloak around her like rolled bedclothes. The moonlight washed over her face as the waves washed up against the rocks, until she too slept.

She awoke to his voice, and sun falling over her from a midmorning sky. Clouds moved across the sky, slow and stately, like a procession of Lords and Ladies. ''Hungry,'' Orien said. ''I'm so hungry . . . and thirsty.''

Birle had never before slept through the dawn. This, she thought, is what it would be like to lie abed, like a Lady.

''My mouth is dry, my lips are dry, and my hands—Birle, look, is my hand trembling?''

She couldn't make out his hand in the brightness of the sun. Her mind wouldn't clear itself, to undertake the day.

''I've been a fool, Birle. I shouldn't have let yesterday go by. We'll only get weaker. There must be something to eat, somewhere in this place. I've been thinking, and if I've the strength I should try to climb the cliff. Before I get any weaker. We can't just sit here telling stories until we starve. Birle? Get up.''

Birle stood. Her legs were unsteady under her, her boots heavy.

''You have your knife? You can watch for fish,'' Orien told her. ''Fish live in water, and there's certainly enough of that. Unless fish, like men, can't swallow seawater. Are you awake? And stay out of the sun if you can. The sun dries you up. Birle?''

Unable to think, unable to awake, she obeyed. She stood in water so cold it penetrated the leather of her boots to numb

87

her feet and calves. She watched through it, for any movement. She saw nothing. And why, with the whole deep sea to swim in, any fish should come to this rocky, shallow water, she didn't know. Every now and then she turned around to see Orien, splayed out against the face of the cliff. His progress was slow. Then it halted. Then he was moving spiderlike back down the cliff.

She too gave up her useless pursuit. Climbing back up onto the rock, she tried to think of how to comfort him. "The pain of hunger passes," she said.

His smile came slower now, and not so bright, but it was still a smile that glowed in his eyes. "I'll welcome that," he said. "But do you know this from experience? Have you been this hungry before?"

Birle shook her head. She'd never gone a day without food before. Or without drink, she thought. At that thought, thirst troubled her again. Her mouth felt pinched and wrinkled, like the flesh of salted fish.

"You look like an old madwoman from the forest," Orien said. "Or one of those who live out under the open sky."

Birle put her hand to her long braids. Her hair hung unraveled. Her hair hung tangled down her back. She almost laughed aloud at the joke of it, with her child's dreams of the wedding day when she might wear her hair at last unbound. Orien looked—Lordly still, even with a rough beard growing on his face, and his hair matted. The blue of his eyes was the only true color in the world.

"Did you never wonder, Birle, why it is that the people must work and the Lords live at ease?"

"Aye," she said, and was surprised when he laughed, and then surprised that he laughed, for his mouth must be as dry as hers.

"A man's bones would ache at the end of every day, and he would know the next no different."

"Aye."

"It is a beast's life, Birle."

She would not have him think her an animal, whatever else he might think of her, not such a beast. "What I used to do

88

was shirk. If Nan wanted the garden worked, or the bed-clothes washed, she would tell me to do it. I wouldn't say no to her but—just because you say you'll do something doesn't mean—saying is different from doing. It wasn't I who wished the linen laundered, it wasn't my linen, I have no linen. If the task wasn't started in time, then the work couldn't be done that day. If a stew burned for lack of stirring, we could still eat what hadn't burned. If weeds grow larger they are easier to pull out. Nan would get into a fine anger, all of them would. And much of the time, they'd find it simpler to do the job themselves than to make me do it. So my own life was in that way made easier.''

''Weren't you ashamed?''

''Why should I be? If I spent the morning scrubbing the floor of the barroom, by night it would be filthy again. What's the good of work like that? If Nan cared to have her floor shining with cleanliness, let her wash it. If they called me lazy, that's only a word and didn't hurt me. I did enough.'' The old anger was there in her voice, she could hear it. It was weak with thirst and hunger, but it was present.

She thought she knew what he must now think, and wanted him to know better of her. ''When I cared for my grandparents, it wasn't—I wasn't—it was easy to say yes to my grandparents, to do the task. They didn't wish me to be servant to their wishes.''

''Nan—she wanted you for a servant?''

''It felt so.''

''What about the others, your father and brothers?''

''They said Nan had the right of it. When the Inn prospered we all prospered. The work had to be done and done right.''

Orien took a while to think about that. ''I begin to understand why you were eager to wed your huntsman.''

''I was a fool,'' Birle told him.

''Maybe. But how could you know. It would be hard if someone else owned all your days, and all your work.''

He understood, he did understand. The Lords need never concern themselves about the people, much less understand,

89

but Orien did. If such a man were Earl . . . but Orien said such a man would be dangerous to the house, and it must be that he understood that too. For which reason, he had left everything behind him, all that was his by right of his high birth. That was much, a third of the Kingdom. She thought Orien must be made of different material from any other man or woman she had known. Even, she thought, her grandparents. Such a man ought to live at his ease, she thought, and his people labor to keep him.

"I'm tired," Orien said. "Hunger leaves me tired. Thirst too, and I am thirsty. I am not well-schooled for this fortune."

"Hunger fades, after its time," Birle told him. "Even if you don't feed it, hunger fades."

"I get impatient, waiting for what will happen next," he said.

What would happen next Birle didn't want to discuss with him. The sun hung high in the sky and there was no shade for them to move to. She didn't know if Orien understood their peril, but if he didn't she wouldn't be the one to tell it to him. Telling would make no difference.

"If we were in one of the old stories," she said, trying to speak lightly, "what would happen next is that Jackaroo would come riding across the water, to carry us to safety."

"How could a horse cross the sea without sinking into it?"

"In a story," she reminded him. You could grow accustomed to almost anything, she thought, surprised. She had grown so accustomed to speaking with Orien that she spoke without thought, and he a Lord. She had grown accustomed to this stony world; her body didn't protest rock for ground and floor, stool and bed. She had learned how to watch the endless sea, with its rising and falling water, she knew what she might expect the sea to do. The music of waves against rocks was as familiar to her now as her Granda's pipe, playing. "It is no more amazing," she said, full of the strangeness of the actual even more than the strangeness of the fabled, "than a boy sleeping forever, forever young."

"Do you ever think, Birle, that the truth of stories is deeper than the truth of the world? Because—a man can be put to sleep by a woman's beauty, and never ask to awaken."

She had never thought of that, Birle thought, sleepy with hunger in the warm sun. "Not actually asleep," she said, to be sure she understood.

"No, but truly asleep."

She wondered if some Lady had cast her spell of beauty over Orien.

"Maybe, then, I'll watch for Jackaroo over the water," he said, but he was teasing. "Do you know the tale of Jackaroo and the prince?"

"No."

He told it to her, of the prince kept in a high stone tower by his jealous stepmother, so that her own son might become king even though he was not the eldest born. The prince was a child when he was stolen away, by guards who did not dare to slay him. The king's grief killed him, leaving the stepmother as queen regent. The prince grew to young manhood in the tower. Jackaroo came, and climbed up the tower wall, a wall steeper and more impassable than the cliffs behind them. He carried a rope, down which the prince climbed, but the rope broke, stranding Jackaroo above. The prince rode away, and it was the stepmother who ended her days in that same tower, where only the bodies of the guards were to be seen when the prince returned with his soldiers, to set Jackaroo free.

"The story makes you smile," Orien said.

Birle hadn't known there was a smile on her face. "I'm thinking how differently Jackaroo serves the people," she said. "Do you know the tale of Jackaroo and the robbers?"

He didn't, so she told it: How Jackaroo had met a woman, struggling through the snow with her babe in her arms. Robbers had set upon their holding, slaughtered her husband and sons, and set the house to flames. She had escaped into the woods while the robbers were busy at their work. Jackaroo took her and the child to a safe house, then rode up into the mountains, into the robbers' stronghold, and captured all three of them. He brought them before the Steward, on a day when people had gathered before the city walls and the Lords had gathered atop the city walls, to watch the hanging of a highwayman. Jackaroo claimed the law to protect the people as well as the Lords. The Steward dared not oppose him, nor could he lay his hands on Jackaroo, who stepped into the crowd and disappeared among the people, who would not move to let him be seen, and taken. "Sometimes the Steward could see the long feather on his hat, moving ever away, like a man walking through a field tall with wheat. But the people kept Jackaroo safe," she said.

All the long hours they traded stories and songs. Not trying to hide her harsh voice, Birle sang him the song about the gay maiden who spurned the lad who loved her true, and when he died of a broken heart fell down dead herself at his burning pyre. Orien told her the story of Jackaroo and the bride, whom he rescued from the wedding her father forced her to and left in the bed of her true love, where once the night was spent her father would not have her back. He sang her the song of the true knight, who laid down his life for his king against traitors, even though the king had ignored his warnings and only with the knight's death knew the truth of him. She sang him the lament of the girl betrayed, whose blossoming belly made her shame known. When dusk fell, their voices faded off into sleep.

Birle awoke to thirst, and moonlight. The cool light fell on Orien, asleep, as if he were a statue carved out of the stone he slept on. She watched his sleep, until clouds covered the moon and she fell asleep herself.

She awoke again, to a heavy gray morning. When the rain, at last, fell over them, they sat under it with open mouths. She licked water from her hands and wrists. She spread her cloak out on the rock, so that after the rain had stopped she might suck moisture from the cloth. That day they spoke little, and moved not at all. After it had fallen upon them, the rain blew across the sky and on over the sea, and away.

Nine

How many days and nights went by, Birle did not know. They might have been many, they might have been few. It made no matter to her if it was day or night. There was a time when it rained, water falling into her mouth, and all over her, soaking into her skin as if her skin itself had tiny mouths to drink in water. Long after the rain had ended, she could suck moisture from her cloak.

Always, Orien was in her sight—except on those rare occasions when one or the other disappeared behind a boulder for privacy. Birle knew that he was growing weaker, as she was, but he would still climb down from the rock to stand at the base of the enclosing cliffs, looking upward. He scratched with his dagger on the stone that was home to them. "Do you think to eat stone, Orien?" she asked him.

He shook his head. When he showed her his work, she saw that he had scratched their two names into the rock—Orien, Beryl—first his, then hers beneath it, "To mark our presence," he said. The sun had colored his face and hands brown. "That's not how my name is written," she said, but wouldn't let him cross it out, to scratch her own name beneath.

Orien kept watch over the empty sea, but Birle did not. He remarked on this, his voice raspy. "You seem at ease, Innkeeper's Daughter. Is it that the people are more skilled at understanding necessity?"

Birle's lips were too dry and painful to make any answer. But she was content; he was correct in that. The sea might blow up white spume as it raced under a wind, or it might lie smooth; it might rise and fall in its restless tides; the sea might never be still, but she was quiet.

"It's hard not to be able to do anything," Orien said. That was his only complaint. He bore thirst and the weakness of hunger without a word.

"Aye, but when all my days there's been someone at my back—goading—to do nothing is not a bad fortune," Birle answered.

Words came slowly. She felt as if she had to walk a long distance into her head to find her thought, and carry out the words for it with great effort. If it had not been Orien who asked, she could not have spoken.

Sometimes, when Birle woke it was night. The stars shone out in their numbers, and seemed to make patterns before her eyes. The moon floated across the sky, with a face that was all sorrow, all the sorrow known to the world. At such waking times, Birle would remember: She began at the first moment, at her first glimpse of the moving shadow, and recalled all that she could from memory. With such a short time left to keep her memories, she counted them carefully. Sometimes, as she lay awake in the night, his voice would ask, "Are you awake, Birle?"

"Yes, I'm awake." Neither spoke any more than that.

When rain quenched their thirst, they spoke with more strength. "I have no wife," Orien said to her, without warning. Birle sat sucking on a corner of her damp cloak. The taste of wool was not nourishing, nor was it good; but it had flavor and in that it was like food. "I have neither son nor daughter. I've left no one in danger behind me."

"You didn't wish a wife?"

"I didn't wish the wives they offered, and they didn't quite dare try to force me to it." The memory made him smile. "Once, I wished it." The smile faded.

Birle didn't dare to ask the question.

"But my father married her himself. He said her lands would come to me in the end, so I had no complaint to make. By her marriage into the Earl's house, the girl's father secured his son's lands, so he had no complaint to make. My grandfather was off with the King at that time, and when he returned it was all done—they were wed and bedded. What's that there? Birle? Is that something—?" He pointed across the water.

Birle looked, and saw nothing. She didn't tell him that, but continued looking, as if waiting to see. She wished Orien could learn not to hope for rescue, but he wasn't the kind of man for hopelessness.

"What of the girl?" she asked. "Did she have a complaint, marrying the father when she thought to wed the son?"

Orien shrugged his shoulders, and she saw how thin his neck had become. "I have no way of knowing what the girl thought. The women stay in their own quarters most of the time. They come out to sit among us in their beauty. To make us hunger. The girl carried three children, but none were born living. Neither did she live, after the last. She's buried beside my mother, and my father's second wife, and now my father lies in the earth beside all three. I think I would rather be burned, as the people are, Birle, than buried in the earth, as the Lords are."

Birle didn't think he had hope of either, but she didn't say that. "What did your grandfather do when he found out?" It was like a story to her, some fabulous tale. She couldn't imagine Da acting so, or—if he did—that either of her brothers would permit it.

"He could do nothing. He was angry at my father—because he had given his word as Earl for the marriage—but he could do nothing to change what had taken place. I think also that he felt sorry for my father. You have to remember, Birle, that if you are the eldest, you are the son who will be Earl. My father had to see first his youth and then his manhood spent in waiting. He was afraid the treasure would never come into his hand. So he granted himself whatever other desires he had. He wished the girl for himself. She had the beauty of a butterfly, delicate, dainty. Fragile. And she had two prosperous villages for dowry, with all the lands attached. I didn't blame him.''

"You should blame him."

"Maybe. But I couldn't, once I got over my own anger. I can't.''

But his heart must have been broken, because he never had married, Birle thought. Maybe Orien was right, maybe he was not the man to be Earl. Not because his father could overpower his desires, but because he had a heart that could be broken. Because he couldn't keep anger at his father, but must understand him.

"It was my father hated the sight of me, not I the sight of him, as he would have hated anyone who was the heir and might live to be Earl.''

Orien might easily have been a different kind of man, living as he had, Birle thought. This was another wonder in him. Lords or people, she thought there could be no other man like Orien. How could she not be content, Birle thought, to spend whatever days remained to her with this man?

How many days lay behind them, Birle could not remember; how many might be left she couldn't guess. She lay on her stomach on their flat rock while Orien picked his slow, careful way along the water's edge. The light in the sky was changing, but whether with morning or afternoon Birle couldn't be sure. It had been a long time since any rain had fallen on them, once again a long time. She no longer felt hunger at all, but thirst left her mind dizzy, as weak as her legs.

As she watched, the little figure of Orien began to wave its arms in the air. She saw him as if he were some insect moving around a candle. It was a curious series of movements, first the arms waving in the air, then the cloak being held up and shaken. It was like the dance of a creature that was not human, with no reason you could

96

think of for its gestures. Birds sometimes flew at one another in the air like that, squawking, circling, then following one another in dips and swoops—Birle never knew why they did that, or what they meant by it. Orien waved his cloak up and down, over his head in just such strange dancing motions.

Something black moved in the corner of her eye. Slowly, she turned her head to catch it; her skin scraped across the stone.

It was a boat she saw, huge, its enormous sail filled with wind. Her head snapped up, and her legs and arms coiled up under her. A rush of energy gave her back the strength she'd lost.

She slid down the rock's side. She stumbled, running across the shore to Orien. He was jumping and waving his cloak. "It's a boat," she said.

"Wave your arms!" he cried.

She was already waving her arms. The wind blew into her face and made Orien's cloak snap.

"They've got to see us," Orien said.

The boat's sail was broad, and square, a heavy red sail. Its mast ran up through the center of the sail. It was bigger than any boat she'd ever seen, at least four times as big as any of the fishing boats. Like the fishing boats, it had oars fitted through holes in its side.

"There's a little boat, behind it, like a dog following," Birle said.

"Keep waving!"

She hadn't stopped. Her arms flapped over her head, like his cloak. Her own cloak lay on the rock, useless.

"They see us," Orien said.

Birle couldn't be sure. The boat didn't hesitate on its way.

While they stood waving, and watching, with their voices blown back into their faces as they called out across the waves, the distant boat passed out of sight around the corner made by the long arm of cliff. They

97

called after it, and waved, even when they could no longer see it.

Weakness overcame Birle. She sank down onto the shore. Her feet were in the water and she couldn't feel them. Orien didn't sit, but he sagged. His cloak dragged in the waves. She couldn't think of anything to say, to comfort him. When he raised his head at last, and turned to look at her, she could not see his thoughts in his bellflower eyes.

There was no use in speech. He reached out a hand to pull her to her feet. She trailed behind him, back from the water. There, they stood side by side, looking at the empty sea.

After a long time he said, "I know they saw us."

After a long time she asked him, "Do you think they'll send help?"

"I'm not thinking anything, Birle."

"Aye," she said.

The waves tumbled onto the shore and splashed against the rocks. Her legs were so weak under her that she sat down heavily, again. Orien sat beside her, his knees drawn up, his head on his knees. His beard was ragged and brown, like weeds growing up already dead.

She felt sorrow for him, sorrow so deep she almost put out her hand to touch his shoulder, in whatever comfort human touch could bring. They were so lost in disappointment that both were surprised when the voice hailed them. "Hoy!" it called, riding the wind in. "Hoy! The island!"

Orien was on his feet while Birle was still finding her legs to put them beneath her.

A man rowed his little boat into the bay. He hesitated there, far out from shore, oars raised. At that distance, he was little more than a shape with a voice. He twisted in his seat in the bobbing boat to stare at them. They stood at the water's edge, staring back.

He put the oars into the water again, and rowed closer.

"Have you your cloak?" Orien asked, his eyes watching the boat's approach. "Better go get it."

She rushed to obey. The oarsman didn't come straight into shore, but turned the boat around when he was still an arrow's flight from them. He looked at Orien, and then his eyes found Birle where she bent to pick up her cloak. He watched her all the time she took, picking it up, fastening it at her neck, returning to stand beside Orien. She didn't like his looking, and she didn't like his looks—a heavy, whiskery face, with little eyes and a thick mouth.

"In trouble?" he asked.

"Yes," Orien said.

The man nodded, but made no move. "Need help?"

"Yes," Orien said.

"Food? Water?" the man asked. The questions were stupid, but those eyes were not. "Rescue?" he asked.

They stood waiting, in their thirst, hunger, and fear. He sat, studying them. Then he put the oars into the water again. Birle wondered if he would leave them, and she didn't know whether she wished him to. But he nosed the boat in toward shore.

"That's my ship, she's anchored behind the cliff," he said. "There might be room for two passengers."

Birle's blood rang a warning in her ears. "Orien," she said, pulling on his arm. "I don't like this."

Orien took her warning seriously, it wasn't that. It was the helplessness of their position that he argued. "I think we must, Birle."

"Course," the man said, still safely distant, "there's a price. For the risk—since there's plenty of dangerous men out and around. There'd have to be a fee. We can't carry you for nothing. Feed you." The eyes studied them and he added, "Give you drink."

"We've nothing," Birle answered him, glad to be able to say no.

"Nothing at all?" He sounded disappointed. "It's not many days. We'd ask little. It wouldn't take much to pay your way."

"I've dagger and sword; she's a knife," Orien called. "We have no choice," he said to Birle.

The man's mouth flickered open in a smile. "There's always something. You just drop them there, at your feet, and step back."

They did as they were told.

He climbed out of the boat and pulled it behind him by a rope. Holding the rope, he studied the knives, carefully. His fingers went over the hilt of Orien's dagger, and he spat on it, then rubbed it clean with his thumb. "Welcome aboard," he said then, with a wide gesture of his arm toward the boat, and that smile that made Birle think she'd be safer starving where she was. "Name's Ker," he said.

"Orien," Birle protested again.

"You can stay, if you must." Orien's cheeks were hollow with hunger and he had little strength for anger. "But I wish you'd come. I don't know how long it would be before I could come back for you."

So she followed him, since he would return for her.

The man helped them into his boat, and sat them side by side on the stern seat. This boat was heavier than the river coracles. Its sides were double-ribbed, its wood thick-cut. Ker grunted with the work of rowing, but said nothing to them. Her own weakness assailed Birle, until she could do no more than sit upright as the boat pushed its way through the waves, and keep her head from falling forward onto her chest.

The ship, when they came to it, rode high over her head. Arms reached down to catch her wrists and she was pulled up over its side. She slid down onto the deck, until hands and Orien's voice urged her to move under shade. When she sat leaning back against wood, out of the harsh sun, Birle opened her eyes.

Two men stood in front of her, thick, strong men in loose trousers and heavy shirts, two bearded faces, two pairs of small eyes. She blinked, but the two didn't become one. Orien was beside her.

100

"This is Torson," Ker said. "My little brother," he laughed. "He's our captain."

Birle couldn't see past them. She could see nothing beyond them but the tall, thick mast, rising. The ship rolled under her.

"You'll see, Brother," Ker said. "A little food, and a little drink, and you'll see what I've brought in."

"Maybe," Torson answered. "Yes, I think this time you may be right." His smile flickered, like a snake's tongue, like his brother's smile. "Little sparrows, you are in luck. We're about to serve the midday meal. Will you join us for it?" He nodded his head, as if their silence pleased him. "Good, yes, that's good. Well then, my clever brother, fetch some food for your two little lost birds."

"And drink," Orien said.

"Ho, boy," said Torson. "There'll always be drink on my ship."

When the brothers moved away, Birle saw that she was at the bow of the ship, under a canopy. Two ill-matched oarsmen faced her, on the rowing seats beside the mast. She saw no more, for dizziness brought her head down to her knees. Ker brought them two wooden bowls filled with ale, and two thick chunks of bread. For a minute, holding food in one hand and drink in the other, Birle could not think of what to do. Then she downed the drink, as Orien—sprawled beside her—also did. It wasn't cool, but it felt cool, flowing down her throat, filling her mouth. She bit at the bread, watching Ker dip her bowl into a bucket, and bring it up full again.

The bread was tough, hard to rip free. Birle filled her mouth with it, and remembered how to chew. Her throat, it seemed, had forgotten how to swallow. She forced the mouthful down her throat, and then emptied the bowl of ale, again.

She lifted the bread to her teeth and ripped off another bite. As she chewed on it, Birle realized she had her eyes closed, but she didn't make the effort to open them. Her stomach did not welcome the food, but she took a third bite and made her eyes open, just as she made herself chew.

Orien sat up now, hunched over his bread. She wondered how he had the strength to eat so eagerly. She wondered at his strength. Orien didn't look at all the man he was, he looked—with his torn shirt and trousers, his scraggly beard—as if he were not at all the man he was. Birle couldn't keep her eyes from closing again, for the spinning in her head, and the buzzing, as if swarms of insects were circling her ears. She couldn't find her hands to bring the bread to her mouth for another bite. She slept.

Ten

I N her heavy sleep, Birle had slipped over onto her side. She pulled herself upright. She knew better than to attempt to stand. The sail had been raised, and now bellied out toward her. The ship moved her backward, with a gentle rearing and falling motion. She had a thirst in her mouth and a thickness in her head, and hunger—the bread was still in her hands. She pulled her knees up.

Her feet weighed like lead. She ripped off bread with her fingers and put it into her mouth, chewed and swallowed. Feeding her hunger seemed to increase it. She fed it more. The bread was gone before she was satisfied, but hunger unsatisfied is different from hunger. If she could only have a drink—but not ale, no more of that ale. Water, she could wish for a bowl of cold water. And why should her feet be so heavy?

She looked at them: They were manacled, and a thick chain ran between the two bands of metal that ringed her bare ankles.

They'd taken her boots. Orien too had been chained as he slept. Birle moved her own feet—it wasn't two handspans of chain.

It wasn't that she was surprised. She hadn't expected any good of these men. She didn't dare to think just what this particular ill might mean, but she wasn't surprised. The brothers were at the broad stern of the ship, now. Ker talked while Torson listened, the long tiller under his hand. She couldn't hear their words.

Overhead, the big sail snapped in the wind. Birle couldn't see much of the sky, between the canopy over her head and the sail before her. Seated as she was, she couldn't see over the sides of the ship, although—as she then understood—she and Orien were on some kind of covered shelf, above the deck level of the ship. The two rowers slept, their hands holding the oars, as if sleep had struck them down in mid-stroke. Her impression had been correct, they were an ill-matched pair. One, with his narrow shoulders and bony legs, seemed a boy, not yet ten years old, she thought. The other—a large oval head with long, wispy strands of dust-colored hair lying along it, shoulders twice the size of Da's and legs thick as tree trunks—he was monstrous large, where he slept.

The rowers too were manacled.

Birle let her head fall forward onto her chest, as if she slept on. Beneath her, the ship rose and fell, so that she was rocked gently backward and forward. When Birle opened her eyes again, the brothers were still talking.

Orien stirred. She felt rather than saw his awakening. His whole body stiffened, and then he moved his feet delicately, secretively. When he looked over to her, she had her face ready.

"I'm sorry," he said. "I didn't think we had any choice, but maybe we did. Maybe if we'd waited—another boat—but there had only been the one in eight days. I'm sorry," he said again.

Apology didn't suit him. "Was it eight days? How do you know?"

"I counted."

The brothers were watching him.

Birle could think of nothing to say to Orien, and he had nothing to say to her. He pulled his legs up, with the dismal sound of chains, and then pulled himself up to stand against the side of the ship. He looked like a starved man, a poor wretch. He stood like one too, his hands grasping the wooden rail as if he dared not let go, his whole body leaning against the sturdy side of the ship as if he couldn't stand unsupported. She wasn't surprised when his legs buckled under him.

"Land's in sight. Close enough to swim, except we'd sink with these." He moved his feet.

The wood of the ship and mast creaked and groaned at its work. Birle wondered if there was any drinking water. It must be afternoon, she thought, watching the shadow of the canopy overhead, and of the sail. Watching the shadows, she knew they must be traveling west. She wondered if they would travel all night and all day, if that explained the rowers' exhaustion. She wondered if she might ask for water.

"I don't know," Orien's voice spoke low, and desperate. "I can't stand—and I have no weapon—and I brought you to this. I the Earl that would be. You should know, Birle—I saw Gladaegal's eyes that night, on me, my brother's eyes; and I couldn't say if he was seeing a murderer or the next victim. To see him so, my brother—so, while the courage was in me, that same night, I left. To give him his earldom. I wanted to do right, Birle."

Birle had never doubted that.

He closed his eyes and leaned his head back, again. When he swallowed she could see the rise and fall of his throat. She didn't know how to help him and she almost couldn't bear to look at him. She looked down the length of the ship, wishing she could summon water.

The large rower had been wakened by their voices. He stared at her. She could do nothing but stare back at him, although out of kindness she ought to have looked away.

She had seen such an expression in the eyes of a dog kicked, or beaten. The uncomprehending eyes were fixed on her face and the lips opened and closed, although the mouth formed no words. He *was* a giant, she saw, now that he sat up on the bench—huge and strong. But his eyes hung in his face, as if they had started to slip down, and been caught up by their inner corners, and the lids hung down over them. She could have wept to see his huge, misshapen face—the projecting forehead and long jawline, the child's nose, and

105

the thick mouth skewed off to the side. The monster threw back his head and made a sound that drowned out the wind and the creaking wood. If he had been a dog it would have been a howl, but because he was a form of man it was a groan. He raised his two huge hands up, and slammed them down as fists onto the seat. His hands too were chained.

Ker rushed forward and jerked from behind on a noose tied around the monster's neck. The monster coughed, lifted his hands to ease his throat, then sat quiet. He turned to his captor, with the eyes of a whipped dog.

"Hoy, Captain! Everybody's awake," Ker called. "Even the boy."

The boy cowered back against the side of the ship, but whether to protect himself from Ker or from the monster, Birle couldn't tell.

"Get up, boy, there's work to do," Ker said. He stepped to the mast and uncleated a rope. The boy stood up, and shuffled over beside him with his manacled feet. He raised his arms to catch the lowering boom, and the falling sail. He staggered as they fell on him.

Without its sail, the ship bounced on the waves, and turned its side to the wind. When it lay like that, Birle could see the shoreline Orien had seen. The shore was green with forest, a thick, dark green of rising land, close enough to swim to, for strong swimmers who were not manacled with iron that would drag them down, under the water.

The wind pulled at the sail, snapping it like linens hung out on a line to dry. Ker cursed and struggled, while the boy staggered, weeping. When Ker had wrapped ropes around the sail, he shoved the boy back onto the seat. "Get to it," he ordered the rowers.

Birle knew they were moving toward land because all she could see was empty sea, moving in waves out to the edge of the sky. After a while, the boy crawled under the platform to drag out the anchor, and pull it to where the monster sat. Without even rising from his seat, the giant picked the huge iron hook up and dropped it into the water. The anchor dragged, then bit and held. The ship swung around.

The boy brought them bowls of water and chunks of bread. The brothers ate by themselves beside the lashed tiller. There, they lit a brazier and roasted chunks of meat over its flames. Despite his size, the monster was given no more to eat than the rest of them—and that he wolfed down. Birle could swallow no more than half of her bread, and Orien had to force the last of his down his throat, she saw. The boy nibbled at his. She held the dark bread in her hand, then made herself rip off another piece. The monster's mouth made chewing motions as he watched her eat, like a mother feeding her child. He was hungry. How long he had been fed so little, no more than the starveling boy who rowed with him, she could not guess. But his huge body must need more food than the boy's, she thought, her mind sluggish. Big men had big appetites, that was what Nan said, and this mindless giant must have a mighty appetite. Her own belly was uncomfortably swollen with the water and bread, as if it had become accustomed to eating nothing.

Birle moved her heavy feet around until she could kneel, then held out the bread to him.

She didn't dare come too close. His huge, chained hands reached out to her. His fingers closed around the bread and brought it to his crooked mouth. Birle retreated.

He made a low grunting noise, deep in his throat, which she took for thanks. Then his mouth moved, one side pulling up. This was a smile, Birle thought, and felt her eyes fill with tears. Hunger and thirst made her weak and weepy, she thought, blinking. Hunger and thirst and the monster's smile, which had a terrible, sad sweetness. She blinked, and tears ran out of her eyes. He held out what was left of the bread to her. Birle shook her head, and held her hands out with the palms facing him, in a pushing-away gesture. He seemed to understand, and crammed the rest of the bread into his mouth, chewing it with little noises of satisfaction.

The boy had watched this, his hands busy as a bird's beak on his own bread. Now he cried out. "Torson! Torson! She's feeding him!"

The giant's eyes grew fearful, and he paddled at the air in

front of him with his hands, like a child paddling at the river's edge.

"I saw her!" the boy cried.

The two men moved up the ship toward them.

"Do I get a reward?" the boy asked.

Ker clipped him a blow on his shoulder that sent him huddling back against the side of the ship. His face crumpled and he wept noisily. "But I told you, I helped you. I'm hungry," he blubbered

Ker wheeled around, and Birle couldn't see his face. The boy could see it, and he stopped his noise. He wiped his nose on the sleeve of his ragged shirt, and bent low on his seat.

The brothers sat down on either side of the platform. Birle moved closer to Orien, who seemed to be taking no note of what went on around him. "You do the talking," Ker said.

"With pleasure," Torson agreed, and looked from Birle to Orien and back to Birle. "I hope you've enough strength to understand us."

"I understand you," Orien said.

Torson ignored Orien's haughty tone. "Well then. You've been saved from certain death, and we are glad to have been of service to you. I hope you'll be glad to pay your debt to us."

Blue waves danced under the lowering sun. The sun turned red as it fell to the horizon, and shone into the faces of the two men, causing them to squint. Squinting, they seemed even more dangerous.

"We paid our passage," she reminded Ker.

"Birle," Orien warned her to silence.

"Birle is it?" Torson nodded as if her name satisfied him. "Well, you'll have to know, Birle, that my brother isn't much judge, and you've already drunk in ale the value of those knives." Birle closed her mouth. This man didn't use words truly; he spoke to amuse himself.

"You owe us your lives, don't you agree? That should be worth some profit to us, you can't quarrel with that. A man can't make his living taking knives in exchange for food, and drink, and passage, can he? But my brother and I have an idea," Torson said.

"And what might that be?" Orien asked.

"Oh, I think you know, little birds. Two little birds, a robin and a sparrow." Torson smiled again at his own humor. Birle did not smile. "I know a market for caged birds, don't we, Ker."

"We'll take four birds to market, then?"

"Didn't I spend hours telling you just that?"

"You dress it up with so many words—I like things plain."

Orien drew himself to his feet. Birle put up a hand to pull him down—they were in the power of these men, it was no time for Orien to try whatever he was going to try. He brushed her hand away. He stood there at the rail of the ship, looking down on all of them. This was as he must have stood in his grandfather's hall. For all the starved and ragged look of him, he stood there a Lord.

"I'm worth more than you realize," Orien announced.

Torson laughed aloud. "Why, this is no sparrow you've netted, Ker. It's a hawk. Tell your story, hawk. Don't keep us guessing at it."

"Orien," Birle said. He paid no attention to her.

"There's a rich ransom would be paid for me."

"Oh yes? Any fool can see that, of course. Anybody would know who Orien is. But I'd like to hear it from your own lips: Who is going to pay this ransom?"

"The Earl of Sutherland."

That wiped their faces clear of mockery.

"Not just a hawk, a peregrine. Tell us more, peregrine. Tell us who this Earl is and where he keeps his strongboxes."

"In the Kingdom."

"And which kingdom might that be?" Torson asked. He had turned to look up at Orien, as if Orien were an actor on a stage.

"The Kingdom lies to the north and inland, upriver. It lies between mountains and forest."

"Oh *that* kingdom," Torson said. "I've heard all about that kingdom."

"Well, I haven't," Ker grumbled.

"But you have, Brother. Where all the women are fair, and all the men rich, you remember. Where crops grow without tending, and no man goes hungry. And the crown worn by the King has a stone in it larger than"—he gestured to the monster—"Yul's fist. A stone as red as fresh blood. If a man could find that kingdom, and if he could find a way to have that stone, he'd never work again."

"That's stories," Ker said, disgusted.

Torson laid his hand over his heart in mocking sorrow. "Do you think so? Do you think our peregrine is just a sparrow after all? A clever sparrow, a bold one—hoping we were too simple to know the tales?"

"But it's true," Birle said.

"And you are one of the fair women," Torson said. Ker snickered.

"The Kingdom is there," Birle insisted. "Merchants have seen it, coming up from the south to sell at the fairs."

"I've heard those merchants, in their cups. Warriors as large as Yul, all in silver armor. The wild men of the forest, whose arrows never miss. The King's golden barge, which he travels down the rivers on. The secret path under the mountain with a stone gate that raises and lowers to a word only the King knows. The merchants love to talk of that kingdom."

Birle had never heard such tales. If she had heard them she would not have believed them.

"There's truth in the stories, for all that they aren't true," Orien said. "There will be a bag of gold for each of you, if we are returned."

"Now it's ransom for both? Where can we claim it?" Torson asked.

"We go north to the river, and thence inland," Orien answered.

"It's wonderful, really, isn't it, Birle?" Torson invited her to join the mockery. "The bottomless sea to the trackless forest, and at journey's end the fabled kingdom. That's enough from you, sparrow. I'd rather hear about Birle."

110

"Aye," Ker agreed, with an eagerness that made Birle uneasy.

"What are you, Birle? Wife, whore, sister?"

For a minute, Orien didn't understand. When he did, his whole posture changed. His proud shoulders relaxed, and he leaned back against the bow. His eyes were mocking, and his smile echoed the smiles of the brothers. Orien became a man Birle didn't know, and not to be trusted. He didn't look at her. "A woman's of more value than a man?" he asked.

"She might be. She can be," Torson said.

"I can tell you this: Birle's no wife—nor strumpet. I'm a patient man." Orien laughed, and pulled at his beard with his hand. "She's but a girl, still. Let the peaches ripen, before you take them from the branch: That's the advice my grandfather gave me."

"Your grandfather, the Earl?" Torson played a game of words.

"If you'd prefer him so, of course he will be," Orien answered.

"You'd no father, then?"

"Ah, my father. Now he was a great peach-picker. My grandfather saved his breath where my father was concerned." They all three laughed at this. In its sound and meaning, Orien's laughter seemed no different from the others'.

Fear rose in Birle, like the tide rising silently on rocks. She looked from Orien's strangely unfamiliar face to the faces of the two men, to the boy watching from his corner, to the monster's bewildered face.

"Have you nothing to say for yourself, Birle?" Torson asked her.

"I serve him," she answered, with as much boldness as her fear would allow her.

Ker leaned toward her. She could back no farther away than she was, on the small platform. Orien stood away, and she was alone.

"Cleaned and combed, she might not be bad," Ker said. "You always tell me, Brother, that only blood can be relied on, when I've said we need wives to answer our needs and care for us. Did you never think that we might take one wife, between us?''

Birle's body couldn't move, but her spirit shrank within her. She could go over the side, she thought, and if she couldn't swim she could drown. Ker's hand moved along the rough boards toward her.

''I take it that a woman isn't worth much, even at best,'' Orien's voice asked. Birle stared at the thick fingers of the hand. ''How much would a girl fetch?'' he asked, as if the answer didn't matter much to him.

''More than a bold lad would,'' Torson said. ''A mettlesome hawk is a trouble and danger, but a plump little robin—''

''Plump?'' There was laughter in Orien's voice.

The hand lifted and came close to her face. Birle's hands clutched at the neck of her cloak. The hand, with its fingers, wrapped itself around her neck and the fingers slid down, under her cloak and shirt. Birle stared at his face; he was watching his own hand. His eyes—there was the same expression she had seen in Muir's, which she had named longing then, ignorant as she was. It was hunger, not longing, and she knew that Muir was little different from this man. She was ever a fool, she thought; she had ever been a fool.

''Stop paddling at her neck!'' Torson spoke roughly.

Ker looked at his brother, and smiled. Birle bit her teeth into her lip to keep from crying out. While he smiled at his brother, Ker's hand stroked down her neck again, and again. Orien stood helpless—angry.

With a howl that turned all of them to him, the monster rose half up from his seat. The rope at his neck jerked him to a stop, but he raised his manacled hands behind his head and pulled. The cleat that held his tether ripped out of the wood, and Yul lunged forward. He had his hands over Ker's head and was pulling back with the chain, choking Ker, before any of the others could move.

What Orien might have done, Birle didn't know. Torson

was the one who moved. He grabbed the rope hanging at Yul's back, and pulled down on it with his whole weight.

For a minute it was a comedy of choking—Ker pulling at the chain that cut off his breathing, the giant unmoved by the rope that cut into his thick neck. Then the giant let Ker drop onto the deck, where he lay crumpled and coughing. "Back!" Torson pulled on the rope. "Witch's spawn! Down!"

Yul turned around to look at him. Torson took the end of the rope, where the wooden cleat hung, and whipped Yul around the face.

"You'll blind him!" Birle cried.

"He'll have to sit then. Sit—you—thing—you—sit."

Yul sat down heavily, clumsily, his chained hands still protecting his face.

"He could've killed me." Ker rubbed his throat.

Torson had no sympathy for his brother. Sweat ran down his red face and into his beard. "Take this rope and tie it around the mast. I should have let him finish you off, if you're not going to do what I tell you. When will you learn to let me give the orders?"

"Hoy, Brother." Ker got up slowly and took the rope, to loop it around the mast and knot it.

"I give the orders, and you obey them."

"Yes, Brother," Ker said, sullen.

"I make the decisions."

"Yes, all right."

"You go along with them."

"I said yes!" Ker exploded.

"Just so you remember." The brothers glared at each other. "They said he was tame," Torson finally said. "They said he was a mouse."

"If he's the mouse, I'd hate to be the cat," Ker said. Then the brothers laughed together, slapping each other on the back, once again pleased with themselves.

Birle felt Orien slip down to sit beside her again, but she couldn't look at him. She formed *thank you* with her lips, soundlessly. Yul didn't understand, then he mimed bringing

113

food to his mouth and smiled at her. Birle smiled back, as much as she was able, and imitated his gesture. His smile stayed on his face, as if it had been forgotten there.

Neither Birle nor Orien protested when their hands were bound by Torson, who said he wasn't going to let Ker near her so the little robin could sleep sound in her nest. The sparrow, Torson said, seemed to have had most of his feathers plucked, and if he didn't want to lose the rest he'd do as he was told. As night deepened, Birle sat silent against the curved wooden sides of the ship. For all that there were five others on this ship, she was alone. Her thoughts were her only companions, and they were not good company to her.

The waning moon looked down upon the ship. Four dark, shapeless sleepers lay before her, and the black mast rose up as if it were driven into the moon's face.

Orien spoke softly beside her. "I was trying—"

"I know." She had thought about his talk of a woman's value and understood what he had hoped to gain by it. She understood that he hadn't betrayed her. "When you asked about ransom, Orien, and then saw that they wouldn't believe you—I almost believed you were such a man, such a—you seemed at home with those two, the same kind of man they are."

"And so I was. I can put on the cloak of the world I find myself in, however I happen to find myself in it. I can sing any man's tune, and you'd believe me. That's my gift." Birle knew this wasn't a gift he honored.

"So you might, in that fashion, make your way safely among strangers, whatever your station there."

"I was a man like my grandfather, in his company; I was an Earl with the Earl. I was a soldier when I trained among the soldiers. A courtier with the ladies, a student with the priests—I think sometimes I am nothing of myself."

"And you might keep yourself safe that way," she said, stubbornly making her hope clear to him. "Why should we both be lost, when you at least might win through?"

They sat there with the moonlight falling upon them, and the ship rocking gently under them. Her ankles were chained,

114

her hands were bound, and each future she imagined for herself was more cruel than the one before. But if Orien could be kept safe—

"So you do know what they mean to do with us?" Orien asked.

"Yes." They were to be sold. They were to be parted. "What was her name?" Birle asked. "The bride your father took from you, what was her name?"

"Melisaune," he said. "Why would you want to know that? Birle, you don't think that it was because of her—? Only a girl would do that, throw everything over for love. That's a girl's reason, not—" He stopped speaking. Birle said nothing.

"You *have* been a fool, haven't you?" he asked.

He shouldn't mock her, she thought. She thought to answer yes, and let him know she thought as little of him as he thought of her. Aye, and then he'd have made her betray herself, along with all the other ill he'd brought her to. "No, my Lord, I have not," she said, and turned her back to him. Let him understand that however he wished.

Part Two

———— ❦ ————

The Philosopher's Amanuensis

Eleven

TORSON led them through an open gateway. Ker made the end of the line of captives. Captives they were, Birle knew. Their hands were tied tight behind them, and each was roped by the hands to the waist of the one behind. Yul still wore shackles at his ankles, but the three others moved barefooted, their legs unbound.

It was like a fenced farmyard, the dirt packed smooth, the herded captives like clumps of weeds on barren ground. The owners greeted one another, eyes assessing the competition of the market that day. There were only two women there, besides Birle, neither of them young. Birle drew more attention than she liked, and Torson was congratulated on his luck.

On the journey, they had fed her as much as she would eat, and given her a bowl of ale at the end of each day, to fatten her. Orien was moved to the oars, beside the boy. Seeing him there, Birle couldn't stay angry at him. It was three days to this city, and Orien was so worn that all he could do was bend over the oar and sleep, whenever the sail was raised or the ship anchored. They never traveled by night.

Birle had grown accustomed to the long, empty days, the slowly changing shoreline, and the endless waves passing under the ship. She thought now that she could grow accustomed to anything. She had been accustomed to life at the Inn, with its labors that had seemed hard to her; then to living on the river in Orien's company; then to the slow death of their stony sanctuary. She thought, standing bound, that she might grow accustomed even to that, even to being on sale, like an animal. Aye, it was terrible how easily she could grow used to things.

Except, she thought, to Orien. Orien was always like sunrise at the end of darkness, ever new and welcome, ever surprising. At the thought, she turned to look at him.

Ragged, exhausted, filthy—he didn't look a Lord. Except for his eyes, she thought, surprising laughter there. "Orien?" she asked, fearful of what he might answer, if his wits had broken under the weight of his fortune.

"Gladaegal wouldn't envy me now," he said.

Anyone seeing Orien now could only pity him. Birle had fared better on the journey. The first morning, she'd been handed a thick wooden comb and told to work at her hair. She had made it into the long braid that hung down her back. Yul had watched her. Whether he rowed or rested, Yul's eyes had stared at her. Birle gave him as much of the bread as she could not swallow, at every meal. She even tried to talk with him. Why she tried to do that, she did not know, except for the gratitude she felt to him. Yul was a simple, but not—as their captors thought—without speech. It was just that the words that came out of his misshapen mouth were twisted into sounds difficult to understand. When he spoke his own name it was a grunting "Ull" sound—forced out from between his lips as if it were food he could not swallow. Her name was little different, when he spoke it. "Url," he would say, to catch her attention.

She had tried to discover where he was from, and how he'd come to his present situation. "Where is your home?" she'd asked.

"Um?"

Birle breathed out the sound. "Huh—huh—"

"Huh," Yul echoed.

"Home," Birle said.

"Hum," Yul repeated, and smiled at her, the monster's smile that lingered on his face, forgotten. His eyes peered

120

into her face in an effort to understand what she wanted him to understand.

Torson had answered her question, from the stern of the ship. "He can't tell you. Some old granny'd raised him—and she died—"

At the word "granny," Yul's big head turned to the stern of the boat. "Grah," he repeated, as if it were a question, or a lament.

"It was a fishing village, up north," Torson said. "A place so dirty, so small—maybe four wretched hovels, and two boats still afloat. They had him tied to a tree, they were terrified of him. They didn't know where she'd got him, only that she'd brought him in from the woods one day. Somebody must have left him there, to feed the wolves. And wouldn't you, if you produced something like that? We didn't have to give them anything for Yul. The boy we paid two copper coins for. Isn't that right, boy?"

Weeping was his only answer.

"Too many children, too many mouths, and I'll tell you, it looked to me like his father was going to drink up those coins before anybody else could have the good of them. The boy's not much but he'll do for the mines. They keep a few boys, for the narrow, deep places underground. Will you like that, boy? With the weight of the earth over you, your candle in darkness. They'll give you something to weep about. I figure, you'll be good for maybe two seasons, maybe less— we'll double our money on that one," he explained to Birle, as if she'd be glad of it. "The rest of you are pure profit. It's been a good voyage, hasn't it, Ker?"

"It'll do," Ker said. "It'll do fine."

Orien slept through all of this, his arms fallen to the deck, his head fallen forward onto his legs. For a minute, Birle watched him, asleep. "What mines?" she asked, although she didn't want to know.

"Gold," Ker said, as if that were a word that filled his mouth better than food.

"They always need men for the mines," Torson said. "Nobody lasts too long. Coughing sickness, mostly," he explained. "Although," he added, his smile flickering, "some of them had the branding festers and they're only good for a couple of weeks." As if he knew her fear he added more. "There's a crescent, here." His finger traced down his cheek. "Maybe not quite so long. No one escapes the mines. They'll want Yul, and pay a good price for him, I'd think a silver coin. They take what no one else will buy, but you don't need to worry about that, little robin. There'll be others to want you, long before the captains of the mines come forward."

Who those others might be, Birle didn't care to think. She stood, bound among other bound captives. There were only captives and masters here. Everybody seemed to be waiting.

When the ringing of bells filled the air, Birle looked up. These were not the bells that hung over wells, to sound alarm for the villages. These were bells that sang out in round, peaceful notes, many of them, not together but at the same time. The notes filled the air like a flock of birds and then, like birds settling into a tree, settled into silence.

At the silence, several men came into the enclosure. Their eyes told what they were—they looked over the captives like people at the fairs looking over an array of knives, or woolens. Almost all were clean-shaven. They wore short coats, in bright colors, belted at the waist. Their trousers fitted to their legs like skin. Then Birle met a pair of eyes that stared at her and she looked down to the ground, and the hem of her skirt, and the dirt on her toes.

The enclosure filled with voices, and more people. Birle had never been at such a market, and had no idea what would happen.

They stood, the four of them, back-to-back—facing out, like beleaguered fighters. She had Orien at her back, for the last stand of their long journey. She didn't have the heart for misery; fear lay so heavy upon her that she couldn't catch her breath. It would have been easier if she had known what it was she had to fear.

Torson and Ker kept a little apart from their captives. They talked at first with other sellers, then with those who wished to buy. Birle heard only occasional words. Ker kept silent, letting his quicker-tongued brother make their profits. The sun was warm, here where the wattle walls kept out any breeze, and dust rose into the air.

Two men, who had walked around their circle twice before, stood in front of Birle. She looked up in apprehension but they were not interested in her. They conferred in low voices, as if she could not possibly understand what they said, as if she spoke a different language or could not speak, as if it didn't matter whether she understood or not any more than it matters if a dog understands. Both men were young and, for this place, plainly dressed, in short brown coats, without any decorations of color or thread. Both had smooth chins, but their hair was long, and tied back. The red-haired one seemed to be trying to convince the shorter, brown-haired man. "He's worth four silvers. He looks as if he's got some wit to him," Red Hair said, "and for the work we need we can't have someone too stupid to learn. There are tricks of joinery, and the accurate measuring of pieces of wood—an error is costly. Tailoring must also need such tricks. We can't afford a witless slave."

"But four silvers—that's all my savings. Wouldn't we be wiser to keep looking out for apprentices, who at least bring payment with them?"

"You know that apprentices go to the guildsmen. Listen, you'll have him from first bell to second. I'll feed him midday and have him the afternoon. Come on, what do you say? If his hands are as clever as they look—beneath the dirt—we'll soon earn our coins back. Give me your hand on it, friend."

It had to be Orien. These were two craftsmen, that was clear. Orien would not be badly off with them—not like the mines, with his face branded; not like these pirates, with their oars and chains. She watched the two approach Torson, and wished them well.

A man waited before her. Of middling age and middling height, he wore a deep blue coat, with red designs woven into its fabric. He looked at her as if he had always known that she would, one day, be brought here, as if—although she hadn't known it—Birle had all her life been moving toward this one day. He had the eyes of a pig.

He thrust his fleshy face toward her. Torson and Ker were occupied with the two craftsmen. His plump hand reached for her throat, but it was only to untie her cloak and let it fall at her feet. He stepped back then, to study her, up and down.

As he examined her, he made an odd little sucking noise with his mouth and cheeks. His head moved up and down, his cheeks puffed in and out; he stepped to one side, then to the other, still making sucking sounds. Then he stood in front of her again, hands behind his back again, sucking.

When he reached out for her face, Birle's head flinched back. She couldn't stop herself. Torson, she saw, watched now, with interest. The hand grabbed her cheeks and pulled her head forward. His fingers pried at her lips. She clenched her teeth together.

Orien's back held her up.

The middling man was angry. The sucking noises ceased and he drew his hand away, and he stepped back, one step.

Then he hit her across the mouth with the back of his hand, and grabbed her face again, prodding into her mouth with his fingers, pulling her lips back to study her teeth. Birle's eyes filled with tears, but she would not weep. Would not.

She looked as far away as she could, which was only to the open gateway. Her cheek stung. Her face felt hot, with shame and helplessness. A gray-headed man was just entering; he saw her and stopped, abruptly, like a drifting boat that had reached the end of its mooring rope.

The middling man, apparently satisfied with her mouth, pulled sharply at her braid—and what he expected to happen when he did that she didn't know—then moved over to talk with Torson. He shouldered the craftsmen aside, and started talking. He never took his eyes from Birle. She didn't look at him, but she could feel his eyes.

At her back, Orien stood tense. They could do nothing, she knew that. They couldn't break and run, to be at least slaughtered quickly—which would be preferable—because

124

they were bound not only to each other but also to Yul and the boy. If she cried out for help, there was no man in the enclosure who would come to their aid. They couldn't help themselves and she could see no way that help might come to them.

The older man was making his way through the crowd. The crowd didn't make way for his slight, stooped figure and he had to weave his way through. Poor as he looked, he looked preferable to the middling man, to Birle's eyes. But he was too late: She saw coins change from the middling man's purse to Torson's hand.

In any case, the older man wasn't looking at her as he moved through the crowds. His interest was probably her imagination, wishing.

He never even hesitated in front of her, but went right over to Torson. His voice was loud, so she heard everything he said.

"The girl. How much?"

Torson answered him.

"What? Speak up, into my left ear, my right ear's gone bad."

"She's sold."

"To whom?"

"This gentleman," Torson said. The middling man smiled, pleased to have in his possession what another desired.

The older man turned to deal with the middling man. "At what price?"

"A gold and five silvers."

"I'll buy her from you," the older man said. His unkempt hair, his worn, dark cloak—he didn't look like a man with many coins to spend.

The middling man looked over the stooped shoulder at Torson, as if to ask who this madman was. The older man's hands pulled at the opening of his cloak, and at his belt, as if he had forgotten where his purse was. He finally found it and counted out five silver coins, and a gold one. "There you are." He held out the money.

125

"Why should I sell her? I never said I was selling."

The older man seemed momentarily confused, then his face cleared. "Yes, of course. Stupid of me. You'll want your profit." He pulled out a second gold coin, which he exchanged for the five silver ones. "There's a profit for you," he said, pleased with himself.

"I said, no sale."

"All right, all right, the silvers too; it's all I've got with me."

The middling man looked at Birle, and winked, as if he and she were playing this game together. If her hands had not been tied, she'd have bitten her thumb at him, if her heart had not been sunk down to her ankles. The older man had no authority, and he had no skill at bargaining. The loss of hope was so cruel to her that she wished she'd never had any, not even for the brief instant it had been hers.

"Loose her, Torson," the middling man said.

"Ours too," the red-haired craftsman said.

"Wait, wait." The older man looked bewildered, as if he hadn't understood anything of what had gone on. "I have more coins, but not with me. I can send for it, however much you ask."

The middling man's fleshy face became the mask of greed. "How much?"

Like a child, the older man spoke eagerly, hastily. "How much do you ask? I've never purchased at market before, so I don't know the prices, or I'd have brought more coins. I'll send to Corbel. When I tell him what it's for he'll let me have whatever I ask, because he's the one who told me I must find someone to keep my house. He told me to come here."

"Who told you?" The middling man's voice had a wary note in it.

"Why, Corbel, as I just said. He'll pay promptly, I warrant it."

The middling man's whole bearing changed, as if all of the plumpness had been sucked out of him. "Just the price I paid Torson, that's all I'll take, no more." He closed his fingers quickly around the coins.

126

"That's very good of you," the older man said.

Birle struggled to keep her face blank. Whoever, or whatever, Corbel was, it was a name to get you what you wished, even here. The older man seemed unaware of the stir he'd made—even Torson and Ker eyed him warily as he turned back to them. "The very large man, how much is he?"

Torson hesitated, and Birle thought she knew why. If Corbel was an enemy no man wanted, then to sell the older man a simple might well prove dangerous. She could almost see Torson thinking it out: If they could get to the ship before they were found out, then they needn't come to market in this city again, not for a long time, not until they had been forgotten. There were smaller cities they had sailed past on their journey to this one. This place had the busiest market, but the others had markets too. Greed and caution chased each other over Torson's face, like two dogs chasing each other. He made up his mind. "One gold."

"That's just what I have. How fortunate."

The coin was given to Torson. Quickly, he untied Birle and Yul from the other two. "Not a word, you hear?" he hissed in her ear. "If you care what happens to Yul, it'll be a longer life than he'd have in the mines."

Ker put the rope that ran around Yul's waist into Birle's hand. He knelt to unlock the shackles at Yul's feet. She didn't know what to do. But she couldn't do anything anyway. If she couldn't, then she needn't.

"And ours," the red-haired craftsman spoke. "Ours too, you've had our money."

"Come along now," the older man said, and without another glance he began making his way back through the crowd to the gateway. He seemed to find nothing odd about Birle leading Yul like a goat on a rope; perhaps he hadn't noticed it. With Yul in his train the crowd parted for him.

As she made her way to the gate, her eyes on the stooped shoulders, Birle had a sudden awful thought. What if it wasn't Orien for the craftsmen, but the boy. If she had been worth a gold coin and five silvers to the middling man, who was a practiced marketeer, then wouldn't Orien have been worth

127

more than four silver coins? If Yul fetched a gold coin? She turned around, to see Orien.

She couldn't find him. She found Ker and Torson, the two shaggy heads; they talked with a man in a blood-red shirt, another beside him whose cheek bore a broad scar, like a crescent moon.

Where was Orien? The boy stood weeping with bent head, but Orien—

She saw his eyes, first. The two craftsmen were leading him away, following the path Yul had made. She saw Orien's bellflower eyes, and his attempt at a smile, before she lost sight of him in the crowd.

Twelve

WHERE she was led, with Yul obediently following, Birle could not have said. There were people, crowds, and their voices filled the air around her. There were houses, lining both sides of dusty streets. She was always climbing up. She didn't have the strength to look around her, nor the heart to care. Her feet dragged. When she stumbled, she barely noticed it. The man she followed walked on, without a word, without looking back, as if he were unaware that he was being followed.

After a time, he stopped before a doorway. The little low house was set in the center of a high wall. He took a key from his girdle, and unlocked the door. Birle followed him into a dim room. Yul followed Birle, at the end of his heavy rope.

The man might have said something to her, but Birle didn't attend. Then he had left them, going out a door opposite the one through which they had entered. She sat down on the wooden floor, and pulled her knees up, and rested her face on her knees. After a time, she noticed that she was weeping. After a time, she noticed that her tears had ceased.

When at last Birle lifted her head, she saw Yul crouched on the floor not far away. Even hunkered so, he looked huge. His eyes watched her, mute and sympathetic, like a dog's. She looked at Yul but she didn't see him. Looking at Yul, she saw only who he was not, and the weight of tears pulled her head back down onto her knees.

It was a pounding on the door that roused her, she had no idea how much time later. The door swung open. A man entered, followed by two soldiers. The soldiers wore red shirts and carried swords. The man strode to the center of the room and stood, looking around him. He was a slight, dark man, with a wolfish face. His cloak was crimson, his red shirt had thick bands of gold at the wrist, his leather boots came up to his knees. His hat fell in soft folds beside his face. For all that he was slender and short, he seemed taller than either of the soldiers who stood behind him.

"Stand up," he said.

Fear penetrated Birle's mind. She obeyed, and Yul—who had crept closer to her—stood too, behind her, as if she could hide him.

The man reached a hand out, to lift Birle's chin and see her face. What he saw did not please him, and he let her chin drop. What Birle saw frightened her—the high-bridged nose and the two cold eyes close beside it. Her blood rang with the warning: This man was like a line of flame, snaking toward its destination, to destroy.

"And this too," he muttered, moving toward Yul, who could have crushed him with one huge hand.

The man wheeled around. His cloak brushed against Birle's arm; her arm twitched back as if from flame. "You men— start unloading, and keep an eye on these two. Although I doubt they'll give you any trouble. You," he said to Birle. "If you move, you'll be killed. Do you understand?"

Birle nodded. This too did not please him. "I should have known," the man said to her. "It's what he always does. He's always been this kind of fool." He went out the rear door, like a line of flame.

In the light of the open door, dust motes circled and danced. Horses and a wagon waited in the street. The soldiers carried in a long wooden box, a cooking pot, a table, four stools, and another box. They left these in the middle of the room, then stood beside the door, on guard, talking.

"I'm surprised the man wasn't taken for the mines—he'd last maybe three seasons, maybe even more."

130

"Look at his face, stupid. He's a simple."

"It's not brains needed for the mines."

"And the girl's no better, if you ask me. Why Corbel has this man . . . brother or no brother . . . in service, I'll never understand."

"We're not here to understand. We're here to get paid for fighting."

"Not carrying around household furniture, neither."

"Corbel brings more living men out of battle than any of the others I've heard of. And each of those men gets booty prizes. If he orders me to carry furniture, I'll do it—long as he's the man who pays me."

The old man stumbled into the room, as if he had been pushed. He probably had been, Birle thought, as the man she assumed must be Corbel entered at his heels, talking angrily. ". . . whey-faced girl—good for nothing but whining by the look of her—and the man strong enough, but a simpleton. What were you thinking of? Don't bother, I know what you were thinking. But leaving them alone in here—Joaquim, they could have walked away, and the coins that paid for them wasted."

"I didn't think," the old man mumbled.

"You never do. You're so busy thinking you never think."

"I'm sorry."

"You always are. You two," Corbel said to the soldiers, "get the collars on them."

Birle backed away from the soldier who came toward her, and Yul made a deep growling noise in his throat. Corbel drew his dagger. "You—girl. Unless you want to watch his heart cut out—"

Birle nodded, without a word. She understood. She looked up into Yul's sad monster face. "We have to," she heard her voice say, and didn't recognize its sound. She made herself stand still while the soldier wrapped cold metal around her throat and pulled it tight. She felt his fingers at the back of her neck. Yul bent over so the taller soldier could reach up to place a gold band around his thick neck. The soldier closed the clasp and stepped quickly back.

131

Birle wondered how Orien was faring, with his two masters, and a collar around his neck.

"Now, girl—look at me."

Corbel's eyes were yellowy brown, deep-lidded, and when she met them with her own, fear ran along her bones.

"You are to get the house in order, and keep it."

Birle couldn't take in what he said; fear deafened her.

"This man will do heavy work."

Birle nodded her head. She would have agreed to anything.

"All who see that collar will know you're of my house," Corbel said. "Know you are under my protection. Thus, also, anyone who finds you will know whence you came. Joaquim is your master and he'll prove a soft one—but remember, you answer to me."

Birle nodded her head. She couldn't move her eyes.

When Corbel turned his back to her, she thought her watery legs would collapse under her. But she held herself straight because the fear of what would happen if she fainted onto the floor—he might well cut her throat and throw her away, as more trouble than she would ever be worth; or take her back to market, and another purchaser—fear of that was greater than the fear she felt of Corbel. She looked at Yul, and could read confusion there. She reached out and put her hand on his heavy wrist, but it was as much to comfort herself as to comfort him.

"I know how you chose this one, Brother, so don't bother trying to explain. She's just like that other."

"But she's not at all—" Joaquim protested.

"You deceive yourself, but that's no matter now. What did you pay for her?"

"A gold and five silvers," Joaquim answered, meekly.

Corbel looked at Birle, then back to his brother. What he was thinking was clear to her.

"There was another man," Joaquim explained. "He had paid as much for her. I offered him even more for her. He wouldn't have done it but that I mentioned your name. He would take only what he had paid."

That statement seemed to satisfy Corbel. He laughed once,

132

briefly and without gladness. "Well, she's young, and if no man has had her yet, she'll be clean. Maybe it wasn't so bad a bargain, Joaquim. And the man?"

"One gold." Joaquim's voice had confidence now.

Corbel's silence burned in the room, but when he spoke his voice was cold. "Who cheats you cheats me. Who had the man?"

"Those same men who had the girl. They were two, with the look of pirates, and the smell, too. Bearded, well-fed men."

Corbel lifted a hand and snapped his fingers. The two soldiers moved out into the street. Corbel turned at the doorway to throw a purse onto the floor and say, "I'll come back, to dine, tomorrow week. By then, the wagons from the south will have arrived and you can show me what you've accomplished, Brother, and I'll see if the girl can keep the house."

He didn't take the time to pull the door shut behind him.

The three he left behind stood for a time in silence, in the shadowy room, lit by sunlight from the two open doors. As fear left her, grief rose up in Birle to take its place, covering her like a heavy hooded cloak. Her master, Joaquim, moved to close the door into the street and then turned, a shadowy figure now. "I expect you want to get started."

Birle wanted nothing. Her chest was crushing her, so that every breath she drew must work to push her chest out, and even then she could not swallow enough air.

He came before her to look into her face. Birle didn't care what he thought. She hadn't the will to lift her head. "You're not ill, are you? Do you hear me?"

"Yes, my Lord," Birle said.

"I'm no lord, child."

"Yes, master," Birle said.

He hovered in front of her for a little longer, then retreated from the room. Birle sank back down onto the floor. She pulled up her knees and wrapped her arms around them, and buried her face in the darkness of her skirt.

Hours later she heard him come back into the room. The odd whimpering noises Yul was making, she realized as she

133

rose to her feet before her master, he had been making for some time. She recognized in Yul's eyes an expression she had seen in the eyes of her little sisters. "Where is the privy?" she asked the master.

The little building was outside, at the far end of a long, low building attached to the house. Yul went into it first, bowing his head at the low door. Behind the house, two shoulder-high walls ran back, as far as she could see, shadowed in the dim light of day's end. Her hand went up to touch the chain at her neck, a smooth band as cool as the grass under her bare feet. The sky behind the house flamed with sunset, and darkness crept toward her over the walled yard. Orien's name was a call she could cry out into the darkness, but it came from her lips as a whisper.

Yul waited while she used the privy, and they walked together back into the house, where her master had lit a candle. Birle sat down on a stool and watched him attempt to make a fire. He arranged and rearranged logs, and at each change patiently struck his flint under them. Finally, he turned to say, "I thought you might have built a fire."

"Yes, master." The woodbox beside the hearth held kindling, and pieces of straw braided together into twists, as well as logs. She made a small pile of kindling wood, then put three of the straw twists under it. Those she ignited with the tinderbox he handed to her. When little flames smoked upward she laid the three smallest logs across the irons; when those had caught fire, and burned, she laid fatter logs upon them. As the flames cradled the logs she sat back on her heels before the hearthstone. She wasn't dreaming, she wasn't thinking, she wasn't remembering—as long as her eyes stayed on the flames, the darkness that threatened to overwhelm her was kept at bay.

"You must eat," the master's voice spoke gently.

Birle rose to sit at the table, where he had set out a round loaf of bread, a round of cheese, a knife, and three metal tankards of wine. Yul ate hungrily and drank thirstily, with little murmuring grunts. Birle could not swallow bread, nor cheese. At her second mouthful of wine, her belly closed up.

134

Her hands, as she watched them, lay still on the table. The flickering firelight flowed over her hands like water.

The master rose from the table, to open a broad cupboard beside the fireplace. "You'll sleep here," he said.

A bed had been built into the thick wall. Birle climbed up into it. She turned her back to the room and fell into sleep

Distant bells roused her. She awoke to fear, and grief, and hunger, and the tangled notes of the distant bells. The room she slept in was empty and dark. The fire had burned out, but the morning wasn't cold. Birle climbed down from her bed and went outside to the privy.

Here, in this southern country, it was full spring. The air glowed with the gentle light of the rising sun. The ground was soft with young grass. Birle's hand went up to the band at her neck. Already she was accustomed to finding it there, to its meaning.

This house had its own well. A low, circular stone wall had a bucket at its side. She dipped the bucket into the well, then drank from it. Clear, cold, clean—the water refreshed her. Was she such a creature to become so quickly accustomed even to this ill fortune?

At the question, grief swept over her again, bringing not tears but a darkening of the morning and a weight on her shoulders she couldn't lift them against. Already the day seemed long to her. She lifted handfuls of water to her face. She washed her hands and as much of her arms as she could reach, then her legs, hiking her skirt up, and finally her feet. She emptied the brown water from the bucket onto the ground and watched it soak in among the tender shoots. She had to go back into the house, she knew it, and that she did not wish to meant nothing. Her wishes meant nothing.

Her master was sitting at the table when she entered. She didn't speak a word to him. She built a fire, then opened the shutters that closed over the windows of the house, to let light in. She brought down the remainder of the bread and cheese, to place before him. She filled a tankard with wine from the jug. Then she stood by the fire.

135

He was not so old as she had thought at first, Master Joaquim. He was a man ripe in years, but not old. What had given her the false impression was his stooping shoulders, the odd, distracted manner of him, and the lack of care he took for his hair and clothing. Now Birle noticed that his hair, though gray, was thick, and his skin, though faded, was not spotted with age.

"Have you eaten?"

Birle shook her head.

"Drunk?"

"There's a well," she told him.

"Sit down, eat. I have to warn you. Corbel will come back, and if he isn't pleased with what he finds he'll sell you. For all that he is my father's son, I wouldn't be able to stop him. Sit and eat, please."

Birle obeyed.

"This"—her master waved his arm around vaguely—"all of it is Corbel's." He wore the same shirt he had the day before, and the same baggy leggings, as if he slept in his clothes.

"The house." Birle wanted to be sure she understood him aright.

"Yes, and other houses, and the city, and the lands around it, and all that they contain. The mines particularly, because of the gold. Corbel has installed me here, in this house, because he has a use for me. I am," he explained, "a philosopher."

"I don't—" Birle started to say, then stopped. It didn't matter whether she knew the word or not. He was her master, which was all that must concern her.

Her unfinished question made him smile, a quiet turning up of the ends of his mouth that made him look as sad and wise as the moon. "Nobody does know what that word means. It means nothing, except that I can claim some understanding, some knowledge of things. Corbel hopes—he's heard tales of a stone that turns base metals into gold."

"Is there such a thing?" Birle asked.

He looked thoughtfully at her, but not as if he saw her.

136

"Men have dreamed of it, although none has ever held it in his hand, not to my knowledge. I cannot say that there is such a thing, no. But equally I cannot say there is not. Why should a man be able to dream of it if it cannot be? If it is so impossible, then what puts it into a man's mind? Greed puts many things into men's minds, and fear does too. But men dream of other things, as well—of justice, of the lost golden age, of an order to their world such as that which orders the tides and seasons, of medicine to cure all sickness. . . ." His voice drifted off into silence, and he sat unseeing, lost in his own thoughts.

Birle waited to be told what she must do. She heard the hooves of horses and voices of people in the street, muffled by the thick walls and closed door. She wondered what had happened to Yul, where he was. She had forgotten him, and remembering, she interrupted her master's silence. "Where is Yul?"

"Who?" he asked. "I don't know your name. Have you a name?"

"Birle."

"Is Yul the man? I sent him to sleep in a storeroom. Is he still sleeping?"

"He might be." She spoke cautiously. "He's a simple."

"I thought those two seemed too pleased with themselves. When he's told what to do, can he then do it?"

"I think so. I'm not sure of it. He rowed, and ate. He's not as simple as they thought, the men who—"

"But we must get to work!" Joaquim rose suddenly, purposefully. "The stables need to be taken down, and—there's much that must be done before the wagons get here, if I'm to do Corbel's will."

"What about me?"

"You've your work in the house. I don't know how it's done but there's the house to keep. Although you might be unhappy, I do hope—he *will* return, Corbel, and he'll make good his word. His displeasure is a thing for all of us to fear."

Birle didn't need reminding. The taste of fear, bitter as

137

steel, had not left her mouth since Ker had first spoken to them. She ought to get accustomed to it, since, she thought—grief lowering over her—she had grown accustomed to so much else strange and terrible and sorrowful. "Master?"

"What is it?"

"I wonder—in my own land, there's a servant's fair, and some are hired while some are purchased." He didn't seem to be listening but she made herself go on and ask the question. "Those that are purchased give six years of service, after which . . ." Birle wasn't sure she had the courage to hear his answer, if his answer was what she feared it might be. "I wonder, in this country, for how long . . . ?"

"How long? Why, for your life."

She was a slave, then. Orien was a slave.

"Unless Corbel sets you free. Sometimes, in return for extraordinary service, a man will do that. Or if it's a woman who has borne children, because a man doesn't want his own children to be slaves and they must be if their mother is, so he might in that instance give her freedom. Otherwise, no." Her master hesitated, thought. "You mustn't mind, Birle."

If she was a slave, then what was the reason to keep the house, to obey? At the Inn, at least, she served the Inn's prosperity, from which they all benefited. Here there was no reason, no necessity—except fear.

Thirteen

FEAR was sufficient reason, given sufficient fear. Birle would have sat on by the fire all day, not for warmth but for lack of spirit; but fear of what Corbel might do—should he unexpectedly arrive, and arriving unexpected find her unoccupied—ran along her bones. Fear kept her on the move—hauling water to sweep clean wooden floors and scrub clean plates and tankards.

At midday the street door burst open and Corbel himself entered. A soldier followed, carrying a fowl by its neck; he bore also a round loaf and a stoppered jug. He dropped his burdens on the table and went back to the street, where the horses stamped their feet. Corbel stood in the center of the room, hands behind his back and feet wide apart, looking around him. If he was pleased with what he saw, Birle did not know it.

"Is your master out back?"

Birle nodded.

"The monster works with him?"

She nodded.

"I hope for your sake that you can cook."

Birle nodded.

Although he had no more to say, Corbel kept looking at her. Then—abruptly—he left. Birle's legs were so weak that she would have sat down, except for the fear that Corbel might return, to catch her out. After a few moments, she tiptoed to the door he had left open, and closed it. How Nan would laugh to see her so meek, she thought, and the thought was bitter to her. Yet it was Nan who made her learn how to pluck and stew a fowl, or roast it. She had never thought she would be grateful to Nan.

Sorrow and fear were what Birle knew of that day—sorrow, fear, and toil. She singed and plucked the fowl, then set it in a large pot to stew. One fowl to feed three—and one of the three Yul—meant that the broth would be welcome. While the dinner cooked, she went up the narrow staircase and found a low attic room, where Joaquim had his bed. This room too she washed clean, and then the narrow staircase. By late afternoon the fowl was ready, so she called Joaquim and Yul to the table. Birle had little appetite. Fear and sorrow filled her stomach. As soon as the meal was done, she climbed into her cupboard bed and fell eagerly into sleep.

A pounding on the door awoke her. It sounded as if someone were beating on the door with two fists. Birle stood beside the door but didn't dare to open it. From behind her, Joaquim spoke, "Open it, Birle."

He had come as far as the lowest step, wearing a long white shirt that fell around his ankles. In the dim light of the banked fire, he didn't look frightened. Neither did he sound alarmed. She obeyed him.

As soon as she had turned the key in the lock, the door pushed against her, and Corbel entered the room, from the dark, empty street. He took his place at the center of the room, looking past Birle as if she were invisible, speaking to his brother. "This place smells like a barnyard," he said. The rich smell of wine came from him, and he swayed slightly as he stood. "You must bathe."

"Yes. Yes of course," Joaquim answered. "I'm sorry."

"Have you a bath?" Corbel demanded.

Joaquim looked to Birle to answer. At the Inn, they bathed in a half-barrel, and she had seen nothing like that in the house. She didn't know if the building where Yul and Joaquim had spent the day contained such a barrel. She didn't know which would anger Corbel more, that they did not know or that they had none. "No, master."

She had guessed correctly, she thought, since Corbel left the house at that answer. By the time she had shut the door, and turned the big key in the lock, Joaquim had gone back to his bed.

In the morning, after they had eaten the last of the bread and cheese, her master turned to her. "Clothing," he said. "You'll want clothing. And I'm not as clean as I might be, nor are my clothes."

"Aye," she said. The morning was fine—the sky clear, the air warm. She could lay his washed clothing out to dry in the sunlight.

"Yul," Joaquim said. "Upstairs, you'll find two trunks. Bring down the one that has a leather strap around it."

He must be as simple as the monster, Birle thought, if he thought he'd be understood. She watched Yul's misshapen mouth twist, to form a word.

"Up?"

"The staircase is behind you."

Yul turned, looked, turned back, nodded clumsily. "Up. D-runk."

"It's the one with the leather strap I want, not the other." Yul shook his head, concentrating on his master's face.

"Ah. Let me see. Leather—what boots are made of. The strap is wrapped around the trunk. The other trunk has no leather strap."

Yul understood. He waited.

"Could you bring that trunk, with the leather strap, down here, for Birle?" Joaquim asked. He didn't seem impatient.

"Yes!" Yul cried, and got up.

"He understands you," Birle said.

"Of course. He's not deaf. Once I've made him understand what needs doing, he does it. It's simple, really—he won't do anything until he understands, that's all. I know learned men who haven't acquired that wisdom. The trunk has my wife's clothing in it. You can take what you need from it."

A wife? But he had the small, narrow bed, and there was no evidence of a wife in the house. "She won't be angry?"

141

"No. She's dead—last fall, in another city. She took the summer fevers, and I couldn't find any physic to make her well. Her garments may do for you, but as to Yul I don't know."

Yul came down the stairs, the trunk on his back, bent over not for its weight but for the low ceiling over the stairs. He set it in the middle of the room.

"Good," Joaquim said. "Now, let's get to the morning's work." Yul followed, as if he understood every word that his master spoke.

Without warning, sorrow rose up in Birle, and beat against her like waves against rocks. Her head fell down onto the table and she had no will to move. It was a dark, darkening, shapeless thing, this sorrow, and she knew its name.

Aye, it would be more bearable if Orien were dead.

But she couldn't sit there, weeping. If Corbel should come—and catch her out—and the soldiers would arrive with provisions and she had no idea how long she had sat there. . . . Birle got up, afraid.

She brushed crumbs from the table and rinsed the tankards clean. She swept the floor, then the stairs, and straightened the bedclothes upstairs. She remembered that she was to open the trunk.

When she lifted the wooden lid, a breath of sweet air come out. Not freshly sweet, as flowers, but old, dry, as if it were the memory of flowers, somehow caught in the dead air of the trunk. She lifted the clothing out carefully: three skirts, one red, one blue, one yellow; six shirts of the same colors; underskirts and chemises of some light fabric; a blue cloak with a worked-silver clasp; and a pair of boots, too narrow for her feet, the leather too dainty for use. Birle lifted the folded clothing out of the trunk and laid it gently on the floor beside her. His wife must have been a fine lady. There were bolts of uncut cloth, some in simple colors, some with several colors woven together, and at the bottom, tucked into a corner, a package wrapped around in a piece of old linen. The cloths, Birle saw, for a woman's monthly time—but these were softer than any she had ever before used, as soft as moss.

Birle held one of the skirts in front of her. She had been almost Birle's height, this wife, and only a little plumper. But Birle had never worn such colors. Her clothing had always been brown, dyed with the barks the weavers knew. In the Kingdom, only the Lords could spare the cost of such richly colored fabrics. She wouldn't dress in them until she had washed—and now that she thought of it, she would welcome a bath.

All that day, one after the other, three wagons drew up before the house. The horses waited patient hours while soldiers unloaded crates and tables. The tables, and some of the crates, were too large to carry through the doorways, so they lifted them over the wall, with Yul's help. He would stand, holding a long table as it rested against the top of the wall while three soldiers hurried through the house to take up the other end; then Yul would join them, to carry it to the building at the rear. Four such tables went into that building, and the afternoon was filled with the pounding sounds of shelves being set into the walls. The crates, too, went into that building, carried by two men, or by Yul alone. The soldiers sweated at their work, grunted and cursed. The last wagon brought also a chair, with back and arms, and the promised bath.

Birle stood staring at this when the soldiers had at last gone. A man might sit in this metal tub, to bathe at his ease. This was the kind of bath Orien had spoken of, in the Earl's house. She was still staring at it when Corbel himself entered, the door flung wide before him. He moved past her without a word. Birle busied herself drawing water from the well, to heat in the cooking pot over the fire. When he returned, Corbel had little to say, no more than, "You'll see that he bathes."

"Yes," Birle said.

"All three of you. There's soap, somewhere, he'll never have thought of it. But I did."

He seemed to want some response to that, so Birle repeated herself. "Yes."

"In two days' time I'll dine here. Unlike the rest of the world, I take my meal after sunset, not to waste the daylight hours. You can expect me then." He reached out his hand and with just a gloved fingertip lifted her chin, until she had to look at him. His eyes frightened her, but she made herself keep looking at him, and it was like making herself hold her hand in fire. Whatever he saw—and he could have seen little more than fear, naked—satisfied him, and he was gone.

Birle closed the door, and leaned against it.

They bathed that evening, in the privacy of the walled yard behind the house. Joaquim washed first. When he reentered the house, his long hair damp, dressed in the clean leggings and shirt she had put out for him, Birle and Yul emptied the bath, then refilled it with fresh water that had been heating while Joaquim washed.

When Birle climbed into the bath, and sat down in the warm water, and the water rose up to cover her, tears as warm as the bath slid out of her eyes and down over her cheeks. The air had turned purple, changing to night darkness. A single star burned over the roof of the house. There was no purpose to thinking of Orien, yet he hung on in her mind, like the star hung in the night sky.

Yul was afraid to bathe. She had to comfort him like a child, with soothing noises over his whimpering wordlessness. She washed him as if he were a child, with soap and cloth. He had no clean clothes to put on, and she thought she might take the uncut cloth, to make him shirt and trousers. As Yul lifted the bath to empty it for the last time, Joaquim came out to join them. Many stars had come out in the darkening sky. Voices, laughing, singing, talking, came from beyond the wall.

"You don't resemble my wife, except for that look of sadness, in the eyes. Look," Joaquim said, pointing, "there's the Plough, just coming out."

Birle didn't know what he was talking about, and she thought he wasn't really talking to her at all. In the morning, she thought, she would take their soiled clothes and wash them. Until the clothes had been washed, they could stay piled against the rear building, so that their odors wouldn't linger in the house, to offend Corbel.

She understood the true situation—she might keep Joaquim's house, but it was Corbel's displeasure she had need to fear.

When the time came to serve Corbel his meal, as guest, the house at least was ready, the meat the soldiers had brought was roasting on a spit over the fire, the little loaves of bread no bigger than her fist—which the soldiers had told her Corbel must have—were waiting in a basket, and the stew of parsnips and onions bubbled in the pot. Birle alone served the two men and then, as she did at the Inn, left them to their meal.

Corbel called her. "Where are you going, girl?" He wanted her to stand silent at the wall, ready to cut meat and fill his tankard. Corbel took the chair, and ate without speaking until all the food had been consumed. For a slight man he had a fierce appetite, Birle thought as she cut the last of the meat from the bone, and scraped the last of the stew from its pot.

"Now you can show me your work, Brother. But be brief; I'm a man with much to do." Corbel seemed well-pleased as he left the room.

He was not so pleased when he returned. "That laboratory—how can my brother do his work in there? If you think I'm going to dress you out in finery . . . and feed you . . . so that you can laze by the fire—"

Birle had never thought that. She hadn't known, no one had told her, she didn't even know what a laboratory was.

"—do the marketing for you, wasting the time of soldiers—"

She hadn't asked for soldiers, nobody had told her anything.

"—and keeping my own cooks busy baking bread for this house too, when they've my own tables to see to—"

She hadn't known where the food was coming from. How was she to know?

"—too whey-faced to leave the house. I give you warning. Joaquim is here to work for me and I won't have your slovenliness interfering. Is that clear?"

"Yes," Birle said. "I didn't know—" she started to say. At her words, his eyes blazed in anger.

"You're not here to know."

He wanted no excuses, and she wouldn't offer him any. He chose to think she had been lazing through the days, and he didn't care what the truth was. Corbel put no value on what she had done; he cared only for what she hadn't done.

"Joaquim isn't fit to go out of doors unguarded, his head's in the clouds and always has been—it's up to you. I leave it to you."

"Yes, master," she said, too frightened to think. A glance at his proud face told her she had answered as he wished.

When she had closed the door behind the guest, and listened to the hoofbeats moving rapidly away, she turned back to the room. Joaquim came in then, carrying a lantern. Behind him, Yul carried a large book. "There's little left to eat," Joaquim said, apologizing. "Yul might have the bone to chew on, and there's the rest of the day's bread. Birle, come and eat something."

Birle shook her head. She needed to start cleaning up.

"But you must. I'm to explain to you where to market, and give you a purse. The money for keeping the house. Please, sit down. You will have the husbandry of it, with Corbel to answer to." He didn't add "I'm sorry," but he might as well have. "When we empty it, we're to ask for more. He wouldn't give us too little, that would defeat his own purpose. He wouldn't want to defeat his own purpose, would he?"

Joaquim waited, but Birle had nothing to say, or to ask.

"Of course he might," Joaquim said. "He might just do that. He might have a purpose I haven't fathomed, and a use for me that isn't at all what he told me, when he summoned

146

me here. Corbel has always had his own plans, and purposes. . . . But this has nothing to do with you."

Birle wished she could believe her master.

"The market square is"—he bent down to pick a piece of charcoal from the edge of the fire, to draw on the table as he spoke—"right against the river, but up from the harbor, so that goods can be brought downriver, as well as up from the ships, and there are roadways, of course. Now, look at this and tell me if it makes sense to you. The city lies on a peninsula of land, where the river goes into the ocean. The land rises, rather steeply on this part of the coast, and it's an old city, which has always been fortified—there are the old walls around the inner section, and then the new walls. Do you follow me so far?"

Birle nodded.

"We are about here." He drew an X near the riverside of the newer city. "The market is down there." Another X. "It's easy to recognize, because not only is it open space, with stones set out for a floor, and the notice post at the center, it couldn't be anything else, but there are also the guildhalls around it. You'll know it when you get there. All you have to do is keep going downhill, and you'll find it. You can't get lost, and if you do all you have to do is ask a soldier for directions. There'll be no difficulty at the gates, not the gates of the inner wall. They aren't ever locked, and they aren't even really guarded, just soldiers on duty there. And nobody would dare to—only those of Corbel's house wear the golden band, you see. You've nothing to fear, Birle."

Birle shook her head; she wasn't afraid, not as he thought she was. She was looking at the rough map he'd drawn. "So that's east," she said, putting her finger down on the river, where it ran by the end of their walled property.

"You can read a map?"

Fear returned. She should have kept her knowledge a secret.

"Birle." He sounded excited now, and his whole face lit up with eagerness, which made him look a much younger

147

man. "Can you read? I mean letters and words. Books. More specifically, can you write?"

She didn't know what her safe answer was to this. Everything was different in this world. Everything had changed from what she knew. What was a danger in the Kingdom might be safety here, and she had no way of knowing before she answered. "Yes," she risked.

"What a piece of luck," Joaquim said. "How did you know which was east?"

"Because the sun set over the house, when we were bathing, and the river was at my back." Surely he must know that.

"Good, good," he said. "That's very good," he said.

Birle was memorizing the map. With a map in her head, she might make an escape. But there was much she didn't know from it. "What lies beyond the outer wall?" she asked.

"Farmlands in the river valley, and forest beyond, then steep, barren hills as the land continues to rise. That's where the mines are. It's the mines, as well as the harbor, that make the city such a prize."

"Does Corbel rule all of it?"

"Yes. It came with his bride—her dowry."

So even if she could get out of the city she would still be in danger. She had no way of knowing how long a journey would take her beyond Corbel's reach. And, now that she looked at it, she could see how much work there would be to get the thick charcoal marks off of the wooden tabletop.

Joaquim took his book, and the candle, and settled himself at the table. He sent Yul out to bed, but before Birle could begin scraping the plates he asked her, "Can you read this?"

It was the first page of the book. " 'The Nature of Disease,' " she read. "Do you know medicine?"

"As much as any man. I would know more," he said, then paid no further attention to her.

Birle went about her chores. If escape was possible, it would be easier by sea; but she wasn't eager to undertake the dangers of a sea journey, even if she could find a boat. If she could escape, she would be leaving Orien behind—wherever he was. At least now they were in the same place, she thought. "Master?" she asked, daring to interrupt. "Is there only the marketplace and guildhall there in the old city?"

"No, no. Don't you remember?" She didn't. "It's like a beehive down there, or an ant's nest, narrow, dark streets twisting and turning, shops and houses, and the poor. All who can have built homes in the new city. In the old city, the night air off the water breeds diseases, hunger breeds cruelty and—but there's no danger for you."

If she went to market, if she was free to leave the house and go through the gates into the old city—

"I'll send Yul with you, for protection," Joaquim interrupted her thoughts. Then he went back to his book.

—she could search for Orien. His masters hadn't been wealthy men, so he was probably there, in the old city. If she could search for him, then she might find him. Her thoughts raced on. If she could find him, then she might see his face again. Her heart beat uncomfortably at the hope.

Fourteen

It was three days before Birle was able to leave the house, three days of toil. She didn't know what would satisfy Corbel, so she dared not leave anything undone. The house had accumulated years of dirt. She made the meals, both the morning meal and the large meal they ate at midafternoon. She scrubbed clothing clean, and stretched it out to dry in the sunlight. In the evenings she sewed a shirt for Yul, a yellow shirt with arms that were too short to cover his wrists, and sleeves unevenly joined, but a clean shirt he could wear. She didn't know if it was because fear rode up on her from behind or because hope shone ahead, but she hurried from one task to the next, never resting.

The laboratory too required cleaning. There, Yul helped, and Joaquim. She and Joaquim uncrated bowls, vials, flasks, wooden bowls with tight-fitting lids, oddly shaped instruments with long and short handles, little metal pots in which a fire could be burned, bellows to increase the heat, and more books. All had to have straw brushed from them, and then be washed, and then rubbed dry, and then set out on the shelves Yul had scrubbed. Birle couldn't rest, unlike Yul, who would curl up like a dog whenever he had no task to do. Even when she lay in her bed at night, her mind roamed between memory and imagination. Hope gnawed at her like hunger.

When at last Birle came out of the house and onto the street, it was midmorning of the fourth day after Corbel's visit. Yul accompanied her to market, for her protection; he followed behind her, a basket in his hand. Birle turned to the right, following the descending street.

Although the air was perfumed with the scent of flowers, and flowering trees, there was nothing to be seen but stone walls, lining the dirt road, and the sky shining blue above. The walls were as tall as Yul's shoulder and ran continuously on both sides of the street, broken only for the occasional set of wooden doors. Birle didn't, for all her hope, expect to find Orien that day. To find one person among the many dwellers in such a city wouldn't be the work of one day. That day she hoped only to begin to learn her way about the city. She hurried on.

As Joaquim had said, at the thick stone wall that enclosed the old city, soldiers stood on guard. They demanded to be told where she came from and where she was going, then they let her pass.

On the other side of the wall, the street ran more steeply downhill, and the houses were small wooden buildings, with thatched roofs, crowded up next to one another. The air smelled not of flowers but of food and sweat and privies. Many smaller streets twisted off the one she walked down. Many people—men, women, and children—were on the street, and in the houses. Red-shirted soldiers rode down past her, and up past her, and the people pushed to the side to let them pass. There were also soldiers on foot, sometimes going somewhere, sometimes standing to talk and watch.

Birle knew the marketplace when she found it. The narrow, dark street she was on came to a large open space, backed on three sides by two-storied buildings. Although streets entered between these buildings, the effect was like walls. On the fourth side of the square lay the river. A tall pillar rose up out of the center of the marketplace, its top pointed like a spike. Three broad stone steps led up to the spike, and an odd shape, like a shelf, stuck out from it. Below it, all around, were lines of booths and tables among which crowds moved. Each of the buildings, too, had crowds moving in front of it, under a covered walkway.

Birle hesitated, and Yul waited behind her. There was too much to see and hear, too many faces and voices, colors and sounds. How you would ever find one person, out of so many, so close together that they hid one another. . . . In a forest, crowded with trees and undergrowth, the one thing that moved was visible. Here in the moving crowds, unless something was still you couldn't find it with your eye. Only the spike was stationary, dark against the bright sky.

Yul pushed her from behind and she turned to scold him. But one look at his face stopped her words in her throat. His eyes, and his mouth gasping like a fish taken from the water—Yul was like a child crowding close to his mother's skirt for safety. "B-irle?"

She thought she could guess what worried him. She answered his question, speaking to him as Joaquim did, as if he were not a simple. "You won't get lost, I can't lose you—you're too big."

He shook his head, frightened. People crowded past them, complaining.

"If I get separated from you, if I lose you—"

"No," he whispered.

"But if I do, if that happens, all you have to do is stand absolutely still. Do you understand what I mean? You're so big, taller than anyone, I can always find you. Stay close to me so we won't be separated."

"P-ra-ted?"

"Apart," she explained. She put her palms together, then moved them apart, to show him. "Separated," she repeated. "Now, what will you do if that happens?"

He searched for words. Birle waited. "Yul—will—stand," he announced, adding with his sad, lopsided smile, "still."

"Good, that's good. And if you stand still, you'll be like the tallest tree, so I'll see you."

"Birle—will—find—Yul," he said.

"Yes," she said.

"Yes," he said.

Birle entered the market. She didn't expect to see Orien, not really. The whole huge square was crowded with people

152

and booths. It was like all the fairs she'd ever been to in her life, all being held at the same time. Once she stepped into it she could see only what was close around her, soldiers, people poorly clothed and well-clothed and some few richly clothed. Ladies with their hair mounted high on their heads were carried through the crowd in chairs; poles extended from beneath the chairs and rested on the shoulders of two servants or, in the case of the grandest Lady, four servants. Barefoot children dashed in among the moving crowd, crying out, the sellers called out their wares, the buyers bartered.

Moving slowly up and down the long rows, Birle thought there was nothing you couldn't buy here. Weavers had one whole row, tables piled high with colored cloths. Some were rough-woven, some smooth, some shimmered in the sunlight while others were as lacy as the froth on a bowl of ale. And that was just the weavers. It was the same with knives, bowls, boots, goblets, plates, soap, and candles. The foods had the same abundance, baskets of onions and turnips, parsnips and carrots, flesh and fowl and cheeses, bread and apples and—more of everything than Birle would have imagined, if she had thought to imagine how much the world could hold.

The crowds led her over to the covered porches. There, the people stood to watch entertainers perform, a singer with his lute, jugglers, even puppets who hit at one another with soft clubs as they quarreled while the audience laughed and cheered them on. All along the side of the raised wooden walkway, beyond its slanting roof, the very old or very young hovered. "Me Ma is sick," they begged, or "Help an old man." Birle couldn't bear to look at their misery, and turned back into the market.

She was almost at the waterside. Looking downriver, she could see the masts of the ships moored in the harbor, around a bend of land. Fishing boats were tied up at the river's edge. The sharp cries of fishmongers reminded Birle of her errands. She stopped before one woman, choosing her at random or perhaps because of a bright red scarf she had tied around her hair. This was a woman of Nan's age, short and plump, with two little children silent at her side. Birle selected three silver fish from the basket, and held them up. "What do I pay you?" she asked the woman.

The woman and her children paid no attention to Birle. They had been struck silent by the sight of Yul. Two little faces peered out from behind their mother's skirt, fascinated and afraid. Their mother looked up at him, then down, then up, and she didn't even hear Birle's question, so Birle repeated it. "What do I pay you?"

The woman opened her mouth to answer. Then she saw Birle's neck. "Why, you pay what you think they're worth," she said.

This wasn't like any bartering Birle had ever done. How was she to know the value of three fresh fish? When the Inn purchased a fisherman's catch—if, for some reason, the Inn's morning haul wasn't enough to feed its tables—her father traded cheeses, wine, ale, or sometimes labor for the catch. If the fisherman wanted coins, then he named how many. "Is three copper coins enough?" Birle asked.

Now the woman seemed afraid of her, and her hands gathered her children closer to her side. This might be a city of madmen, Birle thought. Would madmen all gather together to have a city of their own? Corbel, with his love of fear; Joaquim, who seemed to attend more to what went on inside his head than what was happening around him; the people all around her with their busy buying and selling, as if the whole world hung on each transaction; and now this woman, who asked the buyer to choose the price; as if all the madmen of the whole world—which was larger than Birle had ever imagined—had come together here, to live in this city.

"Three coppers is fine."

Birle had the feeling that if she had said three gold coins, the response would have been the same. Or if she had said one copper. She put the three coins into the woman's hand.

"Thank you." The woman's tongue wet her lips. "Thank you kindly."

But why should the woman be so afraid at selling Birle

three fish? Birle asked where she might find a baker. The woman pointed in the direction of the center of the market-place, where the thick spike rose up over the heads of the people.

"What is that?" Birle asked.

The woman shrugged, and did not answer.

With Yul close behind her, Birle moved through the crowd. The only people who moved more smoothly were the soldiers. People made way before a soldier, or a group of soldiers; they parted and fell silent. Yul's size had the same effect on them.

At the baker's table, Birle was again asked to name the price she would pay, and again the price she named was accepted without question. At the vintner's she finally protested. "I don't know the value of the coins. I don't know the value of your wines."

The vintner was a man of ripe years, with a proud face and a richly colored shirt. There was bitterness in his voice when he answered, the bitterness of a man who thinks otherwise than he speaks. "The Prince's house names its own value for the goods it needs." He spoke to her neck, and the gold band around it, and at last Birle understood. The metal at her throat marked her as clearly as a brand. "I would give fair value," she said.

"It's Corbel to say what's fair value these days."

He wouldn't help her, Birle thought crossly, so she put down two copper coins. If he wouldn't help her, then she couldn't be concerned about his fair profit for labor. She looked up to tell Yul to add the stoppered jug of wine to his basket, and her eye went beyond Yul's head to the even greater height of the spike. Then she saw what she hadn't noticed before: Placed where all must see and any who cared to mount the blocks of stone could reach it, a hand. A man's hand. The hand had been nailed to a board, the board like a shelf coming out from the spike. The hand stopped at the wrist, and it was black, and its blackened fingers curled up around the black palm, and the little shelf was stained black with blood. In the palm lay a gold coin.

155

Birle looked back to meet the vintner's eyes. His own hand, its living flesh browned with sunlight, fingered the woven silver chain that hung across his broad chest. ''What is that?'' she asked him.

''A hand.''

''Aye, I can see that. Whose hand is it? Why is it here—displayed like that?''

The vintner didn't wish to answer, and was not going to. Bells rang, first slowly, then gaining speed. The vintner gathered his jugs together.

''Vintner,'' Birle said, ''I would have my questions answered.'' Although why she wanted to know she couldn't have said. In fact, she didn't wish to know; she wished she had never seen the thing placed there for all to see.

''Then ask your master.'' He wished not to answer, but didn't dare risk silence.

''Vintner,'' she said again. Fear rose in his eyes. For all his plumpness and prosperity, he feared her. The chain at her neck claimed Corbel's power. Aye, and she had no right to it, but she would still use it. It gave her pleasure to watch fear force this sullen man to her will.

''Whose hand it is, I can't say, not knowing the man's name. I know only his crime. There were two of them, and if you care to see the other's hand you have only to step around to the other side of the spike. There's a gold coin there too. Two men, who cheated Corbel. Their hands are here, and their heads one on each side of the slave market—until the birds finish with them. What they looked like before Corbel caught them—they had a ship and thought they'd make an escape by sea—that I don't know either. They were strangers, pirates likely, men more greedy than wise. I told you true, I don't know their names.''

Birle thought she did. Aye, and it satisfied her that the brothers had come to more harm out of this than she and Orien had. But the swift surety of Corbel's justice—

She turned, and hurried back to the twisting street where she had entered. The market was emptying now, as if the

156

bells called the people away, buyers and sellers. The sun was high in the sky.

The most terrible thought of all was to know that the two gold coins would be left untouched in the hands that seemed to offer them to any who would climb up. So great was the fear of Corbel: and Corbel knew this. Even the beggars, who could move under the cloak of darkness, even the soldiers, who counted life less than coins, none would dare to mount the broad stones. They would cheat themselves at market before they would dare to cheat Corbel, or let Corbel think they might have cheated him.

Even if she could find Orien, somewhere in these twisting streets, there was nothing she could do. She couldn't escape. The same power that let her move so freely, and purchase what she would at the price she chose, held her helpless.

Birle and Yul joined the departing crowds, and the people stepped aside to let them pass as if they were two of Corbel's soldiers.

She had no trouble retracing her way, Yul now at her side. She kept her eyes on the street under her feet, winding up the hills and through the guarded gate, past the walled houses, to the Philosopher's house. Inside, before she could unload the basket, Joaquim summoned her from the doorway. "Come here."

It was full midday under a warm southern sun. Grass sprang up greenly underfoot and the breeze carried the smell of the sea and of flowerings, but the sweetness of the day didn't penetrate Birle's heart.

Joaquim glared at her, and at Yul, as if they had displeased him. Birle studied her master's lined face, with the gray hair straggling down beside it to lie on the shoulders of his black robe, and waited. She didn't fear Joaquim's anger.

"A garden," he said. "Placed here, a garden at least forty paces on all sides. You can keep a garden?"

"Yes, master," Birle said.

"The land is level enough, it's close enough to the well for watering should the summer be dry. The grass grows so green, the soil must be good, and I will have a garden. Yul,

157

you will turn the soil over, and break it up fine. Deep, as deep as to my knees. Do you understand?''

In a moment, Yul answered, ''Yes.'' As if afraid he might not be understood because the word, however plain, was distorted as it came out of his mouth, he also nodded his head eagerly, up and down.

''Right away,'' Joaquim said. He seemed agitated, irritated.

''What will you plant?'' Birle wondered.

''Herbs,'' he answered, impatient. Then he took a deep breath, like a child at the end of its weeping, and smiled at them. ''I shouldn't be cross, it's none of your doing. How can I expect you to understand when I haven't explained it to you?'' He answered his own question, but no longer smiling. ''My brother summoned me here, to this city, because he has his use for me. As if I were—he tells me to discover the secret law by means of which base metals can be transformed into gold.''

''But you said that was a tale, a story,'' Birle reminded him.

''There are men who claim to have discovered it. Some other men believe it, Corbel among them. Alchemists—that's the name they call themselves, those who make the claim. There is a name also for those who believe what they say, my brother among them. Which I am too wise to speak, and you should follow my example.''

''Yes, master.''

''While Corbel uses me, as he thinks, I will make my own use of this place. I understand sickness, and the herbs to heal or ease. And I would . . . if I write down all I know, the appearance and use of each herb, that book will make life easier for all men, in all times. That book will be better than a child, to keep my name alive long after I have gone from the world. It will be greater than a string of conquered cities living in fear of my name. A greater greatness. I'll illustrate the appearance—the young plant, the plant in flower, the plant in full leaf, its roots. I'll write out how to prepare and how to apply it. However, Corbel must see me working on

158

his alchemy or he'll—I never know what my brother will do, when the world doesn't go his way. He must think that I work to his purpose.''

"Even if it can't be done?'' Birle asked.

"But maybe it can. Iron, stone—that's the marvel of the idea, that you can transmute the most common matter into the most precious. Whether the secret waits to be discovered,'' he said, no longer looking at her, "is a question I can't answer. This world is rich in marvels that I can't understand. The sun circles overhead—did you never wonder? What holds the sun in the sky?''

Birle had never thought to wonder, although she thought Orien might have. Orien would have been a better choice for the Philosopher's house.

"You put a seed into the earth and a plant grows there, onion or rye, roses—how does that happen, onion or rye or rose from a tiny seed. A tree from an acorn. How can that be, something so tiny transformed into something so large? Think of a man and a woman—they come together and he places an infant into her belly. What makes that marvel? A man comes to the end of his days—through age or illness or accident—and when he dies, what becomes of that which made him the man he was? There is flesh and there is spirit, but I have seen the body of a dead man cut open, taken apart, and never his spirit to be seen in it. The principle of life, the living principle . . .''

Birle, with wonder growing in her, had nothing to say. She couldn't answer his questions.

"So you see, it might be that within every kind of matter there lies gold. It might well be that, could we understand, we might be able to release the gold within lead. Or,'' Joaquim added, with a smile that was as much sad wisdom as laughter, "it might be that there is lead within each kind of matter, that the secret would reveal not the treasure within but the baseness within. I will make trial of the possibility of transmutation, at Corbel's will. I'll make fair trial, the best I can devise. But I will also,'' he said, resolute, "make my book of herbs, and for that I need your help.''

"My help?"

"Yes, yes, that's what I've been talking about. Don't you understand? If you can read, and write, then you will be my amanuensis. Yul will be my arms in the garden, and you will be my hand to record and copy. Corbel may have his will of me, and his purposes, but we three—"

Birle felt then as she thought Yul must always feel, as if she couldn't understand enough, as if she could see but dimly what was clear to others. She knew what she did understand, however, and that was the simplest of things: that for whatever reasons of his own, Joaquim had given her luck when he chose her at the market. She knew what Yul had seemed instinctively to understand, that their master was a man whose use of them wouldn't be harsh, or hard. The middling man would not have used her so, and she had only hope for Orien. Birle had never heard of an amanuensis and couldn't have said what it might be, but she knew luck when she held it in her hand.

Fifteen

I F she could have forgotten Orien, Birle might have been content with her fortune. But she could no more forget him than she could forget her own belly. How she might discover where Orien had been taken, she didn't know—except by searching every street in the city. What she might do, if she *could* find him—she had no idea. All she hungered for was the sight of him, to see his face again.

As spring ripened and then bloomed into summer, Birle wound her way down different streets as she went to the marketplace, as she returned from it. She had little time for the search. Labors awaited her return to the Philosopher's house, as labors had preceded her leaving it, keeping the house and the laboratory. Meanwhile, Yul dug up the garden and, with Birle's help, enriched the soil with manure the soldiers brought them in cartloads from Corbel's stables. Meanwhile, Birle laundered and mended; in the evenings, she practiced writing, under Joaquim's critical eye. In all else he was not a demanding master, but in the writing he required all to be as it might, at its best, be. He taught her how to make the thick black ink and how to cut a goose's feather so that it would draw the lines of the letters without blots. He gave her pages of his alchemy books to copy, odd configurations called formulae. He made her do them over and over until each page was perfect.

Birle welcomed the never-ending toil. It filled the many hours when she could not be, for however many minutes she

161

could steal, walking down a street or alley, looking to right and left into doorways and passageways, marking fountains on her memory's rough map of the city.

On Midsummer Day, when the light would last longest, a soldier brought a cart to the door of the Philosopher's house, at Joaquim's request. They were going out, beyond the city. Birle and Yul sat in the rear of the cart, on empty cloth sacks. Joaquim rode beside the driver. They left the city through the one gate in its outer wall, which was taller and thicker than the inner wall, a stronger defense. As they were going out, people were entering, bringing food and livestock to market. The soldiers at the gate, who stopped each farmer to look into his wagon and take a share of the goods he brought, let their cart pass without question.

The track they followed went through level farmlands, then up the rising land into the forest. There, Joaquim told Birle, were the mines. If they followed this track for two days they would come to the mines, where gold was taken out of caves that ran deep under the mountains. If they took the fork to the right they would come to cities under the rulership of Corbel's bride's father. It wasn't safe to travel to those cities.

Their destination was the forest edge, and the uncultivated meadows before it. The soldier waited with the cart, while Joaquim and his slaves gathered herbs. They stopped neither to eat nor to rest, all that long day. "The gate is closed at sundown," Joaquim explained. "If we must require the guards to open the gates to us after dark, Corbel might hear of it. I have only this one day for my purposes."

"What if he comes while we're away?" Birle asked.

"But he won't, now it's summer," Joaquim told her. "Yes, those two, that's palsywort, and take that one too, dragon's herb. Gently, Yul, you mustn't bruise the leaves, the goodness in the leaves mustn't be lost."

Yul knelt down to work with his fingers at the soil surrounding a ragged little plant.

"He and his soldiers have gone into the service of a prince whose city lies a week's fast journey to the south. He'll be campaigning all summer."

162

"But his soldiers are still in the city."

"Those were left lest the city be attacked. Corbel is away, I promise you. There—see it? Those, Birle, it's a wondrous healer, aloe, more sweet than garlic and better for burns. While Corbel is safely away, I can work on my own great task, we both can, you and I. Be tender with them. To be transplanted so is a shock to them."

Birle's back ached from bending over the low plants. Her shoulder ached from carrying around the sacks, grown heavy with their load of plants and soil. Yet she welcomed the work. The heavier her duties, the more tired she would be. The more tired she was, the more easily sleep came to her.

Along the edge of one meadow, half in leafy shade and half in warm sunlight, lay a thin patch of blue. Birle's heart smiled to see that. Bellflowers, of a blue that brought before the eyes of her imagination Orien's face: that first morning, when he had opened his eyes from sleep and smiled. Misery threatened her at the memory, but she set it aside to take— while it was there before her, more real than meadow and trees and the two men, more real than the ache in her back— the joy.

"You're smiling." Joaquim's voice drove the vision away. "Now you've stopped. You look different if you smile, you look—glad. You should smile more often."

All summer long Birle searched for Orien, in the twisting streets of the city, with Yul at her back. These streets wound, joined up with one another and then forked apart, ended abruptly—it was so confusing that Birle often found herself lost. As summer went on, however, she began to have a good map of the city in her head. The streets came together at fountains, like the spokes of a wheel at its hub; each fountain was different, in shape or statuary. There people gathered to fill buckets and bowls, and to talk, under the eyes of the soldiery. At the fountains especially, the bright red shirts of the soldiers stood out among the dull, patched clothing of the poor and the rags of slaves. Slaves at the fountains wore chains at the neck, to mark them for what they were. Slaves

163

huddled together, furtive, as if to be caught in speech was a danger. Birle's eyes searched these gatherings of slaves, for a pair of high, proud shoulders, for a certain slenderness of neck, for a pair of bellflower eyes. Among such men and women, he would stand out.

At the marketplace, Birle always walked first along the long walkway, where the entertainers performed. In the presence of the entertainers, the wealthy mixed with the poor, slaves with soldiers, countryman with city merchant. Singers, puppeteers, jugglers, dancers—the voices of the entertainers crowded against one another, crying out for attention and coins. There, Birle thought—if it was possible for him—Orien might like to stand, and watch.

Birle went often to market, to purchase household needs. It amazed her that city dwellers would pay coins for things they might make for themselves—soap and bread, candles, chairs, bowls, everything was purchased at market. But they loved making purchases, bargaining, passing the coins between two hands. They loved their coins, and called them by as many names as fond parents give children. The gold coins could be asked for as kings or sovereigns, masters, or goldies. The silver were also known as ladies, sillies, beauties, or—for some reason—truemen. The coppers they named little men, or mannies, or littles, pennies, twigs, kiddles, dogs. "You can't pass a dog off for a man," they said of any item where the price was too dear. But if Joaquim succeeded for Corbel, Birle thought, then a dog could be transformed into a king.

As summer swelled, the air lay hot and damp on the marketplace. Tempers grew short, and the greens the farmers brought to market wilted in their baskets. The market became a dangerous place, although that didn't keep anyone at home. The fear of plague that lay over the city made men foolhardy. If we are to die, they seemed to think, at least let it be with a full belly, whatever its price. Daily, new heads appeared on the spike: thieves, spies, slaves who had attempted insurrection or escape. Birle studied each head, hoping not to recognize it.

Fights were frequent, for everyone simmered with anger ready to come to the boil. It was not unusual to mark blood on a man's face—or on the chest of a man killed before the soldiers could get to him through the crowds—nor to hear women's voices shrieking out, in quarrel or in grief. Birle moved warily through the volatile crowds.

The large buildings, with their smooth pink facades, were the guildhalls, Birle learned, and she learned to stay well back from their carved wooden doorways. When a guild-master strode out from his hall, surrounded by his servants and apprentices, he might be mobbed by angry craftsmen, demanding to be given work. First words, then fists, then cudgels and knives and swords—and as the fight spread over the marketplace Birle fled with the rest of the people into the narrow streets around it. She was protected by Corbel's golden chain and by Yul's size, but in the heat of his anger a man might not see her neckchain, or her companion. Birle feared all, but feared more than anything that she would not find Orien. Every day left her feeling more hopeless as she went doggedly through the streets and among the dangers, never finding him.

The Philosopher's house was a safe haven from the disease, hunger, and fears of the city, not only because the wall with its guarded gates kept the misery within, but also because Birle's work there filled the hours with purpose; work of house, laboratory, and now also garden. Yul and Birle tended the plants, at first plucking those that didn't survive the transplanting, then weeding and loosening the soil around those that grew strongly. Summer rains fell generously onto the garden, and hot sunlight. They harvested the leaves and spread them out to dry, under Joaquim's direction. More grew to replace those that had been taken.

In the long summer twilights, Joaquim would walk beside the rows, bending over to pinch a leaf and smell his fingers, or to break off a twig and chew it. He named them for Birle—lungwort, pennyroyal—and sometimes questioned her to know what she remembered. "This?" "Comfrey," she might answer, or "Garlic," or equally often, "I don't know."

He spoke of ointments, infusions, emetics, and vermifuges, of which herbs were useful in root, flower, or leaf. Birle listened attentively, because her mind, like her body, welcomed the work. Work had the power to distract, and distraction eased her heart. Some of the plants were dangerous, in part or in whole, and those Joaquim made sure she knew: wolfsbane, dwale, poppy.

Often, during that long summer, Joaquim left the house during the day, to take medicines to the ill or wounded of the city. How he heard of the need, Birle didn't know, nor how those in need knew to ask him for help. Word of his knowledge seemed to have spread on the very breezes that blew from the sea and the river over the city, to the Philosopher's house.

There seemed to her nothing Joaquim didn't know. He knew the map of the sky, and was teaching it to her. She could find the Plough now and follow its directions to the star that stayed fixed at the north, the only fixed star in the sky. She knew now, because Joaquim had shown it to her, that the stars did move, arcing overhead in the same fashion as sun and moon, although more slowly. Joaquim had shown her the Wings, which looked like the letter *W* spread out against the blackness, and the seven Flowers, clustered together in a sky bouquet. In the cold seasons, Joaquim told her, she would see the Hourglass, with its three stars marking the narrow passage of time from yesterday to tomorrow.

In the night, while she copied pages of herbal lore, or read in the book of alchemy so she could write down the experiments for Corbel, Joaquim undertook to teach Yul to speak. Just as he knew which plants could soothe a sick body, and the temperature at which water would be transmuted into air, Joaquim knew the proper shape of bones under skin. He had looked into Yul's mouth, and explored it with his fingers. It seemed that Yul's mouth wasn't shaped as other mouths were; even there, his bones had grown monstrously. Joaquim tried to learn how Yul might twist lips and tongue to shape more rightly what words he spoke. Patiently, Yul did as his master asked, repeating sounds over and over. Probably, Birle thought, Yul was happier than he'd ever been before in his life. He had food, shelter, work, and companionship. He was treated kindly.

The summer lasted long, and the heat didn't ease. The marketplace was a cauldron of rumor and quarrel, violence and fear, buying, selling, display, and entertainment. Frequently, the bells tolled to announce a death. The bells made no differentiation between one man or another, a man or a woman, adult or child; whoever the victim, the bells tolled.

Birle knew that Orien might likely be one whom fever took, or one of those who bled to death in an alley, but she didn't let herself believe it. She continued her search, until she grew familiar with the city streets. She even began to recognize some of the entertainers, and to have among them those whom she always stopped to watch; she didn't know if they recognized her, and Yul, among their audience.

The puppeteers, she thought, must know them, for Yul was never content to stand at the back of the crowd, but moved—as if drawn there by a string—up next to the little high stage where the dolls acted out their adventures. All the time he watched, Yul's sweet smile stayed on his face. His eyes were filled with wonder. Birle didn't hurry him away, but stayed close beside him lest some mischance befall him, or her.

She too enjoyed the workings of the dolls at the ends of their strings, and their voices that seemed to speak. Some master carpenter had carved the puppets. Their wooden parts fitted together so that their arms and legs, knees and necks, moved up and down when a string was pulled. They were dressed in bright scraps of cloth, to give them greater resemblance to living men and women. The stories the puppets acted out were of every kind, some to cause the audience to laugh and leave coins in the basket that was set out at the foot of the high stage, some to make the women weep and leave coins, some to cause all to gasp in fear and dread—and leave coins in the basket.

Summer passed on into autumn, marked by a sun that rose later and set earlier. The city filled with rumors of Corbel's return. Birle finally asked her master for true news, on a night when he had taken her outside to show her the Hourglass, spread out across the southern sky.

"Any day now, yes, but I'm not uneasy. I've many papers to show him, so he'll be satisfied with me. He'll have been well paid, if—as I hear—his battles were victories, so he'll not be disposed to be angry. I'll not think of him now, this night, and neither need you, Birle. Show me what you know of the stars."

Instead of answering his question, Birle told him, "My grandfather once told me there might be people who lived among the stars. Do you think it could be so?"

"I can't say no, can I? There are some who believe that the spirits of men rise at death, to become stars. I can't say no to that either, being a living man. You have a grandfather, do you? A man who wonders at what might be. Where did you come from?"

"A land to the north and the east."

"Has it a name?"

She knew now it was safe to tell him, in part because of the kind of man he was, and in part because he might not believe her. "No name that I know of. The people know it as the Kingdom. It lies far from the sea, hidden deep in the land, protected by forest and mountain."

"Like the Kingdom in the stories?"

"Aye." Birle waited to be asked about the snow dragon, whose breath froze any living thing below.

"Where the King rules the Lords," Joaquim asked, "and the Lords rule the people, and the Law rules all?"

Birle didn't say anything. She didn't know if that was really true of the Kingdom, although she knew it was not entirely false.

"And war is unknown, so the land lives in peace," Joaquim's voice went on. They were both gazing out at the distant stars. Yul was asleep in the laboratory, curled up on his pile of straw.

"Where the King has a library of all the books ever known,

168

which a man may spend his life in reading and this is enough to earn his keep."

Birle didn't think this was true, although she couldn't answer certainly. She said nothing. Joaquim was lost in his own thoughts again.

"A land so hidden, that even death has trouble finding it."

"Aye, master," Birle said, "if this is the Kingdom of the stories, there is death in it—sickness and age, accident. It is no magical kingdom."

"What were you, in your own land?"

"The Innkeeper's daughter."

"But how came you here?" he asked. "To this," he added.

"Through fortune."

"It was an evil fortune then, if you tell me true."

Birle didn't know if it was evil or good, only that it was fortune. "I'm telling you true," she said. "But you might not believe me."

"Why should I disbelieve you?" he asked. "It may well be that the unmapped lands of the world are more numerous than we guess. In this world—where the son my father got upon my mother's serving maid has become a prince among princes—why shouldn't there be storied kingdoms, hidden away from the greed of the world?"

"Master, there is greed, and jealousy, and pride there—fear and misery, too."

"Then I am the readier to believe it's real," Joaquim answered. Birle heard a smile in his voice. "But meantime, in this land, we have our work to get done, you and I, before my brother returns." Joaquim had shown Birle enough so that she could go ahead with the work of the Herbal, as he named it, even after Corbel had required him to return to alchemy. Birle drew the herbs, so that any who saw her pictures could identify the plants. She memorized all Joaquim told her of an herb's goodnesses, and at night she wrote it all down in carefully shaped letters, so that anyone who could read could understand.

Corbel returned on a day of autumn storm, when wind and rain drove the last leaves from the trees. Birle had just returned from the marketplace, from searching and purchasing. She had just set the two pairs of boots, hers and Yul's, to dry beside the fire when the door flew open, as if wind and rain demanded entrance. It was Corbel, returned. He pushed the door closed behind him.

Birle stood up but didn't speak. Corbel moved to his accustomed place at the center of the room, and gave the room his accustomed perusal. He wore a metal breastplate and his hair hung down wet under his helmet. Boots, leggings, the red shirt with gold circlets up to the elbow, gloves, and even his face were stained with travel; where he stood, water dripped, as if exhausted, onto the floor; but the man didn't seem tired. The smile on his face was greedy and glad, like a wolf with the blood of his prey running down his jowls. Joaquim rushed into the room.

"I'm here for your news," Corbel said.

"Then come out to the laboratory. There's much for you to see."

Corbel shook his head, and water sprayed around him. "Tell me the one thing: Have you succeeded."

"Sadly, no."

This didn't please Corbel.

"Not for lack of trying," Joaquim said. "I can show you the records of every experiment I've performed."

Corbel shook his head again. "Not this day, Brother. I'll go home instead—to bathe, and eat, and sleep. Maybe my wife has stopped her weeping by now, although my spies tell me not. I'll return, Brother, and soon."

"I await you," Joaquim said.

Leaving, Corbel took with him the summer-long ease of the house. Now there was danger wherever Birle was, in the city and in the house. As autumn turned colder, her sense of danger grew, and her urgency; her search seemed hopeless, futile, and for that reason the more desperate.

There were only two ways she could ease her spirits. The first way was to work. Work was one way of forgetting. The other was a way of escaping, for a while, the thoughts that troubled her. The puppets could give her this temporary escape.

Birle now lingered as eagerly as Yul did by the puppets. Only one puppeteer still performed in the sharper weather, before a smaller audience, for fewer coins. While the dolls acted out their stories, and their words, sang their songs, came to their sad or glad ends, Birle could forget her own fears and worries. She now stood as rapt as Yul while the miniature world went through its changes on the stage before them.

So it happened that one gray day, when the wind off the river had sharp teeth in it to bite at her face and hands, Birle looked away from the stage, where a puppet wife chased after a puppet husband, and saw him—his bellflower eyes—

—and his face was bearded now—

—and hunger had hollowed his cheeks—

It seemed that her heart leaped up into her throat and then fell back, to its accustomed place. It seemed that her heart stopped, to see him. He smiled, and bowed his head to her. Then the smile faded, leaving his face as empty as a sunless sky.

Her eyes took in everything and yet never left his face. He stood among others like himself—rough, ragged brown shirt, no cloak against the wind, feet wrapped round with cloths, an iron chain at his neck, and his face so thin that even the beard couldn't hide the pallor of hunger, his hair long, uncombed. Like the others, he looked unclean, unhealthy, wary and weak; she almost wished she hadn't seen him. She almost wondered why she had sought him. His hands rubbed at his arms for warmth, crossed over his chest as if to protect himself. His shoulders hunched forward. His eyes were the only living thing in his face and they stared at her as if she were the last hope he had in the world; but surprised, too, as if until he saw her he hadn't known there was hope for him in the world—his bellflower eyes—

Birle took two steps toward him. He didn't move. As she watched, a hand reached over from behind, to grab Orien by the nape of the neck as if he were a dog. The hand turned him around, to load the purchases from market into the woven basket Orien wore strapped at his back. The hand pushed at Orien's shoulders, to lead him away, like a dog at his master's heels.

Orien didn't look back at her, or up, or around; he kept his neck bent, his head bowed, like any other slave. She couldn't follow, or try to speak to him, without bringing danger to them both—and for a moment she didn't even want to. Around her the crowd laughed at the quarreling puppets.

Orien was alive, still alive, and she had just seen him, she told herself that. He was hungry, ragged, probably cold— and winter hadn't yet settled over the city. His spirit might have been broken. That too she told herself. Birle didn't know how to feel. The gladness to have him within her sight, however briefly, brought with it a pain to know his fortune, and to lose him again, and an anger to know that there was nothing she could do to ease his life, and the fear to know that she might not ever see him again.

Sixteen

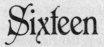

THE joy of seeing Orien was a pain as sharp and bright as a knife. How could he have allowed himself to become what she had seen? It was all luck, she knew, and she knew also that her own luck had been good. But that didn't ease her. She wished she could forget the slave she had seen, and remember only the young Lord she had followed.

This thought troubled her, when she couldn't keep it at bay by work. Winter settled down over the city, a season of sunless days, cold winds, rains of ice, and an occasional dusting of snow. Even though winter kept them close inside, there was much work for the Philosopher's amanuensis. She copied the records of Joaquim's experiments in the Great Art. She wrote the pages of his Herbal. The neatly written pages, of formulae or of herbal lore, gave her pleasure. It was the same pleasure she felt when she and Yul had finished the house for the morning, and the rooms shone. It was the same pleasure she felt smelling the cleanness of clothing as it dried beside the fire. It was the pleasure of a task her own hands had done, and done well.

But always, at the back of her mind, like a rat gnawing to find food, was that image of Orien. She tried not to think of him.

Hadn't he, she asked herself angrily, run away rather than be what he must be? He might have stayed where he was, to be Earl. But he had abandoned the earldom and its people to a brother he knew would be a harsh master, like Corbel.

Winter and inactivity made Corbel a frequent visitor to the Philosopher's house. Birle wished she could hide away from him, as Yul did. His eyes followed her with the hunger she had learned to fear.

One winter evening, as she watched the two men eating bowls of stew, soaking up the rich gravy with the tiny loaves of white-flour bread Corbel required, Corbel spoke out. "I have to admit it, Brother, the girl was good value."

Joaquim, his mind elsewhere, ate on.

"You didn't waste my coins on her. She keeps the house well, keeps you looking more respectable than I've ever seen you—better than that wife of yours did. She is herself clean. She cooks as a man likes to eat. . . . Doesn't complain. She's a treasure, Joaquim."

The Philosopher seemed at last to sense the danger Birle had known from Corbel's first words. He raised his head from his food, to glance briefly at his brother. Birle knew the Philosopher wasn't a match for the Prince, that the knowledge of the one would always be overborne by the greed of the other. Corbel knew that too, and the knowledge pleased him.

"A king and five ladies, wasn't that her price? It seems to me now that I got a bargain." Corbel watched Birle's face as he said this.

Birle was frozen in fear beside the warm hearthstone. The luck she had was not her own. With a word, Corbel could take it from her. How could she have forgotten that?

Joaquim put down his spoon to hear what his brother would demand.

"Celinde has her name day soon." Corbel spoke as if the idea were just occurring to him. "I've been troubled over what I might give her, on her name day. The kind of gift a generous husband might give his young wife—so that her father's spies can't report her ill-treated, slighted, dishonored, to fuel his anger with that false rumor. Have you bedded the girl, Brother?"

"Why would I do that?" Joaquim asked.

Corbel threw back his head and laughed. He laughed until

he coughed, and then he drowned both cough and laughter in wine. Birle hurried forward to refill his tankard when he put it back down on the table. She wished she had the courage to pretend to trip, and thus spill wine all over his finery, and thus earn his anger, and thus go free of his desire. It would be useless, she knew, pouring the wine in a red stream into the tankard, to throw herself on her knees before Joaquim.

But what would become of Yul if she was taken to Corbel's house? And Orien? The answers came quickly. Yul would be safe with Joaquim, she knew; he might be saddened at her going, but he would be safe. And Orien—nothing worse could happen to him. So what happened to her didn't matter, and she would be fooling herself to think that it did. Just as she had been deceiving herself that she had deserved her luck. Birle stood stiff. The fire crackled behind her.

Corbel smiled at his brother in just the way that the Steward smiled at the fishermen, come to pay their taxes into his hand.

"If you choose to take her, then you will do it," Joaquim said. He picked up his spoon and dipped it into the bowl. Putting the laden spoon into his mouth, he emptied its contents, and chewed on the chunks of meat and fowl in the thick gravy. "I'll have to find another amanuensis then, which I imagine I can do—by at least the end of the spring. The slave markets open up again in the spring, don't they, Brother?"

Corbel leaned forward and reached out his hand to stop Joaquim from taking another bite. "Amanuensis? Don't speak in riddles to me, keep it plain. What is she to you?" He was suspicious, and he was not pleased.

"The girl takes down the records of experiments, what matter I have used in what weight, the temperature, whether it is treated to fire, earth, water, air, what changes result—"

"She can write?"

"Yes, yes, and read of course. What use would she be to me as an amanuensis if she could not?"

Corbel thought about this, his face shadowed by his hand,

his eyes flickering between Birle and her master. "I don't believe you."

"Don't you wonder at how much I've accomplished?" Joaquim asked.

"No," Corbel said.

"Which only reveals your lack of knowledge." Joaquim spoke haughtily. "It is one thing to lead an army in battle, Corbel, but if you would discover the secrets Nature keeps locked in her treasure-house—you can't just fill your belly and rush forward. You must write down what you have tried, and what learned. You must keep records. Otherwise, you merely repeat the errors. Birle keeps my records, she is my amanuensis. Fetch in the book," he said to Birle.

For a moment, outside, Birle thought she might go not into the laboratory but down the walled yard, past privy and garden, past bare trees, and over the steep, stony bank, to the river. But she didn't know what she could do then—except perhaps drown. The confusion of stars over her head reminded her of another choice, and she found the Plough at the sky's peak and, following the line from the end of the Plough, she saw the northern Star in its fixed place. Birle went into the laboratory quietly, so as not to waken Yul. The book was so heavy it required both hands to carry it back inside.

"All right, show me. If you can," Corbel greeted her. His forefinger jabbed at the table. "Put it down here, girl, and show me."

Birle opened the book. Using her own finger to point at each word, lest Corbel doubt her, she read. "The stone, which had rested four days in a quicksilver bath, to loosen the binding of the four elements within and give dominance to its volatile element, was placed in a sulfurous fire to discover its fixed element. There was no change over a red flame, none over a yellow flame, and none over a blue flame. The stone was ground to powder, in a mortar of agate, then mixed with salt in equal measure. This, with seven times its measure of water, was sealed in a flask. The salt dissolved in the water, but no change occurred in the stone."

Corbel wasn't satisfied. "I hear nothing of lunar and solar presences, nor *materia prima*," he complained to his brother. But he seemed to have forgotten about Birle, in this new quarrel.

"When you summoned me here, Brother, I told you I was no alchemist, with incantations and star-readings and talk of the black of blacks, the peacock's tail—I told you, I believed none of that. If you would like to send me away and have one of your magicians back—"

"No. Not yet. Not quite yet." His eyes went from Birle to her master, measuring.

"If you must take her," Joaquim said, "then you must. But it will hamper my progress."

"This progress is no progress," Corbel said.

"I told you, Brother, that if this thing can be done at all, it can only be done with great difficulty. If you wish to abandon the hope you have only to tell me."

"When I've used so much gold to make your laboratory? To feed you and your slaves?" Corbel asked. "You don't know how many times I've been told by some fool that a battle was lost, that my army would be destroyed—if I'd listened to them, where would I be? Corbel doesn't turn aside from his chosen route. I don't leave things unfinished. But I should warn you, Brother, that the sooner the safer, for you. The mines give less every day and that at greater expense in slaves. I've a need for gold."

"I know that," Joaquim answered.

Corbel rose up, out of the chair he'd been sitting in. He leaned on the table to study Joaquim's face. "It can be dangerous, knowing things. Dangerous especially if you talk of what you know." Then he relaxed, and stood erect. "But you don't talk—and who would you say anything to, anyway? And you would tell me that it can be equally dangerous not to know, perhaps especially dangerous not to know how widely a secret has spread, and with what effect. . . ." He turned and left the house.

"Thank you, Master Joaquim," Birle said. Even her voice shook.

"I could not bear it if the Herbal were not to be completed," he said to her. The smile on his face was bitter. "If in his pride and greed he . . . He thinks of nothing but victory, and princedoms. If he was displeased, he'd destroy a man's lifework—in his angers—even if he knew that preserving it would—I can't bear to think of it," he said.

Joaquim had not protected her. If she had not been useful to him, he'd have let Corbel take her off without a word or even a thought. Birle remembered Orien, then, seeing him as clearly as if the room were the marketplace, and she wondered how many such moments had bowed him down. She had been thinking harshly of Orien, but now she thought it was a wonderful thing that he could still lift his head to smile at her, helpless across a crowd of people who had no care for either of them.

"Corbel is right to suspect what the city knows," Birle said. As long as she was useful to her master, she had hope for safety. As long as she was safe, Orien was at the other end of a slender thread of hope.

"Right also to think that the city would rejoice at his fall," Joaquim agreed. "Corbel knows it's only his soldiers that give him rule over the city, and open its purses to his hands. The guilds would rise against him—except that they know how quick and cruel his revenge would be. And, of course, they hope Celinde's father will rescue her."

"Is Celinde his wife? Why would her father rescue her from a husband?"

"Because Corbel stole her, for his bride. He took her for the dowry, the city and the lands around it, the mines. He holds her prisoner."

"I've never heard anyone speak of Corbel's Lady," Birle remembered.

"Ah, well, that may be because she's a child, not a lady."

"A child?"

"A child, of eight, although it's been a year, so she would be nine now. He did steal her, out of her father's castle, out from the care of her father's servants, although there must have been traitors among them, because she was roundly guarded. Her father had planned a proud marriage to a prince with ancient lands. Celinde's father doesn't like the idea of a mercenary for son-in-law, a man whose only claim to worthiness is his army's victories. So he plots her rescue, as every man knows. The city waits for his move. As does Corbel. It's her father who keeps Celinde safe from Corbel. Until she's of an age to be gotten with child, he won't bed her. As long as she hasn't been bedded, her father can hope to negotiate the marriage he wishes of her . . . and he'll move carefully, so as not to risk her safety at Corbel's hands. They're like two men at either end of a balancing scale.''

The girl in Corbel's stronghold, for all her high birth and riches, was no different from Birle. She too had her life determined by the desires of others, and she too stood at peril. Birth and riches were a burden to her, and a danger. This thought didn't comfort Birle. In fact, it made her fear Corbel more. ''Why haven't I heard anything of this?''

''Didn't you wonder where the priests are? The bells ring, but not to call the people to worship. Didn't you wonder at bells with no priests?''

Birle never had.

''The priests fled the city. Corbel doesn't care about priests, but the guildsmen do, and the merchants, the citizens, and the poor. . . .''

''But what will happen?'' Birle asked.

''There will be war. I think it will be the more cruel, because there are some in the city whose profits increase under Corbel. Crops burned, famine, looting, disease and death and men maimed—I'll go back south, whatever Corbel says. There is a community, of philosophers—I had to leave it when I wed—but she's dead now.''

''And me? And Yul?''

''That I can't say. You can't come with me. No women are permitted, nor servants. You might offer yourself to one of the guildmasters. The rich will usually survive times of peril and chaos. They will betray the city from within, if they can, the guilds will. If they think they are strong enough, that's what they'll do, to avoid destruction of property and goods.

179

You're a young woman, attractive enough—especially when you smile. If you remember to smile, to look well, you might save yourself. Yul,'' he continued, thinking aloud, ''is strong, and he works willingly.''

Birle had thought that she was, at least in this house, safe. Whatever else, she had thought Corbel's power would provide protection. Now, suddenly, it felt to her as if the whole world were a dark and stormy sea, where danger was approaching fast upon her. ''But, master, if you go to your philosophers, who will be your amanuensis?'' she asked. ''Could I not go, I could go as a boy—if I were careful, who would know I wasn't?'' He was shaking his head. ''It will take time to teach another all that you've taught me, and your Herbal will have to wait while you do that.'' His head shook slowly. ''Is Corbel certain to lose the city?''

''Nothing is certain,'' Joaquim told her. ''Not until it is past. Corbel is strengthening the fortifications, increasing his soldiery—which is why he has such urgent need for gold. But Celinde's father has friends, with dowried daughters of their own, who would have the world know a daughter cannot be taken so. They also amass an army. And Corbel is no fool. He fears the enmity of the city.''

Birle walked back and forth in front of the fire, trying to catch and hold her breath. ''I've heard nothing of this in the city, at the market. Nobody even speaks of Corbel.''

''Would they, to you? You have his chain around your neck, and who's to say that a slave can't be a spy, even though she's a girl? You have eyes and ears, and a tongue to carry tales. The city cherishes its mistress Celinde and would have no harm come to her. Fear of what Corbel might do keeps it obedient. The city awaits war, and its outcome.''

''When will this happen?'' Birle asked.

''Not until early summer, at the soonest. Troops and supplies take time to gather. Celinde's father might wait even longer, until he can destroy the crops in the fields—and starve Corbel out.''

''Isn't there anything Corbel can do?''

180

"You can be sure he has his plans, you can be sure of that."

"What are they?" Birle would have liked to hear that Corbel had such strength, such cleverness, or such luck, that he would never be defeated.

"He doesn't tell me. All that I know is, whatever he does it will be bold."

Seventeen

In two days, notices went up on the spike at the center of the marketplace, and on the doors of the guildhalls; soldiers made the announcement at the fountains: The Prince would give to his city a feast, to mark the first year of his rule. The Prince invited the city to his castle grounds, for food and drink, entertainments and dancing, on the day of the second night of the next full moon but one.

Word spread quickly, like fire across a hayfield, until the talk of the market was only of the feast, and winter, winter and the feast. It would be spring then, and spring was cause for hope. Winter had no hope in it. Food was scarce, fuel was scarce, only sickness was plentiful. Disease spread in winter, not with the speed of summer fevers, but slowly, like a river rising.

Sometimes, during those days of waiting, Birle was awakened from sleep by a quiet knocking at the door that led to the walled yard. In dire need a wife, or mother, child, even friend, would creep up along the riverbank where no guards watched, under cover of darkness, to ask the Philosopher for comfrey to knit a bone; a plaster to spread over someone's chest; even a single spoonful of the ointment that, dropped into boiling water, made a healing vapor that eased a choking cough; or dwale to ease a death. Birle would rouse Joaquim, and together they would go out to the laboratory to gather what was needed, and explain how to use it.

Thus it became known in the city that Birle was the Philosopher's slave, not Corbel's. Speech was less guarded in her presence, and smiles more easy. If she was about to pay too much for something—candles, a piece of meat—there was a quick shake of the head to alert her. She learned to read the more subtle signals of eyes or mouths when she was about to pay too little. When Birle was asked a question she could answer about treatment of symptoms, she did so. When she could not answer the question, she carried it home with her and brought the Philosopher's advice back to market. The Philosopher's maid, they called her, and the name gave her protection.

At the market, much was said about the feast, and Birle began to understand that Corbel had been not only bold, but also clever. The fishmonger had heard that the Prince planned to slaughter an entire herd of goats, to be roasted in deep pits in his own gardens. "Imagine, he'll give us meat. Meat, children." Other voices joined in.

"Bread, mountains of bread. And they say it'll be made from the finest flour, it'll be the same white bread that he himself eats."

"Ale as plentiful as river water in the spring floods."

"I heard it was wine."

"He'd never spend his barrels of wine on us."

"But I heard so, and I thought, hearing it, that the Little Mistress would want it for us, for such a feast."

"We'll eat and drink and take our leisure—I've heard that the minstrel from his own hall will sing that day, for us."

"—puppeteers from the great cities to the south—"

"A man can change, and our Little Mistress is so good she must make any man better."

"The goldmaster's wife has ordered new dresses for each of her five daughters, but I'm thinking it'll take more than fine clothing to catch husbands proud enough for those girls."

It was as if the promise of a feast to come made the winter days warmer and brighter than they were. It was as if, with a promise ahead of him, a man could bear his present miseries more easily.

The hope that she might see Orien at the feast, and might

speak with him among the crowds—she didn't dare to think of it. Thinking of it slowed the moon's cycles, and kept spring at bay. Birle worked and did not think. She awoke one morning to discover spring, unexpected.

In the Kingdom, spring drove winter off, with sharp winds and thunderstorms. In this southern city, with the sea at its feet, spring moved with soft, slow steps, like a girl at a dance. She held out her hand to the old man and he could do nothing else but take it, and be tamed to her will. In this southern city, spring danced winter out the door. Flowers slipped up from the ground, first the low-growing violets and then—just moments later, it seemed—the taller, brighter, prouder blooms. Little leaves came like tears out onto the branches of trees.

Birle felt like that old man, with her unwilling eagerness. Waking, at night, she would do the only work possible for her to do during the long hours of darkness, waiting for the next day to begin to run its course. She would light a candle and bring down from its shelf the Herbal, quills, and the pot of ink. As she sat at the table, carefully forming the letters and the lines of words, she could feel her spirit grow quiet. Aye, and why shouldn't she be proud of the pages she had written so flawlessly, and the drawings as much like life as she could make them? And of the house, too, gleaming in its cleanliness, and the laboratory, with its shelves of medicines, the herbs dried and hung from the rafters, the next day's experiments, which she had set out for her master to perform.

How Nan would laugh to see her now, Birle thought. When that thought rose to her mind, she laughed softly in the darkness, to see herself.

At last the day came. The sun shone, as the city had known it must; the wind blew gentle, and warm. Yul was afraid to go so Birle left the house alone, to join the crowds going up the hilly street. Joaquim had been called to his brother's side early in the morning. Birle wore red for that day, the red skirt and shirt, and even a red ribbon she had purchased at market to braid into her hair.

Corbel's castle rose high atop a hill among hills. The wealthy approached the castle, to mount the carved stone steps and go within. Birle and others moved around to the left, following the crowds before them. Hills sloped steeply down and then rose steeply. Everywhere, people milled around, going to the tables for food and drink, exploring the grassy hillsides, the orchards, and the woods beyond, drawn over to a raised wooden platform, where musicians played on instruments. The smell of roasting meat was in the air, and faint music, when Birle listened for it. Tables had been lined up, some with barrels beside them, others piled with loaves of bread. Each guest had brought his own tankard or bowl, to dip again and again into the barrels; each guest might eat and drink his fill, many times over.

Birle, standing still, was jostled from behind and from the sides. Many—and those the poorest—crowded around the food tables, too hungry to wait for roasted meat, so hungry they could see nothing of the occasion but the bread and ale spread out for them. Hands reached out over the platters, to grab bread and take it to mouths and reach out again for more. Servants in Corbel's livery poured ale from jugs into the cups that surrounded them.

Birle watched the throngs at the food tables, guessing that Orien would be among the hungry. Why, she wondered now, was she so certain he would be at the feast? A master could refuse his slave the day's pleasure.

One of the indistinguishable throng at the table turned around, and his eyes met hers as if he had known where to look for her. Birle couldn't be sure, at the distance, of the color of the eyes, but she knew. She hurried down the hillside, pushing past people, to where Orien was.

When she came there, he was gone. But she knew he had seen her. Why had he not waited? People pushed roughly at her, in their haste to get to bread and ale. The stench of unwashed bodies and clothing filled her nose. She fought her way free.

She looked back to where she had been standing, at the top of a rise of land. He was there, watching her, and she lifted her hand. She understood—he had gone to find her even as she was hurrying to find him. He didn't raise his hand in answer, but she kept her eyes on him as she hurried back. When she was sure he had seen what she was doing, she attended to making her way as fast as she could, against the flow of people. But when she got there, he was again gone.

Orien didn't wish to meet up with her.

If Birle hadn't needed to warn Orien, she would have left the feast right then, gone back to the Philosopher's house. But it was the poor of the city who would suffer most, if it came to war, their perils would be greatest. If she didn't warn him—

She went slowly down the hill to the entertainers' platform and became one among the many who watched. She kept herself to the rear of the crowd, and off to one side. Puppeteers had the stage.

These were puppets the likes of which Birle had never seen before, carved with so many joints that when they walked they seemed to be alive. When the puppets stood in line upon their stage, and bowed, Birle stamped and clapped her approval with the rest of the audience.

A singer followed the puppeteers, a fine young man, handsome enough to set the women murmuring and the men grumbling. He looked into the crowd as he sang, his hands plucking melody from the gleaming lute. He sang about a mother whose three sons were lost at sea but came back ghosts to tell the sad news. He sang of two brothers in a field, from which only one brother came back alive, and was compelled to leave his lands forever, for his crime. Then he sang a song Birle had heard before, the song about the ravens and the dead knight. "As I was walking all alane," his sweet voice sang, "I heard two corbies making a mane." In this song also, only the hawks and hounds and lady fair knew where the knight lay, but the hound had gone hunting to fill his own belly, and the hawk had returned to his perch, and the lady—Birle listened, remembering—had taken another mate. So the corbies were going to pick clean the knight's body, like the heads on Corbel's spike—even his golden hair would be taken to line the nest. It was the same song, only everything was changed.

Birle would have wondered about that, but she saw, at last—Orien. He hadn't seen her, she was sure of it. If he had, he'd have gone elsewhere.

By the time she stood behind him, the singer was finished. He was letting the crowd praise him, a handkerchief held to his nose. Birle stood at Orien's back. Two festering boils stood out red and puss-filled on the side of his neck. Birle wished she could take him back to the Philosopher's house, and heat him a bath, and dress him in clean clothes, and make compresses to draw out the infection from the boils. But that was only a fleeting wish. She didn't know how long he would give her to speak with him, and she had a warning to deliver. She spoke into his ear, her voice quiet under the crowd's noise. "Orien, I would have only a few words for you."

The head went up. It was a long moment before he turned around. When he did his face was not glad to see hers. He was afraid, she felt that. But why should he be afraid of her?

Orien grabbed her roughly by the arm. "Come on, then," he said. He pulled her along the path. When they were alone among the trees, out of sight of the feast and beyond its noises, he sat down on a rock and looked up at her. "You know the danger you've put me in."

Birle stood, uncertain. "I've put you in no danger."

"It's little you know, Innkeeper's Daughter, living safe as you do in Corbel's service. For the others of us, anyone who deals with Corbel's house, except for profit, is suspected of spying." He had tied his matted hair at the back of his neck with a leather thong. His beard was as matted and stained as his hair. His words were angry, but it wasn't anger she saw in his eyes. His eyes were too filled with hopeless sorrow to leave room for anger. There was a smell of city filth all over him.

"I'm not Corbel's slave. I'm the Philosopher's slave, and I live in the Philosopher's house."

187

His hand reached out as if he would touch the chain at her neck. He didn't have to say anything.

Birle spoke more quietly. "You can ask, ask anyone at the market."

"I don't go to the marketplace."

Birle sat down on the ground. "I saw you there."

"Sometimes, I go to the fountain to fetch water, but that's as far as I go. The one day was—my master had business with me."

That reminded Birle. "Listen, Orien, Joaquim has told me—"

"Who is Joaquim?"

"The Philosopher."

"You call him by name?"

"You've heard of the Little Mistress? Corbel stole her—and her father will come to take her back, and take the city back too. That means war. War means—"

He was shaking his head, slowly. "It doesn't concern me."

"But it does, because a city in war—"

"I've been sold to the mines," Orien said. At that, he smiled—his smile not even a ghost of the one she remembered, his smile a rotting corpse.

"When?"

He shrugged.

A terrible urgency fell down over her. "Then you have to escape."

"How can I?"

"Go to the river."

"I don't know what lies beyond the river, I'm too weak to go any distance, an escaped slave, when he is captured. . . ."

"Listen, the Philosopher's house backs onto the river. Orien? Yul is there, you remember him? We could hide you, I'm sure of it." Orien didn't seem to be listening, but she went on talking. "The house is small, and it stands right up against the front wall, unlike all the others. You can recognize the house easily, when you get there. This wood must go as far as the river."

188

"You've forgotten the soldiers," he reminded her, and she had. "The difference is, Birle, that you have no need to remember the soldiers, but I do. No matter how poor my master is, they will find me for him. Before the soldiers bring a slave back . . ." He swallowed, and didn't finish what he was saying. "Even if I could get as far as your Philosopher's house, what would I do then?"

Birle's spirits were being ensnared by his so that her own ideas seemed hopeless to her even before she gave them voice.

"I don't know," she told him. "I could show you how to read the map of the skies, and we know we came south and west from the Kingdom—"

"I almost disbelieve in the Kingdom," Orien said. "It has been four seasons now, a full year. Did you note that, Birle? No, you wouldn't, it wouldn't be needful for you to think back, to say, 'Only a year ago, a year and a little more, I was such a man.' To think of what I was. The Earl that would be, and who would believe me if I tried to tell them? I should never have left, Birle. If I had it to do again . . ."

"Aye, but you don't." There was nothing to be gained by this talk.

"Yes, but if I did. I sometimes think of it. I often think of it."

"Why is your master selling you to the mines?" Birle asked.

"To pay his debts. The carpenter put himself into apprenticeship. He had to—otherwise he would always be poor, never have a wife. As an apprentice, he serves his seven years and then he can become a member, if they find him worthy."

"You seem to envy him."

"How can I not?"

"Because you're not a craftsman—you're an Earl."

At that he gave her the smile she remembered. "No, Birle, 'm a slave, slave to a tailor whose work is so poor that his uck matches it." He rose, as if to leave her.

"You have to escape," she said.

"I can't."

189

"You did it before, you escaped the Kingdom."

"Yes, but then—you might have had your master whom you call by his name buy me, Birle." His voice was bitter now. "You might have sought me out."

Orien walked away. She was not going to follow him, to make explanation and excuse. If he thought that of her, and so bitterly. If he would just walk away from her that way. Aye, and hadn't he always turned his back on those things that weren't as he wished?

She walked on through the trees, away from the feasting, to be alone with her sorrow and her anger. He would let himself be led to his death in the mines, like a goat to the slaughter. He complained that she hadn't found him, but she had—what else had she done, this day? He complained that she hadn't helped him, but when she tried to talk of escape he would say only that it couldn't be done. He complained of his luck—

Aye, and he had the right to complain. She stood now at the river, which flowed far below her. Three soldiers stood guard, and she turned back into the trees. Orien had much to complain of in his luck; if complaining would do any good, she would have complained with him, and lamented.

When Birle came out of the shadowed woods into the sunlit grounds, she joined the crowd around the entertainers' platform yet again, because there she was least likely to be noticed. A tall, dark man strode over to the edge of the platform and stood there, waiting for the silence to grow ripe. "Today," he spoke in a voice like the calling of horns, "You are privileged to see those things which—until this afternoon, until this very hour—only the great of this world have had set before their eyes."

"Fine speech," a man from the crowd called out. "But I never gave a kiddle for fine speech. And I'll wager Corbel didn't either." The crowd laughed at the challenge.

The Showman wasn't upset. "Let my wonders speak for themselves, and so they will, without any speech at all." He lifted an arm into the air and turned, his long red robe flowing around him. A wagon, with two horses, had been pulled up at the back of the platform, a bright yellow wagon with a yellow house built on top of it. "Wonders!" the Showman called, his voice ringing out, "Reveal yourselves."

The door opened, outward.

Nothing happened.

The audience, which had been temporarily quelled by the Showman's voice, hooted and cried out.

At last, a man crawled out of the door, on his hands and knees. Then slowly, like a seedling unfolding from the earth, he stood up. The crowd fell silent. The man was taller by far—taller by half the Showman's height—than the Showman, tall and as thin as a birch tree. Before the audience could respond, another figure ran onto the platform, to stand beside his fellow. This man came up no farther than the tall man's knees. The two were dressed alike, in red leggings and yellow shirts, which only emphasized their great differences. The little man had a head as large as a grown man, but all the rest of his body was no larger than a child's. He was no bigger than one of Birle's small sisters. A third man came to join them, a man as thick and strong-looking as the trunk of an ancient oak. He dragged a heavy chain from his hands. When he pulled on the chain, a snarling creature who moved on all fours like a wolf was dragged out at its end. Whether that was a man or a woman, Birle couldn't tell. Its long hair hung down over its face and its head moved like a wild animal's, back and forth. It leaped out to the end of its chain, snarling at the crowd, and the strong man jerked it sharply back.

The crowd moved backward, pushing against Birle. Even then, the Showman held his pose. "And now," he called out, his voice like a bell over the silent, staring crowd, "the last and best."

Through the low doorway stepped a woman, the likes of whom Birle had never seen before. She was a delicate thing, with her hands slipped up inside the broad sleeves of the green gown she wore, with gold-slippered feet that minced forward in tiny steps as she bowed up and down from the waist. Her costume had a wide sash at the waist, and fitted her legs closely as it fell to the floor. The material was intricately embroidered in gold and white, with flowers and clouds and a huge golden dragon with red flames coming out of its open mouth. The dainty woman had long, thick, straight black hair that reached almost down to the ground. Most wonderful was her face—the skin almost a golden color, the eyes slanting upward at their ends. She stood at the end of the line and the Showman—knowing how captivated his audience was—named his wonders. "The tallest man in the world, the shortest man in the world, the strongest man in the world, the wild man of the north, and—from lands so far to the east that you would have to journey a lifetime only to arrive there—the Emperor's Daughter."

The crowd sighed with satisfaction.

"What do you have to say now, man?" the Showman called to his heckler.

"I say," the voice answered, "If I had a kiddle to give, you'd have it."

"Birle."

His voice spoke in her ear. She shook her head.

His hand tugged at her elbow. "Just for a few words," he asked.

She turned and made her way through the crowd, following him. He led her a few paces beyond, where they could speak without anyone attending to what they said. She stood stiff before him; let him have his few words, she had nothing more to say.

"I wouldn't have us part thus," he said. His bellflower eyes spoke what his words didn't. "For two who have journeyed so far together, that was an unworthy parting."

"Aye, it was," she agreed. Birle had no more heart for anger. Pity and sorrow were all that were in her heart, and her heart was his. "You deserve better, my Lord."

"And you deserve the luck you've had," he said. "Can you really read the map of the skies?"

He didn't want to talk any more about luck, or the future. "Only a little. I know only a few of the star patterns, but one of them is a pointer to the fixed star in the north. Joaquim—my master—"

"I remember."

"He knows many more, and how they move through the sky in their seasons. Which fountain is it you go to, Orien?"
He hesitated, as if he didn't wish to answer.

"There are so many, in the city, but each one is different," she said. If he were to wonder how she came to know that, that was not a question she would answer, to tell him what he ought already to have known. She waited.

Orien hadn't used to be so slow to decide if he would speak or no.

"I could bring an ointment, for the sores on your face, and one to draw the boils—and food, I could bring food."

"Even Corbel's power won't guarantee your safety, where I live."

Birle shook her head impatiently. "But Joaquim's name will. He takes medicine to the sick, and they know I serve him. Actually," she told Orien proudly, "I'm his amanuensis."

"Ah," he said, teasing now, so that he was almost the young man she had first seen, "his amanuensis, are you that?"

As if some giant's hand had grabbed her heart and squeezed shut around it, there was pain in Birle's breast. If she could have gone to the mines in his place—if she could have lived this last terrible year for him—she would have done it. "They call me his maid, in the marketplace. I'll be safe, I think." She didn't care if she wasn't.

He made up his mind then. "The fountain has four tortoises at the corners, and a frog spitting up water at its center. One tortoise has no head, and the street comes in by that headless tortoise. My master's—house—is on your left as you walk away from the fountain."

"How will I know it?"

"You'll know it. If you risk it, bring Yul for protection."

"Yes, my Lord," Birle said. That was the only way she

knew to tell him all that she was thinking. That was the only gift she had to give him.

He drew his shoulders up, and bowed his head to her. "I'll go now," he said, his voice gentle, and sad. But why should he be sad, knowing she would be bringing him food, and medicine?

"I never asked you to give me your heart," he reminded her.

"And I have never asked for yours," she answered.

"So we make a good parting," he said.

He turned, looked back to smile for her, and was gone.

Eighteen

BIRLE slept deep and dreamless; she awoke just as the last darkness was leaving the sky. The stars were fading away, the air hovered: It was the silvery time of day.

Quietly, quickly, she dressed, in her plainest skirt and top. She went out to the laboratory, to find ointments; garlic to draw the boils, chamomile for healing. Yul wakened at her first step into the room. "It's early hours. Go back to sleep," she reassured him.

He put his head back down on the straw and closed his eyes, but then she decided to tell him. "Yul? Do you remember Orien?"

He shook his head.

"When we were all on the sailing ship?"

He remembered nothing, his face said.

"With the two—when you rowed, on the sea."

The memory frightened him.

"There was a man with me, do you remember? He rowed too."

"Yes. A man. Not the bad men."

"That's right, not a bad man. That was Orien."

"Or-ien."

"He needs medicine, and food; I'm going to take them to him, in the city. That's where I'll be. Will you tell the master where I've gone?"

"Yes. Yul will tell the master." Yul sat up in the straw. "Birle will—come back?"

195

"Yes, I will, of course I will." But he wasn't listening, he was wrapping his fingers tightly around a fold of her skirt. Birle bent over to gently loosen them. "I wouldn't go away and leave you behind, Yul."

He shook his head. "If Birle dies. Gran died, and didn't come back."

"Aye," Birle said, "if I die, I can't come back, can I? If I live, I promise you, I will come back. I think today I will live," she said.

"Yes." Yul lay back down, rearranging the straw under him to make it more comfortable, and closed his eyes.

From the food stores in the house, Birle added bread and cheese to the medicines in the basket, then a jug of wine. She unlocked the door and stepped out, pulling it closed behind her.

It was not until she arrived at the guarded gateway into the city that she remembered the soldiers. It was not until the two guards ranged themselves before her that she remembered she needed some reason to be going into the city at this hour, long before the morning bells had rung. She had no tale ready to tell them.

One of them was older, with gray in his beard and eyebrows, the other young. Both had their hands ready at the hilts of their swords and both yawned, sleepy after a night's watch, but both red shirts were as clean and unwrinkled as if they had just been put on. The older one stood in her way. "And where do you think you're going, girl?"

Birle tried to think of an answer, but her mind was sluggish. She could think only of Orien. She made her face a mask of fearlessness as she sought for the reason that would satisfy the soldiers.

"Well?" the younger asked, more suspicious the longer she took to answer.

"I must go into the city," she said.

"We will know your errand," the older said.

"Aye, but—" Birle couldn't find any ideas in her head. If she had to turn back now—she couldn't bear to turn back, and wait for the bells to ring. "I must," she repeated.

The young soldier looked at her, and laughed. "Some man, I'll wager. She's from the castle, slipping out to meet some man, and if Corbel knew that one of his slaves—"

"That's not true," Birle said. She wasn't slave to Corbel.

"Or she's been sent out to find him another maid from the city. I told you, didn't I? When battle draws nigh, Corbel's appetites increase—and so do mine, but I can't feed them as richly as the captain. So I wager we'll pass this little missy through more than one time. The city is full of maids who'd be happy to lie in Corbel's bed—he'll not thank us for hindering her."

"Let it be on your head, then," the younger soldier said. "Because if she's a spy—"

"If she's a spy, then it never hurts to have done the enemy a good turn, should fortune's tides turn against Corbel. You have your way, girl, you can pass. If it's a lover you go to meet, treat him well, in memory of two poor soldiers with no girl to come to their beds. And maybe, by summer, we'll not need beds, for being tucked up forever in the earth. If it's a girl for Corbel you fetch, we can all hope she'll give him good sport. And if it's the enemy you serve, remember how we two let you pass, with no word spoken."

Birle just nodded her head. She cared no more than they did what was false and what true in their words, just so they let her pass. She didn't mind if it was Corbel's chain at her throat or the soldiers' whim that gave her passage. She didn't care if it was she who made things turn out as she wished them to, or if it lay in somebody else's power to do that, so long as they did turn out as she wished. When the soldiers parted to let her pass, she went through without any thanks or farewells.

Birle knew where to look for the tortoise fountain—in the poorest part of the city. No one was yet about on the streets. It was as if the whole city slept, full-bellied for once. Those who slept out on the dirt streets or in doorways had carried within them their burden of food and drink as far as they could, then collapsed under it.

By the time she came to the tortoise fountain, some few

197

women had come to stand yawning in doorways, and children's voices could be heard. Birle didn't remember if she had been on the street that wound away from the headless tortoise before. Wooden huts, carelessly built, most leaning against one another for support, the doorways sometimes pieces of rough-fitted wood and sometimes only cloth hanging over the opening—this looked like any of the city streets. She studied the dwellings on her left, walking away from the fountain. He had said she would know it.

She did know it. As soon as she saw the shed, she knew this must be the place. Even on those streets it looked mean, uninhabitable. A thick chain hung from a ring on the doorpost. Without asking anyone, she knew it, and knew who had slept at night, thus chained, at his master's door, and knew also that the hut was empty.

Orien might have spared her this, she thought, and then she knew why he hadn't. Aye, if she had known he would be gone before the morning, she'd have insisted that he act, make some attempt at escape, she would have . . . It didn't matter whether cowardice or concern for her safety had led him to deceive her, since the end result was that he had already been taken to the mines. Taken to his death.

She had thought that it would be easier if he were dead, and she were to know it—but it was not. Aye and he was no coward, to bid her farewell in that fashion.

Birle stood staring, the basket heavy on her arm. He had told her clearly enough, but not in words—in the fact of his absence he made sure she must know. He thought to spare her, but he didn't know her heart. He measured her heart by his own.

How long she stood there, Birle didn't know. How long she stood, helpless in her understanding, she neither knew nor cared. The piece of cloth hung for doorway across the street was pulled aside and a woman demanded, "What are you after?"

She was not an old woman, although her eyes looked old and tired. Her clothing was ragged and bright, like finery someone else had worn the goodness out of before giving it away. Birle tried to swallow down the lump in her throat, so that she could force words out.

There was something in Birle's face that made the woman willing to speak. "You needn't bother asking for the tailor. He's gone to Corbel's armies. Well, he won't last long there—he'll make no more of a soldier than he did a tailor. I wouldn't waste my tears over him."

"And his slave?" Birle could barely put words to the question.

"Well, he was the bonnier of the two, I won't say you nay." The woman had a ragged smile, like a rose as its last petals fall. "But you'd best forget him. They took him off to the mines at sunset yesterday. Him and others. Corbel decreed that they might go with their bellies full, in honor of the feast. If I'd had the four kiddles, I'd have bought the lad for myself—he was biddable, and he told tales well, and for his eyes. Tears for that one wouldn't come amiss. Well, and the truth is I shed a few myself when I heard he must be sold."

Birle had no tears. She had not thought there could be a grief too deep for tears, but now she knew it. She nodded her thanks to the woman and turned to make her way back to the Philosopher's house.

It was midday when she opened the door into Joaquim's kitchen, the basket still on her arm. She didn't remember finding her way back through the streets, or passing through the gates. She didn't remember seeing or hearing anything. She didn't remember how long she had been gone, or why. She replaced the food she had taken. Yul was digging in the garden and didn't notice her, but she couldn't make herself go to greet him. She went into the laboratory to put the medicines back on their shelves.

Joaquim was stripping dried leaves from a bunch of comfrey. For an infusion, Birle thought. She had no desire to help him. A beaker bubbled over a low flame at the far end of the table—the liquid in it was golden, and a handful of pebbles rumbled in the liquid. She would have gone back into the house, but her master called her name.

199

"What is this story Yul told me? Who is this man, Orien?"

Birle didn't care that he was displeased. "It doesn't matter."

He looked up at her. "What has happened?"

Birle shook her head. Nothing had happened.

Now his voice was gentle. "Is there some harm my knowledge can mend?"

"There's nothing to be done," she told him. She didn't want to talk. She was having difficulty enough forcing breath down into her chest.

"There are some," Joaquim told her, "who say that the Lady Fortune has a wheel, and all men are fixed upon it. The wheel turns, and the men rise, or fall, with the turning of the wheel."

Birle nodded her head. She would agree with those who thought so. She would agree that she was bound to such a wheel, and—being fixed upon it—must follow its turnings. She felt as if the wheel's weight were on her back, as if at the same time she must ride it, she must also bear it. She would agree that it was thus for her—but what of Orien? She could not accept that Orien must be fixed to such a wheel.

"Who is this man?" Joaquim asked again.

"He's been sold to the mines," she said. Joaquim's face told her what she already knew. But having spoken so much, she said more. "In the Kingdom, he would have been the Earl Sutherland. There are two Earls, who serve under the King and rule over the Lords and people. Orien was heir to the Earl Sutherland; he was the eldest son."

"What happened?"

"He left it all behind him."

"And you came with him."

That was near enough to be the truth.

"And you were both, somehow, captured, and sold into slavery."

She nodded.

"But now he's been taken to the mines. And now the best you can hope for him is that he will die quickly."

200

Birle gave no voice to her anger—how could he say it so? Even if it was true, to say it so, as if it were no more than any of the other ideas he uttered so easily.

"I thought last night—you smile so seldom, but last night there was springtime in your smile. Maybe they are right, Birle, and we are bound to the wheel until death frees us."

As if she had hoped that her master would be able to do what she knew could not be done, Birle's heart flickered like a candle, and went out.

"I must," she said, "prepare the meal. I must. There's work must be done." How she could bear the weight of the hours, she didn't know. But if there were no toil she must think of Orien—a tiny figure bound like all the others to a wheel of iron, and his eyes the blue of bellflowers.

Those days Birle labored long, late and early. She didn't know how many days there were, she only knew that there was no easing to the grief. All she could do was bear it, through the long days. Yul worried for her; she saw his worry without being able to ease it.

Joaquim too worried, but not over Birle. Her master was often out of the house, but doing what she didn't know and he didn't say. When he was at home he didn't work in the laboratory but wandered restlessly about whatever room he was in. Birle thought Joaquim was afraid, but that didn't trouble her. Neither was she troubled at the changes in the marketplace, where fewer customers—and none of them the wealthy of the city—paid more than goods were worth, and paid the sums without question or complaint. Fewer red shirts patrolled the streets of the city, watched over the marketplace, guarded the gates. Birle had no thought or care for any of this. It was the most she could do to thank Yul when he brought her in a handful of flowers grown wild in the grass of the yard. She sat up by candlelight, copying pages into Joaquim's book, until her head fell forward onto the table and she could sleep.

Beyond the open door to the yard, a heavy black sky hung like a curtain, pricked with stars. The wavering light of the candle flowed like water over the sheet of paper, and the pen

scratched steadily, as letters and words—carefully shaped—
came from its sharpened tip. Sleep would find her there, and
carry her off before she had time to notice its presence.
Sometimes when she slept she dreamed, and sometimes when
she dreamed she saw Orien, and once he was laughing. When
she awoke from that dream her face was wet with tears.

She lifted her head and saw that her tears had blotted the
page, so that it would have to be redone. She went outside.
Once again it was the silvery time of day, but this morning
a fine rain filled the air and brushed against her face. On her
way to the privy, she saw that Yul had put a bundle of clothing
out, up against the wall of the laboratory. She would launder
that day, then, and never mind if it was not fair. She would
heat the water to scalding over the fire, so that when she put
her hands into it there would be a pain she could put a name
to. It was not until she was coming out of the privy that Birle
thought to wonder why Yul, who had never before bundled
his dirty clothing in that manner, should do so, or to remember—with a suddenness that squeezed the breath out of her
chest—that there had been something like a stick across the
top of the bundle, as if to hold it in place in a wind, or like
an arm.

Until she had pulled the arm away, and turned the listless
head to face the rain, she didn't dare to know it was Orien.

There was no time for gladness. When she turned his face,
the one eye that could open opened, and didn't see her. His
tongue flicked between his caked lips, to taste the rain. The
right side of his face was an open sore, red and festering so
that the eye—caked with pus and dirt—couldn't open. He
was burning up with heat, with fever. The sore that was his
face smelled like rotting meat.

Birle crouched on the ground beside him, just for a minute
or two, until the joy that made her hands tremble and the fear
that made her heart beat painfully fast had both receded.
Then she decided what to do.

She went into the laboratory and roused Yul. "Help me,"
she asked. Yul carried Orien back down the grassy yard and
laid him on the ground under a cluster of bushes, grown so

tall that their branches formed low rooms. Birle sent Yul to bring blankets, and a bucket of clean water, and cloths.

She washed Orien's face and neck. He turned and complained under her hands, but he didn't know who hurt him so. He spoke no words, and if he had she would not have heard them. They had branded him, the wound had infected—as if half his face had been held in the fire. She didn't think of that. She thought only of cleaning his poor face, gently, gently, bathing it in cool water and dripping water from her hands into his mouth when it turned, like a sucking babe, toward the coolness of water.

His wrists were chained together with iron loops two fingers thick. She didn't think of that. The little rain pattered down.

Leaving Yul with Orien, she went into the laboratory for medicines. Garlic ointment—it would pain him but it would clean the wound—barley water . . . she didn't know what she might use, she thought, but then she realized that she did. The pages she had copied were copied into her memory. Thinking quickly, she took down the vial of dwale. A drop or two, in the barley water, would give him sleep. Too much— and her hand shook—would kill him; but dwale in small measure—she watched one drop, then two, fall into the vial of water—would ease him, and let him sleep.

While he slept, she would cut away the hair from his face, then she could apply ointment with less pain to him. She didn't know if Yul's strength would be any use against the chains on Orien's wrists.

She could only hope that her master would be too distracted by whatever was worrying him to notice that something was going on. She must put a meal on the table, but it wasn't time yet. If Orien was sleeping a drugged sleep, she could leave him safely hidden there, for the time it took to feed her master.

If Birle had been less distracted by her own misery of the preceding days, she would not have been so surprised at her master's announcement as he sat down for his morning bread and wine.

"Today I leave," Joaquim said. "I leave the house, the city, this warbegone countryside—and the false alchemy too—and I leave my brother's rule. You've no reason to look dismayed, Birle. I warned you."

"I had forgotten." They would have the house to themselves, then. That suited her needs. "What should I pack for your journey?" Orien could have Joaquim's comfortable bed. There was medicine and food to hand.

"You'll pack nothing. And you'll say nothing either, not to anyone. Corbel won't know until nightfall that I've gone, he mustn't know. When the soldier brings a cart to the door, you and Yul must put the sacks into it—as we did last year. Where is Yul? Have you woken him? I'll put my Herbal in one of the sacks, that's all I need to take with me."

"Will the soldier let you leave the city?"

"He won't know until I don't return. I wouldn't think of giving the order. Only Corbel has the power to exact obedience. I'm like your lost Earl—I have no desire for power. It's my brother who desires that. He counts the cost well spent that gets him what he desires."

"Aye, and so do you, master," Birle said. She knew this, because she knew it of herself. "And so does every man." The only difference lay in what the object of desire was.

"I've no time for talk," Joaquim said. "As for you, and Yul, it would be well for you to be away from the house by sunset. I don't know where, or how you can hide yourselves, especially Yul. It might be that you ought to go separate ways, for your safety. I've silver coins to aid you. Don't let Corbel find you. Unless you think you'd be safest in his house, in which case you should wait here for the soldier to bring the news of my escape to Corbel. Corbel will come here first. He'll be angry."

Too much was happening, all at once. Birle couldn't take it all in; she could think only of Orien.

"So I'll say farewell to you," Joaquim said. He left his food uneaten, and held out a small purse to her. "I wish your future fortune happier than this one."

If Joaquim left her here, Orien would be trapped. She must

204

urry, to fetch Yul, and think of how they might hide Orien, hey must hurry before they lost this last chance to leave the ity, before war and Corbel—

"No." Birle's voice was as harsh as a raven's, strong and ure.

Joaquim turned back to face her. She said it again, lest he misunderstand her. "No, master. You won't leave us behind."

Nineteen

JOAQUIM answered her impatiently. "It's the world, the way of the world. If I could change the world I would, but in warning you and giving you coins, I've done all I can." Until she heard how his voice trembled, Birle hadn't understood how frightened her master was. He gave out fear just as a fire gives out warmth. "I'm helpless. Don't you understand?"

Birle was as frightened as he was. Joaquim was their only hope. The only power she had was the power to touch his heart so that he would, for pity of her, help her escape from the city. For the same reason, he might also help Yul. But Orien—

Birle wouldn't leave him behind. She'd left him behind once, but she'd had no choice then. Was she any less helpless now? For all his kindness, Joaquim had still used her for his own purposes. His purposes were not cruel ones, but they were his own and not hers. Pity didn't move him. Her weepings would fall on him as the rain did. He would take them as he did the rain and make out of them something to wonder at: What caused them? Where did the water come from? Why should it be salty? Why should women weep for what they wished, and men fight?

Joaquim would neither weep nor fight. He would obey when fear forced him but go his own way while obeying, make his own secret uses of whatever occasion his fortune or his brother forced upon him.

"There is yet one more thing you must do," Birle told her master.

He turned away, but she snaked her hand out to hold his arm. He would have pulled the arm away but she gripped it tightly with both of her hands. He raised his other hand as if to strike her.

Birle knew he wouldn't do that. Joaquim had the strength of knowledge, and no more. Even then, he would belie his thoughts with words if danger threatened. He must not know of Orien, because in Joaquim dangerous knowledge meant betrayal. He was right to value his Herbal above all else: The actions that made up his life would never be the best of Joaquim; his life was not his great work, his book was.

"You can't stop me," Joaquim claimed, even as her hands held their grip on his arm.

Not pity then, but fear. For this time, her own will, born out of her own fears, would rule him. He was a man easily ruled.

"You'll be punished," Joaquim warned her. "You're a slave."

"That I'm not. Master," Birle said, "I'm not a slave because you've never made me one."

"And this is how you repay my kindness?"

"It wasn't kindness. You couldn't have done otherwise, so you can't claim to have chosen to be kind. No, you must take us with you, as you did before. The soldier won't suspect anything, because it is what we did last spring. But this year I'll drive the cart."

"Do you know how to do that as well?"

"No, but I will," Birle said. "Once we get to the hills beyond farmlands, you can leave Yul and me to make our own way. You can take the cart yourself, and make a quicker escape."

"You don't understand, Birle. You belong to Corbel. If you were mine I'd do as you ask, I would. But—don't you understand?—if I make off with Corbel's property, as well as myself slipping away, he'll—"

Birle cut him off before he frightened himself into useless

207

idiocy. "If you leave me here," she said, making him her promise, "I'll waste no time in telling Corbel. I'll tell him everything. I'll tell him about the Herbal, the hours we spent on that, which were every one of them hours we didn't spend searching for his stone. Do you think he'll allow you to preserve your work, done at the expense of his? What—in his anger—do you think he'll do . . . if he were to know of it?" she concluded. "You must take us out of the city," she told her master.

Joaquim had shrunk inside of his robe. "Yes, I must. I will." There was no trickery to him; he didn't have the courage for deceit. "Call Yul, to tell him that we're leaving, gather what you need—"

"No," Birle said again, harshly. She dropped her hands from his arm, because she didn't need force to hold him now. "I need a day to get ready. So when the soldier comes, tell him to return tomorrow, at first light. Today, send him back."

"He won't obey me."

"He will when you give him the order in Corbel's name."

"I warn you—it's on your head if we've left it too long, if tomorrow we can't get out of the city. It'll all be your fault."

Birle feared that as much as Joaquim did. If the war came before the morrow, if—she had to get Orien out of the city, take him away into safety, and the day's delay might lose them their only chance—

But she needed the day, for her preparations. If she just went running off, without any thought for what she might need or whatever journey lay before her—she would purchase food from the marketplace, gather together garments for the three of them, and medicines, and the cloths for her time of the month. She would sew the silver coins her master had given them into her own skirt, so that no one would know she carried them. She needed to try to explain to Yul what they were doing, and if in doing so she gave Orien a day's healing rest, that was to the good. She needed to try to think out what way their journey should take them—three of them, runaway slaves, with war coming down upon the city, and one of them so weak he couldn't walk—

And a knife, she must have a good sharp knife in her boot—

Orien must have boots—

And a tinderbox—

As they moved over the top of a low hill the last farm dropped out of sight. They had passed the fork where a road led off to the north and now only double tracks led away, to the mines and westward. A fine rain fell over them. Birle pulled the horse to a stop.

Joaquim had not spoken a word to her since the morning before, but this wasn't the silence of anger. Joaquim was afraid, his whole body curled over the book he held at his chest. His face was hidden by the hood of his cloak. When he turned to look at her, Birle pitied him. "The horse is old and easily guided," she reassured him. "You'll have a whole day's head start. Corbel won't know until nightfall that you've fled the city."

The Philosopher shook his head. "Sometimes, he suspects. And if he does, and if he sends a soldier to look in the house—"

"The soldier this morning was glad to be returned to his company," Birle reminded her master. "The lady Celinde's father must be nearer than Corbel has let the city know. He won't have a thought for you today."

"He'll know where to find me," the Philosopher confessed. "My brother has never forgotten an injury done to him. I could almost wish him fallen in battle, if I dared. And he my only brother."

Birle couldn't help him with that. She put the reins into his gloved hands and climbed down from the high seat. She motioned Yul to help her lift off the layers of sacks they had covered Orien with, before she called Joaquim out of the house. One of the sacks was fat and heavy; that one she put at her feet.

"I should never have done this," Joaquim was saying. "I should have known better, I should have stayed where he put me, because he'd protect me—my own brother. I'm not a soldier, so why should soldiers wish to harm me? What was I thinking of?" Joaquim asked.

Orien, wrapped round with a blanket, lay on the floor of the cart. How much he understood of what was happening to him, Birle didn't know. Even in the early morning, his body had been hot with fever, and his eyes hadn't opened. He had swallowed a few spoonfuls of cool water, and tried to squirm back from her hands as she spread ointment on his swollen, oozing face, but he wasn't aware of anything. Birle spoke soothingly, but she had no hope that he recognized either the words or her voice.

Yul took up the inert form that was Orien. He held Orien cradled in his arms, as a weaver carries a bolt of fine cloth. Birle lifted the heavy sack and hung it over her shoulder by its wide leather strap.

Joaquim stared down at them, his face white. "What have you done, Birle? What is it, who? It's the one from the mines, isn't it? Do you know the danger he puts us in? No man escapes the mines."

"Aye, this man did." Birle said it proudly.

Joaquim didn't hear her. He was lifting the reins to urge the horse along the track, to put as much distance between himself and them as he could, as fast as he could. The cart creaked and rattled away.

Birle looked about her, accustoming herself to the weight on her back and to the lie of the land before her. At waking, she had been sorry for the rain. As they drove out of the city she was glad of it, because it kept most people indoors and made the soldiers at the gate hasty to get back into the guardhouse. Now she was sorry for it again, because rain concealed the sun, which made it hard to know direction, and if it held it would conceal the stars, which would make it impossible to travel by night.

The track along which the cart hurried curved off to the left. To the right, a meadow fell down the hillside, and there the forest made its sparse beginnings. North and east, those were her directions. Yul waited and she tried to smile for him. "We'd better be going on," she said.

"To the Kingdom?" Yul asked.

"To the Kingdom, if we can," Birle answered. They set off, side by side, the gentle rain in their faces.

Once under the trees, and far enough within their shelter, Birle stopped. "Set him down, Yul," she said, adding—even though it wasn't necessary—"gently now, gently." The medicines had been the last thing she packed, so she had only to reach into her sack to find the flask of barley water. Yul held Orien's head up, so she could open his slack mouth to pour in what she thought was the right dose. Orien coughed, swallowed, and didn't awaken. This was not, Birle knew, true sleep. This was the sleep of fever, as Joaquim had explained it to her. The spirit hid deep within the body while the fever burned. Like a fire, the fever fed on the flesh; it would burn itself out and if, in its passing, it had consumed too much of the flesh then the sick man would die. Thus, you treated fever with waters, as you might pour water on flames to extinguish them.

After the first taste of barley water, Orien's mouth opened for more, and she hoped it might have eased him. "Now we'll go on," she said to Yul. Birle was grateful that the giant didn't have the wits to ask where they were going that day, because she had no answer. He was contented to know that they would travel to the Kingdom, if they could.

Birle was not contented, and not easy. She wasn't sure of her direction, except that it should be away from the city of their slavery, away from the armies about to join in battle. She wasn't even certain which way the north lay, or the east. Unless the skies cleared she wouldn't be able to guess at that. And she did know that the sick man would heal best if he lay quiet and sheltered and undisturbed; but that ease she could only give him at even greater risk to his life.

All that day they followed a path through the forest, stopping only to give Orien medicine. At evening, they came to a little brook. Birle led Yul away from the path, to a thick-trunked oak that spread its branches over the brook. "Men made that path," she explained. "We don't want to be caught there, unaware, if there should be any-one traveling along it."

Birle studied their situation, as Yul placed Orien on the ground. Orien lay where he had been put, like a dead man wrapped in his shroud. "If anyone does come, Yul, if there's danger, climb up into the tree."

Yul looked up from where he had seated himself beside the sick man. "Yes, Yul can climb that. Yul can lift Birle up." She hadn't thought of that. "Not with Orien," Yul said, sad.

"We'll hope no danger comes," Birle said, which was the only answer she could give.

They had no fire and only their clothes for warmth. She thought that her fears would keep her awake, as they had the night before while she sat at Orien's side, unable to heal his sickness but unwilling to let him lie unguarded, unaccom-panied. But that first night, the bread and cheese sat warm in her stomach, and the air of late spring was warm around her, and Birle slept most of the darkness away. Beside her on the ground, Orien too must have lain quiet, for he didn't waken her.

At dawn, the rain had ceased although low clouds still covered the sky. Birle noted where the sky turned rose and they headed off with that over her right shoulder, following the path, which ran in their direction. There was a stillness in the woods that Birle didn't like. There should have been birds, and small scurrying creatures, but no sound came to her ears. She didn't know what might cause such stillness, but even the wind seemed to have frozen into immobility, listening. All Birle could hear was her own heavy footsteps and the sound of her own breathing as she carried the weight of the sack along the rough path, stumbling on roots and stones as the path rose steeply up and fell steeply down, crossing the forested hills.

Yul carried his burden easily. He held Orien's head close against his shoulder, to protect it from branches. The feet, filthy and full of deep cuts, hung out at the end of the blanket.

By afternoon, Birle's own feet felt hot and swollen, and she knew there were places where she would find the skin rubbed raw if she took her boots off. She had no time to think of that. The path ran northward, she thought, but no sun broke through the clouds to confirm her hope. How many days they must travel before they could stop—that she could only guess at. Where this path led—that too she didn't know. It was dangerous to stay on the path, because it had been made to lead to some destination, for those traveling to or from Corbel's city. It was just as dangerous to go as slowly as they would have to, if they stepped off the path and journeyed through unmarked forest. In the forest, you could go in a circle and arrive exhausted at the very place you had left.

But she didn't know how long it would be before traveling so weakened the sick man that the fever would consume him. She didn't even know if she should wrap him more warmly, to sweat the fever out of his body, or uncover him so that the air might cool him, she didn't even know—

"Birle."

Yul, who hadn't spoken for most of the day, spoke her name. His voice was low, a whisper that was almost a growl.

"What's the—"

His face was a mute snarl. It silenced her. She had never thought to fear Yul and she looked quickly, to see that Orien's head was still gently held. Still and silent, she heard what Yul's whisper had warned her of. A heavy sound, as if an iron wind dragged itself slowly toward them.

Birle drew back from the path, back into the shelter of the trees and undergrowth. She took no care to move quietly, because the approaching noise covered any sound they might make.

The noise overtook them so rapidly that she could only sink to the ground behind a tree and motion Yul down beside her. Closer came the noise, until she could hear that it was a jumble of differing sounds—feet, hundreds of feet, and hooves, voices in conversation and the clink of weapons. It

213

sounded like an army, but she couldn't see any army. She could see down to the path they had abandoned, and the army was not on that—unless it were an invisible army; an army of dead men and horses, going off to fight some long-ago war.

Laughter, a snatch of song—this was no army of the dead, if there could be such a thing. Birle scolded herself. There was danger enough to be dealt with, without creating imaginary fears. This was an army of living men, moving to present battle. It seemed to be moving beyond the path, although in the path's direction back along the way they had come. Toward Corbel's city. It didn't matter whose army it was, friend or enemy to Corbel—the whole world was enemy to escaping slaves. But at least, Birle thought, she needn't worry that they were being hunted here. Even Corbel in a fit of anger wouldn't waste an army chasing down three slaves. Yul sat bent over his burden, his eyes like a dog's in terror. "We're safe enough, or so I think. We are safe for now, Yul. Safe," she said.

Orien moved restlessly, stirring in his blanket like a moth in its cocoon. Birle put her hand on his forehead, his neck: The skin burned dry under her fingers. She could have wept for helplessness but she made herself speak softly. "Hush now, quiet now, sleep now. Hush, easy, be easy, my Lord. Good, yes, quiet now." As with Yul, it took a while for her words to penetrate.

All the long afternoon they crouched in their fear while the army passed, filling the air with heavy dragging sounds. Birle dared not move back onto the path, although she thought they might pass unnoticed. She dared not risk making the wrong choice. If the choice proved wrong, that was the end of their chance. Darkness was settling over the forest before Birle felt it was safe to move again. It might also have been safe to stay where they were, for the night, but she didn't think she could sleep so close to danger. Yul gathered up Orien, with a muted clanking of his wrist chains, and Birle once again lifted the sack onto her back. The muscles of her shoulders and back ached; it hurt to move legs stiffened by the hours of motionlessness. Birle moved her feet cautiously in the dim light, making her way back to the path.

She forced herself to keep walking, and distracted herself by thinking about the path. It must run hidden beside a broader roadway, a roadway so broad an army could march along it. Why should there be two such ways through the same forest? Unless the path had been made by those who didn't wish to be known to be traveling from the one city to the other. The bare earth under her feet gave evidence that there were many such travelers, moving into and out of Corbel's city.

Soon they walked in darkness, with no star to guide them and no moon to light the way. Birle led, slow, careful, cautious, her ears straining to catch even the smallest noise. Somewhere, off at a distance, an owl called, and that eased her. She listened for the sound of water. When they came to water they would stop. They must stop soon, in any case; she could hear Yul stumbling.

But the thought of the army behind her, moving toward battle, the thought of the way the devastation of battle might overtake them, moving swift as a forest fire—Birle made herself go on, even though she doubted the wisdom of following this path too far. This dark path must have a destination. Whatever that destination was, it was not Birle's.

Shadows moved among the crowded trees; the path ahead was a dark shadow.

When shadows around her closed in, she was too dull and tired to know her danger. Before she could draw a knife— before she quite knew what was happening—an arm across her chest and cold metal at her throat told her what had happened. From the darkness behind she heard men struggling, and incoherent sounds from Yul. "Don't drop him," she called. "Yul, can you hear me?"

A voice spoke at her ear. "I'll cut her throat, man, if you don't give it up." She almost knew the voice. "I'll kill her."

The struggling sounds ceased.

The knife's blade stayed at her throat. "That's the price paid. He is a monster though, isn't he? And what's he carrying? She's got a sack on her back but he's not carrying a sack, is he?"

"A child, it looks like," another half-familiar voice answered.

"All right then," the voice at her ear spoke. He shifted his grip on her so that his one arm hooked around her neck while the other kept the knife handy. "You'll come along with us, peaceful like. You'll do that?"

She nodded her head.

The knife pressed into her cheek. "Say it, so the monster can hear you."

"Yes," she said. Yul echoed the word.

"He'll behave himself as long as she's with me. She'll be safe with me as long as you behave yourself, monster. Do you understand me? I'll slit her throat right here if I have to."

There was a short silence, two heartbeats long, before Yul's voice came again. "Yes."

"It's not so far, lass," the voice at her ear said, and the man shoved her into movement, along the dark path.

Birle obeyed the knife and the voice. She knew what was familiar about it, even though she knew it couldn't be the same men—she had seen their hands at the marketplace, they were a year dead. These weren't the same men; but they were the same kind of men, by their voices.

It was all to begin again. Birle had led them back into captivity. But there were differences, this time; she knew more, and could estimate the dangers more accurately, and she feared less. She had a knife at her boot and she would put it into Orien's heart before she would let him be sold again.

They hadn't gone far when she saw a light among trees. As they came closer, leaving the path and crushing bushes underfoot, with no attempt at silence, she saw that the light came from a small fire. Behind the fire stood a wagon, carrying a small house on it. Shadows disguised the face of the man who stepped across the fire to greet them, but she knew him. Even though he wasn't wearing his brightly colored robe, he walked as if the small, dark clearing were an elevated platform and all the world stood below him, looking up in wonder.

Twenty

I<small>N</small> the darkness that crowded onto the clearing, the man gave his orders: "Release her. Take the child, one of you."

"Don't hurt him," Birle asked. "He's ill, he's—"

Yul growled and clutched Orien closer.

"Yul," Birle said. "Put him down. Gently, Yul."

No sooner had Yul knelt to place the blanketed figure on the ground than there was a knife at his throat. Birle shed the sack and grabbed at the arm that held the knife, and pulled back on it. The man shouldered her away. Her arm was grappled from behind, and twisted up, until the strain at her shoulder made her cry out. She couldn't think, she couldn't think at all, in the shadowy light, among strangers.

"I know you," she said to the tall man, who now stood before the fire. "I know you," she said again, not knowing why she repeated it.

"I'm sorry to hear that," he said. She couldn't hear in his voice what he was thinking; she couldn't see his face to read his nature in it.

"It's no child, Damall," a voice reported. "It's a man, bearded."

"How do you know me?" Damall asked.

"I saw you at Corbel's feast."

"She's telling the truth," the voice said. "He's in the sweats."

"What do you want of us?" Birle cried out, desperate.

Yul attempted to rise and come to her side. Birle shook

218

her head at him. "Yul? Don't let yourself be harmed, stay there. What do you want of us?" she asked Damall more quietly.

"Release her," was his answer, and her arm fell free to her side.

They hovered at the rim of the fire's light, Damall and his wonders. One of the figures was the size of a child, another like a tall birch tree: She recognized them. The wild man seemed tame now and the Emperor's Daughter wasn't there. But she could see none of them well enough to guess what kind of danger the escaping slaves had come to. Firelight made shadows out of the cloaked bodies and sent shadows like clouds over the faces, keeping their thoughts and characters secret. Aye, and she would be happier to see the Emperor's Daughter appear, she could hope that a woman might have more mercy in her heart than a man would.

"Come," Damall said, in his showman's voice and with his showman's smile. "Come sit by the fire. I can't offer you food, I'm afraid. We set off in such haste, and there is food in plenty for us at our journey's end—but come, sit, and your large companion too. Yul? Yul, come sit with us, and keep warm."

Yul left the dark shape that was Orien at the clearing's edge; Birle asked, and received, permission to tend to him. "I can use a little time to think you over," Damall said. He wanted her to be uneasy, Birle knew; he wanted to be sure that she knew their danger. "I would rather that you hadn't recognized me—what is your name?"

"Birle," she told him, looking up from where she sat with Orien's head resting on her arm while she dropped barley water into his mouth.

"Birle," Orien said. His hair was damp, his skin was damp, but his one good eye was open, and looked at her. It was so dark the eye looked black. "What—?"

"Hush, my Lord," she said, wishing to quiet him. "Drink this," she said, hoping he would hear their danger in her voice, and be guided by her judgment. "Then you'll sleep, think."

219

He must be mending, if he knew her, to call her by her name and maybe even recognize her face in the shadowed light. He didn't speak again, but neither did he close his eye. She smoothed the ointment over his blistered cheek and he flinched, but didn't protest. For all anybody watching would know, she thought, Orien was asleep in his fever.

Birle returned to the fire and sat down next to Yul. There were six of the troupe also at the fire, and Damall moved to sit next to her. Over the shoulders of those opposite her she could see their wagon, and three horses hobbled nearby. One of the horses had a lumpy, misshapen back, which must, she thought, be the necessaries they carried with them. She took in as much as she could, waiting for Damall to speak; she would need all of her wits about her. For the moment, however, she felt no danger, from Damall or his wonders.

"Birle," he said. "And Yul—a creature of prodigious size, so I am sure I've never seen him before—and the third?"

"Orien," Birle said.

"I won't harm you unless I have to," Damall reassured her. "Do you believe me?"

"Yes," Birle answered, because it was what he wished to hear. If he could say that it might be necessary to harm them, then she would be a fool to believe his reassurances; that was her thought.

"You wear the neckchain of Corbel's house," Damall said. "So I conclude that you're a slave, escaping—"

"The man wears iron, and his wrists are chained," a voice across the fire reported.

"Ah," Damall said. "That, I hadn't expected. Tell me: Who are you, and where going. If you lie I'll know it—it's only fair to warn you of that. I have friends of my own in the castle Corbel thinks is so secure."

"They won't know of me, or Yul," Birle said. "We are from the Philosopher's house."

"I'll believe that, I've heard of this Philosopher—I've a wife in the city, she spoke of him because he knew how to heal illness. Does he?"

"Aye, although not all illness." Birle was speaking one

220

hing and thinking another. Damall had ears in the city and
n the castle, and he dared to light a fire close to where a
road army must be camped. He would be a spy then, for
Celinde's father, perhaps. At the least, he would have friends
n that army. He would then be no friend to Corbel.

"Where's the Philosopher now? What did you do? Did
ou murder him?"

"We did nothing. He's fled the city—against the coming
var."

"I doubt Corbel gave his brother permission to be gone."

"You know that they're brothers?" Birle asked. Damall
lidn't seem reluctant to talk, and the more she knew about
im the better her chances of winning their release. Or, she
varned herself, the worse their chances.

"I've taken my wonders to the castle, many times in the
ast year. The Little Mistress often asks for us, and Corbel
leases her, and himself too, in this. My little company has
raveled the roads freely."

Why would such a thing please Corbel, Birle wondered,
nd had the answer before she had completed the question:
Damall brought Corbel news of Celinde's father; Damall was
Corbel's spy among the enemy. If she was correct, then
Damall was playing a dangerous game.

Damall stared into the fire, listening intently to discover
ll that voice could tell him about her. Birle asked him a
question of her own. "Where is the lady, the Emperor's
Daughter?"

Damall chuckled, pleased to answer, "Right here." He
ointed to the man at his side.

"But—"

"People would rather see a lady in captivity than a man,
nd they would most like to see a lady of the highest birth,
n Emperor's Daughter."

Now that Birle leaned forward and looked carefully, she
ould see the broad cheekbones and curiously angled eyes,
nd note how slight he was, for a man. "Is he the Emperor's
on?" she asked.

"Any man—take him far enough from his home, let him

221

be strange enough to the world he walks through''—this was Damall's showman's voice speaking—''and he'll be a prince. Or princess. The world would have things so.''

Damall was a man in love with danger.

''Where are you going, Birle?'' he asked in his ordinary voice.

''Northward.''

''Now I know the direction. And I think you know that no city lies northward. There's nothing but unmapped forest there, and mountains too, they say. But when they talk in the same breath of the snow dragon who roams the mountain—freezing men to stone with his breath—then I believe everything they tell me. Why would you go into such country?''

''It's the land I came from. I would return to the Kingdom.'' To name it was a risk, but she judged the risk worth taking.

He turned to study her face. ''The Kingdom,'' he echoed. ''Are you a bold liar, Birle?''

''If I were to lie I'd be as bold as I dared, but this isn't a lie.''

''I've heard that in the Kingdom, the entertainers are honored and wealthy men. That there are fairs, twice yearly, where coins can always be taken. There the great princes dine with entertainers.''

Birle answered carefully. ''If we speak of the same Kingdom, life is as hard for entertainers there as it is here. And as easy.''

''Are you a great lady in the Kingdom, Birle?'' He was mocking her.

''I was the Innkeeper's daughter.''

''No slave then, nor servant.''

She didn't say anything.

''And Orien, what is he? Husband? Brother? Sweetheart, and you are the old song—the maid who travels untold distances to rescue her beloved from dungeons where he is kept awaiting a ransom his brother will not pay.''

Birle thought the truth would please Damall. ''In his own

land, Orien is a Lord. By birth he is one of two Earls who serve the King.''

Damall smiled. "And you?''

"I serve him.''

As if preferring his own ideas, Damall asked her no more. "And Yul?''

"Yul was also a slave in the Philosopher's house.''

"I'll believe that, he accompanied you to the marketplace. My wife thought I might like to purchase him. Gentle-tempered, she said, if simple.''

Birle said nothing.

"I thought at the time that I would like at least to clap my eyes upon this man-monster. Little did I think he would come to find me.''

Birle said nothing.

"And Orien, did he also serve in the Philosopher's house?''

"No, he didn't have the luck. He belonged to two crafts-men, first, then to one of them when the other put himself into apprenticeship. Then he was sold to the mines.''

Damall's teeth gleamed in the firelight. "And you rescued him?''

"No, he escaped.''

"Then he's one of the few ever to do so.''

"They said none ever had.''

"Do you believe, then, whatever anyone says to you? I'll tell you what I believe. I believe that if I had the luck, and the wits, and the courage and strength to get free of that place—I'd not return to the city to boast of it. Doubt what they say, whatever they say.''

"Aye, I do,'' Birle assured him, with a smile she couldn't conceal. Birle's smile answered his own and she told him, "Even what you tell me, that too I doubt.''

Again he laughed for pleasure. Under this laughter, Birle thought more boldly. It might be, after all, that she could win them free.

"Will you marry me, Birle?'' he asked.

"Aye, but you have a wife.''

"Aye,'' he mocked her, "but I have two wives. A man

223

should not be without a woman to comfort him, and pleasure him, a man should have home and bed to go to, wherever he might be going. And you are a fair lady by firelight. Of course, all ladies are fair by firelight," he said, mocking both her and himself.

But he would wed her, if she said yes, even though there was no hunger to fear in his eyes. "No," she said.

"Because of the man you serve, because of Orien," Damall guessed.

Birle didn't answer.

"I would like to know this man. If he lives, I would be interested in sharing his company, learning how a man earns such faithfulness from a woman. But that doesn't solve our problem. What am I to do with you three? How do I know you aren't Corbel's spies, sent to test my loyalty. How, I might wonder—if I were inclined to doubt even you—how did three such unsecret travelers make their way out of that guarded city? How did you manage to avoid the army that marches down on it?"

"Luck," Birle told him. "And fear, turned to our own uses."

"You couldn't buy your freedoms of me," he suggested, with regret.

The coins were sewn into the waist of her skirt, and Birle almost thought to risk it. But if Damall knew she had coins, he would see her differently. Now he saw her as bold and weaponless, and that he approved. To admit to having coins— she judged that a risk as perilous as drawing her knife from her boot. She clamped her jaw shut, and said nothing.

"Not that I have anything against letting you go free—if I knew beyond doubt that you speak true of yourselves."

There was no way Birle could convince him of that.

Damall stood up. Without warning, he rose to his full height, and held down a hand to lift her to her feet. Birle preferred to meet her fortune standing up, so she took the hand. "In the meantime," the Showman said, "let's have these chains off you. Two of them are gold and the third must be heavy to bear. Friend Ling, bring me the shears, and a

224

hammer for the man's chains. You three are a question that will be answered before daybreak, but even if I must kill you here you need not die slaves.''

If she was going to die, Birle didn't see that it made much difference. ''Besides,'' she pointed out, ''gold is gold, melted down so none can say where it came from.''

Again Damall laughed, and answered her with mockery. ''Do you doubt me?''

The slight man went to the sumpter beast, which was tethered beside the two horses that pulled the wagon by day. He reached into a saddlebag and returned to the fire. The hammer he gave to the strong man, while he approached Birle with a pair of long-handled shears held out before him. She held her long braid aside as she knelt before him with bowed head.

Not until she felt its absence did she understand how the band had weighed upon her. At her own insistence, Birle herself cut the band from Yul's neck, while the hammer rang on Orien's iron chains. For all that he lay quietly, without the restlessness of high fever, Orien didn't waken.

When the operations were completed, they stood silent. The fire crackled. The seated men seemed to sleep where they sat. Yul waited in patience at Birle's side. Orien slept.

''I'd like to let you go free,'' Damall said. ''But I lack a guarantee. I'd feel better if I had a guarantee.''

''A promise is not enough,'' Birle said, to let him know that she didn't hope for that but to suggest it to him, in case he hadn't thought of it.

He shook his head. ''A promise is made of air. That's too light a matter to carry the weight of a guarantee, don't you agree?''

He waited, but Birle had no other suggestion to make. She waited, to hear his terms.

''If, on the other hand, one of you stayed on with me . . . and the other two knew that he, or she, stood at hazard? Then, even a cautious man like myself might feel safe.''

Quick as a rabbit fleeing the fox, Birle's mind considered the possibilities. ''I can't carry Orien, and he is too weak to

225

walk. Yet he needs the medicine I know how to give him, if he is to live.''

"I can't keep all three of you, that's too risky, entirely too risky. Besides, I have no use for you.''

"Although you might for Yul,'' Birle said.

"You follow me most precisely.'' Damall smiled. "I can see it—a human tower, he's quite strong enough—and Jacko on the very top, or perhaps Ling? That's a show that would draw people to it, don't you think?''

Birle didn't think she could abandon Yul, just go away and leave him behind. She didn't know why she shouldn't—there was no argument to convince her she shouldn't, and many to let her do what her mind told her was the only choice she had. Yul sat huge at her feet. He didn't understand what was going on, the twin dangers that threatened them. How could she hesitate to save herself and Orien, two out of three, just because Yul was the price to be paid?

"You have one more horse than you need,'' she told Damall, who was growing restless with waiting for her decision. Birle knew that if all three stayed here, then he must get rid of them all.

"Horses are valuable, even a sorry nag like that one.''

"You have two gold chains in your hands, more than the price of a war-horse,'' Birle pointed out. "Orien could be carried on horseback.'' Even while she tried to think of some other way, Birle knew she had no other choice. "If it must be,'' she said. "Yul will stay. You must promise—when I return for him, you must promise to give him up to me.''

She had surprised him, but he masked it quickly. "Of course, yes, of course, when you return for him. I agree.''

He didn't think ever to see her again. "Are you a man of your word?'' she asked him.

"When I can be, yes, I like to be.'' His smile mocked her. "Of course gold, or jewels, or—profit always makes it easier to keep my word. On the other hand, you don't have to doubt the care I'll take of him. My wife, the one I go to now, not the one I left behind yesterday, keeps a rich farm. He'll be quiet enough there, and well fed when we aren't on

226

the road. I take my wonders up and down the coast,'' he
added. ''The three great cities of the coast keep me and my
wonders. I can be found at any season in one or the other of
the cities—once this war is finished, as it will be soon, one
way or the other. I tell you that so you'll know how to find
Yul. When you come back for him.''

Birle didn't think he would have agreed so readily if he'd
thought she would return to claim his prize from him. She
wondered at herself, to think that she was selling Yul into
further slavery, and the price paid to her her own freedom.
She wondered that she could so quickly change from slave
to slave trader.

And she hoped she had judged rightly. She judged it was
all live or all die—at Damall's pleasure. Her choice was based
on that judgment.

''If you wait until he falls asleep, then you can leave quietly,'' Damall suggested.

Now Birle was surprised. ''Leave without telling him?''

''Don't be a fool, girl.'' Damall seemed at last out of
patience with the game. ''Ling, let's unload the sumpter
beast. If the girl is actually going to leave, she'll want to do
so at first light. If she doesn't—we'll need shovels to dig
graves. Women,'' he said, for Birle to hear, ''girls. A man
would rather sleep and they make him dig graves.''

Birle laughed. Then she turned to Yul, and stopped laughing. She didn't know how to explain to the simple man what
was going to happen, so that he might understand it and not
be afraid. Yul stood, like a small hill, still as a hill. Even in
sunlight his face couldn't be read like that of an ordinary
man. In firelight she had no hope to know what he was thinking. But Yul was smiling, and the sight of his shadowy, sweet
smile almost made her turn around to tell Damall that he'd
better dig his graves after all.

''Yul will stay. With the man,'' Yul said.

Birle couldn't speak.

''Birle will come back—if she lives,'' Yul said, still smiling.

''The man's name is Damall,'' she told him.

"Dam-all," Yul repeated obediently.

"He's an entertainer, like the puppeteers, remember? Only Damall doesn't show puppets, he shows people who are strange-looking, like you. If you will stay, there will be people staring at you. You'll be up on a platform, with these others, and people will stare at you."

Yul thought about that and at last he said, "Yes."

"Because Orien is sick I have to take him with me."

"To the Kingdom," Yul said.

"Yes. Can you wait? A long time, maybe, many summers and winters."

"Yul can wait."

"Damall says he will treat you well, and I think he will. But Yul, hear me. If he doesn't—if he is cruel, if you are hungry—then you must take your hands and crush his head. Do you understand?"

"Forewarned," Damall spoke. She had forgotten he might hear. But he was amused, not alarmed. "Forewarned is forearmed," he said, "but it won't come to that, I think. I'm not a bad man, Birle. I care well for my investments, my wonders. And there's no murder in your giant's heart, I think."

"There's more in Yul's heart than any of us guess, that's my thought," Birle told him.

"I'll believe that, yes. The hearts of men—who would ever dare to guess at them. Now women, their hearts are easier to see," Damall answered. "I've always been an admirer of women's hearts."

Birle understood then why he was letting her go, with Orien. It would profit him, however it turned out, that was true; but she thought it also suited him to send the two of them off, into unknown perils, to fail or succeed together, like sweethearts. She didn't disabuse him. And he wasn't, after all, more than half wrong.

They slept what hours of the night were left and were up and about before daybreak. In the dim light before sunrise, the tiny clearing in the trees seemed crowded with people. There was no breakfast, so once she had given Orien the barley water—laced with a drop of dwale, that he might sleep

228

the day away—and anointed his face, Birle and Yul hoisted him over the horse's back, and tied him there so that he couldn't tumble off.

Birle made her farewell to Damall, who bowed from the waist before her, causing her to laugh despite her sadness. At last she stood in front of Yul. "Pick me up, Yul," she asked. His huge hands lifted her until her face was level with his own. Her feet hung useless, but it wasn't her feet she thought of. She put a hand on the side of Yul's face and made him her promise. "Friend," she said. "You are my friend."

"Yes," Yul answered, with a smile that lingered, forgotten on his face long after he had put her down again.

She shouldered her sack, and Damall put the horse's lead into her hand. "Maybe, after all, we'll follow you to the Kingdom," he said. "It would save you the long journey back."

"The Kingdom has no employment for spies who serve two masters," she answered. Damall did not fear her—aye, and why should he?—but it would benefit Yul if Damall knew what she understood, and that she might, at her choice, with luck, be a danger to him.

Damall welcomed the risk. "Then I'd have no livelihood," he told her, laughing. "Go now, Birle, before I decide that I can't bear to part with you."

The sun, rising in the east, gave her direction. She led the horse off to the north, stepping into the pathless forest without a backward glance, her sack heavy on her back.

Part Three

The
Earl's
Lady

Twenty-one

As long as the sun rode in the east, Birle could be sure of her direction, even through this trackless forest where the land underfoot rose and fell sharply. They made slow and twisting progress, she with her sack on her back and the horse's lead rope in her hand, the horse with its limp burden. She kept the sun at her shoulder. Thus they moved always farther from the seacoast, and the cities of the coast.

At midmorning they halted. She dragged Orien down, to lay him on the ground with her cloak spread beneath him and his blanket over him. She poured water by drops into his mouth, then wiped clean the side of his face to cover it again with the ointment. At least he no longer smelled like rotting meat. Now he smelled sharply of garlic, which she hoped was an improvement for him. Certainly she preferred it.

All across the middle of the day, they rested. Orien slept fitfully. The horse, tied to a low tree branch, grazed the forest floor. Birle tried to sleep, but could not—for listening to the forest sounds, should any of them signal danger. She was listening not only for sounds she might hear, but also for the kind of silence through which they had gone yesterday, the silence that pooled out around a moving army.

Her plan was simple, and immediate: to go deep into the forest, deep enough so that no matter what happened in the world, they would be safe. There they would stay, for however long it took for Orien to heal, and regain his strength. That particular day, her task was to be sure they kept the right direction, to care for Orien, and to remember that—however ill he was—he lived.

When the sun began to slide down the western part of the sky, she hefted and shoved Orien back over the horse's back, shouldered her own sack, untied the horse, and they went on, with the sun at her left shoulder. They halted again at twilight, but only until the stars came out. Nighttime progress was even more slow than daytime, but always, Birle knew, they were moving away.

They stopped at last, high on a rocky hill. Once again, Birle gave Orien medicine and covered him with a blanket, tied the horse and thought of sleep. The distant sky glowed orange, like dawn. Except that dawn didn't paint the western sky, midway through the night. For a minute Birle was too afraid—was the edge of the world aflame?—to understand that most likely the city was in flames. Whose army was burning it, she neither knew nor cared. Orien was safe away, Yul was under Damall's care, if the city burned what was that to her?

But thinking of it, imagining the crowds of the city trapped between river and wall—the fishmonger and her children, the young woman who would have kept Orien from the mines if she'd had coins, the entertainers, and even the guildsmen, and even the soldiers—aye, if that was the city, and if it was going up into flames, all that would be left would be the spike in the marketplace, and the stone walls, and she did care.

The second night, when she climbed up a tree and looked back to the west and south, the horizon lay dark. Orien slept deeply, quietly; Birle hoped it was a healing sleep, not a continuation of the dwale-induced sleep into which she put him for travel. His head was not cool but it no longer heated her hand like a flame. For the first time since leaving the city, Birle felt hungry. She cut herself some bread and cheese, gave herself a little of the water from the bag she had filled at the well in the Philosopher's faraway house, and slept.

They came the next morning to a small clearing where

234

three huge boulders rose up from the earth, two side by side and the third facing. Between them, a little stream rolled down the hillside. There, Birle thought they might stay. The boulders stood like walls, to protect. The ground was soft with moss. Although no fish would live in so small a stream, the little clearing and the forest around would provide some food, when the bread and cheese gave out.

She pulled Orien down from the horse's back. She hobbled the mare's front legs and turned her free to graze. Then she looked around her, to determine what needed doing first. Sunlight spattered over the boulders and rode down the stream.

"Birle," Orien said.

She crouched where he could see her, should his eyes open. "We're going to rest here, until you're well, my Lord," she said. She didn't know if he understood her.

"I keep—I'm here, and then I'm gone away elsewhere," he said, but whether in apology or complaint she couldn't tell.

"Sleep, my Lord," she said. "Sleep."

"But—" He struggled to raise his head. The eye on the blistered side of his face could now open fully, she noticed. Aye, and she didn't know what she had to be smiling about. She pushed him gently down onto the soft ground. "Sleep, my Lord."

He obeyed her.

The first thing Birle did was to lie on her stomach, and drink her fill of the icy waters. Then she set to work.

She built a circle of stones, for a fire, and gathered small branches to start it, then larger pieces of wood to keep it fed. She walked twenty paces into the trees behind the third boulder, and with a stick and her fingers she dug a trench for a privy. She spread out the contents of her sack, food and medicines, the cooking pot, the spoons she had taken from the Philosopher's cupboard, and the mortar and pestle. The clothing, including the boots she'd purchased that last day at market, she left in the sack.

Birle didn't have the skill to build a shelter, with roof

235

and walls. But for the time, the season was favorable—warm days, and the chill of nights easily kept at bay by a fire. It was early summer, with warmer days and nights to come.

That night by the fire, Birle thought of Yul, and her thoughts troubled her. But she had made him her promise, which she would keep if she could. Yul trusted her. He was right to trust her, she knew. What she didn't know was if she was right to trust Damall, and all she could do was hope the man's sense of where his profit lay would keep him honest.

For the time, being able to do nothing about Yul, she dealt with Orien. She bathed him, warming the water in the cooking pot, gently removing all of his clothes, using the cloths for her woman's times—aye, he'd never know so it wouldn't embarrass him, and the cloths were soft and clean. She bathed him as if he were a baby, and could have wept to see how little flesh lay over his bones. But she didn't weep. She dressed him in one of Joaquim's fine, soft shirts and a pair of Yul's trousers, which she had cut off short. Even drawn close at the waist, the trousers fit Orien like a skirt.

When she had done, and he was back on his cloth pallet, under the blanket, his eyes opened. "Where is Yul?" he asked. "I seem to remember—" He slept again before he could say what he remembered.

The fever left him gradually, as a fire burns itself out. Some mornings he was cool to the touch, and the fever seemed to have gone; but by midday it would have returned, although not so hot as before. Orien coughed sharply, and his breathing was harsh. Birle fed him what he could eat. She had found in the woods nearby an abundance of marshmallow, with the roots of last year's growth thick beneath their dried stalks. These she brewed into a soup, into which she dipped crustless pieces of bread for Orien. The broth both nourished him and eased his cough. When he was well enough to sit up for part of the day, and to willfully walk alone to the privy, she knew that however long the healing took, he would be healed—even though he returned pale and shaking with weakness from the short walk into the trees.

Orien slept, days and nights, and Birle foraged for wood and food. She was glad of the weather. It rained seldom, and then gently. Most days the sun shone down warm. In woods and meadow food plants grew abundantly—early onion, the tall marshmallow, fat garlic bulbs beneath their slender shoots, and the piss-a-beds that sprang up wherever sunlight touched the ground, as if they would soon cover the whole floor of the world with their ragged long leaves and bright, hairy-headed yellow flowers. The horse grew fat with grazing.

There came a day when Orien returned from the privy and did not immediately fall down exhausted on his pallet. Instead, he sat back against the boulder. "Where are we, Birle?"

She was surprised at the question. For more days than she had counted, he had spoken only of thirst, and sleepiness, the need to visit the privy, and sometimes hunger. "My Lord?"

"Where are we?" he repeated. "Where is this place that you've brought me to?" Her surprise pleased him.

His question pleased her. "Three days north of the city. We're safely away, in an uninhabited forest—if I can believe what I was told."

"And where are we going?" he asked.

"North, and east," she said.

"North and east?"

It wasn't that he didn't understand her words. His eyes shone in his face and his mouth twitched with laughter he wouldn't let out.

"To the Kingdom," she said.

"To the Kingdom," he echoed.

"Aye, my Lord, with luck."

"With luck." Then he smiled, saying to her, "Birle, you have a smile like a girl with a glad secret at her breast, you have a smile that Spring must wear—I can see the lady Spring come creeping to the edge of winter, and looking over the landscape she's about to take from winter—with that smile upon her face. A minx's smile, Birle."

"Aye, my Lord." She laughed.

"You used to know my name," he said. "Shall we be on our way?"

"On our way where?" It was as if Orien had left her a sick man and returned from the trees a well one.

"Why north, and east. To the Kingdom. Home," Orien said.

"But you can't, not yet. You can't try the journey until you've regained your strength, because we don't know what lies ahead."

"There's the horse. I could ride."

"No, Orien," Birle said.

The eyes danced like bellflowers under a summer breeze. "You didn't used to be so cautious, Birle. You were—quite hasty, when we first met. So you've learned that hastiness leads to grief. Do you regret having been so hasty?"

"Not now, I don't. Not at this time, in this place. But I have, at other times and places in between, and so I think must you have."

"Yes," he said, all laughter gone from his face. Then he smiled again. "But, like you, not now. So I'll be patient, if I must, and regain my strength, as you tell me to do. I'll obey you in this, Birle."

"Aye, and you'd be foolish not to," she told him.

Oddly, it was when his body was healed that Orien's sleep grew troubled. During the day he would do what work he could with the strength he had. He kept the fire, watched over the pungent broth, and went for walks into the woods, to find fuel and to train his legs to their former strength. During the day he kept busy. But at night, with only sleep to occupy him, he turned and muttered, sometimes whimpering, sometimes in anger, sometimes with sounds like the beggars in the marketplace.

His distress wakened Birle, who sat silent, to wait out the time of nightmare and be sure he slept quiet again. One night, however, he screamed—like a pig being slaughtered—and she rushed over to where he lay screaming, to shake his shoulders until he woke up.

He sat up, completely awake, and wiped at his face with his hands.

"What is it?" she asked him. Her heart drummed from the sound of his voice, screaming into the night, so she could imagine how much worse he felt. He had seen the dream; she had only heard its effect on him.

Orien shook his head. He wouldn't answer her.

"Can you go back to sleep?"

He shook his head. His face looked pale, and he shivered in the warm summer night. If he had been a child, she would have gathered him into her arms and rocked him into restful sleep. But he was Orien, so she directed his attention to the stars that burned white in the sky beyond the black mass of boulder. "The Plough is there, four stars and then three for the handle, can you see it?" After a while, the voice in which he asked his questions grew thick and sleepy.

In the morning, he still refused to speak of his nightmares—as if he was ashamed. Neither would he speak of his life in the city, although he questioned her about hers, and about their escape, and about the Showman. Birle told him only part of the truth. "Yul chose to stay, with others of his own kind. Damall traded the horse for the man."

They had some variety in their food—berries and nuts, and fat peas to cook in with the greens and roots—now that summer filled the forest with ripeness. They made a game out of what food they wished most to have, if they could have any food they wished. Would it be duck, chicken, or meat? Perhaps a cheese, but if so should it be toasted over the fire? Although there was much Orien would never speak of, it seemed to Birle they were always talking. His tongue healed to its full strength long before the rest of him, she complained. "How else would I talk with you?" he asked, as if that were a sensible question.

Orien walked longer, as his strength returned. He would be gone for the space of the morning, or the length of the afternoon. Then one afternoon he returned with two silver fish, one in each of his hands, his fingers hooked into their gills.

Birle didn't know what to say. He was always surprising her. His smile was like the sun shining out of his thick brown beard, and if he hadn't been Orien, returned to health, she would have thought he looked entirely too pleased with himself.

"I found a lake," he announced. She tried to remember when she had last seen him look so proud, in that tall-standing way, or if she ever had. "Birle? It's not so very far—will you let me show it to you? It's filled with fish so eager to be eaten that I had only to stand in the water"—he lifted a wet leg to show her—"and explain how welcome one or two would be to us, if they could bring themselves to the sacrifice."

Birle laughed out loud, at the fish they would eat and the gladness in his eyes.

"Lady," Orien said, "I lay these at your feet." He went onto his knees before her.

Birle understood his teasing game, as if they were puppets performing on a stage. "My Lord," she answered, "I thank you for the gift."

"And with them, I plight you my troth," he said.

"Aye, my Lord, and there is no need for mockery."

"Aye, my Lady, and I do not mock you."

Birle knew she ought to look away from his eyes, for she saw in them the hunger she had learned to fear, and it was also longing. Or maybe what she saw was longing, which was also hunger. She ought to take her own eyes away, she knew, and look at the boulder, or the running stream, look away—but she didn't. She couldn't, and she didn't want to.

"I would have you for my wife, Birle," Orien said. "Will you have me for husband?"

She had no heart for this game of his. "Get up, Orien. I'll teach you how to scale and gut a fish."

He obeyed her but she didn't know what it was he saw in her own face, and eyes, that made him look at her so. "There's inequality between us, my Lord," she reminded him, since he seemed to have forgotten.

"Aye, there is, and ever has been. You gave me your heart and I gave you nothing in return, so now I give you mine—and we are equal."

He had deliberately misunderstood her.

"You will not say me no, Birle."

The word was on her lips. She knew that no was what she ought to say. But she chose to obey his will. "No I will not," she said. "I will say yes to you, and gladly."

When he clasped her into his arms, she couldn't tell if it was her own heart beating so fast that she heard, or his. He spoke above her head, and she couldn't see his face. "I will be your husband, Birle."

She answered in kind. "I will be your wife, Orien."

Then he stepped back, to take her by the hand. "Do you know what a lake is, Birle? Come on, come with me. A lake is not merely where fish can be caught, it's also a bath. Larger than we're used to, and colder too than most, but still a bath. Would you like a bath, Birle?" he asked, laughing. "Did you ever think, Lady, my heart, how sweet the body is when it's clean—like meadows washed by rain, and the sweet, clean earth. I would be so for you. You don't need to fear me, Birle," he promised her. But Birle was not afraid.

When he came to her as a man does to a woman, she was not surprised to find in herself a hunger that matched his.

Nothing changed between them yet everything had changed. They lingered in the forest, neither one eager to leave. They slept on one pallet, as man and wife, and

241

Orien didn't often dream. When he did, Birle knew now how to comfort him, aye, and soothe him more than words could. She also had now the will to make him tell her what the dreams were. In the telling, the dreams began to return to the dark places from which his memory had dragged them.

She learned the chance of his escape, by the good luck of the brand infecting. Seeing this, the soldiers had kept him aside among others who were also too weak with sickness or infection to go back into the mines. If he lived, they would use him. If he died, they would bury him. The soldiers thought he was too weak to escape—and so he was, but he crawled away anyway, and crawled on in a shallow ditch that ran beside the cart track until he couldn't remember what he had done. He couldn't walk, but he braced himself up with a stick, and walked. He remembered walking so, but he thought it might have been a dream. "It was like being consumed by flames that froze," Orien told her.

Birle didn't wish to know these things. When he spoke them, he gave them to her in a way that made them her own, as if it were her own fingers that had been twisted in the carpenter's vise for punishment. "I learned the craft quickly," he said, his voice low at the memory. The memory, and the shame, were hers now too, as if she too had begged weeping to be fed, had sat sewing from sunup to sunset, her legs crossed beneath her until any movement was pain.

At the branding, two soldiers would hold the man down while the third stood above him—waiting, waiting—then slowly lowering an iron that shone red-hot—until the slave screamed and screamed and screamed—first in terror, then in pain. The branding lay in Birle's memory now, as it lay in Orien's. It seemed they must both carry it, otherwise the burden would be unbearable.

There came a day when they both knew, without a word between them, that it was time to travel on. "The season is

242

changing," Orien said, and Birle agreed. "It would be wise to be in the Kingdom before winter."

"If we can find it," Birle said.

"I think we can, although I've no good reason for thinking that," Orien told her. "And you think the same, for no better reason. Why do you smile, Birle?"

"Because," she said. "Because—I've sympathy now for the goats in their season, billy and nanny—and for men and women too." As he laughed she answered his question. "It would be better to have shelter over us, when winter comes. Shall we leave in the morning, Orien?"

Perhaps because they never doubted, their journey was easy, and they took it at ease. Sometimes Orien rode the horse with Birle walking beside, sometimes Birle rode while he walked, sometimes they rode together. That, however, they did seldom, because the sack was heavy for the horse, and it seemed harsh to add the weight of two people. They crossed a range of steep hills. When they came to a river they followed it north, until they found a ford. After that they went directly east for a few days, to correct their direction. Birle didn't think they were in any danger of arriving unaware upon the port. Her guess was that they would come, at some time, to the great river that ran into the forest, where the Falcon's Wing was. "How will we recognize the river?" Orien asked.

"I'll know it," Birle promised him.

As they traveled north and east, the year traveled on into autumn. Nights grew longer and colder. Even at midday, a chill lay in the forest shades. Then, one morning, they crested a hill to see a broad, grassy meadow spread down a hillside, with forest again at its foot.

Orien put his hand on Birle's arm. "Look." He pointed.

Birle looked. From the elevation, a thick forest spread out, rising and falling as the land beneath rose high, then fell. In the far distance, the horizon was a jagged line.

"The mountains," Orien said. "Those are the mountains,

and this will be the forest beyond Northgate's city. We're home, Birle.''

Standing beside him, Birle caught his excitement. The distant mountains shone white in the sunlight. She didn't doubt his word, even though she'd never seen this part of the Kingdom.

"Let's finish this journey, Lady," Orien said to her.

Twenty-two

$\mathbb{N}$ow it was Orien who set the direction, without need of sun or stars to guide him. They traveled from the first light of day until darkness had settled heavily down over them. He gave little time to gathering food, and they went to sleep hungry. On the third day they stood at Northgate's city. The stone walls were bathed in the golden light of the lowering sun.

Orien reached over to take her hand. "Shall I go in and buy some food? Bread, Birle, and meat, or chicken?"

"You're bearded, and you're poorly dressed," she warned him.

His laughter rang out. "Poorly dressed? Birle, I'm the shabbiest man in the whole Kingdom. But, we have no coins to pay for food."

"Aye, but we do." It was good to be able to surprise him, for a change. "Sewn into my skirt."

Birle used the time he was gone to take the remaining coins from their hiding place. Orien returned to spread a feast before her—a tall, round pastry, filled with meat and fowl, a jug of cider, and new apples. He told her the news. "The fair is recently over and the inns prepare now for Hearing Day, for the custom that brings. I hadn't thought your coin would cause such talk."

"What did you say, then?" Birle asked, reaching over to take the jug from his hand, and drink from it.

"I said I'd gotten it from one of the merchants, when I

245

bought a piece of cloth from him. I described that cloth most carefully, do you want to hear what it was like?''

''No,'' she said. ''Did they believe you?''

''Why shouldn't they?''

''Because it isn't true,'' she pointed out. ''Because you don't look the kind of man to have coins to spend. I think I wouldn't have believed you.''

''But you've grown doubtful. Before,''—he didn't need to specify before what—''you would have believed me, if only because you wanted to. Aye, they didn't entirely believe me either, although they lacked the courage to question me. The people are not fools. If it isn't birth, Birle, that makes a man a Lord, to rule over the people, what is it? Here, in the Kingdom, I am a Lord—and because the eldest born I am the Earl, though Gladaegal is more fitted to the place. And if it is not to be birth, then not just a younger son but any man of the people might rule, and maybe rule better than the Lords. And if that might be, and maybe even should be, how do you determine what boys will become such men, and prepare them for the work? That's if the Lords would ever give over their power, which I don't think they ever will. Did you never wonder, Birle?''

''So you didn't tell anyone who you are,'' she asked.

He was a dark shape close beside her. She couldn't see his face. ''I thought—I don't know what I thought. I couldn't think. I wouldn't know what to answer, were anyone to ask me who I am. Even if I wished to answer truly. Can you say who you are?'' Orien asked her. ''Now?''

She knew what he meant; he meant now, after everything that has happened to you. Birle thought she knew her answer—she was his Lady. His betrothed. His wife that would be. But even as she thought her answer, pictures rose in her mind. The places where that person stood—his Lady, his betrothed, his wife to be—was hidden in shadows. She couldn't see herself there, giving shape to the place. Birle was glad of the darkness that hid her face from Orien.

''When you talk of the city, Birle, and the house, and of Joaquim, it always sounds to me as if—you could have been contented, there, for all of your days. The Philosopher's amanuensis. I could be jealous."

He was mocking, but there was something behind his mockery. "I was often contented, my Lord. Even though . . . There was work to be done and I was the one who did it. Who could do it," she explained. "So to be a slave, and worse, to be Corbel's slave in a world Corbel ruled, that was only part of it. There was you, too. I couldn't rest easy— even contented I couldn't be easy when I thought—"

"That at least was easy for me. Until that day I saw you— remember? Until that day I didn't dare to think of you. Then when I saw you—you looked so proud, and clean, and fat with good food, and—you smiled as if all the world's ill were just a mischief. I couldn't wish you ill, Birle, but I wished you ill."

"Aye," she remembered, "and you spoke me ill too, and bitterly. But you made a good parting."

She couldn't see his face in the darkness.

"So you did well by me."

"How could a man wish ill to the lady who has his heart? Unless it is because she holds it, and how can he then but do well by her?" He gave her no time for answer, and Birle had no answer to give. "I don't know what has happened, at home," he said. "Grandfather was ill, my brother was to wed—if we travel quickly, we can arrive on Hearing Day. If we can arrive then, I'll see—something of how things are."

"You'd better take these, then," Birle said, putting the four silver coins into his hand. "Among the people, the man would carry the coins."

"I've no purse to carry them in," he protested.

"Aye, you slip them into your boots," she told him.

They traveled long days and long into the nights. They slept in inn yards or on the grass at the roadside. The horse grew lean again. The journey became, for Birle, a succession of days that flowed like a river. There were inns—the Ram's Head, where the Innkeeper had hair the color of flames, and his wife's apple pastry was so good Birle ate herself sick on it; the Running Bear, where the Innkeeper's wife came to sit with them and look at Orien with hunger in her eyes so brazen that her husband sent her to the kitchen; the Pig's Ear, with its bitter ale; the King's Arms, where a man lay drunk across the doorstep; the Priest and Soldier, which was famous for roasted duckling. There was the King's city, which seemed small to her after the greater city where she had lived the last year and more. There were people they met and passed every day, faces and questions, names, whole lives she touched, in the way that one wave touches another before both move on. They went always on foot now, she and Orien, with the sumpter beast behind them. Their story was that Orien was a groom, delivering himself and the horse to one of the southern Lords. Even with that story told, there were those who looked at the two strangers as if they might be other than they claimed.

On the ninth day of their journey, with the sun hovering overhead and a cold wind blowing down from the mountains, they came to a castle that had been built on a mound rising up from the broad plain. A narrow river wound beside them. The castle, with its city spread around it like a lady's skirts, was the stronghold of the Earls of Sutherland.

Orien led her along the packed dirt streets of the city, then through the broad gateway into the castle yard, where a guard said only "You're late, best hurry," and to a building as long as three stables laid end-to-end. He tied the horse among the other horses at a railing there, leaving the sack on her back. Birle followed him through the doorway.

The high-ceilinged room was crowded with people. Orien stepped along the back wall, with Birle beside him. "Hearing Day," Orien whispered, "was started in my great-grandfather's time."

The hall had a platform built at one end of it, taking up a quarter of the room. On the platform, lined up on benches, sat many Lords. On a carved chair at the front, a dark young man leaned forward. His clean-shaved face marked him as a Lord, his place marked him as the Earl. Below, with all of the Earl's attention on him, stood a sturdy man of full years.

"That's the Advocate, who speaks for the people. He presents the cases. Have you been to Hearing Days?"

"The Inn is too far away, the village had no quarrels we couldn't settle among ourselves rather than make the journey to the Earl's castle." But even as she explained this to Orien, the Falcon's Wing seemed to Birle to be something she barely remembered, something she had heard about once in a story.

Orien spoke to an old man who sat on the benches set against the wall for those too weak to stand for the long day. "A farmer asked a girl to wed, and then at the fair he said he would not have her," he told Birle. "Her father brought the case, claiming that the farmer has found a bride with a larger dowry. They're waiting for the decision."

The whole room waited, with quiet conversations. The Earl, in his green shirt with a wide-winged golden falcon sewn on it, at last stood up before his chair. "The man," he said, "must give this girl five gold pieces, for her shame, and he must also wed her—if she will have him. For she might not wish to put her life into the hands of a man who would shame her so. Furthermore," he went on, in a cold voice that carried to all the ends of the great hall, "the man must also give his second betrothed five gold pieces, for he has dishonored her as much as the first. Her he may wed, be he free, if she will have a man capable of such deceit."

This was a heavy sentence. Even the wealthiest of farmers took years to amass ten gold pieces, after he had paid his taxes to the Earl. It seemed to Birle that if neither girl would have him now, this man might never marry, and she wondered if the Earl too had thought of that.

The Earl sat down again. "Next case," the Advocate called. This was a plea brought by a weaver, who said he had paid his seven silver coins for taxes to the Steward, but the Steward had come back after only three days to say he'd only paid five of them, and to demand the other two. The Steward was not at the Hearing Day, but his Lord was. The Lord said that five was the number written down as paid, in the long book. The Advocate reported that the man's wife, and three neighbors who were after him in line, all swore that he had paid seven. Because they couldn't read, they couldn't say what the Steward had written down, but they could count from one to seven, and seven were the coins that had been placed by the Steward's hands on the table.

"Sir," the Lord spoke, "in the long books several such short-payings have been noted, but never more than one in any village."

"Aye, then he writes down falsely," an angry voice called, and the Advocate turned quickly, to catch the speaker.

The Earl ignored the interruption. "Send to the villages, to hear what these others say. There might well be one error, in all the work of collecting taxes. There might even be two. But more than that will identify a guilty party, if there be such a one. If there be such a one, the law will deal with him. Does that satisfy you, Advocate?"

"It satisfies me, my Lord," the Advocate replied, without hesitation. "Last case," he announced.

"Hearing Day used to go on, late into the night and sometimes into the next day." Orien sounded surprised.

"Is something wrong, then?" she asked.

"Or it's been made right," he answered.

The last case involved two farmers, who were also neighbors. The one had sold the other a sow, thinking she was a gilt. But she had been pregnant, and now he claimed to own the piglets—arguing that while he had sold the sow he hadn't sold her piglets, not at that price. Two men, both as round-bellied as pigs themselves, shoved to the front of the crowd behind the Advocate, and punctuated his summary with their own claims, and their anger at each other. "Greedy pig," and "Swindler," they called each other. "A pigman without the wits to know a gilt from a pregnant sow," one said, and the other answered that that was a mistake he'd rather make with his pigs than his wife.

The Lords raised gloved hands to rub at cheeks and noses, concealing smiles. The crowd laughed openly. Even the Advocate was ashamed of the case. Every sentence he spoke to the Earl had an apologetic "my Lord" tacked on to its beginning or end.

The Earl rose, interrupting the Advocate, silencing the farmers. "This is no case to bring to Hearing Day," he announced. "The Lords have nothing to do with these quarrels." At the sound of his voice, all smiles fled all faces. Even the Lords sat up straighter.

"You two." The Earl pointed a finger at first one farmer, then the other. The two tried to shrink back into the crowd, but nobody would give them room to hide. "You two will settle this between yourselves. In three weeks' time my Steward will come to find out your settlement. He will know if it satisfies the Earl's justice."

The young Earl looked out over the crowd, as clapping hands approved of his judgment. At Birle's side, Orien smiled. "That's my brother," he said to Birle, and she heard pride in his voice, and laughter too. His smile, sent over the heads of the crowd like a beam of sunlight, caught the Earl's eye.

The Earl stiffened, stared.

There was something here Birle didn't understand. Then she could understand it: Unfinished between these two was the matter of a father's death. More than that: This Earl could not be the Earl, once Orien had returned. Birle stood at Orien's side. She had a knife at her boot.

"Hearing Day is completed," the Earl announced. "Let the hall be cleared," he said. Behind him, the Lords stirred and rose. Before him, the people turned, to crowd out of the door. "You, man," he said, not needing to point for Birle to know to whom he spoke, "wait where you are."

"Aye, my Lord," Orien called back in answer.

The room was quickly emptied. Some of the people cast curious glances at Orien, where he leaned at ease against the wall, but most hurried away, back to their own labors and their own lives. Birle stayed beside Orien, who ignored her. Even when the hall was emptied, he didn't move or speak.

It was the Earl who jumped down from the platform, to cross the empty floor. He was a darker man than his brother, with black hair and eyebrows, but his eyes were a much paler blue. He approached slowly, with no expression on his face. A few feet away, he stood to stare.

"Orien?" he asked.

"Aye, my Lord," Orien answered. He didn't move.

At that response, the Earl laughed aloud and his whole face lit up, as if he had shed solemnity like a cloak. "Aye, my Lord indeed, Brother." He held out both of his hands, to take the one Orien held out to him now. "I give you greeting, my Lord," he said, and his voice was stiff now. His eyes shone cold, perhaps angry or perhaps afraid. Before Birle could decide, he spoke again. "Brother indeed," the Earl said. "And you're back, you've come back."

He was glad of that. He hadn't even noticed Birle, so glad was he to have his brother in his sight. Orien was in no danger here. This dark man was no guilty murderer, whatever else he might be.

"A little travel-stained," Orien said.

"A little—" The Earl laughed again. "Yes, you might say that and I won't gainsay you. You look—" He reached out and turned Orien's head a little to the side. "What's that mark? As if you've been—" Quick as flames in dry branches, anger took the place of gladness on his face.

"I'll tell you the story sometime, Gladaegal. For now, it's enough to say that no beast in my house will ever again be branded. No, Brother, the men who did it are well beyond your reach, and I count it enough to be alive. Brother," Orien said, to distract the Earl, "you sit well in judgment."

"Yes, I think so," his brother answered, all pride. "Yes, I know I do. It's the second time I've had the Hearing Day and already fewer bring their quarrels. Orien, you must see Grandfather."

Birle looked at Orien's brother. Then this was not the Earl, if the old Earl still lived. Orien must have known it all along, but she didn't know how he would have. For just a minute, selfishly, she wished they were once again beyond the Kingdom, just the two of them, equal in the forest solitudes.

"I owe him an apology," Orien said.

"Him and the rest of us too."

Orien held up a hand. "You don't need to say it. I've learned—" Without saying what it was he had learned, he turned to Birle, and took her arm. "This is my Lady," Orien said.

"Your Lady?" Gladaegal echoed.

"My Lord," Birle said to Orien, "can't it wait, shouldn't you go to your grandfather if he's alive to greet you?" She thought she might slip away, take the horse, and be out of the city before he had time to notice she was gone. She thought he hadn't known what would happen here, when he had returned to his rightful place; she knew she hadn't thought of it.

"Birle," Orien said, "let me present my brother."

"I give you greeting," Gladaegal said. But he paid no more attention to her than Orien did.

Birle took the arm Gladaegal offered, although she was well able to walk without it. She was in a world she knew nothing of. If, in this world, a woman took a man's arm for support when she walked, then Birle must do as the others.

They went along a long corridor, where the only light came from candles set in the walls. They entered a hall where fires burned in fireplaces large enough for three men to stand abreast, and great woven hangings covered the walls. Men sat or stood near the fires, and all turned to see them enter. "Orien?" one asked, and all came forward.

Gladaegal summoned a maidservant. "Take this lady up to my wife," he told the girl. "You'll join us at table, won't you, Lady?"

He was only interested in his brother, and Birle thought that was right. She too had her eyes on Orien, but he was occupied with the Lords who closed around him.

"I give you greeting, my Lord," they said, one after the other, kneeling in turn.

The servant led Birle up a broad stone staircase and down a long hallway. They were bid enter a room where a tall Lady rose to meet her. "I give you greeting," she said. "You are welcome to this house." Then she spoke only to the servant, to give orders. Birle didn't take offense at being slighted. She didn't know that—had it been asked of her—she could have spoken her own name.

Birle followed the servant into another room, where beds stood against the wall, each one surrounded by heavy hangings, and a fire burned. Behind the privacy of screens, Birle was unclothed, and then bathed in a metal tub set before the fire. She didn't know what she was supposed to do, or say, so she did as she was told and said nothing.

They dried her hair before the fire, combing it free. They dressed her in a fine shift, then lowered over her head a red dress that fitted close up under her breasts and fell in folds down to the floor. Birle ran her hands down over it, admiring the way the long sleeves hung down from her wrists. She had seen such dresses, on Ladies at the fairs. They put soft leather shoes on her feet; the shoes were too long but they stuffed the toes with pieces of cloth to make them fit.

When she was ready, Birle was led down the hallway and down the stairs, back to the great hall, where long tables were set out. The Ladies sat along one side, the Lords along the other, and at the high table were only three—Orien and his brother and Gladaegal's wife. Birle was given a seat among the women.

Servants moved up and down the room, carrying platters of fowl and fish and flesh, baskets of breads and pastries, jugs of wine. They put food onto the metal plate before Birle, and she tried to eat it, but had no appetite. It was enough trouble to keep the long sleeves out of her food. They poured wine into the metal goblet, and she raised it to her mouth, but could not swallow. None of the others at the table had any desire to speak with her. Their talk was all of Orien, and his return, the scar on his face—which they had heard he earned in battle, or maybe in a fight to free himself from pirates—and the mystery of his disappearance.

When she dared, Birle raised her eyes from her plate, to look at him. Orien too had been bathed and clothed. His beard had been shaved off. As he ate and drank, as he spoke laughing with his brother, while his brother's wife sat unnoticed between them, Birle recognized him for what he was, the Earl that would be.

She didn't want to sit gawping at him, so she turned her eyes back to her plate. It was as well that no one asked, for she didn't know what explanation to give of herself. The meal went on, and on.

Birle's plate was taken away and replaced with another. Servants came by with wooden platters of cheese, and baskets of apples, and bowls of sweetmeats. They put food onto her plate. She lifted her goblet and drank as much as she could. Then there was a movement of chairs from the high table and from across the room. Birle looked up.

All around the hall, the men were standing, with goblets raised in their hands. The ladies didn't stand and Birle followed their example. Gladaegal gave the toast. "To my brother, returned. You are welcome to this house, Orien."

Everyone raised goblets, echoed him, and drank. "See?" an excited voice said, down the table from Birle, "it's me he's looking at."

"No it's not," someone answered. "You're always such a ninny about him. It's her he's looking at."

Birle raised her eyes to meet Orien's bellflower glance, almost as she'd first seen it. For a brief time, only heartbeats long, it was as if nothing had changed.

"He's not married yet," the wistful voice said. Then Gladaegal's Lady rose from her seat between the brothers, and all the Ladies rose to follow her out of the hall.

Birle moved among them, although she had no idea why they were leaving, or where leading. She was taken back to the room upstairs, her fine gown was removed, and the shoes, and the shift; a long white dress was put on her. She was put to bed in one of the beds that lined the wall. She was asleep before the curtains were drawn closed around her, on that bed softer than even her imaginings had thought it might be.

Twenty-three

ON a windless winter morning Birle stood by a high window, looking out. Smoke rose from city chimneys into a clear blue sky. Beyond the city, fields and hills were blanketed with snow, and the frozen river looked like a long gray snake, asleep in the winter sunlight. The air on her face was cold.

Birle had everything she had imagined, and more: That was her thought as she listened to the voices of children playing in the snow that covered the castle grounds, and the sounds of servants at their work. She had somehow found for herself everything she had wanted, and better than she'd dared to dream. At her back lay the apartment of the Earl of Sutherland, where a broad fire burned, where tapestries hung over the cold stone walls. The Earl himself had just asked, "Come sit by me, Birle, and read to me."

She would never have imagined it. She would never even have thought to imagine it. But if she had, she wouldn't have thought that she wouldn't be contented.

Birle turned around. The Earl sat by the fire, in a tall carved chair, with a blanket over his legs. Two woven tapestries, hanging out from the wall on long wrought-iron poles, kept him out of drafts. The Earl was an old man, with sixty-one summers behind him. The skin on his face was as papery as the dried skin of garlic bulbs. His body was weak with age and sickness, but his mind was not weak, or dull. At their first meeting, the Earl neither gave her the customary greeting nor pretended that he hadn't heard of her. Even weak as he'd been then, he had fixed his pale blue eyes on her with a boy's direct glance, and said, "I knew your grandparents. I was sorry when they died."

Birle had learned already not to give voice to questions. Why did he not speak to her in formal manner? Why should he know Gran and Granda, and even so, why should he remember? She had asked nothing of the old man in the high bed, pillows piled behind him to help him sit up. She had stood silent beside Orien, trusting Orien to show her how she should behave. In the castle, every word spoken seemed to mean something more, and also less, then the word itself.

"Doesn't she speak?" the Earl had asked Orien.

Birle felt the Earl's impatience, and she saw it in the way he scratched at the backs of his pale hands and arms. She thought she might make him formal greeting, but the words were clumsy in her mouth. She felt always clumsy these days, her hair loose and needing frequent attentions from the servants, her hands and mind without occupation. Even though the dress she wore had been made especially for her, it seemed to fit her ill. The seamstress, she had learned, might do that, if she didn't like you. She might pretend to be doing her best, but the finished gown would make the girl look awkward. Birle didn't know if the seamstress had disliked her, or even if the dress did fit badly; all she knew was that she felt awkward and clumsy, and she couldn't think of any words to speak, even though her silence was making the old man in the bed cross.

"Say something. Say anything," he had commanded. "Say your name."

The woman who sat in a chair beside the bed had spoken then. "You already know her name, my Lord." Her hands were busy with knitting needles and fine wool. The blanket she knitted lay like snow on her lap.

It was not her words but the laughter in her voice that made Birle lift her eyes from her own clasped hands to look at her. The woman wore a gray dress, soft as rain clouds; her hands held the needles ready to begin their work again. A gray silk band was wound into her white hair, and her eyes, under white eyebrows, were a deep, bright blue. "I'm Orien's grandmother," she said.

"He never said he had a grandmother," Birle protested. She turned to Orien, her tongue unlocked by anger and curiosity. "You never said." In the days she had lived in the castle, she had seen him only across the dining hall; when they did pass close enough to speak, there was only time for his quick question, "Are you content?" and none for her answer.

"Why didn't you tell me?" she demanded. Then she heard her own voice and was ashamed, and fell silent again. She felt sad, and sick at heart at what she was beginning to unwillingly understand. Orien must regret asking her to be his wife; he had never said so to her, but since they never had opportunity to talk, she couldn't console herself with that thought. It seemed often as if she were a puppet on a stage, being presented before the people of the castle, who observed from their places in the audience how the doll performed. Gladaegal's Lady, who had the duty of instructing Birle in the running of the household, referred frequently to "Your foreign customs," as if she refused to know who Birle was. Birle had been lost in unknown lands, and lost among strangers, but she had never felt so lost as she did here, in Orien's home. He stood beside her, now, but as the Earl that would be, not as the man she would wed.

"Orien doesn't know this," the Earl said. "but your grandparents saved my life, and my father's."

"The girl should have a seat," the Earl's Lady said. A servant brought a chair forward, setting it beside the Lady's. Birle sat down gratefully. The Earl seemed to be waiting for her to say something.

"I never heard anything like that," Birle said.

"If I were given a goblet of wine I could tell the story. If you'd like to hear it. Would you?" the Earl asked.

"Aye, my Lord," she said.

"You probably should hear it, since you seem to have stolen this boy's heart from him."

At his way of putting it, Birle could have laughed out loud.

So that was what the castle said she had done, stolen Orien's heart, as if she were an enchantress. To think that the castle believed that made her want to laugh.

"And you look just like your grandmother when you smile," the Earl said. "Just like her."

Birle heard his pleasure in his voice. That it pleased him satisfied something in her, so that she dared to ask, "What is this story?"

He drank the wine, and told the tale, of long ago feuding in the castle, and war in the lands as brothers fought for the title. He and his father had fled to the north, where they had been caught by a blizzard, and the Innkeeper's daughter had kept him safe in an isolated house they chanced upon, and the Inn's servant had brought his father safely through the blizzard. Birle listened, trying to imagine Gran a girl of sixteen and Granda a servant. As the Earl described the long days of being snowed in, she wondered if this was how Gran and Granda had learned to read. The Earl had been then just a boy, he said. A boy might not know that the people were forbidden to know letters. "My grandson tells me that you know how to read," the Earl said.

"And write," Orien added. Both he and the Earl were watching her, as if they had agreed about something she didn't understand.

Birle had had enough of feeling that everyone knew and understood things of which she was ignorant. "I think it must have been you who taught letters to my grandmother," she said to the Earl. "And given them the books that were in the cupboard in their holding, and the maps, and also had them taken away when the house was empty."

At least she had surprised the smug expressions off their faces. "Now that Birle has given us her greeting," the Earl's Lady said, "we would ask you, Lady, to tell us something of this foreign city. Orien tells us nothing of the time, except that you brought him out alive from slavery. He said your master was a philosopher. What does that mean?"

It was this question, and Birle's answer, and all the questions and answers of that first long afternoon, that made the

Earl's apartment the place in the castle where Birle most liked to be. It was a place where the map of the skies could be mentioned, and the ideas of alchemy considered. Here too Birle had a use—for while she couldn't heal the Earl, she could make him more comfortable. She knew that aged cider added to his bath water would ease the itching that tormented him, and that the sores she could soothe with an ointment of comfrey and honey would not appear if he moved from his bed. She advised hot infusions of chamomile and catnip for sleeplessness. In the Earl's apartment, Birle had work to do. Although the Earl was won more slowly, his Lady had—from that first meeting—seen into Birle's heart, and smiled upon her.

The Earl's Lady shone like sunlight over the people of the castle. Birle understood why Orien had never mentioned his grandmother—she was too close to his heart to speak of. The Earl's Lady was the treasure at the heart of the castle—for Birle and for all of the others, servants and Lords alike; all came to her for her wisdom, or for her help, and just as often to bring her some gift. Only Gladaegal's wife was unchanged in the presence of the Earl's Lady, almost as if by her stiffness she hoped to curb Gladaegal's spirit. Birle had studied Gladaegal, watched and listened. She thought now that Orien had been right to doubt his brother—not for what the dark young man would do, but for what he must feel, being the younger brother, to whom the title would not come, whatever his worthiness. In the presence of the Earl's Lady, Birle could see clearly what might otherwise have kept hidden—that Gladaegal admired his brother more than he envied him.

It was the Earl's Lady that winter afternoon, when Birle had returned to her seat to pick up the book from which she had been reading, who didn't allow her to return to the task. "I think, my Lord, that Birle has something more important than reading to discuss with us."

"With us?" the Earl grumbled. "You mean with you."

"I mean with us," his Lady said, "and that is why I said it."

"Then it will be bad news," the Earl said. He shifted in

his chair. "I'll tell you how I know, so you won't have the trouble of asking. If it's good news you simply tell it to me, when you judge the time is right. Only bad news needs discussion. So it won't be anything I'll be pleased to hear. Well, Birle, what is it?"

Birle took a breath, and waited for just one moment more, hearing the soft wooden clicking of the needles, feeling the warmth of the fire on her back, seeing her own white hands as they held the book open on her lap. Then she made herself say it. "I would ask your permission to leave the castle, my Lord."

"You don't have it," the Earl said. "There now, that's settled, let that be an end on it. You're laughing at me, Lady," he complained to his wife. "Well, Birle, is it that you wish to visit your family? I could give you leave for that."

"I ask your leave to go, and not return."

"I've answered that request."

"I think, my Lord," the Lady said, "that if you forbid her she'll run away from us."

"Just like Orien, they're as alike as two peas. Never a warning and never a word of explanation. One day he's here, and the next he's gone, and when it pleases him he comes back." Then the Earl changed the subject, but whether to divert her or to ask a question that troubled him, Birle didn't know. "Do you know why he left, Birle? Did he tell you?"

"I know what he said about it," she answered carefully. "But I've learned, here, that what is said often masks the truth."

"Can you tell us what he said?" the Lady asked.

"He feared that he would be too gentle an Earl, which he feared wouldn't serve the lands and the people well."

"Like me." The Earl spoke what she hadn't.

"Like you, but not to judge you harshly, Lord. Orien admires you, and your service to the people. What he said was that two such Earls, one after the other—that was where he saw danger."

"He doesn't seem troubled by that any longer," the Earl said.

"No," Birle agreed. "He doesn't." She didn't know what was in Orien's mind; he was most often away, visiting the southern Lords, hunting, talking with the priests and Steward, drilling with the soldiers—he was seldom at the castle. "And there was his father's death, the manner of it, and his father's jealousy, and he feared Gladaegal. For what Gladaegal might desire."

"Foolishness," the Earl announced. "He should have known better."

"What about you, do you fear Gladaegal?" the Lady asked.

"No, I don't."

"Why not?" the Lady asked.

"Because—because Gladaegal holds his honor dear to him. If he had murder in his heart he'd do it openly, before everyone. If I feared ambition's hand," Birle added, because in this room she could speak her mind openly, "I'd fear his Lady. But she would never dare to plot harm, because she also knows that Gladaegal is a man who would give his own wife to the executioner, if honor required it."

"In fact," the Earl told her, "it was murder, as Orien feared. But the huntsman wasn't suborned. The huntsman meant murder, to revenge his daughter's shame. He was brought to law, and hanged. The truth didn't come out until after Orien disappeared, but how was I to know what he was thinking? He never said—he never explained or asked—he just disappeared. Have you told Orien your desire?"

Birle shook her head. She would not have dared to put the question before Orien, the Earl that would be, to make formal supplication, to stand before them all to hear him answer her.

"Are you so unhappy?" the Earl asked.

"How could I be unhappy? It's only that I'm not content. I have no work," Birle said. How Nan would laugh if she could hear Birle saying that, Birle thought. She tried to explain. "Among the people, a man and his wife work the holding, or the loom, or nets, or whatever the work of the house is. Among the people, a man and his wife are both

263

necessary to the well-being of the house. I can't change myself into a Lady, any more than my master could change stones into gold. I can act the part, but—'' She put the book down on the floor and stood up, because she thought it would somehow be more possible to make them understand if she was standing. "Do you know it was fully ten days, when I first arrived, before I remembered to inquire about the mare who had carried us here?" For which Yul had been sold, she thought, but didn't say. "We left the beast tied up on Hearing Day, and then—I didn't remember her for ten days."

"Was it not well cared for?" the Earl asked.

"But I shouldn't have forgotten. I never would have anywhere else. Also," she went on, "I am with child and I didn't even think of it until I noticed that while all the other Ladies take to their beds for the length of their woman's time, away from the company, I never have needed to. Not that I wish to spend the days abed, not that I would need to do that. It's not that. Also I am with child," she said again. She stood before them, waiting for their anger, or their pity for her shame.

"What troubles you is that you didn't notice, or think of it?"

"Yes, Lady."

"I think you ought to give her the permission she asks," the Lady said to her husband. "I think you ought." Tears rose to Birle's eyes, for sorrow and relief, both; she brushed them away.

"What about Orien?" the Earl protested. "You'll break his heart."

"I don't think that," Birle said. "Now that he's back here, home, himself again. . . ." She didn't know how to let them understand what Orien didn't wish them to know. "My slavery was as much a gift as a burden. But Orien had all taken from him, strength and honor, all hope. He was a slave to ill fortune, and now he is—again—Fortune's favorite. Now he will be the Earl, and he'll find a Lady to wed." But she didn't want to speak of that, or think too precisely about it. "If I thought it would break Orien's heart, then I would stay."

"It is his child you carry?" The Earl was angry now.

"Yes," Birle said, remembering. "Yes, it is Orien's child," and proud too. "A betrothal can be broken off. A marriage cannot."

"But—" the Earl waved his hand impatiently.

His Lady interrupted him, and didn't let him finish the thought. "The Ladies of the castle live apart, even wife from husband. The Earl's Lady, perhaps most of all—it is only in these last years, my Lord, that you and I could spend long hours together, in the friendship of our hearts. You liked it no better than I did, my Lord," she reminded him. "The children of the castle sleep in the nursery, and are left to the care of servants. I often wished for myself that it were not so, for the good of the child and of the mother."

Birle said, "Lady, I think you know my heart."

The Earl had fallen back into his chair. "My Lord," Birle said, "it troubles me that Orien didn't need to leave, but thought he did. He never had to run away, but he didn't know that."

"I should have guessed his mind," the Lady said.

"He didn't wish you to," Birle said. Once again she took a deep breath. "I ask your leave to go."

The Earl spoke to his wife. "You tell me I must give it?"

"There is no must for the Earl of Sutherland," she answered. "I tell you only that I think you ought. Do you wish to go home, Birle?"

The Earl didn't allow Birle to answer. "If we should give leave, and I will," he announced, "then I will tell you how it will be. As your Earl, I tell you. You will have the holding your grandparents had." He held up a hand to silence her. "At the first of spring, you may go there, not before. You may not travel until winter has left the land. I'll send you under the care of a messenger and servants. No, Birle, you must let me do it this way, so that you have supplies to keep you until the holding can do that, so that you travel safely and live comfortably."

Birle sat down at his feet. She hadn't thought the Earl and his Lady would want to help her; she had hoped only for their consent. "I don't want to dishonor Orien," she said. "My idea was that if the people of the castle were told that I was sickening for a sight of my homeland, and the grip of winter disheartened me—they would ask no questions. Although they know the truth, they don't believe it."

"They don't wish to believe," the Lady explained. "The Ladies so seldom leave the protection of castle and servant that they know nothing of the world beyond, the world beyond is no more than what they imagine it to be. The Lords let the women tell them what to think on matters such as these. The Ladies understand that a Lord might find a servant fair, and he might desire her, and she might give him pleasure. But not wed her—that he may not do."

"So I will be forgotten."

"Will Orien forget you?"

"Aye, Lady, I hope I will become a memory that makes the other memories of the time better for him. I would be no less than that," Birle said. "But no more."

"So I will equip you for a journey to the south," the Earl said.

"But not with a messenger," his Lady suggested, "or with servants. There must be no talk. If servants know the journey's end, word will spread. Birle wishes to disappear, but how could she do that if there were rumors to fly after her and hunt her out? And how could Orien undertake the earldom, with rumors to feed hope?"

"I can travel alone," Birle assured them.

The Earl had his own plans. "You'll go with Gladaegal, then. His word will be his bond. That is my will, Birle—for I wouldn't sleep easy not knowing that you were safe. That's settled, then. At the first of spring, when Orien goes to bend his knee to the King, you and Gladaegal will travel the River Way, into the south."

"Aye, my Lord," Birle said.

The Earl's Lady stopped her knitting. "Orien will expect a wedding when he returns from doing obeisance to the king. What will you tell him?"

At the question, so gently asked, Birle's eyes filled again

with tears, which she couldn't wipe away. "I'll tell him what I can, to give him ease," she promised them.

After that, there was only waiting, for the time. The waiting passed quickly—or so it seemed to Birle. One day, icicles as thick as a man's arm hung down outside of the arched windows, and then they were gone, washed away by days of cold rain. Patches of furrowed earth appeared from under the snow, and the bowed golden grasses of last year's meadows. The first flowers raised timid heads in the castle gardens. "This is the sixty-second spring of my life," the Earl said, on a morning when he was too weak to get out of his bed. "Can you smell the new year in the air, Birle?"

"Yes, my Lord," Birle said. She was reading to him again, to pass the time, the old stories of animals who spoke and acted like men. This was her sixteenth spring, she thought. She wondered if it hurt the little flowers to have to push up through the covering earth. After the long, safe sleep of winter, it would be hard to be naked to the air again.

"The year turns on a wheel, like Fortune's wheel," the Earl said. "What would your Philosopher say about that, Birle?" He didn't wait for an answer. "Orien goes to the King in the morning, do you know that?"

Birle could barely lift her head under the weight of that knowledge. But the plans had been carefully made, and so she stood with the others, Lords and Ladies, to bid farewell to Orien, who would be Earl. When she took in deep breaths, the dress she wore stretched uncomfortably tight around her ribs—another month and she wouldn't be able to conceal the child.

Another month and the child's father would be long out of her sight, long and forever, she thought, and watched him bow over the hands of the Ladies and exchange a word with his Lords. When he stood before her, she could do little more than look at him—tall, strong, proud, and glad, the curved scar at his cheek, a man who carried his power like the sheathed sword at his side, the promise of ringing steel—and

267

his bellflower eyes smiling down at her. "Lady," Orien said, "it's a short journey I make, too short for sorrow."

"I would make every journey with you," she told him.

"You have much to do here in preparation. It will not be for long, Lady."

"It seems long," she told him. "It will seem very long."

"With a wedding at the end of it," he reminded her.

"Aye, my Lord," she said, her voice so quiet only Orien could hear her. "Until we are wed I will carry you close in my heart."

"And after?" he asked, laughing.

She didn't begrudge him his gladness but she answered sharply from her own heavy heart. "After will have to take care of itself. Your men grow impatient, my Lord."

He bowed over her hand and walked away. But when he came to where the groom held his horse's reins out, he turned and strode back, Orien in a shirt as green as summer leaves, with the golden wings of the falcon outspread across his chest—the Earl that would be. He bent his mouth close to her ear and said softly. "Do you think of the forest bed, Birle? I do, and of the nannies and billies."

Then Birle did laugh. "Yes, my Lord," she said. "And is this your good parting? Is this memory going to make the time less long?"

"Lady, you know me too well," Orien said.

"I hope so," Birle answered. Later, when he thought of this parting, he would understand her meaning.

Twenty-four

BIRLE sat on the broad stone doorstep. Sunlight fell over her. The little spring bubbled quietly and the stream flowed out from it, across the grassy meadow. The house waited behind her, its door open and windows unshuttered. Bird-songs and the hum of insects were all the living voices the breeze carried.

Soon she would have to rise and go inside to change into the skirts and shirts chosen from the stores that clothed the castle's servants. She would comb her hair and braid it again. But not, she thought, into the two braids to be wound around her ears. She wished neither the two thick braids crowding the sides of her head, nor the bother of hair hanging loose. The fashion she had made for herself, her slave's fashion of a single braid, that was what suited her.

There was much to do—the cart that rested on its two long shafts beside the stone house must be unpacked, the house needed airing and cleaning before she stored away the sup-plies that had been packed for her at the castle. The horse, her own sumpter beast, grazed the meadow; her front legs were hobbled, but that seemed not to trouble her, not with the new grass and cold water. There was much for Birle to do, but for a long time she sat unmoving, after the long journey. Here at the southern edges of the Kingdom spring had settled in, and the air in her mouth tasted of all of spring's remembered sweetness.

Longing and regret would return to her, Birle thought, and

the longing was the worst. But for these few minutes, her heart was quiet. She listened to the spring, and didn't know if the water wept or laughed.

What Nan would think of the summons Gladaegal brought, Birle didn't know. The summons he carried asked the Innkeeper's wife to go out to the holding, when she could spare the hours. It might be days before Nan had the hours to spare. Birle didn't mind putting off the scolding Nan would give her. Aye, and she deserved this scolding—but she was glad to have many days in which to whet her appetite for the humble pie that Nan would serve her. She stood up, and stretched.

A woman came hurrying along the path out of the trees. She hadn't even taken the time to remove her apron, or put on a cloak, or roll down her sleeves.

This would be a fine fury, then. Birle stood, waiting.

When Nan looked up and saw her, her feet hesitated. Nan had a face like a chipmunk, cheeky, with round brown eyes. "Lady?" she asked, and then shook her head briskly, as if to clear her sight, and scurried up the path. "Birle!" she cried, and her feet ran the last few steps.

Birle found herself wrapped around by Nan's plump arms, and hugged tightly. "Aye," Nan said. "Aye. Aye." What she meant by that Birle had no idea, but her own arms were around Nan, holding her father's wife close. When they drew apart Nan's face was bright, her round cheeks pink. "Look at you," she cried. "Just look at you. And me, I look a mess, I abandoned the pastry half-mixed, just look at me."

Birle looked. Nan's forehead was damp from the exercise of rushing along the forest path, and she was breathing hard, as if she'd run. "Here, sit down," Birle said. "Don't worry about how you look, you look fine, you look just the way I remember."

Nan sat, and her fingers fussed at the lopsided braids.

"Only you're shorter than I remember," Birle said.

"It's you that's grown taller. It's good to see you, Birle. I thought I'd never see you again, and never know that I never would."

"I thought you'd scold me." When Birle sat down, Nan's

fingers went out to feel the wool of the gown. "I thought you'd be angry at me."

"Aye, well, maybe when I've got used to knowing that you're safe I'll have a thought to spare for anger. Are you a Lady now, Birle?"

"No." Birle smiled.

Nan was studying her—hair, dress, hands, boots—"You could be."

"Aye, I could, but I'm not. So if you like the look of me you'd better look now, for I was about to fold this finery away in the cupboard."

"I like the look of you," Nan said. "Ouuf. Now I've my breath back, that feels better. Now I've my daughter back— don't look at me like that, I was there at your birth. You were the first I ever birthed, mine or another's, and your mother too weak to do much for you those first weeks. Will you be living here, then? Has the holding been given to you?"

"Yes," Birle said.

"And the man?"

"What man?"

"For the holding."

"Why does there have to be a man for the holding?"

"You're as contrary as ever, aren't you, lass."

"But Nan, it's a question worth asking. If a man dies, his widow keeps the holding. So all know that a woman can work a holding alone. A man doesn't need a woman to have a holding, why should a woman need a man?"

"Why can't you accept the way things are?" Nan scolded.

"I can," Birle said. "I do."

"Why do you always want to change your life?" Nan asked, not listening to Birle or, Birle thought, not believing her.

"I don't," Birle said. "Things happen, Nan. But why shouldn't things change, why should things always stay exactly the way they always were? I have been given this holding, for myself," she said proudly.

Nan looked over her shoulder and into the house. "Aye, it looks it."

"Nan, I just arrived. I was resting after the journey. Thinking."

"What's there to think about with all the work that needs doing, I ask you that."

Nan hadn't changed. It made Birle smile, because she wouldn't want Nan to change.

"Thinking," Nan grumbled, "it just makes trouble. Like asking questions. It's better to get things done."

"Well then," Birle said, "I'll put these clothes away, and you sit here to rest from your walk, and then we'll get done what needs doing. I'd welcome the extra hands."

Nan's chipmunk face was filled with little circles of surprise, and she had nothing to say.

As they worked—to carry the mattress outside, to wash floors, cupboards and walls, to unpack the household supplies and clothing—Birle told Nan her plans for the holding. A milking nanny; a hive of bees; chickens and ducks; a garden for turnips, onions, cabbages, parsnips. A garden for herbs that she would make into infusions and ointments.

"Who'd buy them?" Nan asked. They were shaking out the bed linen, filling it with spring air. "What do you know about the healing herbs?"

"I was a slave," Birle began.

Nan's arms stopped moving.

"It was in a faraway city, where—my master taught me about herbs, and how to prepare them, and how to use them."

"I thought you were a Lady," Nan protested.

"I was." Birle thought she knew what Nan's answer would be, but she asked the question anyway. "Do you want to hear about it, Nan?"

Nan's arms moved again, "Aye, no, it's enough that you're back. Now you're back, it doesn't matter."

Birle didn't agree, but there was no purpose to a quarrel.

"I'll send your brothers to dig the gardens for you."

"There's no need, I can turn the ground over. There's a spade in the cart, and I know how to use it."

"Aye, but that's something you shouldn't do, not unless you have to."

"Why not?"

"Because of the child." Nan gathered the sheet into her strong arms.

Birle followed her into the house and they spread the sheet over the mattress, tucking it firmly under. "How did you know?"

"How do I ever know? You've the look about you. When are you due?"

"Summer, I think. I think early summer."

"And there's no man for the holding." Poor Nan didn't dare to make it a question. "You won't come back to the Inn?" Nan asked.

"No."

"Aye, then, I'll come out here to be with you, when your time comes close," Nan decided. "For I won't have you giving birth alone."

"I'd be grateful for that," Birle said. "That's more than I hoped for."

"What you'll tell your father, and brothers, and sisters," Nan said, again not asking.

"There's nothing to tell." Birle had thought about this, and decided that she must say nothing. They would think whatever they would think, and she would have to let them do that. If she were to tell a story, there was danger that bits of the truth would be put into it. The truth—Orien's name, for example—was a thing that must never be spoken.

"There's three new families in the village." Nan began telling her the news. "Your da has named Reid his heir. Ware will ask the Steward for a holding in the forest, where he can raise pigs. Muir's not been seen since that spring fair when you weren't there to marry him. Aye, at the first, I was afraid Muir had stolen you away in the night—he was like a wolf with his hunger for you. But when he came up to claim you, aye, slavering like a wolf—"

"You disliked him so much?"

"So much, and more. Your da had planned it out, we were going to tie you up in your bed and tell Muir you'd the spotty fever, anything to frighten him away and give you time to

273

come to your senses. Da was going to give him the gold dowry coins, to leave you alone. Aye, we disliked him for your husband. You'd not have wed him, lass, not while we lived.''

"I didn't know that. I had no idea.''

"If you'd had any idea, you'd have run off with him, just to have your way. So when you did run off—''

"I didn't mean to,'' Birle said. She wouldn't say she was sorry, because she couldn't be sorry for it. But she didn't want Nan to think she had no care for the people of the Inn. Although, now that she thought of it, she hadn't taken any thought for Nan or Da, and she should have. "I'm sorry, Nan.''

"Well, it's done and behind us now, so we can forget about what might have happened—wolves, drownings, robbers taking you away for their pleasure, aye, we thought of everything that can happen to a girl alone.''

"All behind us now,'' Birle reminded her. "Why are none of my brothers wed?'' she asked, to distract Nan from remembered sorrow.

Nan had no questions and there were also no questions at the Inn, when she went there to greet Da, and her brothers, and the little girls. There were no questions because that was the way of the Inn. Birle had returned, she had the holding, she was with child—that was all they cared to know.

For company in her solitary life, Birle had the books and maps the Earl had given her; and for work she had her gardens, growing seeds from the Inn and tending the plants she transplanted from the forest. Spring swelled the land, and Birle's belly swelled. The child moved within her and she didn't feel alone. When longing, and hunger, for Orien threatened to weigh her down, she reminded herself that she had known from the first that they must part, and she reminded herself that she had held his heart for a time, which was more than she had had reason to hope for. The weight of the child she carried gladly.

The time for the spring fair came, but Birle didn't make the journey. Everything was waiting, until the child was born, even the problem of Yul. But in the fall she would have oint-ments and infusions to sell, and it would be good to have some coins in her boot when she went south. In the meantime she tended her gardens and kept the house clean, she made pots of soup, and cut wood, for the cooking fire and for her winter woodpile.

At night the stars shone silently over the holding, the Plough and the Wings, the high Northern Star. Under the day's sun her herbs grew strong in the rich soil of the mead-ow—knitbone and garlic, marshmallow, foxglove, spire-ment, chamomile, henbane, each clustered with its own kind. Underground, turnips fattened and above ground the cab-bages grew round. Carrots sent up ferny leaves.

Nan had been with her only a few days before the child's time came. Nan had told Birle what to expect—rolling pains that grew ever closer each to the one before until there was no rest between them, and then the labor to bring the child out into the world. Even then, Birle must not rest, not until the afterbirth too had been expelled. Nan had told Birle what to expect, and Birle had seen cats, dogs, and goats at their birthings—but still she was surprised. For a whole day, from dawn until late afternoon—a day that seemed as if it would never come to its close—she lay on the bed while pain held her in its fist. There was only her body and its pain, a fist clenching and opening. Birle heard Nan's voice and felt Nan's hands on her forehead; she obeyed Nan, because Nan stood outside of the grip of the fist. When at last it was finished, and Nan had tied a knot in the cut cord, and placed the damp child on Birle's breast, Birle didn't even move her arms. Her eyes were fixed on Nan. When Nan went to the door, Birle called out in protest.

"Ay, Birle, I'm burying the afterbirth," Nan said. "No fear, you've done the work, rest now. All's well," she prom-ised.

Birle's belly and arms were exhausted. Her mouth was dry as stone; the palms of her hands were raw from clenching the birthing straps. Her hair felt sodden with sweat. The naked babe lay across her chest like a fish. Birle looked at

275

its back, where miniature ribs spread out and then contracted, in breathing as small as a bird's. The babe lay bloody and as exhausted as Birle. Those little breaths were the cause of it all, Birle thought—they were in miniature the same clenching and unclenching of the labor. She put her hand down on the tiny back, to feel the rise and fall as it breathed. Her hand could wrap around the babe, encircling its delicate ribs.

Nan bustled back into the house, smiling. She took the babe up in her hands.

"What are you doing?" Birle protested, and struggled to sit up.

"I'll wash her, and put cloths on her, and swaddle her. It'll only be a moment, the water's ready."

"She's a girl?"

"Aye, Birle, I told you that."

Birle had never felt better. She felt terrible, but never better. "I didn't hear you. That's why they call it labor, isn't it, Nan?"

"Aye, that's why."

"Nan, in the cupboard, under that gown I was wearing the first day, there's a blanket to wrap her in."

Birle watched Nan gently wash the baby clean, and listened to the howls of protest. The little arms waved meaninglessly in the air above Nan's lap, the little feet kicked. Nan put the baby in Birle's arm and went to the cupboard.

"Where did you get such a thing?"

Nan held the little blanket out in front of her, a thing as fine as lace, but thick and soft. It looked like floating snowflakes. Nan's fingers stroked the wool. She stared at Birle.

"Her great-grandmother knitted it for her," Birle said. Nan asked no more. "Why is her hair so dark?"

"It'll fall out. That's the way of babies."

"Her eyes are blue."

"All babies have that, that and those squeezed-up faces from the birthing. Your eyes were blue too. All babies look alike at first."

276

"Her eyes will be blue," Birle said, even though it was only a hope. "Shall we call her Lyss?"

"It's a pretty name. Your da would be pleased."

"And you?"

"Aye, your own mother was a happiness to everyone who knew her. To me as well, even if I was only the servant."

Birle had never thought about Nan's life, as Nan had lived it. Now, with her child in her arm, she did. "I think my mother would have been glad to know she left her children in your care, Nan," she said.

Nan humphed, and her cheeks turned pink, but she didn't say anything. Her response was practical. "You'll bleed for a few days, as if it were your time of the month. But you'll have no woman's time while you nurse the child. That's the way of it."

Birle could not for long stop thinking of the wonder. "Yesterday there was only me, and today—just now—now there's another. How can that be, Nan?" If Nan had asked her at that moment, Birle would have told her all about Orien, and the wonder of him.

But Nan didn't ask. "A babe is what happens, when a man and a woman lie together," she said. "It's time you gave her the breast, Birle—that closes the womb, you'll feel it—aye, and you have to show her how to fill her belly."

For a few days, Nan stayed on with Birle and Lyss, to cook, to wash the baby's clouts, and to scold. "If you don't bubble her, she'll have colic," Nan would say. "Aye, if you pick her up every time she cries it won't take her long to learn to weep and wail for what she wants."

Birle didn't know why she had ever minded Nan's scolding. It was just the way Nan cared for things, and kept the empty air from being lonely. But she was not sad to stand in the doorway of the house, with Lyss in her arms, and watch Nan turn to wave for the last time before she stepped into the trees.

She stood in the doorway, with the weight of the babe in her arms—aye, and in her belly this same child had seemed heavier by far—and let the silence fall over her like rain. Orien must have given her back her heart, she thought, because she had it to give to the child: She didn't know whether to rejoice or weep over that. She wished she could ask someone—to ask if all of life was changes, like alchemy, transmutations from one thing into another, as she had been transmuted into two, herself and Lyss. She would know if alchemy rested on that truth, and she would know where it had degenerated into magic. She would know—aye, she would like to know everything, and give the knowledge to her child. She would give—

Her eyes rested on the meadow, where the cress-choked stream wound its way into the forest under a sun-filled sky. She would give Lyss, from Orien, his way of doubting, to ask questions when everyone said something must be so, and the courage that enabled him to endure without hope, that brought him to her from the mines. From herself she could give only her own heart. Aye, and she had already done that, given it completely and without warning. As with Orien, it had been wholly given in the blink of an eye, her heart gone into this babe's keeping without a thought. And once again, Birle's whole life had been changed by the gift.

Twenty-five

THE wind rushed across the meadow and on into the black branches of the trees. Dark clouds raced across the sky. Birle had been drawn out of her bed, but she wasn't alarmed once she had taken the measure of the night. This was fall, like an army on horseback, driving out the last of summer.

The wind caught at her cloak, whipping it around her. If she looked through the door she had left open behind her she would see Lyss's cradle in the shadows beside her own bed. Under her blanket, Lyss breathed softly in sleep, her hand curled up beside her mouth.

The wind couldn't trouble Birle any more than it could trouble the stream meandering across the meadow. The stream had its own source, and its own direction; it was too small a thing for the wind to waste its strength on. Birle also had her own source and her own direction.

In the spring, or next fall at the latest, Birle would go south again, to the cities of the coast. To find Yul. Since Birle had promised to return, she must. It might be that Yul wouldn't wish to return with her, but she had to give him the choice.

Birle stepped out along the path, to let the wind blow all around her. She had thought, at first, that she could take Lyss with her on the journey. She had told herself that she needn't leave her child behind. She could bind Lyss on her back, or carry the child in a sling across her chest. But Birle had always known that she couldn't take Lyss into the chances of the southern cities, helpless and innocent. The thought of Lyss at the slave market—even just imagining it—that, she couldn't bear. So she knew she would leave Lyss at the Inn, under Nan's care, when she traveled south with the merchants and entertainers from the fair, in the spring or next fall.

If she never returned, then Nan would raise the baby as one of her own. It pained Birle to think of that, but the pain was for her own loss, and hurt less than the thought of harm to Lyss.

Birle had argued with herself. She had tried to convince herself that she must forget Yul. She had tried to tell herself that the simpleminded giant would have long ago forgotten her. She had assured herself that Yul would be safe with Damall, safer than Birle would be while she searched for him. The hazards of the search far outweighed the chances of success. Birle knew that.

She also knew that when she wasn't there, there would be no one to give medicines to those who came asking. Word had spread, and now there was never a week that went by without someone coming to ask for a soothing ointment, or a cough-comforting infusion. The little house was hung with drying herbs; its shelves were lined with wooden bowls Birle had carved to hold the ointments. If she were to go away, and not return, who would answer the people's need?

But she had no choice. She couldn't give herself the choice because she had given her word, and because she wasn't the kind of person who could forget. Aye, and she wished she were, she wished she could.

Most of the time, as she worked, and tended Lyss, Birle didn't remember, for the time. Most nights she slept deeply, tired by the day's work. But sometimes, as on this windy night, her thoughts troubled her. Birle stared out into the night.

A shadow moved, at the edge of the meadow, like a land-bound cloud among the trees. Birle backed away, into the darkness that surrounded the house. Her heart was racing with fear. She needed a dog. She would have a dog from the

280

Inn's new litter, she would choose one. No, she would have two, for two would make twice the protection of one. Tomorrow, she would take Lyss and they would go to the Inn. Peering into the darkness, holding her cloak quiet around her, Birle thought that it was no shadow she had seen among the trees after all. It might have been a sapling bending with the wind, or just the movement of a low, leafy branch.

But it was a shadow, a shadowy figure that moved slowly onto the meadow, its own cloak blown by the wind. Birle reached down to pull the knife from her boot. He was alone. He would think she slept helpless within. She moved back until the stone wall stopped her, keeping well away from the faint light that tumbled out of the doorway onto the stoop. Her hand wrapped around the handle of the knife. She would surprise him, and that would give her the chance. She had never killed a man but she didn't doubt that she could.

Drawn by the faint light, he moved forward, his feet unsure on the dark path. The wind caught and pulled at his cloak, so she couldn't tell how large a man he was, or if he carried a weapon—knife, staff, or sword. She waited her time, watching. He would have heard them talking about the woman in the woods, and the coins people brought her for her medicines. They would have exaggerated, as they always did, so he would think she had riches buried under her hearthstone, his for the taking. She thought it might have been his thought that wakened her, as he crept toward the solitary holding; she thought that the danger in his thoughts had reached out to awaken her as surely as an alarm bell ringing out across the night.

Just beyond the light he halted, as if deciding what to do. Birle hoped he couldn't hear *her* thoughts, where she waited like a wolf ready to spring out of the darkness.

He raised a hand and pushed his cloak back from his head, and stepped forward.

"Orien?" Birle asked.

She had surprised him, and alarmed him. His hand went to his sword, briefly, before he reached it out to her, and reached out his other hand too. Birle took them both and said his name again. "Orien."

"What's that, a knife? That's a fine welcome, Lady, to have me bleed to death across your doorstep. My knees won't hold me, Birle," he said, and sat down on the stone step. Because he held her hands, he pulled her down beside him.

Birle dropped the knife so that both of her hands could lie in both of his. "Why have you come here?" she asked. "How did you find me? Who told you?" she demanded, now trying to pull her hands free.

"Lady, I needed no one to tell me. You yourself told me, in your voice, when you talked of your grandparents and their holding. Where else would you go?"

"I neither am nor want to be a Lady," Birle said. She had to tell him that, so he would know what was in her heart.

He let go of her hands then, and turned his face to her. His eyes were dark, and his face as much shadowed as illuminated. "If that is what you wish," he said. "But what about the child? What child did we have, Birle?"

Fear went to her heart, like a knife. Suddenly, she felt alone, as if she stood naked in a dark and windy world, with her naked child held against her chest, helpless, both of them. "They promised not to tell," she cried. If he were to say that Lyss must go with him, what choice would she have?

"They kept their word, rest easy. The Earl could never tell now, even if he wished to. He died in the summer."

"Then you're the Earl Sutherland." Everything was changing. With each word Orien spoke he changed everything. Birle thought that she ought to stand up before him. She thought she didn't know how to address the man who had lain in her naked arms, sleeping and not sleeping, who was the Earl Sutherland.

Orien said nothing.

Birle understood then. In the kindness of his heart for her, which she had never doubted, he had come to tell her he was to be wed. She had thought that she would hear this news, if she ever heard, from someone unconcerned, telling the tale at the Inn, or announcing the birth of the heir. Orien said

282

nothing now because his honor troubled him, to tell her this. She could spare him that, she thought.

"Are you to be wed, then, my Lord."

"No. I am already wed."

Now Birle couldn't speak. Even though she had known this must happen, to know it had already happened stopped her throat. He had not, then, given her back her heart, as she had thought. The wind blew and she could find no words to speak.

"It is in the power of the Earls," Orien explained, "to say the words over a couple who wish to wed. The law gives this power, to the Earl that is and the Earl that will be."

Birle didn't know why he was telling her this.

"If the pair speak their will to wed, to be husband and wife to one another, in the presence of the Earl—or the Earl that will be—then under the law they are wed."

Birle was remembering, and she understood now why he explained this to her.

"Does any of that remind you of anything, Lady?"

She nodded. She could have wept for the trap they had put themselves into. "You didn't tell me," she said. And she could have laughed, for gladness. "The Earl knew, though, didn't he. Aye, and the Earl's Lady too."

"You are the Earl's Lady," he told her. "If you wish it. But you don't wish it, as you said. Has your heart changed?"

"No, my Lord," she told him. She had thought her heart had been given back to her, to give to Lyss, but in fact she knew now it had merely become more to give. And when Orien smiled at her, as he did now, her heart pressed against her ribs, and up into her throat, as if it were too large for her body to contain it.

"Then it's simple," Orien said. "If you will not be the Earl's Lady, I can't be the Earl."

"But you are," Birle pointed out.

"Give me your hands again, just—yes," he said, holding both of her hands in both of his. "And I'll tell you a story. About the young Earl, who even when he was no more than a slave in the south won the heart of a maiden there. She was perhaps a wealthy merchant's daughter, or the only child of one of the great princes of the south, or an orphan with wide lands who was a ward of greedy priests. The slave who was an Earl won her heart, by his—well, however a man does win the heart of a woman, whatever his station may be. The lady rescued him, taking him out of slavery, leaving everything of her own behind. He took her to his glittering castle, high on the hills of his own country, to make her his wife. But the northern lands were cold and she was a delicate creature of the flowered south. Also, she had her own lands and people to care for, and thought of home, and her heart broke with every step of the long journey.''

"But they know better than that," Birle said, wondering.

"They know what they wish to know. Except Gladaegal."

"He gave his word never to speak. I would have trusted his word."

"I say it again, Lady: Nobody told me anything. I needed no one to tell me what my heart guessed. Hoped. But you haven't heard the end of the story."

Orien was enjoying himself, and Birle was content to sit beside him with his hands wrapped around hers, and hers around his.

"The young Earl had no peace without his Lady. No song lifted his heart, and his feet forgot how to dance. Flesh nor fowl nor sweetmeat could coax him to hunger. There was nothing anyone could do, except watch him weaken and fade toward his death."

Birle laughed. "I don't believe it. I might believe the song and the dance, but never the food."

"Let me tell the story," Orien insisted. "So at last they understood that the young Earl would have to ride into the south again. He named his brother regent, and announced to all that—under the law—if he had not returned within the year, his brother must be Earl, and the brother's sons Earls after their father. The young Earl rode off with a troop of soldiers, the pennants waving above them in the early-summer breezes. They rode off with a thunder of hooves, away into the south." Orien stopped speaking then.

Birle turned her hands in his until she could feel the narrow bones that ran down the backs of his hands to join with his wrists. It was the dead of night, she knew that, but the world seemed as bright as if it were full noon. This was Orien's way with her, to give her joy, as if he were himself the heart of her. "It's a pretty tale, my Lord," she said, unable not to smile.

Orien bent his head forward, until their foreheads touched. "I would stay here with you, Lady. If you will have me."

"I will have you," Birle said. "If you would stay." If this was the fortune he chose, then she would live it with him, and gladly.

For a moment, her heart beat with happiness. Then she remembered, and all the brightness went out. She wished to forget, but having remembered, she had to speak. She had no choice. "But I must leave you here for a while—not until after the spring fair, Orien, but I have to go back to the cities. For Yul," she explained.

Orien shook his head slowly, his forehead held against hers.

"Aye, and I have my word. I lied to you about it, because you were sick. Yul didn't choose to stay with Damall—he was kept for ransom, until I would return with gold to buy him free."

Orien's head moved back and forth.

"You can't say me no in this," Birle told him, as gently as she could. But her mind was racing, considering. "Unless—if you think a man might travel more safely, would you go yourself? Would you do that? I can, and will, but if it would be better for a man—" She didn't know which would be hardest, to leave him behind—again—or to watch him go away without her, again. She thought that it would be cruel to ask him to go again into the land of his slavery, to risk again dangers whose faces he now knew, and knowing must find more terrible. "It's a pity the soldiers are only in a story."

"But they aren't," he said. "Or, they weren't. I knew you were lying, Birle, and I knew why you lied. Those were

285

waking moments for me, in Damall's camp. So the story is true—or why would it be a whole summer's journey to find you? How could I do less for Yul than he had done for me? I did ride south with a troop of soldiers, and I wish you could have seen Damall's face as we came up upon him, on the highway between the cities, I wished you were there with me. I gave him three of the green stones, beryls—a great price, but Yul looked well, and it seemed right to give Damall beryls from you. Yul has come back north with us. He remembers you."

There were no words to thank him for this. Orien had honored her promise for her, before she asked the gift of him.

"Where is he then? And the soldiers?"

"They're camped half a day south of the Inn. When I rejoin them, I'll send the soldiers back to Gladaegal by a roundabout way. Yul and I will come on alone, to ask at the Falcon's Wing for the daughter who lived in the cities of the south."

"Won't the soldiers carry the tale?"

"They don't know where I've gone, and their guesses will be just another story." Orien sounded certain of this.

"You've thought of everything, my Lord."

"I've thought of everything because I've thought of little else, Birle, you and the child I guessed at. We'll be a couple from the south, in time, when the Innkeeper's daughter has been forgotten. Our ways will be strange because we will have come from the strange-customed south. I've no wish to go bearded, nor for you to grease your hair and wrap it around your ears. I like to see you wearing colors and I am myself vain, and care for softer clothing, and—in the cities of the south, remember? There were more than Lords and people, there were craftsmen, and guildsmen, entertainers, and even your Philosopher. And slaves," he said, his voice falling with the memory.

"What will you be, then, Orien? If you are not the Earl and not one of the people. Since," she reminded him, "there are no craftsmen, nor philosophers, nor slaves here in the

Kingdom. If you've thought of everything, have you thought of that?''

"Of course I have. You know me better than to doubt that, Birle. I'll be—'' Orien stood up. He threw back his cloak to assume the Showman's pose, with an arm outflung. "I'll be the puppeteer,'' he announced. "Yul and I bring a cartload of goods—fabrics, and wood, string, and even a puppet, to study how it's made. I wouldn't be content to work a holding, Birle.''

Orien stood there, as if waiting for her answer. The wind blew around him, lifting his cloak, blowing his hair into his eyes. He had once again surprised her. He knew himself better than she thought he did, he knew himself better than she knew him—he was always surprising her, and now he had again. She didn't doubt that he could carve, join, and clothe puppets, and learn to pull their strings. His puppets would tell tales of castle and holding, slave and prince, pirates and ladies, merchant, soldier, craftsman—every kind of person. And the puppeteer would know, from his own heart, what kind each person was.

Orien stood before her with their life in his hands to give her, and Birle—as contrary as Nan said—could think only of herself. What of her own life? What of her own work? What of the years she had thought to live with her daughter, the two of them, on the little holding distant from all the rest of the world. Must she give that up?

Birle could have laughed at herself. She had gone beyond a place where the world could tell her *must*. Aye, and they both had. Whatever Orien's work, she would grow the herbs and prepare the medicines, she would be herself and his wife too, and the mother to Lyss and whatever other children they had. She would be each of these, in the same way that Orien would be each of his puppets. And maybe too, she would undertake the Philosopher's task: to write an Herbal. Not so that her name would live, but so that the knowledge would live. That would be work worth doing. Her life was in her own hands.

Orien had no idea of what she was thinking, and her silence worried him. "I've thought of it, Lady. I couldn't be content to live in hiding, working a holding—nor for my children to live so. Any more than you could live content as the Earl's Lady," he said.

Birle rose to stand before him, and to reach her hands out to him. "Aye, my Lord, but I am the Earl's Lady. Just as you are the Earl, because you have been." She thought she was beginning to understand the way of fortune, and change, in the world.

"Then I am also a slave."

She knew the true answer to that. "The one slave who escaped from the mines."

His face was shadowed, but she could see the smile growing there; she didn't need to see his face to see his heart. "Shall I make a story out of that too? Even that? Shall I turn it all into stories for the puppets to tell? A man could spend his life at that work, Birle."

The wind blew around them, where they stood together. This night wind might blow in a storm, or it might blow in a clear morrow; there was no way for Birle to know. She could know only that a dark wind was blowing around them, and it was time to go into the safety of the house.

Orien seemed to think the same, for he took her hand and pulled her toward the open door. "You didn't tell me what kind of child we had."

"I had," she corrected him.

He ignored her, shutting the door behind them and—for all that he spoke of the baby—his bellflower eyes hungry only for her face.

"A girl," she said. "We have a daughter. We've named her Lyss, after my mother." She put her hand against his mouth, to quiet his laughter. "She has her father's eyes," Birle told him, "but she's asleep for now."

He held her hand and spoke softly against her fingers. "And should not be awakened, I think. But may I not waken her, Birle?"

"If you do that, she'll stay awake."

"Then we'll watch the night through with her," he argued, "all three together. There are worse fortunes to be had, and few better, as I think. What do you say, Birle, do you say yes? Lady, my heart, when you smile like that—let the child sleep, morning will come soon enough, all of the mornings to come will come in their time and for now—"

But Lyss stirred in her cradle, disturbed by the voices. Birle turned to pick the baby up, her heart glad to put Lyss into Orien's arms even while she wished Lyss might have slept on and left the two of them undisturbed. "When I've fed her she'll sleep again," she promised Orien, giving his child into his hands. For just a moment, their arms encircled Lyss, as if they were dancers at the fair, or themselves the wheel that turned.

ABOUT THE AUTHOR

Cynthia Voigt is the author of fourteen other novels, including Newbery Medal-winner *Dicey's Song* and Newbery Honor Book *A Solitary Blue*. Mrs. Voigt lives in Maine with her husband, Walter, their son, Peter, their daughter, Jessica (a student at Bryn Mawr), as well as their dog, Rosie, and their cat, Bongo.

Mrs. Voigt is the recipient of the 1989 ALAN Award, given by the Assembly on Literature for Adolescents by the National Council of Teachers of English for significant contribution to the field of adolescent literature.

Acclaimed reading
for young adults
from
CYNTHIA VOIGT